MOVIE STARS SHINE
BRIGHTEST IN THE DARK

JILLIAN THOMADSEN

To Analise,

Happy Reading!

Jillian Thom

MOVIE STARS
SHINE BRIGHTEST
IN THE DARK

JILLIAN

AUTHOR OF THE AWARD-WINNING NOVEL ALL THE HIDDEN PIECES

THOMADSEN

Chapter One

Vetta Park Light Industrial District
September 15, 2022

WHAT DID anyone really know about Cecilia Cinvenue? She was a beautiful, world-renowned actress. She was a performer, a box office rainmaker, a full-lipped, blonde-haired, long-legged ambassador of the arts…and now she was dead.

The world didn't know of her death of course – not at first. The first person to arrive at the scene was Dalton Beck. Beck worked at the quarry where Cinvenue's Italian-engineered sports car had landed after its vault over a jagged cliff.

Beck was a barrel of a man – thick, wide-sloped shoulders, full cheeks and a shiny bald head. He wore the same outfit to work every day: yellow helmet, bright orange blazer, ripped t-shirt and long jeans. On that day in mid-September, it was particularly warm for Eastern Missouri, and Beck was aggrieved to be hauling limestone and sediment under an unrelenting heat advisory warning. He had just gazed skyward to curse his situation when he heard the engine of Cinvenue's cherry-red Ferrari.

Beck didn't know much about sports cars but he knew

something was amiss, and it sounded like a fast-moving vehicle in some type of distress. The next few seconds occurred in a haze – so improbable, he was unable to process exactly what was occurring. First, he heard the gunning engine and then he saw the mesh of red and silver titanium plunge into the quarry's craggy rock – descending in the most violent, horrific way before finally coming to a stop just a few feet away from him.

Beck stood silently at the scene, staring at the car, his mouth ajar, his legs wobbly. He was sufficient to just stand there and take it all in – nearly frozen from this cryptic delivery from the heavens – when he heard the small, mousy cry from the driver's seat.

"Help," the driver said softly. "Help."

Beck raced over and saw the petite woman crushed against the center console. Her hair was bloody and matted against her sweaty forehead. There was blood on the steering wheel, on her clothing and on the door. Dalton Beck had seen Cecilia Cinvenue on movie screens and red carpets numerous times throughout the past few decades but this woman looked like a mangled, battered version of the star.

Still, he knew it was Cecilia – perhaps by the way she stared at him with those familiar, anguished, eyes. Perhaps it was the way her unblemished skin blanched into a ghostlike pallor at the loss of blood. He had seen her tremendously successful action movie in the early 2000s, and all the bleached pancake makeup in the world couldn't hide her beauty. Then, just as now, Cecilia Cinvenue was stunning and vulnerable, and Beck's every instinct commanded him to save her from this car. Especially now that the aroma of fuel was wafting into the air.

Unfortunately, Cecilia was trapped by a passenger door that wouldn't open – a crushed chassis that pinned her in the driver's seat, obscuring her from the waist down.

"Cecilia Cinvenue! Ok, ma'am...I can't....I mean...I'm gonna try to help you out...I mean...what happened?" Beck fumbled with words, while he ran to the passenger side to try another way to make the extraction. He was strong and determined, but the aluminum was just as stubborn as he was, and it proved unrelenting.

Beck peered through the shattered passenger window – his nostrils infused by the sweet benzene odor of leaking gas. It delivered an almost-immediate light-headedness that drove him a few steps backward.

Cecilia hadn't said a word since *help* but Beck acted as though she had. "Well, we've got to get you out of there," he said, knowing full well that there was no way he could get this woman out of her car. The prized, imported tour de force had become a metal straightjacket, preventing her from moving, wrapping its sharp alloys around her in a macabre embrace.

Beck was just pulling his cell phone from his pocket, just starting to dial the authorities, when Cecilia Cinvenue turned towards him and spoke her last words. Her eyes were glassy and her speech was garbled, but there was no mistaking what she said. These words would launch speculation and investigations – a wide-reaching inquiry by two police departments that plumbed the depths of Cecilia's tragically truncated life.

Cecilia spoke these words to the stranger standing three feet from her passenger door. Then the car's engine erupted in flames. The fire licked and danced around Cecilia's body, eventually engulfing her in its blaring fireball.

By the time the authorities arrived, Cecilia Cinvenue was gone.

DETECTIVE ROBERTA HOBBS ARRIVED AT THE SCENE ROUGHLY forty-five minutes after impact. She gripped the cruiser's steering wheel while she navigated the main streets out of Vetta Park's residential areas and into its Light Industrial District.

The cruiser's siren was wailing, its lights were flashing red and blue – an almost patriotic display of pageantry. And yet, there was no one to witness such a display, just as there was no one to displace to the side of the road. The sidewalks of Vetta Park's Light Industrial District were lined with abandoned lots and grassy patches sporadically littered with empty bottles.

Hobbs sped past warehouses and facilities – utility storage sheds and flat one-story edifices of dubious establishment. When she finally reached the quarry, it was a long, gravelly path to the bottom – one she winded and weaved while clutching the wheel, praying her tires could hold up.

At the bottom of the quarry, Roberta could see that an ambulance and fire truck had beat her to the scene. She saw five men in hard hats and overalls spread around the burned-out shell of a car. The stench lingered in the air and smoke plumes billowed from the sports car's remains…but at least the fire was out.

One of the men caught sight of Roberta and wandered over. "Hey, are you Vetta Park PD?" he asked. Roberta noticed that his cheeks were black, bits of ash dripping downward from his mustache.

"Yes," she answered, and briefly swept the corner of her blazer, revealing a badge that was affixed to her belt. "What have we got here?"

The fireman tipped his head towards the car. "Well, I'm sorry to say that there was a driver in there. A female. By the time we got here, there was nothing we could do. But she did say a few words to that guy."

The fireman gestured towards a truck, and Roberta Hobbs got her first look at Dalton Beck. He was standing outside of his construction vehicle, nervously nibbling on his nails, his round head soaked in sweat.

Roberta thanked the fireman and walked over to the man. "Hey there. I'm Detective Roberta Hobbs with the Vetta Park Police Department." She brandished her badge just as she had with the fireman: a quick sweep of the corner of her jacket, which revealed the silver, shield-shaped enamel. Then she reached into her back pocket and pulled out a small spiral-bound writing pad and a pen. "Okay if I ask you a few questions?"

The man nodded and dropped his hands to his side. "I didn't expect it to flare up like that," he said. "I woulda tried to save her. I mean…I…I wanted to save her. I tried. She was stuck inside. I feel awful. Really awful."

Roberta nodded and saw that he had tears in his eyes, a ruddy complexion, perhaps worsened by the sun. He was breathing quickly and his fingers were quaking – their nails bitten down to nubs.

"Can we start with your name?" she asked.

"Oh…yeah…sorry…Dalton Beck. Most everyone calls me Beck. I work here loading dirt onto rock trucks usually. Usually have at least two other guys but they called out sick today. So it's just me today."

"Okay, Beck, can we move the conversation to over here?" Hobbs asked politely, but didn't wait for an answer. The sun was beating down, and she could feel sweat beads start to drip down her back. She walked Beck to a shady patch of land, dry rock sheltered by a protruding cliff overhead. Perhaps it would be disarming for him to be further from the scene.

By then, more fire trucks had arrived – their conduit down the gravel path assisted by the firemen who had arrived first. It had become noisy by then – the barking orders of men mixed with the cry of an ambulance.

Roberta was at first surprised to see the ambulance depart with its lights and sirens triggered. From what she understood, there was, distressingly, no duty to perform, no reason for speed. But as the ambulance skidded its way north against the toil of fire trucks headed the opposite way, she saw the reason for it to announce its presence to vehicles that were twice its

5

size – tires milling against rock while slipping across an unpaved trail.

To Hobbs' credit, Beck did seem to calm down once they were a few more feet away. He crouched down and ran his fingers over his head, and when Hobbs asked a follow-up question – "Can you tell me what you saw?" – Beck appeared more lucid, more forthright in his response.

"I saw a sports car," he said. "A really nice, expensive Ferrari go over that cliff over there." Beck gestured towards the top of the cliff – the very spot where Hobbs had descended into the quarry, where fire trucks had been ambling down at a cautious pace, where the ambulance carrying the body of the car's driver had finally summited.

So much for a clean crime scene, Hobbs thought to herself, with a whiff of annoyance. If the road had remained unsullied, she and her partner could track down a tire expert, who could look at the dirt and determine whether the sports car's driver had tried to apply brakes before going over. But every emergency vehicle carving its tire tracks into loose ground – rewriting the forensic evidence of this incident -- made that scenario less probable. Hobbs would still try, but she doubted the effort would lead anywhere.

Beck swallowed hard. "And I want to say...the driver gunned her engine," he said, his voice wobbly. "I heard the engine goin' – loud and clear – right before I saw the car jump."

Hobbs nodded and made a few notes in her spiral notebook. They were quiet for a moment – Hobbs with her head bent down and Beck sniffling and rubbing his eyes – when Hobbs saw her partner, Ray Martinez, appear from the tawny haze.

Martinez was swatting dust off his pants while he made his way over, his eyes watery and his gait protracted. "What's going on?" he addressed Hobbs. "I didn't even see you at first; it's so dusty down here. Took me forever to get down that road." Then, seeing Beck, he swiveled and offered his right hand. "How're you doing? Detective Ray Martinez."

Beck shook the man's hand, stated his name, and then retreated a few steps back. He found a spot of shade against serrated rock and bent his head. Hobbs had seen this type of behavior before and she knew he was dealing with the trauma of what he'd seen. There would be nightmares and coping mechanisms, flashbacks and wanton guilt. She wanted to suggest therapy to him, but first they had to get through the rest of the interview. Her softer side would have to wait.

"This is a witness, Dalton Beck, and he was just telling me about what he saw," Hobbs told Martinez. "He was just saying that he heard the engine rev before the car went over."

"I see," Martinez said. "Did you see what type of car it was?"

"Um, I think it was a Ferrari," Beck offered. "Red. Looked real nice, real expensive." Then he shuddered as if reliving the moment of impact.

"Had you ever seen the Ferrari around here before?" Hobbs asked.

"Nah, never," Beck said. "I'd remember."

"Did you get a chance to take a look at the driver?"

Beck nodded and looked solemnly over at Hobbs. She felt like she had pressed at his most acute vulnerability, that his dark brown eyes – now rounded– were going to pour forth a cascade of tears.

"I saw her," Beck said, trying to subdue the quavering of his chin. "She was…uh…she was sad. Looked like she'd been crying. And…you're gonna think I'm crazy when I tell you this…but I'm pretty sure it was Cecilia Cinvenue. You know, the movie star."

Hobbs nodded and continued writing in her pad while Martinez pivoted and surveyed the rock behind him. She knew that Martinez was suppressing a smile – that he was maintaining his best stoic stance in the face of distress.

Hobbs put the odds of the driver being Cecilia Cinvenue at about one in a million, but Beck's assertion didn't necessarily surprise her either. Beck had been shocked out of his morning work by the sight of a horrific tragedy – and his brain was likely stimulated into delusions and mirages from what he'd seen.

This was why witness statements weren't as reliable as the state would like to believe. This was why she and Martinez were determined to maintain the appearance of normalcy, that there was nothing comical or unfeasible about placing Cecilia Cinvenue in a rock quarry in Eastern Missouri.

Had there ever been a celebrity sighting in Vetta Park? Once, Hobbs had heard rumors about a straight-to-video movie that was filmed in a series of abandoned lots near Vetta Park's seasonal farmers' market. She had driven by and seen all the trappings of a movie set: trailers stationed at the side of the road, lighting setups and at least three different types of movie cameras. Still there were no actors and no scenes being shot, no fans asking for autographs and no subsequent write-ups of Hollywood's dalliance with this tiny Midwestern town. When Hobbs drove by again a week later, everything was gone – the lots as deserted as a stretch of untended farmland. She never did learn the name of the movie that was supposedly filmed (or at least *partially* filmed) in her hometown, and this was the closest Vetta Park had come to having a slice of fame – at least to Hobbs' knowledge. So Beck's claim that he had seen Cecilia Cinvenue behind the wheel was about as believable as if he'd said he'd seen an alien spaceship spring from the quarry.

But Beck's claim wasn't a total loss. Most likely, the driver was someone who looked like Cecilia, and this would provide a fair bit of identifying information. Perhaps – like the actress – the driver had long blonde hair, bright blue eyes and pale skin. Perhaps she was small and dressed impeccably – prone to wearing form-fitting designer outfits and cutting-edge fashion.

Hobbs made a note on her pad to get Beck with the PD's sketch artist. If the driver was so beautiful as to be mistaken for a movie star, it probably wouldn't take long to make an identification.

Also, there was the issue of the license plate. Hobbs hadn't seen a front plate, but she had glimpsed a license plate on the ground near the back of the burned-out car's contorted husk. Once one of the uniformed officers ran the license plate, it probably wouldn't be too difficult to trace a line back to the driver.

Ray Martinez brought his gaze back to Beck and asked, "This…uh…this famous actress who was behind the wheel. Did she say anything to you?"

Beck nodded. "Yeah, she did. She said someone was chasing her."

Hobbs kept the tip of her pen on the pad while she considered this. If Beck had heard correctly, it was a huge piece of evidence. "Did she say who?"

"Naw," Beck said. "I couldn't ask her either…cause then the car blew up."

"So, she didn't get a chance to say anything else?"

"That's right, ma'am."

"So, to be totally clear, she told you that someone had chased her off the cliff?"

"Well…naw…not that someone was chasin' her *off the cliff*. Just that they was chasin' her. Maybe they peeled off earlier in the chase and by then it was too late for her to stop."

"And you didn't ask by whom?"

"You serious? Look, Officer, I ain't had a chance to ask her anything after that. The car exploded, end of story."

Hobbs could tell by Beck's testy tone of voice that she had pressed him enough. But the identity of whoever was chasing this mystery driver – Cecilia Cinvenue's doppelganger – could have been a juicy enough nugget to clear the case right then and there. Of course, Hobbs was going to push, and of course she was going to feel pangs of disappointment at Beck's deficient detective work.

By then a uniformed police officer was waving them over. She and Martinez left Beck by the cliff's wall and walked towards the maelstrom of officers, first responders and charred metal.

"You're not going to believe this," the officer said, motioning down at his notes.

Hobbs glanced downward and saw some letters and numbers scrawled in black ink on the man's pad. He had written out *California* in looping script underneath the cryptic characters.

"Is it the plate?" Hobbs asked.

"Yeah, the station just called it in. You'll never guess who this car is registered to."

Hobbs didn't have to guess. "Cecilia Cinvenue," she stated as though it were fact.

The officer looked dubiously at Hobbs. "Yeah, that's right. I'm thinking it might actually be the actress. You knew she was out here?"

"Our witness ID'd her," Hobbs said, and then she turned towards Dalton Beck. He was crouched over, fumbling with a cigarette, sweat dripping from his glistening head.

So Beck had been right about Cecilia Cinvenue. It was, in fact, the starlet who gunned her engine loud enough to distract a man who was hauling rock. It was Cecilia who careened, full-tilt, off of an elevated platform, rather than face whatever was chasing her. *Whomever.*

Hobbs had a starting point but not much else. A well-known name – a beautiful face whose semblance had been tacked onto billboards, movie posters and magazine covers for at least three decades. The key to this case rested in her ability to answer one simple question: Who was chasing Cecilia Cinvenue?

Chapter Two

Los Angeles, California
November 15, 1977

IT IS *with great joy that we announce the birth of our baby.*
  Name: Cecilia Marie Cinvenue.
  Born at UCLA Medical Center, Los Angeles, California
  Date / Time: Tuesday, November 15, 1977 at 11:57am
  Weight: 5 Lbs, 3 Oz
  Parents: Richard and Betty Cinvenue

CECILIA MARIE. THAT WAS THE NAME HER PARENTS HAD agreed on if she were a girl. Named after her mother's mother. If she were a boy, she'd have been Bernard Edward Cinvenue, named after her father's beloved uncle, who had died after a dreadful bout with tuberculosis.

But, as luck would have it, she was a girl. No sooner had the obstetrician pulled her into the world, gave her a once-over and declared that she was healthy and well-formed, than Cecilia's mother determined that this baby was destined for fame.

She was only minutes old, of course, but Betty Cinvenue could tell that her beautiful new baby had what other babies lacked: a wide-eyed expression, a velvety complexion, a charming disposition.

When Cecilia Marie rested next to her mother for the first time, she looked around as though assessing her surroundings, basking in the adoration the doctors and nurses heaped upon her.

Betty Cinvenue stared down at her daughter with tears in her eyes and ambitious plans taking shape. Betty had tried for years and failed to make it in Hollywood, but Cecilia Marie was going to succeed. Cecilia was only five minutes old, but her destiny was ordained. *Gosh*, Betty thought to herself. *How lucky is Cecilia.*

WHETHER THROUGH LUCK OR TALENT, CECILIA LANDED HER first commercial by the age of two. Hired to sell diapers, her role was to crawl voraciously across a hardwood floor – cooing and giggling while her diaper remained firmly in place. This was a job Cecilia was made for. The bright lights didn't intimidate her and the repetition didn't bother her. Over and over, she enthusiastically crawled across that walnut-hued floor, as if she were Pavlov's dog responding to a stimulus.

Cecilia never saw her first commercial, but it was the launching pad for all that was to come – a rectangular strip of card welcoming her into the actor's union as well as a signed contract with both a management company and a much-coveted Hollywood agency.

Cecilia's toddler years were spent in various waiting rooms in tall, glossy buildings. Betty tried to keep them both occupied while they waited. Little girls filtered in and out of the door leading down the hallway, and Betty compared each of them to her precious Cecilia.

None of those girls had the grace, the poise, the looks to accomplish what Cecilia could, Betty postulated. They didn't have the rose-colored cheeks of a cherub, or the flaxen locks that curled just above their ears. Further, they hadn't appeared in a *nationwide* diaper commercial and weren't represented by a well-respected agent– not like Cecilia.

Unfortunately, for all of Betty's upselling and coaching efforts on Cecilia's behalf, her clever, talented little girl didn't land a single television or commercial role during those years.

Those terrible Hollywood casting directors, Betty thought to herself, after she invariably heard the news from Cecilia's agent. The telephone cord coiled along her left hand, a sleek lit cigarette dangling from her right...Betty knew what these casting directors did not. Her Cecilia was a star, predestined for the stage or screen. And it wasn't just because of her attractiveness. Weren't all toddlers adorable? Cecilia was especially precocious – her high-pitched little-girl voice sounded like the accent of a crooning nightingale. What's more, Cecilia wasn't nearly as troublesome as those other little monsters. Oh, how Betty had seen those little girls carrying on in the waiting room, satiated only by gobs of sugar and overindulgent parental promises.

Every time they waited, Cecilia sat dutifully next to her mother while they anticipated the call for her name. And when that call finally came, and Cecilia had dazzled and delighted the people sitting behind the table – Betty always left feeling confident. *This* was going to be Cecilia's next break.

Betty's certainty could be measured by the width of their smiles, the excited lilt in their voices while they thanked mom and daughter...sometimes profusely.

So there had to be some reason why the follow-up phone call always bore bad news. Perhaps it was nepotism, Hollywood favoritism, or simply bad taste.

The feedback quoted by Cecilia's agent was never helpful anyway:

The casting director was going in another direction.
They wanted a child taller / smaller / older / younger.
Cecilia did a great job, but wasn't exactly right for the part.

The problem was, Cecilia didn't seem *exactly right* for *any* part, and at this rate, her stint as a clambering baby was likely to be the apex of her professional career.

Betty simply could not let that happen. She enrolled Cecilia in acting classes, hired a voice coach, prepped her for pageants and modeling competitions. Betty knew what the other mothers in the neighborhood thought of her when they caught sight of little Cecilia in a pageant dress, or outside running lines for her latest audition. She saw their judgmental faces, their derisive scoffs.

But it was *everyone else* who was wrong – not Betty. She wasn't one of those strident, loudmouth stage moms – pushing an unwilling child to perform. Cecilia was the very definition of obedient. She was diligent, deferential. She worked hard at her lessons and improved her game. Betty was giving her child all the necessary tools to succeed in a very harsh, competitive world. If Cecilia hadn't wanted any of it – if she had pushed back at any time – well, that would have warranted a very serious discussion. But that was the thing about Cecilia. She never pushed back.

———

BETTY KNEW HOW HARD IT WAS TO SUCCEED IN HOLLYWOOD because she herself had never caught a break. A star performer by the age of fifteen – at least, by the standards of her local community theater – Betty had moved out to Los Angeles as soon as she was of legal age. Back in the sixties, acting opportunities were much more limited. Trying to get signed by a studio was like trying to catch someone's eye from a thousand yards away. There were only a handful of studios and so many charming, exquisite, striking young women vying for their attention.

Betty Carlson was a talent, to be sure, but her talent never took her anywhere. By the age of thirty – unsigned, unrecognized, uninspired – Betty stopped trying and settled into a life of domestic simplicity. She married Richard Cinvenue and settled into a bungalow just east of the 405 freeway.

At night, Betty would lie in bed next to Richard and imagine that the humming engines of speeding cars were really the swells of the ocean. During the day, she would wander around their tiny cottage and imagine that they were living in their guesthouse while their adjacent mansion was under construction. Betty's mind carried her to all sorts of decorations for her fictitious domicile. There were gardens, gables and fountains, columns and marble staircases – all cleverly hidden behind magnificent gates in Beverly Hills. These were the rewards that life as a successful actress would bestow.

Betty hadn't made it but she still ached for the bounties of her mislaid dream. When she showed up at her doctor's office after a week of nonstop vomiting, and the man had given her the news she already somehow knew – *you're pregnant!* – Betty left the room with an irrepressible optimism. This was the first time she'd felt that emotion – was it *hope?* -- in years.

More than just the approaching duty of parenthood, this soon-to-be bundle of joy supplied a direction that had been lacking in Betty's life. The effort hadn't been pointless. This child could pick up the metaphorical football where Betty had left it and run with it. The fact that they already lived in Los Angeles was a significant advantage. This child would be beautiful and talented, and would be raised by a mom who already knew the ropes.

Driving home from the doctor's office with a growth the size of a pea taking form inside of her, Betty tied her only silk scarf around her head and rolled down the windows. She floated back to her house, grinning wildly from the secret that only she carried…the future that only she knew.

IT FINALLY HAPPENED IN 1987. ENTERTAINMENT MAGAZINES would describe Cecilia's success as "overnight" but this was only true if overnight could be interpreted as having taken a decade.

Betty spent ten years driving Cecilia to auditions and waiting – always waiting – while Cecilia performed behind a closed door. First there was the initial wait, and then there was the longer wait. The drive home, the everlasting evening, the restless night of sleep while possibilities tugged at Betty's brain.

She kept the telephone unencumbered during these waits, which meant Richard had to drive to the office if he wanted to speak with his family back in Michigan. It meant that whichever telemarketing agent called during "the wait" would be swiftly berated and hung up on.

"We have call waiting, Betty," Richard always insisted on his way out the door, peeved that he couldn't plainly communicate with others from the comfort of his own home. "Cece's agent can get through even if you're already talking to someone."

But Betty knew it wasn't just about freeing up the telephone; it was her state of mind. She couldn't think clearly while she was waiting for the news, and no conversation with a friend or relative was going to distract her until she knew for sure.

For years and years, the wait ended with the chime of the phone and the same banal excuses from the same nasally voice of rejection that Betty had grown accustomed to for years.

Until – one day – the voice said something different.

Friday, April 24, 1987. Betty picked up the phone and got

the news that she'd been waiting for – not just for that night, not just for that audition. She got the news that she had waited *ten long years* for. And, if you counted Betty's truncated foray into show business, the news she had waited over twenty years for.

Cecilia Marie had been cast in a pilot. She was going to play a ten-year old girl in a blended family comprised of ten children: siblings, step-siblings and half siblings. Betty could already see Cecilia's name in the opening credits montage.

The pilot hadn't even been picked up by a network yet, and Cecilia's agent had warned against premature optimism. "More pilot episodes get rejected than picked up," she had cautioned Betty. "So, you should view this as an opportunity that opens doors for future opportunities. If this one doesn't get picked up, she's more likely to be cast in another one. It's a great thing, Betty, but don't put the cart before the horse."

Betty heard these words but she *knew* – in her gut, in her very essence – that this show would make Cecilia Cinvenue a household name. Everyone loved a mixed family sitcom these days, and this particular program would be helmed by a burgeoning comedian in the role of Dad. This show had all the trimmings of high entertainment, and any test audience or marketing executive worth his weight would understand that.

Cecilia Cinvenue – her hair a luscious mane of blonde silk, her golden skin that blushed and shined– would easily stand out among her nine TV siblings. If Betty carried one axiom in her heart, it was as true from the day she learned she was pregnant to the day she signed the contract on her daughter's behalf. Cecilia was going to make it in Hollywood. It was *finally* happening.

Chapter Three

Los Angeles, California
1987

CECILIA REMEMBERED her life before she'd been cast in *The Family Next Door*. The mornings were early and filled with preparation. She dutifully rose before dawn, when the street behind their house was quiet and stars were still scattered above their tiny bungalow. She got dressed and made herself breakfast, and reached for the small wad of papers that her mother unfailingly left for her.

Character names in all caps, dialogue typed neatly underneath, with perfect left-adjusted margins. Depending on the day, Cecilia was Stephanie, or Angela, Michelle or Kimberly, perhaps hundreds of other names she was meant to inhabit. She was willful, loyal, energetic, stubborn or emotional.

The various coaches her mom had hired for her throughout the years helped her establish how to occupy the right persona. Not that it mattered. For years, Cecilia's diligence had resulted in absolutely nothing.

But Cecilia endured the ritual all the same. There was audition practice and then there was school – several hours a day where Cecilia was just a kid, roaming the tiled hallways of her elementary school. After school, there was dance class, pageant coaching, voice instruction.

Oftentimes, Betty showed up at school office to sign the little girl out. Auditions happened during working hours, and so Cecilia had to miss hours of regular instruction every pilot season.

Cecilia saw her classmates – watched them gaze at her as she meandered past their metal desks on her way to the office. She knew she was different from them by enduring this sacrament. To her knowledge, none of her peers had to leave *Capture the Flag* or *Heads Up / 7 Up* early to run lines with a casting director.

Later in life, several interviewers would ask her to reflect on this period of fruitless auditioning. Did she hate it? Or did she view it as the necessary prerequisite to a successful career?

Cecilia was never able to provide any particular insight, since she had been auditioning from as far back as she could remember. It was part of the landscape of her early life, just as the peeling yellow wallpaper in her bathroom or the soft thrum of the cars that drove past her bedroom window in the mornings.

Auditioning, practicing, performing – these weren't verbs to form opinions about. They were just *there* – part of what she did before she was even sentient, crawling around audition rooms while wearing a bonnet and diaper.

Interviewers also frequently asked her what landing that first role was like, and this was a question Cecilia could answer. She remembered arriving home from school that day and finding a kitchen full of celebratory balloons. She remembered Betty's jubilant face, her outstretched arms as she gathered Cecilia and swung her into a tornado's eddy of joy and pride. She even remembered the weather outside – sunlight glimmering through their kitchen window, while Cecilia twirled and spun, chasing and throwing the balloons Betty had purchased for her.

Cecilia remembered the flurry of phone calls – Betty perched on a dining room chair while Cece danced and glided around her. Betty called relatives and friends, acquaintances they had met on the audition circuit and pageant rounds. Betty was doting and appreciative in spreading the good news, and her voice absolutely dripped with ebullience.

Cecilia Cinvenue remembered this moment in intimate detail for the rest of her life. It became a photograph – one that starts off luminous and immaculate, and then...with years of experience and age, begins to look a different way.

This moment in Cecilia's kitchen when she was ten years old – at first it was pure exhilaration. It was the day that all her efforts paid off after years of exhaustive striving. This was the moment that her career truly launched. It would take years before Cecilia saw this moment for what it really was... the jumping off point for everything that followed.

Chapter Four

Vetta Park, Missouri
September 15, 2022

ROBERTA HOBBS WAS TIRED. It had been a long day.

In typical cases of fatalities, once law enforcement identified the body, they had to notify next of kin. Hobbs absolutely hated this part – despised it with such intensity that it caused her to question her chosen profession. She remembered the first time she'd had to do it – her stomach churning as she stood on the doorstep of a stranger's house, about to deliver the worst news of their lives.

At least Cecilia's residence was five states away, and this meant they would be able to send California state patrolmen to the Cinvenue's doorstep. Hobbs could envision the passive faces of the officers, their sullen gestures of comfort while they said that a woman matching Cecilia Cinvenue's description had been in a car accident, that the ensuing casualty *might* be their daughter.

It was *maybe* until it was absolutely confirmed – with DNA analysis or dental records. The patrolmen – their wide-brimmed, cinnamon-colored hats in their hands – would ask whether Cecilia's parents had spoken to their daughter recently, whether she had been morose or anxious lately. They would collect all manner of clues while offering condolences for the outcome that had likely occurred – which the celebrity gossip blogs would surely print had occurred – but which the respectable, uniformed police couldn't *confirm* had occurred. Not yet. It was terrible to be on either end of that conversation.

The next of kin had to be notified before word got out – but, like everything else in Cecilia Cinvenue's life, the mechanics proved more tricky than usual. Who was Cecilia's next of kin? Her parents – Elizabeth and Richard Cinvenue – had long since passed away. Cecilia had no siblings; she had never married and she'd had no children.

Who would be the forlorn, stricken face on the doorstep? The man who clutched his heart at the news, the woman who brought her hand up to her ashen face, tilting against the doorframe for support? Hobbs didn't know, and it would take some digging to find out.

HOURS PASSED WHILE HOBBS REMAINED AT THE VETTA PARK Industrial District. In the previous five hours, she'd spent more time there than she'd cumulatively spent in her decades of living in the municipality. She and Ray Martinez canvassed the district to ask about doorbell cameras and odd sounds that employees might have heard.

Distressing but not surprising, no one had heard or seen anything. And no one had doorbell cameras either. This wasn't some fancy, high-traffic quarter where valuables were stored or exchanged. The businesses out here had skeleton crews for their staffing. There were lumber and equipment storage yards, sheet metal shops, a tractor repair shop and two chemical manufacturing plants.

The employees who came to the door were chatty and cooperative with Martinez and Hobbs, but the little information that they shared was entirely useless to the investigation. Hobbs was reluctant to reveal more than what was necessary. Her opening line, delivered with bureaucratic formality: "We're investigating a nearby car accident" – was met with uneven brows and casual concern.

Soon enough, these employees – and the world – would learn what had transpired less than five miles away from their little district. Hobbs didn't see the need to bring these people into the fold any sooner than necessary. If they had some helpful information to share, then sure, *maybe* she would share some details in exchange for some details – an instructive back and forth. But there was no need to even think that far ahead. No one knew a thing.

———

Hobbs and Martinez returned to the Vetta Park precinct later that day. They had uncovered one and only one solid bit of evidence – the tire track marks. The Vetta Park police's tire track expert happened to be available that afternoon, and he sped over to the quarry on his motorcycle after getting the call.

Tall and weighty, with wisps of white hair peeking out from a St. Louis Cardinals hat, Charlie Blackburn met them at the top of the quarry. This was after the neighborhood canvass, when Hobbs was deflated and not expecting much of anything. She showed Charlie the general area of gravel where Cecilia was perceived to have hurdled into the chasm. After several fire trucks had forayed a track path from the gravel into the pit, one of the officers had finally sealed off the general area with bright yellow police tape. Since then, the emergency vehicles had to navigate a windier track downward, but at least they were no longer tainting the crime scene.

Charlie Blackburn got to work as soon as Hobbs explained the task at hand. When she left the Vetta Park Quarry, he was still at it – furled over rock-strewn wheel imprints, his camera shuttering as though he were paparazzi.

Charlie Blackburn was the first call that Hobbs got when she was back at her desk. "I can't tell you definitively just yet…" he said, his voice trailing off behind what Hobbs envisioned was a puff of the Copenhagen tobacco he always chewed.

"What can you tell me non-definitively?" Hobbs asked.

"It doesn't look like the driver braked at all," Charlie said. "That sports car sped up before it went over. Usually, we see evidence of braking and wheel rotation just before the edge. Not this time."

"Hmmm," Hobbs said, letting the news digest. So Dalton Beck had been right about this as well.

"Did you see any tire tracks other than the sports car?" Hobbs asked. "Any indication that there was a car chasing the sports car?"

Charlie sighed. "Well, I'll say no, but I also want to caveat it. The road turns to gravel maybe thirty feet before the quarry's edge. If there had been a car chasing the sports car, it's possible they could've turned off before hitting the gravel. And if they were a far enough distance behind the sports car, it's entirely possible they could've gently applied the brakes without leaving tire marks. Do you see what I'm saying here? I don't see evidence of a second car, but I also don't see a *lack* of evidence of it either."

Hobbs bit the inside of her cheek and then asked, "So, if there were a second car behind the sports car, you wouldn't be able to tell me anything about it?"

"That's correct, Detective."

Hobbs thanked Charlie and quietly set the receiver of her

phone in its cradle. Charlie had been somewhat helpful – at least able to corroborate Beck's version of events – but not so helpful as to provide a useful lead.

Hobbs sighed deeply and sat back in her chair. She was just conjecturing about next steps in the case when her phone rang again.

"Roberta Hobbs," the detective answered.

The voice on the other end was deep, husky, familiar. He seemed almost out of breath – but maybe it was just quick exhilarations that frequently accompanied a terrible panic. "Roberta," the voice said, "I'm in trouble and I need your help. Meet me outside the Vetta Park precinct in twenty minutes."

Hobbs had no ability to respond since the voice dissipated – an audible click as the actualized period at the end of his sentence. Was it a sentence, or more of a demand? Either way, she wouldn't hesitate to comply.

The chair squeaked beneath her as Hobbs made her way outside, into the fresh sunlight. She recoiled from the infernal air by seeking shelter underneath a rectangular awning. The parking lot stretched out before her, as languid as ever. Shift changes were going to occur in a few hours, but nothing was happening yet.

Hobbs sighed and glanced at her watch. Twenty minutes never felt so long. All she could do was stand, stare and wait for him to arrive.

Chapter Five

Los Angeles, California
1988

CECILIA SAT in her dressing room and looked at her reflection in the mirror. She was eleven years old and caked in makeup, her hair severely pinned into place with barrettes, bobby pins and hairspray.

Eleven years old and she was already a star. For starters, she had outgrown her initial agent and was now represented by a much bigger player in Hollywood – Anita Livingston. Anita was a dealmaker with a long roster of clients, including several whose names had lit up movie marquees before Cecilia was even born.

In addition to Anita, Cecilia had a publicist, an on-set tutor, and various acting and voice coaches who still provided guidance. And as for her manager? Betty Cinvenue filled the role quite impeccably. The woman negotiated with the other adults in the room; she signed Cecilia's professional head shots; she managed the little girl's income; she was the CEO of the Cecilia Cinvenue brand.

Cecilia didn't push back on her mother's role. If anything,

it was reassuring to have a familiar, intimate person managing so much of her life. When Cecilia whined that the work was too hard, that they had to run through the same drills repeatedly, inexorably, to the point of exhaustion, it was Betty who reminded the girl that *The Family Next Door* was a winning ticket.

Picked up by one of the networks, and auspiciously deposited in a prime-time lineup of successful shows, *The Family Next Door* had slingshot to the top of the Nielsen ratings, and with it, Cecilia's star power.

There was no room for grumbling or discomfort, Betty scolded the girl, reminding her of the throngs of eager hopefuls who could easily replace her. Even on a successful show, even mid-season, writers had been known to thrust familiar – even beloved – characters down elevator shafts or into humanitarian missions in Siberia. Studios had no forbearance for haughty, overconfident little girls, and so all the indignities and discomforts Cecilia faced would have to be suffered – not in silence but in appreciation. *Appreciate the long hours and repeated run-throughs*, Betty had told her, *because they're better than the alternative.*

It wasn't all bad. In fact, at the beginning it could be quite good. Betty brought Cecilia her fan mail between rehearsal and filming, and the two sat together in Cecilia's dressing room reading what was mostly fawning praise. Most of the letters were from little girls with big dreams, who lived in far-flung areas of the U.S. that Cecilia would never visit. Ohio. Kentucky. North Dakota. Cecilia's response to fan mail was always the same – a glossy head shot with a flourishing signature that her mother signed on her behalf.

Most days were full of work, but on the occasional evening out, Cecilia commanded all the attention in the room. All the heads swiveled towards her; all the faces seemed delighted just to be in her presence. Cecilia Cinvenue had become the center of the earth, tugging everything in her direction.

She arrived at an awards show in a limousine – the fabulously long kind, which seemed to stretch in every direction. When she and Betty emerged from the vehicle, there were photographers clamoring for her attention – begging her to answer their shouts of "Cecilia!" by looking in their direction.

Cecilia's eleventh birthday party had been a huge deal. She didn't know who had hosted it, but the mansion was tucked away in the foothills of Malibu. It had a sprawling outdoor pool and an immense lawn, which more than accommodated the pop-up carnival rides. The guests were her on-set siblings and other Hollywood pre-teen and teenage luminaries. Photographers snapped away while Cecilia and her onscreen siblings floated through the air with effortless delight.

When it was time for cake, Betty brought in the two-tiered chocolate confection while everyone gathered around Cecilia. She beamed after blowing out the candles, realizing just then that none of this would have been possible without *The Family Next Door*. Not the mansion, not the rides, not the casual familiarity with same-aged celebrities. Previous birthdays had consisted of a round of bowling with three friends and twenty minutes at the arcade. This was exceptional.

Betty cut the cake and passed around slices, but there was none for the girl of honor.

"Hey! Where's my piece?" Cecilia asked, and she saw the shock and consternation that her question had posed – broadcast across her mother's face.

Betty ushered the young girl into one of the marble bathrooms and locked the door behind them. "I can't believe you asked for cake like that in front of the photographers!" Betty hissed.

Cecilia instantly knew that she had done something egregiously wrong; she just didn't know exactly what.

"But I just wanted my piece of cake!" she insisted. "It's my birthday! Everyone else got cake!"

"You can't eat cake, Cecilia! Your contract stipulates that

you are to maintain a weight of *seventy-five pounds*. Do you have any idea how much you've already eaten today?"

Cecilia had no idea how much she'd eaten that day. Her thoughts had been lost to the whirr of carnival rides – the drift of crisp Los Angeles air across her face while she hovered and dipped. Her mind had been distracted by doting guests who looked at her with gratitude and thanked her for the invite. She hadn't invited these kids – some of them she'd never even met – but she basked in their praise, their pleasure of being in her orbit. She felt important, revered and well-liked. And that day – up until the cake incident – had been the best day of her eleven-year-old life.

"Okay," Cecilia said softly. "I won't have any cake."

She and Betty left the bathroom together, arm in arm, back to the party. This united front was betrayed by the tears forming in the corners of Cecilia's eyes – although she had the presence of mind not to allow them to fall, certainly not before this assortment of photographers.

It wasn't so much that she had been denied cake at her birthday party, but that she was confronted with the notion that she had done something inescapably *wrong* – something that she had previously considered a fairly banal childhood ritual.

And the only thing worse to Cecilia than the idea that she was being disobedient – acting out against the rules, which she never ever wanted to do – was the first kernel of realization that childhood rituals were a thing of the past. Sure, she was only eleven – not even old enough to sit in the front seat of the family car (although Betty still let her) – but she was well aware that all that lay in front of her was adulthood.

"OKAY, CECILIA, KEEP YOUR EYES CLOSED…NOW ONE, TWO, three…open them!"

It was nine o' clock at night after a particularly rigorous week of filming – and Betty had promised the girl a surprise once they got in the car and drove off the Burbank studio lot.

"Is it a party for me?" Cecilia asked eagerly from the passenger seat. "Or...the pair of boots I asked you about?" Her mom had instructed her to keep her eyes closed for the whole ride, and backstopped this request by tying a handkerchief around the top of the girl's head.

Curiosity got the better of Cecilia, and she occasionally opened her eyes and peered out, but the passing L.A. scenery – especially when cloaked with a blood-red film – gave no hints.

Finally, they reached their destination, and Betty pulled the car to the side of the street and guided her daughter out. They promenaded past what Cecilia assumed was a mailbox, and then onto a concrete path. At the top of the path, Betty raised the handkerchief from Cecilia's face and said, "Ta! Da!"

It was a single-family house, two stories high, with brown paneling and a caramel-colored awning. They were standing in front of the one-car garage, facing a green, well-manicured lawn shaped like a square of cheese. The front door – also painted brown – was wide open.

"It's a house," Cecilia stated, rather flatly. She had been hoping for a pair of high-ankle cowboy boots that she'd seen one of her castmates wearing. And she didn't quite understand the meaning of this surprise or who they were visiting.

"It's not just a house; it's *our* house, silly!" Betty said. And then she grabbed the girl by the hand and led her through the front door.

The inside of this house was impressive, to be sure. It had shiny, hardwood floors, a grand kitchen – big enough to eat in – and large, floor-to-ceiling windows. Even at this hour, Cecilia could imagine the sunlight streaming in at daybreak, illuminating breakfast at the kitchen table they didn't yet own.

Their tiny bungalow was, by contrast, much older and drabbier – but it had been home for Cecilia's entire life.

"What about our house now?" Cecilia asked.

Betty smiled. "Why, we'll sell it! Isn't this much better?"

Of course, it was. The rooms were bigger, the paint was newer, the lights were brighter. Cecilia drifted throughout the house, marveling at the future they were to behold at that residence. It wasn't until she walked outside that exhilaration truly overcame her.

There, several yards behind the sliding glass doors, was an L-shaped swimming pool, with rippling blue waters and a diving board at one end. Cecilia screamed with excitement when she saw it – a noise so piercing that dogs in the distance started barking, and Betty came trotting outside to calm the girl down.

"Please! Cecilia!" Betty scolded. "They'll call the police if you scream like that!"

Cecilia began jumping up and down, hopping like a rabbit stretching for a dangling carrot. "We have a pool! We have a pool! We have a pool!" She exclaimed. She couldn't remember the last time – if ever? – she had behaved so unmindfully, had been so unrestrained.

"Yes, Cecilia. Yes, we have a pool!" Betty said with a smile. "I'm glad you're so happy about it!"

"But how could you afford it?" Cecilia asked. She knew absolutely nothing about the family finances, had no knowledge of what her television paycheck contained or where it went. Richard and Betty didn't talk about that sort of thing in front of her, so the bulk of Cecilia's knowledge arose from the chatterings of her on-screen family. Many of her television siblings lived in rented apartments near Burbank, and parroted their parents' concerns about the price of California real estate. Cecilia felt, at that moment, especially lucky. *Blessed.*

"*You* did it, Cecilia! It's because of *you* and your success that we can afford this amazing house with the amazing pool!"

When they later went to the local dessert and coffeehouse to celebrate – decaf coffee for the girl and a buttered croissant for her mother – Cecilia felt like she was going to burst with delight. The coffeehouse was sparsely attended, but those who were there took notice of the young star. They smiled reverentially at the girl, and mostly left her and her mother alone, until the very end. Just before Cecilia and her mom prepared to leave, two middle-school age girls approached and asked for Cecilia's autograph.

"We watch *The Family Next Door* every week," one of the girls said. "We absolutely love it…and you."

Cecilia smiled broadly and left the coffee house, back to her new house with its incredible backyard swimming pool. Everyone she met seemed to admire her, and she was the one who made all things possible. It was a heady, intoxicating feeling; so potent, it seemed like it could never evaporate. The type of feeling that really made a person feel valuable. The type of feeling that – when chased – could lead down a dangerous path.

Chapter Six

Vetta Park, Missouri
September 15, 2022

ROBERTA HOBBS WAS JUST ABOUT to give up. She had waited for forty minutes already – leaning flaccidly against a plastic awning column while work churned inside. There was so much to do, and she had little time for this – for the man whose voice had been nearly hysterical with urgency, now making her wait for his car to arrive.

But eventually it did. She spotted the old navy-colored station wagon as soon as it puttered into the parking lot. She watched carefully as a familiar face appeared – shaggy graying hair, a disheveled beard, eyes that mirrored her own.

It was Harlan Hobbs, her brother – or, more precisely, the youngest of her older brothers. After the three Hobbs boys made their appearance in the world, Roberta's birth had been a mistake (*a gift*, her mom always insisted). But even though Harlan no longer inhabited the role, he had still always acted like the baby of the family.

Throughout her life, Harlan had been the neediest of the Hobbs children – the one who took up residence in his parents' basement, long after the others had moved away. Harlan was the one who solicited advice from their parents – guidance really – even after he turned forty, and had been married and divorced with a son of his own.

Roberta wasn't surprised that her brother had called her needing help with something – but there was something about the worry in his wavering voice that signaled a deeper concern.

If he'd been anxious on the phone, he was a jubilant and unvexed in the parking lot. "Roberta!" he called out, then walked up to the police steps, stepped under the awning and lifted her into a tremendous hug. "How are ya?"

Roberta brushed her hands over her clothes after she was reunited with the ground. "I'm good, Harlan. How are *you*? You seemed kind of upset over the phone."

At once serious, Harlan pressed his lips together and nodded. "Uh-huh. Yeah, I've got a real situation on my hands, Berta, and I'm going to need your help. You know I wouldn't ask unless I was really desperate."

Roberta invited him inside the building, to one of the interview rooms. At least there, he could ask her to borrow money without the threat of eavesdroppers and gossipers. Sometimes, the Vetta Park police department resembled a middle school lunch room. Particularly in colder months -- when active calls abated and the bustle of activity slowed to a standstill – the employees of the department would entertain themselves by whispering about each other. Roberta didn't need that kind of scrutiny in her life these days.

She led Harlan through the main precinct room, past shabbily decorated cubicles, white board metrics and filing cabinets. During the walk, she had a chance to think about her bank account. How much money was she willing to lend her older brother anyway? Money she knew he would guarantee to return, and money she was certain she would never see again.

And of course, he would be in need of a loan. Harlan had gotten married a year earlier to a woman he'd met at the dingiest bar in South County. He always spoke about their introduction with an inflection of pride – as though it was miraculous that something so monumental could emerge from a diminutive shed with sawdust on the floor and blinking neon advertisements in the windows.

But whereas Harlan saw it as serendipity, the rest of the Hobbs clan saw it entirely differently. Of course, he would have met Shanna – Shayna? – at that bar, because that's where she spent most of her free time. The fact that she had two young daughters made the situation even worse. Shanna / Shayna left them in the care of an older neighbor, while she let loose on the dance floor, knocked back tequila shots, and thrust herself into the arms of lost middle-aged men like Harlan.

Perhaps Roberta wasn't capable of a charitable view of Harlan's whirlwind romance, because she still viewed him as the boy who refused to grow up. He was still the tangle-haired goblin of her youth – the boy who chased her girlfriends around their farmhouse with fresh pig feces, the teenager who rode shirtless on the tiller whenever she had a party, hoping to get noticed.

Roberta had spent her recent years hoping Harlan would become smitten with a woman who would knock sensibility and maturity into him; instead, Shanna / Shayna appeared to be just as bad as he was…and they had doubled down on their impetuous ways. This included a hasty romance, a hasty Vegas wedding, and a hasty pregnancy announcement. It was no surprise that Harlan would come to her asking for money.

When they reached the interview room, Roberta closed the door and they both took seats at the desk across from each other. Roberta had to remind herself that just because the setup was designed to be antagonistic – cop versus robber seating, bright overhead lighting, empty walls and chipping white paint – she and Harlan were on the same team, in the same family. There was no need to be as punitive as the room would suggest.

"What do you need, Harlan?" Roberta asked.

Harlan sighed. "I need help – a lot of help – with Nick."

"With Nick?" Roberta repeated. Nick was Harlan's son from his first marriage. The boy had to be… twelve? Thirteen maybe? Roberta hadn't seen him since before the Covid pandemic, and even then, he had been a quiet kid, always shrinking away from her, from all familial interactions.

"How old is Nick now?" Roberta asked.

"Fifteen," Harlan said, in a way that enunciated both syllables, as if to suggest there was something shared and knowable about a fifteen-year-old boy.

But Roberta had no children of her own, and didn't know the first thing about them – particularly not teenagers. And particularly not *this* teenager, whose interactions with her since the age of ten had most recently consisted of grunting a perfunctory greeting behind the glow of a cell phone screen.

"Harlan, I don't how I can help you," Roberta said. "I don't know Nick at all."

"I wouldn't come to you if I wasn't really desperate," Harlan said, and Roberta saw the shift of color in his face, the mist of tears on his cheeks, his swollen eyes.

She leaned forward and squeezed Harlan's hand. "Okay… well…Tell me what kind of trouble Nick is in."

Harlan tilted his head back and ran his eyes back and forth over the walls of the room before finally looking back in her direction. "He's out of control," Harlan said, and his voice caught on the last word. It was as if he was capitulating, accepting his fate as the parent of a balky teenager, one who couldn't be *controlled*.

"How so?" Roberta asked.

"He's just angry…angry at us. Angry about Shayna's pregnancy. Angry at having little sisters. He's incredibly rude to Shayna. He doesn't listen to either of us. He cuts school. He goes out and doesn't tell us where he's going. I think he's failing school, by the way. He's miserable and I'm really worried and I don't know what else to do."

"What about Mireille?" Roberta asked.

Mireille had been Harlan's first wife, and Nick's mother. Roberta remembered the pregnancy announcement with easy clarity. On heavy cardstock, a barefooted, blonde-haired woman was frolicking in golden-brown Indian grass next to a Caps Lock announcement that she and Harlan were having a boy.

Things seemed so simple back then. The pregnancy had happened quickly, but Harlan assured his family that he and Mireille were in love and that everything was occurring exactly as it should. When Nicholas Daniel Hobbs emerged several months later, the impetuously-settled family seemed as blissful as could be hoped for.

And then, just as quickly as the domestic harmony had come together, it all broke apart. Mireille showed up at Mr. and Mrs. Hobbs' Kansas farmhouse, infant in tow, and charged their youngest son with the crime of shirking his parental responsibilities. Harlan didn't help his case by showing up several hours later – soused and enraged – yelling inanities about love and commitment before stumbling into the living room couch.

What followed was a marital annulment and a détente between the warring factions. Mireille headed back to her Connecticut hometown and Harlan relocated to a Stamford suburb, and they spent the next decade taking turns raising the young boy. Roberta didn't see much of Harlan – or Nick – during this time. On several occasions, she purchased plane tickets to Connecticut, but some unopened case, or pending trial, or life event prevented her from boarding the flight. For his part, Harlan rarely came back to the Midwest during those years, claiming the need to save every last penny in his bank account.

It was only once Nick turned eleven or twelve that Harlan finally made the trip home – and this time, the marital dissolution was unquestionable. When Roberta showed up at baggage claim, she noticed that her brother was heatedly pulling suitcase after suitcase from the carousel.

"Mireille decided to move to Canada," Harlan had explained, an overstuffed Longchamps bag draped over his shoulder. "So, I moved back here and I'm going to raise Nick by myself."

Roberta had only nodded at this news, certain that any expression of delight or concern would irritate her brother – especially in the crowded space of St. Louis Lambert Airport. But in actuality, Roberta had felt both delight and concern. She daydreamed unrealistically about Thanksgiving dinners and family visits – times when the Hobbs clan could throw back a nice California Pinot and reminisce about the olden days, without feeling like a piece of the puzzle was displaced to the East Coast.

But Roberta had also been worried. It seemed Nick was going to have no interaction and limited communication with his mother. Roberta tried to get more details about this situation but Harlan clearly didn't want to share. He rashly threw his suitcases onto a cart and bolted out of the airport terminal – his son and sister charging behind him to try to keep the pace.

At the short-term parking lot, Harlan was just as reticent.

"What about Mireille?" Roberta asked while Harlan rammed his bags into an already-cluttered trunk. Harlan responded by ceasing all activity and contemptuously glaring at his sister. "Exactly," Harlan said. "What about her?"

In the Vetta Park precinct interview room – just as in that airport parking lot – Harlan simply didn't wish to reveal any insight into their co-parenting arrangement (or lack, thereof).

"Mireille hasn't been in Nick's life for years," Harlan said. "I would rather send Nicholas to military school than rope *the devil* into this."

Roberta chose to ignore Harlan's epithet for his ex-wife, failed to point out that Mireille was more of a ghost than the devil. As far as she knew, Mireille was absent, invisible – her influence only perceptible in the slight ways her son unwittingly duplicated her mannerisms.

"Is that what you're thinking about doing?" Roberta asked him. "Military school?"

Harlan took a deep sigh and clasped his hands together on the table, and this is when Roberta realized that all the antecedent dialogue had been preface for the Big Ask.

She knew Harlan's ways, and the manner in which he prepared himself for these types of solicitations. He gave a show of being nervous – of tousling his salt-and-pepper hair, then rubbing his hands over his face as though they were devoid of circulation. Then there was the long silence while he seemingly prepared his words – although Roberta knew that this, too, was part of the act. Harlan knew exactly what he was going to say and how he was going to say it. The blank space between them was meant to convey his solemnity over the whole deal.

Finally, able to stand it no more, Roberta broke the silence. "Harlan...*what?*"

"I need you to take Nick for a little while," Harlan said – the words lurching out of his mouth in a single exhale.

Roberta's response was much more deliberate. She was sure to clarify each syllable. "Take...him...where?"

"Take him off my hands. Roberta, please."

Harlan stared at her piercingly, his tanned face now blotchy and tear-stained. "He can't live with us anymore, Roberta. Not with the baby on the way and two other little kids. I thought we could handle him but we can't, and I have nowhere else to turn."

Roberta noticed that Harlan had neglected to mention the precise ways in which Nick's behavior made him untenable. Harlan had to occupy the narrow margin of space between Nick's requiring a new home and Nick's behavior being too disorderly to handle. Because if the boy's own father couldn't even take care of him, what hope did Roberta have of reining him in?

"Can you elaborate on what has Nick been up to lately?" Roberta asked.

Harlan sunk his head in his hands and then, after a few seconds, looked up at her. "He runs away...all the time. He hates living at home. Says it's too loud. One of the Sheriff's deputies returned him to our place last night after he was caught at a bar down the street trying to use a fake ID. He skips school and then just wanders around the neighborhood. He doesn't get along with Shayna and she's at a point now where she said he's got to go."

Roberta saw the pained expression on her brother's face. His melancholy was almost too much to bear. It brought her back to nights in their childhood home, when wild storms threatened to rip through their curtains, threatened to fracture the delicate window panes that separated their serenity from the ferocity outside.

Harlan had always been the most afraid of all of the kids. He had been the one curling, shrimp-like on their mother's lap, burying his head beneath hers until the storm passed.

Now, just like then, he was unmoored – breathless and panicked. Roberta could see the young face in the man's countenance. When he breathed deeply, she remembered their mother's relaxation exercises. When he held his fingers to his mouth and closed his eyes, she saw the numbers that he counted to track the interval between lightning and thunder. When he opened his eyes again, Harlan was calm. He spoke carefully.

"Roberta...listen to me. Nick skips school and he's gloomy,

yes. But he's not a bad kid. He's not into drugs or alcohol. Yes, he got caught in the bar, but he hadn't been drinking. He doesn't even have a *driver's license*. Right? He's only fifteen. He doesn't capture wild animals or play with guns or any of that. He just doesn't want to be at home, and Shayna doesn't want him there, and with a new baby about to enter our lives…it's just too much. Roberta, please, I am your brother and I am *begging* you. Please."

"What makes you think that I'll do any better with him?" Roberta asked.

"Because he gets along with you. He loves you."

Roberta threw her head back and scoffed. Her previous experiences with Nick had been fine, satisfactory. She would describe them as fulfilling the obligations of familial interactions…to the barest degree. Was there love? Sure…the way someone loves a relative they barely know and only see (via a screen) a few times, and can acknowledge a degree of genetic connection. The way a person generally expresses love out of obligation and necessity – a love that has absolutely no feeling.

Roberta knew that she and Nick did not share the kind of love that would foster a relationship – that would facilitate an easy co-habitation in a two-bedroom apartment. They were essentially strangers – she and Nick – so for Harlan to claim that they *got along* was entirely a fabrication of omission. They had gotten along in the past because they barely knew each other.

"And there's no one else that can take him in?" Roberta pressed. "How about Nash and Tucker?"

Nash and Tucker were the older two boys of the Hobbs clan. They were so much older than Roberta and Harlan, that occasionally she had to correct herself when revealing how many siblings she had. Yes, she had three brothers, not just one – but really it had been like two sets of kids at a time. Growing up, it had just been her and Harlan running around their parents' bucolic farmhouse outside Leavenworth,

Kansas. Her older brothers were apparitions – phantom creatures whose lacrosse balls had dented the wooden doorways, whose scrawling had scratched the Formica countertops. Now, just like then, Nash and Tucker were affable and loving, but also physically withdrawn. They had their own lives, and Roberta felt like the minor character who'd come along in the third act.

Harlan shook his head. "Nash and Tucker have young kids too. I think what Nick needs – just for a little while – is an empty place."

"My place *isn't empty*," Roberta said, her voice inflecting with prickliness. "I have a boyfriend, remember? And, I have to say…I don't know how he feels about kids."

"Oh, right…Dennis."

"No. His name is Dean. Dean Adams."

Roberta's tone was harsh, but she was starting to feel a bit relieved – that she could use the boyfriend card as an excuse to evade Harlan's request. She didn't *have* to bend to his request because there were technicalities. Officially, Dean Adams *was* her boyfriend – although their liaison had cooled as of late. He was a Lieutenant at the Vetta Park Police Department – several years younger than her, although technically more senior than her.

Whereas Roberta had initially despised this young man – his uncomplicated ascent through the department ranks, his clever acumen that made clearing cases look like a breeze – Dean had won her over. In addition to his other attributes, Dean Adams was jovial and charming. He gave blithe smiles and great advice, and when he drew her in for a hug the first time, he smelled delectable – like peppermint and dark roasted coffee.

In 2018, Roberta and Dean went official with their office romance, and every one of their colleagues seemed to support the duo. After all, the Vetta Park PD was a bit of an incestuous agency, what with all the late nights and long hours spent with each other.

Now, four years later, the story of Roberta and Dean defied easy categorization. They spent the night at each other's apartment...sometimes. The initial heat of their attraction had long since worn off, and there was neither talk of marriage nor pressure for it to ever materialize. Were they still boyfriend and girlfriend? Friends with benefits? Roberta never asked these questions, and neither did Dean. She felt that their romance had evaded every practical accepted conduit and every foreseeable pitfall. And perhaps she felt lucky about this. But there was a singular law of physics that she accepted as the rule of her own life -- the earth slowly drifted away from the sun in its course of orbit – just as she and Dean were experiencing a slow-motion divergence.

Harlan shook his head and said, "Oh, I didn't realize Dean lived with you."

"He doesn't," Roberta corrected. "He's just over a lot."

"I see. Well...I wouldn't ask you for this if I wasn't desperate. I know it's a big favor."

"For how long?" Roberta asked curtly.

"I don't know. Let's see how it goes."

Roberta shifted in her seat and then stood up and faced the wall. She was annoyed at the presumptuousness of Harlan's response. *Let's see how it goes*...as though the situation were already agreed-upon. She hadn't said yes...yet. Although Harlan was probably mindful of the fact that she hadn't said no either.

"What am I supposed to do with him?" Roberta asked. "I have absolutely no experience with kids."

Harlan placed his hands against the wooden desk, flattening them over the smooth surface. "You don't need any experience with kids to do this, Roberta. Take him to school in the morning. Pick him up afterwards. Or, better yet, have him walk or take the bus. He goes to school. He comes home. That's it."

What was left unspoken in Harlan's summary of Nick's daily itinerary was the boy's lack of adherence to it. The entire reason Harlan needed help was that Nick *wasn't* going to school – and they had no reassurance that a change in geography was going fix a thing.

She didn't say what she really wanted to ask him – *and what if he skips school out here, too?* – because Harlan seemed convinced of his own irrationally optimistic scenario. All Nick needed was a quiet apartment and he would be set on the right path of obedience and conformity. Maybe straight As and an Ivy League education were to follow, and – while he was at it – why not a distinguished career as a Nobel Prize-winning astrophysicist?

Roberta didn't say anything because Harlan had always been this way – in search of the expedient fix, a purchaser of his own snake oil charms. And she didn't want to raise the issue of Nick's truancy because she knew exactly how she'd handle it. Unlike Harlan's toadying subservience, Roberta wouldn't hesitate to track down the boy in her police cruiser. Perhaps some blue and red lights, a howling siren and a night in the Vetta Park drunk tank would teach him a lesson. Her apartment was not going to be some kind of free-wheeling teenage sanctum. It was going to be a place for tough love and hard work – the kind of values she had grown up with on the farm. But maybe Nick would actually be better off this way.

*Maybe he would be better off...*she couldn't stop herself from thinking it. A structured setting, a room of his own, a firm consequence to poor behavior. Nick – this child that she didn't even know well enough to picture in her mind. He was a blurred vision, faint dark hair above peach-colored skin, but she imagined it anyway...a distorted specter finding his peace in her guest bedroom. If all he needed was a metaphoric kick in the boot, she could certainly provide that.

"Fine," Roberta said with a heavy sigh. "I'll take him. But if he gets to be too much trouble, I'm giving him back."

"Thank you, Roberta! *Thank you thank you thank you*! I'll bring him by tonight after dinner, around seven p.m. You are a lifesaver! Thank you!"

Harlan turned and nearly skipped out of the room. He walked with the elated buoyancy of a man who'd just gotten a stay of execution – a man who'd just received a second chance at life.

And Roberta – who by all means was a good person – who had taken an oath to commit her life to the service of others, could only feel the weight of an untold future in the near distance. She wanted to feel happy for offering her sisterly assistance – for the exhilaration that she alone had bestowed upon her brother – but the only emotion coursing through her body was fear. She swallowed hard and glanced at the time, as the countdown to seven o'clock began.

Standing up, Roberta felt unsteady as she drifted back to her desk. She caught sight of Dean Adams and mentally began preparing the words for the uncomfortable, stressful discussion they were going to have to have. But instead of formulating articulate arguments on behalf of opening her doors to a rebellious adolescent, Roberta could only focus on one unpleasant, recurring thought: *What have I just done?*

NICK WAS DROPPED OFF AT SEVEN P.M., RIGHT ON TIME. It seemed funny to Roberta, as Harlan had never been punctual about anything in his entire life, as far as she was aware. But there they were, as promised – on her doorstep and waiting to be let in. Harlan, wearing a backwards baseball cap and wide smile, draped in backpacks and miscellaneous luggage. And there was Nick, his dark hair shoulder-length and uncombed, bangs hanging over his right eye. Whereas Harlan was weighted down with the accoutrements of a long-term expedition, Nick was carrying only a cell phone.

"Here, why don't you guys come in," Roberta said, and shepherded them through the front doorway. She took a few bags from Harlan's shoulders, and allowed the two to walk around the space. It wasn't much. She had a narrow kitchen to the right of the doorway that led to a breakfast nook, an open living area that housed two beat-up mushroom-colored couches and a desktop computer, and then two bedrooms and a bathroom. The walls were beige and mostly undecorated, save for a few framed prints that Roberta had picked up at the local artisan's market.

"I guess you guys haven't been here before," Roberta said rhetorically.

Harlan sat down on one of the couches and tapped his thumbs together while Nick hoisted one of the backpacks and padded towards the bedrooms. "Which one's mine?" he asked, his voice a low murmur.

"The one on the right," Roberta called out, and she and Harlan locked eyes while Nick disappeared.

"Thanks again," Harlan said. "I can't tell you how relieved Shayna is. Honestly, it's any day now with the baby and, well…this is a real help to us."

"I'm glad I could help," Roberta said. "Is there anything I should know about? Allergies? Medications?"

"No and no," Harlan said.

"When's his…uh…bedtime?"

Harlan threw his head back and laughed. "He doesn't really have a bedtime. Goes to sleep about midnight, I guess."

If her questions were absurd, Roberta hoped that Harlan would consider changing his mind. Maye he would appreciate what she had been trying to tell him in the precinct room – that she was all wrong for this role, that she knew absolutely nothing about children, that this whole arrangement was an inauspicious plan.

But Harlan simply heaved himself off the couch, wandered into the guest bedroom for a quick good-bye, and then gave Roberta a quick hug. Not thirty seconds later, she heard his truck's engine turn, saw the reflection of white backup lights through the partially open curtains…and then he was gone.

Dean showed up thirty minutes later. He had a bottle of Shiraz in one hand and a chunk of shrink-wrapped butcher meat in the other. When Roberta opened the door, he burst through and set the items down on the kitchen counter, then drew her into a tight hug before exclaiming, "Sorry, I'm late. I know I'm late."

Roberta took a few steps back and had to remind herself that they'd made a date for that evening. So much had happened, she'd completely forgotten about their plan for grilled ribeye under the recessed balcony lights, accompanied by the latest shipment of Shiraz that the wine store guy had been peddling for over two weeks.

Dean could sense her hesitation. "Berta – is everything ok?"

"Yeah. I just…I forgot about tonight. I'm so sorry."

"You forgot? I thought we agreed on a standing Thursday evening together. Do you want me to go?"

"Um…well…"

"Is someone here?"

"Yes, but it's not what you think. My nephew Nick is here. Harlan dropped him off about half an hour ago."

And then, perhaps because he had heard his name, or perhaps because he'd sensed the imminence of food at this twilight hour, Nick emerged from the second bedroom. He walked into the kitchen and opened up the refrigerator door –

neither acknowledging the stranger in the kitchen, nor articulating any sort of a greeting.

Roberta placed her hand on the kitchen doorframe and gestured towards the refrigerator. "Dean, this is Nick, my nephew. Nick, this is Dean, my…boy…my…boy…*boyfriend*." She'd said the word with an unconvincing inflection, as though she were unsure about the accuracy of the label. That was the thing about introductions; they forced categorization, premature pigeonholing. Of course, she and Dean had been together for four years now, so it seemed silly to think of anything regarding them as premature. If anything, their status should have been decided by this point. Maybe if they'd followed the pathway that most good-natured, red-blooded Americans adhered to, they would already be hitched by now, cohabitating in a single-family house in a trendy St. Louis suburb. But that was not their path.

If Dean was at all perturbed by Roberta's stuttering, he didn't show it. "How're you doing, Nick?" Dean asked, good-naturedly, and then watched as the teenager took a quarter gallon carton of milk from the fridge and guzzled it.

"Nick, in this household, we use glasses," Roberta said, with as much authority as she could muster.

Nick turned to look at her, but didn't say a word. The one eye that wasn't obscured by greasy hair follicles grew slightly wider – a register of disbelief at his aunt's tone of voice. He seemed to finish the milk but still returned the empty carton to the fridge, then closed the door and shuffled back into the bedroom.

"That kid has no manners!" Dean said incredulously. "Didn't even say *hi* to me. What time are his parents picking him up?"

"Um, well, that's the thing…" Roberta said, and then she led Dean to a spot on the sofa, but not before placing the pink, marbled steak in the refrigerator. It was a delicacy that she deeply wished she were indulging in at that moment – instead of litigating her case for a situation she hadn't wanted to begin with.

"Nick is going to be here for a little while," Roberta continued. "His mom is out of the picture and his dad – my brother Harlan – is about to have a baby with his new wife, and Nick's been having kind of a hard time on the home front with all the transition going on and all the noise in his house… so I agreed to take Nick in for a little while…until things settle down."

Dean nodded but avoided looking in her direction. He kept his eyes on the wall opposite the sofa, frowning at a framed enlargement of the St. Louis Arch. The silver structure gleamed and glistened – towering over ornamental turf grass and assortment of trees carefully curated beneath it.

"You took on a kid without asking me?" Dean finally asked.

"Well…Harlan was really upset when he came by this afternoon. He was actually literally begging me. I didn't really think he would take no for an answer."

Dean placed his forehead into his hands, as though he were praying, bowing down before this monolith of St. Louis architecture. Though his knuckles obscured the side of his face, Roberta thought she could detect a trivial nod, an acceptance of family obligation.

"How long is a little while?" Dean then asked.

"Sorry…what?" Roberta responded.

"You said the kid would be here for a little while. How long is *a little while?*" Dean asked. He stood up from the couch and wandered around the living room, staring aloft as though mentally calculating the square footage. Then he disappeared into the kitchen and returned with red wine in his hand, strangling the bottle's neck while tapping the burgundy glass against his thigh.

"I don't know," Roberta said softly. She knew that the answer to Dean's question was a key component to his calculations. He wanted certainty, the ability to circle a date on the calendar, the solution to the question of how long – and how far away – he should flee before it would be safe to return.

"I can't do this," Dean said. "You know this. The kid thing…it's not for me. We've talked about this before. Let me know when it's just you living here again." He turned around and took a few steps into the foyer, then said, over his shoulder: "Keep the steak. I bet the kid's hungry," and then closed the front door behind him.

Roberta stayed in her same spot for a while. She should have gotten up and marinated the steak, pre-heated the grill, rubbed some spices into the hunk of meat, but instead she stayed seated on the couch.

A profound feeling of loss overcame her, but Roberta couldn't precisely pinpoint its meaning or its origin. What, exactly, had she lost? Before performing his swift escape, Dean had implied his eventual return. She trusted that he would make good on that pledge too. Years of erratic push-pull intimacy with Dean should have prepared her for this. But still, she felt the heavy blanket of melancholy. Staring at the walls, which now seemed beiger and emptier than before, Roberta wasn't even able to find solace on the now dull-seeming St. Louis Arch. It seemed everything had lost a bit of color.

Roberta stayed like that – pinned in her reclining position by the invisible cloak of misery – until Nick eventually emerged from the bedroom about an hour later. He surveyed the refrigerator and the cabinets with a brusque ravenousness and then walked into the living room.

"Is there any dinner in this place?" he asked in a quiet, dispirited voice.

Roberta shook her head. "There's a ribeye, but I'm too tired to make it. Do you know how to cook?"

"No. I only know how to make toast. And cereal."

This is how, on Roberta's standing Thursday date night, she ended up eating dry Rice Puffs cereal and toast with peanut butter. Nick sat down at the table and ate alongside her, and the two of them had dinner without saying a word to each other.

Friday morning, fresh sunlight flared through the open shades of Roberta's apartment, and blanched Nick's blankets in the shape of slatted shutters. It took Roberta three tries to wake the teenager, and she only eventually succeeded by loudly threatening to find and break into his electronics.

While the boy was taking his sweet time getting ready, stumbling around the apartment – oblivious to both his unkempt cowlicked hair as well as his rumbling stomach – Roberta was tending to a flurry of text messages.

First, she heard from Ray Martinez, who had cryptically texted her at 4:15am: *Word is out.* Then Dean, who seemed to have forgotten his dramatic exit the previous night, guilelessly texted her a longer explanation.

Berta, one of the tabloid websites got word about CC and has already posted three stories about it. Going to be a media zoo today. Be prepared.

Roberta wanted nothing more than to dash to the precinct, where her colleagues were unquestionably already gathered in Captain Weaver's office. She could imagine them clustered around his walnut-stained desk, poring over news reports, coordinating with their central Public Relations team, which was certainly already dispensing advice over the speakerphone.

And where was she? Herding a vexingly unhurried teenager through the three simple tasks of eating, dressing, and brushing teeth. His deliberate nature – the way he seemed to lose track of everything he was doing at the moment of doing it – provided no shortage of frustration and fury for Roberta. When pleas of *Hurry!* And *Come on!* proved futile, Roberta eventually set the oven timer for five minutes and announced that upon its alarm, she was going to muster her police training to drag Nick out of the apartment and to the local high school – pajamas or not.

Exactly five minutes later, Nick joined Roberta at her car. She was ecstatic to see that he was appropriately dressed and heaving a heavy backpack. His disheveled, uncombed hair would be a discussion for another time.

"What's in the backpack?" Roberta asked him, as she steered her car out of the apartment complex.

"Just some papers," Nick said. "My dad gave it to me to give to the school. Stuff like my birth certificate."

When they reached Vetta Park Central High School, Nick handed her the sheaf of papers and took his time getting out of the car. Roberta leaned against the car's frame while she waited, and stared up at the brick-red structure. It was two-story and freshly-painted – a boxy but inviting building, with a giant American flag fluttering wildly and three stationary yellow buses in the front of the parking lot.

"Nick. Come on!" Roberta said impatiently, and mentally forced herself not to do the math of how many times she'd said *Come on!* that morning. It was only seven forty-five.

Nick emerged slowly from the car and looked up at the building as though it were a foreign prison in a foreign country. He stumbled behind her with similar indolence, staring at the ground while they made their way into the front office.

Inside the building, Roberta noted the contrast in security between this high school and the one she'd attended several decades previously. They endured several rounds of buzzing before they were allowed inside, and layers of plexiglass fortified the main office's reception area. This place was perhaps as structurally garrisoned – perhaps more so – than the police station where she worked.

"Can I help you?" a tired-looking woman standing behind a mahogany counter asked.

"Yes," Roberta said. "I'm here to enroll my nephew in ninth grade."

"I'll need his vaccination record and your driver's license and you'll also have to fill out this form *in its entirety*."

Roberta obliged and then took a seat on a straight-backed plastic stacking chair to the right of the reception area. While she filled out the application, she could overhear the whispered chatter behind the reception area.

They said she was seeing a regular guy – not a movie star – who lived around here, and she was out here visiting.

They met online.

I have heard that celebrities sometimes come out here because nobody expects to see them. Think about it! There's no photographers, no gossip columnists, no nothing!

I wonder what would make someone drive off a cliff like that.

Tragic Hollywood story. Drugs and booze. Live fast and die young.

This is what our town is going to be known for. The place where Cecilia Cinvenue died.

Transcript!

Roberta had her head stooped downward, eyebrows wrinkled as she fought the desire to hang on to every whispered word about Cecilia. It was as though the administrators' gossip were a totem – anchoring her to the work she should be doing at this moment. Instead, she was tiring out her right wrist with addresses, emails and emergency contact details. Details about Nick's birth were included in his birth certificate – right down to the doctor who had delivered him. But the pertinent information about previous schools, illnesses and preferences – the questions that pages two through five of the high school application form were beseeching – those she had no idea how to answer.

"Transcript!" The voice barked again, and only then did Roberta realized that the registrar was addressing her, asking her in impatient staccato to provide details of Nick's previous schooling.

"Nick, do you have your transcripts from your old school?" Roberta asked, and then Nick nodded solemnly and handed her a crinkled page from his backpack.

OFFICIAL TRANSCRIPT
RANDALLWOOD HIGH SCHOOL

Hobbs, Nicholas
9th Grade
DOB: 3/21/2007

Art Drawing: B
English 9: World Literature: D
Foundations in Writing: D
Pre-Algebra: C
Physical Science with Lab: Biology: D
Physical Education: C
Spanish 1: C–

"NICK, THESE GRADES…" ROBERTA STARTED AND THEN stopped herself. What type of parental authority did she have over Nick, anyway? Yes, she was his guardian – temporarily. But this implied the need to fulfill the very basic parental duties: feed the kid, clothe him, shelter him. To argue with him over grades was somewhere up much higher in Maslow's Hierarchy – a segment of the pyramid that she didn't know how to appeal for.

And the fact that her phone was buzzing with urgent entreaties from the office – that the people behind the high school reception area were buzzing for the same reason – all of this placed the issue of Nick's abysmal grades at the bottom of her priority list.

Roberta handed the transcript to the woman behind reception and took some solace that the woman had neither recoiled nor sighed plaintively at the data. Instead, the woman spent ten minutes punching her keyboard with militaristic authority while Roberta and Nick stood quietly and waited.

Finally the woman grabbed a printout and handed it to Roberta from beneath the plexiglass. "Here's his schedule," she said. "And you live too close for bus transport, so you'll have to drive him or he can walk."

Images of Nick holding court with his fake ID at the local bar deluged Roberta's mind. The closest drinking establishment was miles away, but Roberta knew how crafty, how resourceful teenagers could be when they set their calculating minds to something.

"I'll drive him," Roberta said, aware that the registrar was simply stating the rules, and didn't care one bit whether Nick was driven or walked, or arrived to school by hovercraft.

"So…" Roberta continued, "What time does school let out?"

"Two-thirty p.m."

"He'll walk," Roberta corrected herself, and then she turned towards Nick, half-apologetically. "Two-thirty is in the middle of the afternoon. I can't take off work…"

"Aunt Berta. It's fine. I'll walk. I have your address. Can you give me the key to get in?"

Roberta fumbled around in her purse for the keys to her building and her apartment. She tried to clear her mind, to consider whether she was making a grave mistake by giving this kid unregulated access to her apartment. She didn't usually get home from work until after six p.m., so this accorded at least three hours of free time for him to do…what exactly? Probably not homework, based on his grades. Search for porn on the internet? Throw a party? Visit that dive bar only a few miles away – the one she'd unfortunately had the displeasure of frequenting due to drunken altercations, sex solicitations and calls about underage consumption?

Keys in her hand, Roberta choked the metal trinket and

revisited her decision. "You know, I can get here at 2:30 and pick you up and take you to the police station. We have several open cubicles where you can sit quietly and do your homework and no one will bother you. That way, you won't spend hours every day by yourself. Okay?"

Nick rolled his eyes – at least, the one eye that was visible to Roberta and not cloaked by a wall of heavy bangs. "Aunt Berta...I know how to take care of myself."

"Oh, I know. Of course. This way is just better."

Nick rolled his eyes again and grunted miserably, then seized the piece of paper from on top of the wooden counter and trampled out the door. Roberta had an impulse to follow him. There were room numbers on the boy's schedule – but no map – and even the best oriented person would spend a while migrating through this structure until he could figure out where he was going. Roberta imagined Nick giving it a lethargic effort until her car had safely exited the parking lot, and then wandering out the front door and into the open streets of Vetta Park.

"Is he going to be okay?" Roberta asked the registrar – not because she thought the woman had any insight about how her nephew was going to adjust, but as a way of registering docile protest. When one of her colleagues invariably dragged the teenager through the precinct doors, at least Roberta would be able to claim that she'd questioned the front desk staff before she left.

The registrar gave a half-shrug in response and joined her co-workers, who were now clustered behind a computer monitor streaming grainy images of the Vetta Park rock quarry.

Roberta turned around and left the office, checking her phone as she walked to her car. She had missed three phone calls and five text messages. The last message was from her boss, Captain Weaver – an avuncular, white-mustached man in his late sixties who almost never texted her unless there was some type of an emergency.

The text read: *Roberta, we've been trying to reach you all morning. I need you to work this case before the media vultures take root. Cecilia Cinvenue has got more skeletons than a graveyard.*

Chapter Seven

Los Angeles, California
1990

CECILIA CINVENUE SAT by herself in her semi-dark dressing room and ran her fingertips over the pages of a thick script. This wasn't an installment of *The Family Next Door.* It was the promise of a soon-to-be produced film with a lot of important people attached to it. Cecilia didn't recognize any of the names, didn't even really know what it meant to be *attached* to a movie project, but she closely followed the advice of her manager, Betty, who insisted that Cecilia just *had* to get a role in this movie.

It had started with a meeting – pastries and petit fours spread across a glass coffee table. Betty, presenting Cecilia as though she were a show pony. "Here she is!" Betty had said when they'd walked through the double doors. Cecilia nodded hello and took a seat at the table, focusing most of her energy on how to clandestinely steal one of the confections from the center of the table. The crumbly desserts were laid bare in the meridian, as if daring her to make an illegal seizure in plain sight of everyone.

"Cecilia?" a skinny, severe woman pressed, and then the young girl realized she'd been daydreaming instead of paying attention to these people. These people who her mother had insisted for the duration of the car ride over were *important* and *crucial to her career.*

"I'm sorry," Cecilia said. "Can you repeat what you just said?"

The severe woman raised her eyebrows. "I asked how you were enjoying being on *The Family Next Door!*"

She had phrased it as a question, but it felt more like a declaration to Cecilia. That the woman had presumed enjoyment – in some variety – and Cecilia's job was to play along and say the pre-written lines. Lines that were crafted by her mother – this time – instead of the usual gaggle of writers, crammed together around notepads and computer processors in a waxen room.

"Oh, I absolutely love it!" Cecilia said. "Every day, I'm so grateful for the opportunity to be on the show! Sometimes it's hard work, but that's ok. The other cast members are so nice to me and I've learned a lot from Bob and Suzanne…you know, the people playing my parents."

Cecilia glanced over and saw – from the corner of her eye – that Betty was beaming. She had executed the mission flawlessly, delivered the lines as though they were her own.

If anyone had really asked – if anyone really cared – Cecilia would have said that she found the work tiring and redundant. That occasionally she caught sight of other teenagers hanging around and goofing off with each other, and she felt a pang of grief for the trivial pleasures she'd never experienced.

A few months earlier, she'd been granted a rare day of rest. There was no filming, no tutoring, no practicing. Cecilia was sunbathing on her front lawn when a girl around her own age approached and asked to join her. At first, this spontaneous consorting was exhilarating to Cecilia. The girl seemed altogether *normal* – unencumbered by the trappings of Hollywood. She went to regular school and had a regular schedule. But as the minutes progressed, all the girl wanted to talk about was Cecilia's brushes with fame and fortune – who she'd interacted with, what her fake siblings were like on set, how much money she made.

Lying on the grass, watching the clouds take shape – the sky rotate with perpetual deliberateness – Cecilia let tears roil down her freckle-dotted cheeks. It was the first of many realizations she would have about her standing in the cosmos – what it meant to be Cecilia Cinvenue. She was too bright a star to even have the most normal interaction with someone her own age. And this brilliance was something she'd spent over a decade working for – longing for – that she was now suddenly beginning to hate. Actually, there were a lot of things she was beginning to hate.

She hated having to wake up before the sun came up, every single morning, regardless of the time of year. Many days, she never saw the sun at all – the closest approximation being the harsh stage lights that blared fiercely from the set ceiling.

She hated the hours spent in the make-up chair, staring at black text that she was supposed to memorize while professionals applied powders and solutions to her face, painting her into someone she was not.

And there was the work of it too. Sometimes executed flawlessly, sometimes executed in take after laborious take. On any given morning, she wouldn't have been able to predict which way it would go – whether she'd be able to run through the lines with easy efficacy or repeat the same scene with painstaking tedium. To make matters worse, there were infinite reasons why a scene could go bad, ranging from technical to human. Perhaps she wouldn't hit her mark on the ground, or a coworker would burst into laughter or a sound technician would drop an instrument off camera that rendered all the work they'd put in to that point futile. It was a protracted, hours-long process – chopped and skillfully curated into a thirty-minute segment with a laugh track...made to look easy. But it wasn't easy.

"I'm so glad to hear that," the woman at the table said, and it took Cecilia a moment to remember that the woman was responding to her avowals of devotion to the craft, her love of acting.

They stayed seated for thirty more minutes around the table, discussing the project, and what it was likely to entail. From what Cecilia could gather, the whole thing seemed uncertain anyway – a promise of something that currently consisted of no more than a script.

She was surprised when, six months later, Betty came sauntering into her dressing room and announced that the movie was moving ahead. The producers had found their director and cast a few of the roles already. Cecilia was to run lines with one of the already-cast teenagers – a young man with powerful command of the teenage tabloid covers.

As Betty described it, Cecilia would have no trouble being cast in this film. She was the girl they wanted, the face they'd envisioned when they'd greenlit the project. Cecilia was *in* – making the legendary leap from small screen into big – cementing the next logical step in her inevitable career as a Hollywood heavyweight. It was as though this great, glorious ladder of Hollywood realization rested in front of her. All Cecilia had to do was keep looking skyward and climb it...and never, never, never think about what it meant...and never allow herself to look down.

IT DIDN'T HAPPEN. TO BE SURE, THE MOVIE WAS unequivocally successful. Starring four or five Hollywood linchpins, the film's plot wittily capitalized on Americans' anxieties about global terrorism, repackaged into patriotic escapism. Opening weekend smashed all expectations and launched the careers of its top lineup even higher into Holly-wood's rarefied A-list. Unfortunately, this lineup did not include Cecilia.

She had run lines with the movie's principal teenager during a screen test. He was square-shaped and awkward, shorter than she'd expected, with a sheen of pale foundation covering either freckles or acne.

When he pulled her close to him, Cecilia recoiled. Not from disgust or disinterest, but because the sheer motion of it all surprised her. One moment, they were bantering back and forth, hitting cues and bouncing off each other like staccato ricochets. The next moment – when the script called for him to sweep her gently into his arms – he practically yanked her from her stasis and forcefully seized her body against his.

Cecilia was visibly startled, but she tried to recover as quickly as possible. She spoke her lines with more intensity than she'd ever used for her character on *The Family Next Door*. Her inflected manner of speaking, her rounded eyes and expressive gestures – all of which she combined to sell a story of young infatuation.

But it didn't work. Maybe it was her reflexive repugnance towards the already-cast young man, or maybe she had over-compensated in its aftermath. Either way, by the end of the screen test, everyone but Betty seemed to comprehend that she had lost the part.

Cecilia cursed herself for the entire car ride home, buried her head in her hands and refused to speak. Betty's misguided optimism only made matters worse. She let the woman's well-intentioned remarks sail over her head while silently counting the minutes until she'd be liberated from this stifling automobile.

When they finally reached her house, Cecilia raced inside and took shelter under her bed covers. Her misery endured for the better part of a week, accompanying her during early mornings and late nights, rehearsals for *The Family Next Door* – which now seemed more puerile and mediocre in the shadow of a non-existent film career.

Like a dedicated – if not naïve – steward, Betty waited patiently until the news was official. A few days after Cecilia's flawed audition, the older woman waited in her daughter's dressing room, seated in her daughter's wingback vanity chair with a stack of letters tucked beneath her arm.

When Cecilia arrived in the room after a particularly arduous day, she expected they would quickly gather their things and exit the studio. Instead, Cecilia saw her mother's expression and instantly felt the blood rush through her veins. She walked over to the large rectangular mirror – which was mimicking her mother's desolate expression – and dropped to her knees. "Momma! What is it?"

"You didn't get the part in the movie," Betty said softly, and Cecilia responded by lowering her head on their enfolded hands. She could feel her heartbeat soften – its ferocious gallop slow into a stable rhythm. She could feel the blood return to her extremities, as though the ability to stand up and walk around her dressing room were a newfangled carnival stunt. She had been terrified into paralysis, but now everything was normal again. And perhaps, her physical ability to accede this news was due to its redundancy. Cecilia had known days previously that she lost the part – felt it at the moment of impact. It was only Betty who had held out dubious hope—holding vigils by the house phone, waiting for a call whose essence only she questioned. Everybody else already knew the answer.

"Oh, Momma, it's alright," Cecilia said, and she found her footing and took a seat on a velvet, jade camelback sofa. "I've still got this sitcom…and there'll be other auditions—"

Betty disrupted Cecilia's comments with a brusque sweep of her arm – the one that wasn't clutching a stack of folded papers. "You don't get it!" Betty scolded harshly, and Cecilia noticed something darker in her voice — a primitive tenor, as though emanating from the very back of her throat or the bottom of her stomach. "You don't get it," she said again, more softly.

"What don't I get?" Cecilia asked.

Betty then produced the papers and handed them to Cecilia. They were letters — mostly handwritten on lined pages, but a few had been typed. Cecilia took a moment to read the one at the top. Splintered bits of paper on the left margin indicated this one had been torn out of a notebook. The writer had a coiling scripted — wide y's and g's — penned with colored pencil. Most likely someone around her own age.

Betty didn't give Cecilia a chance to read past the first paragraph. "It says you've gained weight," she paraphrased. "They all say that. You're lovely and talented and have the whole world in front of you, but baby girl, you need to lose weight."

Her eyes fixated on the curlicue font, Cecilia didn't look up at her mother. Instead, she continued to read. The first paragraph had been fawning praise — the type of admiration Cecilia had grown accustomed to reading. But all of the accolades were simply prologue for the hammer drop.

Your so pretty but youve gotten really fat. My friends and my dad say so too. We watched last season and compared it to this season and Alison doesnt even look like the same person. Please loose some wait. Because I loved your caracter last year and I want to again.

The impact of this letter felt like a battering ram — it's heavy steel surface knocking Cecilia's temples. She felt a rush of warmth and frigidity both at the same time — a chilliness that made her start to sweat. With shaking fingers, she placed the top letter next to her on the couch but the second one — typed with callous 10-point font — was no better.

I hate your character's weight gain this season. I don't think it works well for the story. She's supposed to be a pretty thirteen-year old girl who's dating a high school freshman. In reality, this freshman wouldn't go out with you because you're too fat. But in the scenes, he's still acting in love with you and it isn't believable.

Cecilia placed the second letter down and fumbled through the remaining pieces of paper. They were all the same. She saw the words *fat*, *big*, *heavy*, *weight* and *ugly* dance and jump off of the page in oversized lettering. These words swelled until they were larger than life, sweeping across her dressing room, mocking her with insufferable disdain.

And everything in her dressing room was an accomplice to the crime – outfits that were one or two sizes larger than what she'd worn last season. Last season, she was a twelve-year old kid – still feeding hackneyed retorts about elementary school to the mouth of simulated laughter.

Now, she was thirteen, and the gods of maturation had been unkind to her. Cecilia had felt it before the cruel letters confirmed it. Whereas there was once a linear passageway from armpit to knee, she now had curves and contours. Her hips jutted out and her breasts flung forward. Cecilia had metamorphosized into a bulging, distending creature – a monster of adolescence that had overtaken her ability to control it.

Now Cecilia's mouth was getting dry, her palms sweaty. She felt the blood drain from her body again—similar to when she'd first entered the room. Back then – was it only fifteen minutes ago? – she had feared the worst. A death or illness in the family. But wasn't this – in some way – worse than that?

As sad as a death in the family would be, at least that was out of her control. There would be mourning and loss, coupled with the sympathy and admiration from others. *Admiration* – a sentiment she had secured from others throughout her entire life. She knew how to bask in it, how to metabolize it, how to grow from it. It was the seed that fed her motivation, her worth.

But admiration had a flip side – *disdain* – and it seemed

that Cecilia was now suckling on that side. She couldn't feign innocence or blame the deities for her misfortune; she had done it to herself. An extra bite of dinner here, an extra spoonful of dessert there. She was broadcasting the results of her overindulgence for the entire nation to see. She was as disgusted with herself as they were.

"I'll lose weight," Cecilia said to her mother. "You don't need to worry. I will lose it really quickly. I've been eating too much. I'll pull back."

"Yes, you have," Betty said, scornfully. And Cecilia felt doubly stricken. Gone was the mother who held her girl in her arms, who swung her around a room, who would have (should have?) swept up Cecilia in a loving embrace and professed her affections regardless of body size.

This woman, instead, was a shareholder of the Cecilia Cinvenue stock – much like her agent, her studio bosses, the whole of America. Cecilia didn't quite understand how her everyday decisions were delicate cogs on a wheel that fed other people's salaries. But this evening in her dressing room, she got the first taste that her body – her life – did not belong to herself. Quite simply, she did not own herself. Had she ever?

The next step for the young thespian – the action that everyone unanimously seemed to agree on – was that she would lose weight. There was no one in Cecilia Cinvenue's life to worry that perhaps in the young girl's quest to become thinner – to obstruct indulgence to the point of non-consumption, to pour all of her energy into occupying less space on the planet – perhaps she would become so *less* that she simply disappeared.

Chapter Eight

Vetta Park, Missouri
September 16, 2022

A PHALANX of reporters and photographers were assembled in front of the Vetta Park Police Station. From a distance – as Roberta was driving closer once the last traffic light turned green – these interlopers looked like one mottled, misshapen group. She saw news trucks parked on the side of the parking lot – where patrol cars usually rested. She saw the brilliance of transitory, retina-searing light, well-coiffed reporters and expensive cameras. And, once she eventually found a parking spot – much further than she usually got to park – she saw journalists milling around the front entrance, asking questions of two of her colleagues. Or was it the other way around?

Her colleague Rochelle – petite and red-headed, was speaking with one of the journalists. Both had spiral-bound notebooks, stubby pencils. Next to her, Dean Adams was speaking with a different person. Again, the redundancy of notebooks, pencils, wrinkled eyebrows, solemn expressions.

Hobbs pushed past the masses and made her way inside the building. The scent of hours-old coffee in their tiny kitchen pantry drifted towards her. Roberta helped herself to a large pour before Captain Weaver emerged and summoned her into his office.

Once inside, her partner Martinez gestured at the empty chair next to him and Roberta obliged. It was just the three of them inside the spacious office. Roberta looked towards the window frame and saw shafts of sunlight beaming over spruce trees, car chassis, grassy lots. Much further away, she could see the metallic curvature of the Gateway Arch – looming over the city and all of its inhabitants.

Weaver sat down at his desk and cleared his throat. "Roberta? What were you up to this morning?"

"I'm taking care of my brother's teenager for a short while," Hobbs responded. "I had to enroll him in high school." She thought of the fact that Weaver could have simply asked the Lieutenant who had effortlessly strode into work on time – easy combed brown hair, wide shoulders pressing against a black button-down, khaki pants, a clean shave that indicated an untroubled, undisturbed morning. Why not just ask Dean Adams – who hadn't bothered to assist his girlfriend's (ex-girlfriend's) nascent foray into maternal serfdom? Surely, he had plenty of free time to answer the boss's questions about her.

But maybe it was preferable that Weaver stayed out of their personal life – that he didn't resolve his queries about her whereabouts by wandering over to Dean's desk. To ask about her would be to inquire about their entire relationship – so frequently were they off and on, like a light switch – that she couldn't blame the boss for choosing ignorance over interference.

But Weaver – for all of his paternal angles, all the times he asked her about her life, her health, her mental health, her sleeping and eating habits – didn't press her that morning about her obligations to her nephew. He was all business.

"I guess you saw that we have quite a circus going on

outside," Weaver said. "Rochelle and Dean are out there questioning the folks."

Martinez shifted in his seat. "They're questioning the reporters?" he asked. "Or they're answering the reporters' questions?"

"A bit of both. The most obvious premise is that photographers chased Cecilia Cinvenue off of a cliff. Someone got word of her being out here and decided to snap some pictures. Maybe a paparazzo caught a flight from Los Angeles or maybe just a local who wanted to earn a few bucks. Rochelle and Dean are out there questioning the people who showed up to the precinct this morning about when they learned that Cecilia was here. Maybe some of them know something, or have a few friends who got tipped off earlier this week."

Hobbs and Martinez nodded, and Weaver continued.

"So, we're approaching this from two directions. The first is local – the Light Industrial District. Rochelle and Dean did some canvassing yesterday and they're going to get out there and knock on more doors later today. Someone in Vetta Park knows something. *Something* brought this movie star to our neighborhood."

"And the second direction?" Roberta asked.

"The second is to look into the life of Ms. Cinvenue – and that's where you two come in, in collaboration with the Santa Monica police department. I want you guys to figure out known associates, business dealings and the like. And, for that, we'll need you to get on a plane as soon as possible."

Roberta sat back in her chair, heard the groan of painted chrome and stressed leather padding. She had never been to Los Angeles before; her knowledge of the city came from television and movies – perhaps some that Cecilia Cinvenue had starred in. She envisioned palm-tree lined streets and endless sunshine, sandy beaches and trendy cafes. She tried – instantly – to change her thinking. This was a business trip borne out of tragedy, not an opportunity to sow her land-locked oats.

And then there was the matter of Nick. Only one day at the local high school and he was going to be sent home again – into the fragile arms of his reluctant parents. But there was no way she could leave him at home in her apartment – not even for a few days.

"Do we know Cecilia Cinvenue's next of kin?" Martinez asked.

Weaver shook his head. "She's unmarried, no kids, no siblings and no living relatives. The Santa Monica police are looking into aunts, uncles or cousins, but they've got nothing so far."

"Do we know who tipped off the press?" Hobbs asked. It was a cardinal rule of police procedure not to release the name of the deceased until next of kin were notified. Of course, police procedure rarely contended with an ultra-famous celebrity – a woman whose simple presence would have alerted the city's denizens of her detection. She was like an exquisite tiger living in an endless safari. Everyone was craning their necks to get a look, trampling friends and neighbors to take a photo. Cecilia was impossible to overlook, so anyone who crossed her path could have made that phone call or sent that text. Any fireman or paramedic at the scene, any hospital worker who wanted to make a few extra dollars. Perhaps Dalton Beck himself.

"We have no idea," Weaver said. "The only folks in our precinct who knew about it were the five of us. I don't think any of us would have done it. Certainly not when you think about the carnival atmosphere it would bring upon the station house."

Hobbs thought about *the five of us*: She and Martinez, Captain Weaver, Rochelle and Dean. She could rule out herself – at least, as long as she was fully cognizant of her own motivations and behaviors. But, could the remaining four be tainted? How readily would they succumb to the juices of money dangling precariously in front of them? And all they'd have to do was provide a few details. Not the whole story: perhaps just a name, a rendering of the deceased's charred vehicle, an inventory of the recognizable items inside. All they had to do was assume the role of expert – savant – knower of things that others would pay dearly to learn. To be *wanted* and to be handsomely rewarded for it as well – how strong were they to resist that forbidden fruit? How strong was Hobbs?

There was a silence that hung over Weaver's office, paralleling the shift of the late-morning sun outside their window. It became darker in the room – a change in the mood while Weaver toyed with the wisps of his moustache and Martinez played with a frayed thread on his slacks.

Finally, Hobbs broke the silence. "You said that Cecilia Cinvenue had skeletons in her closet? I think you had learned something about her background that would give us a good place to start?"

Weaver clapped his hands together and nodded his head. "Ah, yes. Our partners in Santa Monica did a house search and they found Cecilia Cinvenue's diary. I probably should have mentioned this sooner…but we are trying to keep it under wraps to the extent possible…tell as few people as possible, even within both departments."

Hobbs said, "Ahhh," and looked down at her notes, her thoughts swimming. In the absence of forensic clues, a diary was the Holy Grail of any police reconnaissance. Hobbs imagined a thick-paged journal, with evidence seeping from every entry. The voice of the departed, bearing Cecilia's inner thoughts, which would undoubtedly betray every glossy interview, every sanguine and prefabricated P.R. puff piece the actress had ever given. This diary had the chance to be investigative gold.

"Where did they find it?" Martinez asked.

"One of the detectives discovered it in the bedroom and

77

I've been told it has a lot of personal details, that it covers the last twenty years. Gets into her relationships, the death of her parents, gets into some sexual stuff, drugs, lots of skeletons is what the detective told me over the phone. I haven't read it."

They were all quiet again, until Hobbs asked, "When can we expect to read it?"

"Well…" Weaver returned to the task of winding his moustache tendrils into twin coils. Hobbs had only observed him engage in this compulsive exercise when he was deeply pensive – or troubled – or both.

"We talked about the contents of the journal possibly getting leaked, and as you know, that would be the death knell of our investigation. Santa Monica's lead detective on the case is going to encrypt and scan the journal. As far as this police department is concerned, only the two of you and I will get to see it. Once it's scanned, the three of us can meet in the conference room to go over it. I'm only going to print out one copy, and I'll keep it in my office safe. Our counterparts over there have agreed to the same."

Hobbs nodded and crossed her arms over her lap.

It was quiet for a few moments and then Weaver gave them instructions to book flights and hotel rooms and adjourned the meeting. Hobbs walked back to her desk and picked up the receiver of her desk phone. Best to get the most difficult mission out of the way.

Harlan picked up on the fifth ring, just before the line gave way to voicemail. "Hey, Berta, what is it?" he asked breathlessly, and Hobbs could hear screams in the background, and other noises – perhaps toddler toys, with their earsplitting accessories.

"Is everything okay?" Hobbs asked. "Did Shayna have the baby?"

"No…no…no…not yet. But the doctor says any moment now. We just converted Nick's bedroom into the girls' bedroom to get them out of our room. So, as you can guess, it's been a bit chaotic here." Behind Harlan's voice, a small child's voice shrieked *GIVE IT BACK!* And the screaming persisted.

"Hold on a second, Berta," Harlan said, and then – transforming from the calm, even-tempered brother who had picked up the phone to an enraged brute, his voice roared into a thunderous bellow. "GIVE IT BACK TO YOUR SISTER RIGHT NOW! BOTH OF YOU! IN YOUR ROOM! NOW!"

Then, as if adding to the chaos with a pre-timed entry, as if this were some sort of audial tragedy that had been rehearsed and scripted for Roberta's amusement – or torture (it wasn't clear which) – Shayna's squawking voice could be heard emerging from the cacophony.

"HARLAN, I NEED YOU NOW!"

"Berta, I gotta go," Harlan said, and then all the screaming immediately disappeared with the grace of a click.

Roberta looked left and saw that Martinez was lingering around her cubicle, hands stuffed into jean pockets, his left hip balancing against her cubicle. "Hey…sounds like you were on the phone with a slaughterhouse. Everything ok?"

Roberta nodded. "Everything's fine. It's my brother. They have little kids and he's about to have another baby."

This mollified Martinez, but Hobbs sank her head into her palms. How was she going to finagle Nick back to his home of origin, given all the turmoil? Harlan had already converted the boy's bedroom.

She massaged her temples as she considered this tragedy, and her inability to escape it. The fact that Harlan hadn't even asked how Nick was doing was not a surprise, not a disaster, but illustrative of the situation at hand. Harlan couldn't even inquire about his distanced son, let alone parent the boy.

Hobbs acceded to her years of police training: *In a difficult situation, consider all of the options and choose the best one; divest any personal emotion.*

So this was where Hobbs landed: Nick couldn't go back home and he couldn't stay at her apartment by himself. She would have to take him with her on her trip to Los Angeles. She was stuck.

THEY MET UP IN THE CONFERENCE ROOM A FEW HOURS LATER — Hobbs, Martinez and Captain Weaver. Halogen lighting shined down from the ceiling and onto the flat, wooden tabletop — lighting its surface and the black leather office chairs behind it.

Weaver approached with a wad of papers in his hand and waved the other two over. He set up an assembly-line system of inspection, which had him reading each page of Cecilia's diary and then passing it to Martinez, who would then pass it to Hobbs. The whole exercise seemed kind of silly to Roberta — a redundant version of pass-along, but Weaver insisted that he only wanted the journal available for viewing at that moment, and he wanted all three eyes on it.

Weaver had provided a note pad in case any of them wanted to take notes, and Hobbs felt like she was in some sort of rare books sanctuary, able to observe the cherished pearl — read it, comment on it — but not recreate it. She was mildly surprised that she was the only one of the three of them to take notes.

Another surprise: The pages in their entirety passed through their fingertips hastier than she would have liked. Cecilia Cinvenue had not been a very diligent journal-keeper; many entries had months, if not years, in between them. She also tended to write abstractly — almost poetically — which was enchanting as a reader enjoying the cryptic gifts of an artist but frustrating as a detective trying to solve a homicide. Like this entry from 2007:

. . .

I AM A BIRD RESTING IN MY NEST, A SOUL THAT HAS AWAKENED. I fly away from what I've always known. I am more alive than ever before. Everything before this was prologue – Now I'm truly living! I finally realize why I'm here, why my breath makes my body rise and fall, why my eyes open in the morning. There's no light outside, but I can see my inner light, hear my voice, feel my heart. I can think about all the possibilities in this infinite universe.

HOBBS SCRIBBLED ON THE NOTE PAD: *SPIRITUAL AWAKENING, 2007, age 30. No names.*

There were no names on any of the entries – not even a first or last initial – and nary a physical description to help the detectives cobble together a narrative. When Cecilia felt alive in 2007…and then seemed to have fallen in love in 2010…was there a single gentleman caller behind both instances, or were these time periods completely unrelated? This was hardly the fodder of "skeletons in the closet" that Hobbs had been expecting. She wanted dates, depictions, evidence – not the flowery reveries of a distracted, spinning mind.

Weaver and Martinez continued to feed the diary's pages through their fingers to Hobbs, and Hobbs took some notes while questioning the practicality of any of it. Cecilia's foray into hallucinogenic drug use was certainly interesting:

X CREATES A RAINBOW ARC. I'M WIGGLING MY FINGERS ACROSS MY face, across this page. They float against the sky and all the colors of the universe follow. It's beautiful and magical and I can make it happen. I feel so happy inside. Hope it never ends. Never ends.

But most of the entries were about sex. And, unlike the ecstasy narrative, these accounts weren't flowery erotica. They weren't passionate, romantic affairs. When Cecilia wrote about sex, it was dry and fleeting, the coping mechanism for an internal struggle.

I had a terrible day today. Couldn't remember my lines and couldn't deliver them and I came home at midnight feeling so miserable that I called up ----- and went to bed with him. Kicked him out of my house an hour later and I now feel dirty and gross. Why do I always do this?

Cecilia may have had compunctions about her behavior, may have questioned why she invariably (according to the diary) clung to sex and sexual situations as an antidote of questionable value to mollify her privation. Sex was a box of sugar pills sold by a charlatan. The pills never worked but she was dependent on them anyway, and committed herself to a lifetime of incurable, continual patterns: Misery, sex, more misery, more sex. And year after year, journal entry after journal entry, Cecilia endured the same.

Hobbs had made it all the way up to 2021 when something finally changed. Captain Weaver let out a sound while the piece of paper rippled in front of him. "This is something!" he said triumphantly, and Hobbs guessed that his giddiness was owed to a break in the never-ending stream of despondency that preceded it.

"What does it say?" Martinez asked, and Weaver started reading aloud.

Is it bad for me to wish harm upon another person?! Because I do! Some people are the absolute worst people and deserve to be obliterated from this planet. Oooh, I am so angry, I could scream. Let it be known, here, on this date, June 25, 2021, that we are at war! It is ON! Mark my words.

"Wow," Martinez said, once Weaver had finished reading.

The three of them sat in silence while they allowed Cecilia's words to sink in. Weaver had read it stoically, devoid of emotion or sentiment, but Hobbs could imagine Cecilia's vehement frame of mind as she'd written it. Hobbs, herself, had hated someone so much as to wish them harm – who hadn't? – and those thoughts, when they were compelling enough to warrant dictation, were always accompanied by tears, shame and wrath. What had Cecilia endured, and who had wrought it upon her?

Hobbs had always marginally envied the lives of celebrities and movie stars. They seemed to have everything so easily – money, power, fame, access. But Cecilia's journal made no mention of the riches afforded the select few – only the melancholy that complemented insecurity and loneliness. To be sure, Cecilia seemed to have plenty of late night callers, but it was clear from her writings that none of them adequately filled the void.

And yes, Cecilia had lived in a huge Santa Monica mansion, with tall ceilings and a back gate that abutted the Pacific Ocean. But Hobbs could tell from these journal entries that there was a flip side to living in a gated estate. Cecilia had written about the need for such security – that every decision to leave the mansion was an invitation to be photographed in unkempt hair and saggy pajamas, with accompanying storylines designed not for authenticity but to sell magazines. The gate was necessary but it was a demarcation that severed her from true connections. She could enjoy views of the Pacific Ocean but not fully experience the water's chilliness. She couldn't feel the sand's crumbling surface beneath her toes without worrying about aerial photographers. She could view the easy undertakings of everyday people – she could even play them on television and in movies – but life for her would never be that simple. Her life was tremendous, exorbitant, but it left her disconnected – sometimes paranoid – and always lonely.

As Cecilia's diary progressed into contemporary times, Hobbs felt a metastasizing kernel in the pit of her stomach. The problem was, she knew how the story ended, and it was upsetting to read the optimistic words of the deceased. Cecilia never stopped *longing*, although she also never stopped relying on her old habits. She never wrote about her talent or her beauty; only the omens of her tremendous self-doubting.

Hobbs wanted to reach through the page and shake the movie star. She wanted to punish all the men in the journal – identified only by clusters of hyphens – who failed to see the value of Cecilia Cinvenue. They were content to enjoy the spoils of Cecilia's sexual compulsions without confronting her motivating demons.

How many men were there in total? It was impossible to know who and how many – just that they existed. Hobbs conjured these guys in her mind – drooling, gaping admirers, men of all ages and backgrounds, who told stories in the murky haze of LA locker rooms and expectantly kept their phone ringers on high volume before they went to sleep at night.

Who were these men? Hobbs had no idea, but she was going to find out. Most of them would be investigative dead ends, footnotes in the sordid story of an unfortunate outcome. But – quite likely – one of these Hollywood men had gone to war with Cecilia – and quite likely chased the talented, beautiful, hopeful and ill-fated movie star off of a rocky cliff.

ONCE THEIR FLIGHTS HAD BEEN BOOKED, HOBBS AND Martinez joined Captain Weaver in his office. They switched a button on the Polycom, and waited a few rings, and then two detectives from the Santa Monica Police Department joined the line.

Hobbs could easily tell the difference between the two by their voices: One, older-sounding, gravelly, as though his vocal chords were laboring across a gritty path. And the other: younger-sounding, higher pitched, an intonation that conveyed his eagerness simply to be invited to the party. The older man was Bobby Frazier and his younger counterpart was Mason Oliver.

Hobbs didn't know what these detectives looked like, but

she mentally arranged hairstyles, facial features and clothing choices while they spoke. In her mind, Frazier was olive-toned and long-nosed, dark hair combed to one side, a paunch belly resting latently over a constrictive belt buckle. And then there was Oliver – new to the job, or the role. When Oliver spoke, Hobbs imagined pale, freckled skin, short blonde hair, a kind of neophyte neatness accustomed to one who's still trying to impress his bosses.

After the introductions, Weaver sat back in his chair and toyed with his moustache while the quartet confirmed logistics. They were going to meet in person the next morning at the Santa Monica Police Station. The next morning would be September 17 – a Saturday – a day Hobbs would have much rather spent sleeping late and wandering around the Tower Grove Farmer's Market in St. Louis.

But this case didn't allow for weekends. It was a fast-moving train with would-be sycophants and leakers at every stop. Those who wanted to make a buck by siphoning information and selling it to the press. And there were the tabloid reporters, who wanted a piece of Cecilia's story – whether she was dead or alive, whether it was true or not. The four detectives had to contend with all manner of meddlers on their factfinding journey, and this was why the investigation had to continue apace until it was resolved, regardless of day of week.

As they began their discussion, it was clear that while the Vetta Park police had been canvassing neighbors (to no avail), and wasting resources fending off newly-disembarked reporters who had appeared from all corners of the country, the Santa Monica P.D. had actually gotten somewhere. In addition to uncovering Cecilia's diary, they had already interviewed Cecilia's best friend.

At least, this woman had claimed to be Cecilia's best friend when she showed up at the police station after hearing the news. She had been heaving and sobbing, clutching her purse and wildly berating all the evil forces in Cecilia's life. It was all a bit dramatic, the detectives acknowledged, and they lived in Los Angeles, so they would know.

"What was this woman's name?" Hobbs asked.

"Sparrow Shearwater," Frazier responded. "Her birth name was Mary Smith...which also sounds fake, by the way... but she's been going by Sprarrow Shearwater since her...and I quote...*spiritual rebirth* at the age of twenty."

"What did she say?" Hobbs asked.

"Oh, all sorts of things. First of all, she wants us all to know that she's a Shaman, and that Cecilia had not properly warded off all of the negative energies in her life. She said that Cecilia came to her seeking spiritual counseling and the two of them used to go to Joshua Tree and engage in some voodoo rituals intended to purify their souls."

Hobbs frowned. "Voodoo rituals—?"

"Oh, I added the voodoo part," Frazier said. "Sparrow just said they were cleansing and purifying. Lots of meditation, chanting, staring up at the stars. She didn't mention substance abuse but I wouldn't be surprised. That sort of thing."

"I see."

Frazier continued. "Sparrow told us that the last of these trips ended several years ago. She said they hadn't been as close in recent years, although they still talked every so often. She said that Cecilia Cinvenue wouldn't properly ward off the material immoralities in her life and that was her undoing."

"Her undoing?" Hobbs asked.

"Yes," Frazier confirmed, and then Hobbs could hear the sounds of ruffling papers. "She said, and again I quote, 'Cecilia was lacking fulfillment and internal harmony her whole life but she turned to dark methods to tame the beast of her highest insecurities. When Cecilia felt like she wasn't measuring up, she flung herself into the arms of the nearest man for validation, instead of looking inward at the shadow aspects of her own personality. She also turned towards the impure vices of sex, drugs and alcohol. I tried to explain that the corporate empire profits off of people entombing their sorrows with artificial substances, but Cecilia wouldn't listen to me.'"

"*Oh*," Hobbs said. "Okay. So maybe she was drunk or high when she went off the cliff. Do we know---?"

"Toxicology report is pending," Weaver interrupted. "We've fast-tracked it and we should have it in a few days."

Hobbs nodded, then leaned forward and bent her head towards the telephone. "Did Sparrow observe Cecilia getting drunk or high in the last few days or weeks?"

"No," Frazier said. "They hadn't spoken in two months. For what it's worth, Sparrow said that Cecilia hadn't seemed under the influence in any of their phone calls covering the past few years. But she couldn't say for sure since they hadn't gotten together in person in a while."

"Did she give any more details on why they drifted apart?"

"Oh, she said a lot about why they drifted apart. She said that Cecilia had come to her for guidance, but then wouldn't *follow* the guidance. Sparrow told Cecilia to look inward, but Cecilia never quit getting and I quote – artificially high from material things – so she finally told Cecilia to look elsewhere for a spiritual counselor. Sounded like she kind of fired Cecilia as a client...the way she tells it. So they called and talked on the phone every few months, but that was it."

"I see," Hobbs said. "These material things...Drugs, alcohol and men...right? That kind of overlaps with Cecilia's journal. Did Sparrow give any clues as to who were the men in Cecilia's life?"

Even if there had been no journal, or no Sparrow Shearwater, Hobbs would have started the investigation with a deep dive into the men who inhabited Cecilia's life. It was the cardinal rule of investigating a suspicious death, and it more frequently than not occasioned a conviction: Always Start with the Significant Other.

"The men? Oh yeah," Frazier said. "She said she didn't know all of them – and she made it sound like there were too many to count -- but she named three. Pencils ready?"

Hobbs affirmed that she and Martinez were ready to take notes, but in truth, she had been writing all along. Every overlap between Sparrow's melodramatic clamor and Cecilia's poignant journal warranted a line of script in Hobbs' spiral-bound notebook. Hobbs had written: *Lonely* earlier in the day, so she added a few underlines and exclamation points when Sparrow seemed to affirm it. Hobbs also wrote *Seeking spiritual guidance* and *Reluctant to follow advice*.

"Behind door number one..." Frazier began. "is a big-time movie producer. Terry Mahoney. Maybe you've heard of him."

Hobbs and Martinez looked at each other and both shook their heads. "Um, vaguely," Hobbs said, since the name did ring a bell. She typically went to the movies a few times a year, and couldn't rule out the possibility – perhaps a refabricated memory—that that name had appeared on one of the screens. Terry Mahoney. She was certain she'd read something about him...was it his largesse? His prowess? His box office command? Hobbs wasn't sure, but something rang a bell.

"Oh, well...he's been around for over thirty years," Frazier said. "He produced a bunch of action movies that featured women in lead roles, and he was one of the first to do that. Remember the movie *Soldier of Payback*? Came out in maybe 2001? 2002?"

Hobbs leaned back in her chair and thought back two decades. Back then, she'd been a reluctant movie-goer – a recent college grad with late-night ambitions and a messy social life. She'd allowed herself scant relaxation time – and a dark movie theater seemed to suggest the exact type of enter-tainment she tended to avoid. Still, there were a few whimsical sprees to the local theater now and then. Hobbs did recall seeing Cecilia Cinvenue's beautiful face curved towards her, weeping while profound prose flowed from her pouty lips. But *Soldier of Payback* did not ring a bell.

"I don't think I saw it," Hobbs said.

"In that case, I think you're the only person in America who didn't see it. It was a huge blockbuster, although I wouldn't describe it as Oscar-worthy. But that was one of Terry's films, and according to Sparrow, Cecilia and Terry were very close for years after that. Sparrow wasn't sure if it was a boyfriend-type situation or what."

"What's the age difference--?"

"I haven't done the math, but safe to say…decades."

"Ok," Hobbs said. "Well, we'll definitely want to talk to Terry Mahoney. Any idea where we can find him?"

"We're working on that," Frazier said. "He's on location somewhere in the Middle East on a shoot. Hoping we can pin him down. Ready for who's behind door number two?"

"Sure," Hobbs said. "Go ahead."

"Next we have Marco Bagnetti – who Sparrow made out to be quite the Italian Stallion. According to Sparrow, the last time they spoke, Marco was Cecilia's boyfriend. He was also her personal assistant, bodyguard and her driver. Sparrow said that Marco was trying to make it as an actor in Hollywood, and he was using his relationship with Cecilia to open some doors. The words she used to describe him are…wait a sec… okay, here we go: *loverboy, opportunist, eye candy*, and my personal favorite…*fornicator*. Apparently, Marco was very popular with Cecilia's female friends and associates."

"Wow. Okay. So we'll want to sit down with Marco."

"Yeah, definitely. He's setting up a candlelight vigil tomorrow night at Westwood Rec, and he's made himself the keynote. I'm not sure who else is going but once Marco delivers his eulogy – or maybe before that – we can sit down with him."

"Gotcha," Hobbs said. "Who's the last guy?"

"Oh, well, I'm sure you know who the last one is."

Hobbs frowned and locked eyes with Martinez, who shook his head. "I do?" she asked.

Frazier snickered. "Come on! People Magazine cover 2012? Star Magazine? Hottest couple, then most surprising breakup? You mean you don't pay attention to the magazines?"

"I try to avoid them wherever possible," Hobbs said, neglecting to mention that she did occasionally glance at the covers, if only fleetingly and the result of checkout ennui.

"Billy Sloan." Frazier said pointedly, and Hobbs did know the name. She hadn't known that Billy Sloan and Cecilia Cinvenue were a couple in the mid 2010s…hadn't seen their sexy red-carpet photo before the 2013 Oscars or the glossy-paged feature from People Magazine, showcasing their ocean-side mansion.

Hobbs hadn't known any of this, and hadn't thought about Billy Sloan in many years. His face had adorned bill-boards and magazine covers for a little while, but at some point, he seemed to drop off the face of Hollywood movie posters and prominent movie bylines.

"Billy Sloan," Hobbs repeated. "Yes of course. I forgot he even existed. Is he still making movies?"

"Nope," Frazier said. "He does the Vegas casino circuit now. Songs and magic tricks. He was doing his show in nowhere, Nevada, for years until someone on the Vegas Strip finally gave him a show."

How far the mighty have fallen, Hobbs thought. Billy Sloan, from his lofty days as a sought-after movie star to a quiet casino residency off the beaten path. Could Billy have blamed Cecilia for the break-up or for his near-total Hollywood disappearance – perhaps the greatest magic trick in his toolbox?

The other guys couldn't be counted out either, according to what Frazier had revealed about them. Perhaps Marco

Bagnetti had been nursing a Disney-caliber fantasy... Cinderella in reverse. The beautiful princess was supposed to fall for him and then consummate all of his Hollywood ambitions. And when that didn't happen...what?

And then there was Terry Mahoney. A big-name producer who'd been around for decades. The age difference between Terry and Cecilia was vast – a crevasse into which her immaturity and his Hollywood domination could be a toxic combination. After all, successful (and successfully married) men had a lot to lose.

But it wasn't just those three. There was another name that Hobbs wanted to add to the list. And this man wasn't a suspect or former lover, but an outside party whom Hobbs suspected of potentially engineering an investigation to his own benefit.

Dalton Beck – no longer the ripped t-shirt wearing, woeful eyewitness. His observation had made him part of the story. Until the journalists and reporters unearthed more details from the sleepy hamlet of Vetta Park, Dalton Beck was their *only* story. And he cleaned up – if not nicely then quickly, and very enthusiastically.

In the twenty-four hours or so since Cecilia's death, this once-quavering man had appeared on three local news broadcasts and two well-known online gossip blogs.

When they were finished discussing the three former lovers, Hobbs asked, "Hey, what do you guys think of Dalton Beck?" and then Weaver brought up the local broadcasts on his computer screen. The trio gathered around the monitor in time to see Beck, now the unappointed representative of the department. He was telling his tale in a deeper voice than Hobbs remembered – and recounted a more manly construction of events, that consisted of partially successful attempts to lift the sports car and shake Cecilia out of it.

The detectives had warned Dalton not to reveal any of the specifics of Cecilia's last words. After all, law enforcement had an upper hand only to the extent that they could rein in the circus. If word got out about a homicide investigation, reporters and journalists in Vetta Park might double and triple in number —cancerous cell clusters multiplying inside of reluctant hosts.

For the meantime, Dalton kept his word, and his retelling of the story revealed very little about Cecilia's final moments and much more about his own athletic background, weightlifting sessions and general commitment to physical fitness.

"How long do you think this guy will hold out?" Martinez asked, and both Hobbs and Weaver shook their heads. They were on borrowed time and they all knew it. At some point, some probing correspondent from Chicago or New York would arrive on the scene and offer to tail the now-famous construction worker for the day. There would be flattery and inquiry, mixed in a recipe of high-cost dinners and top shelf liquor. At some point, the journalist would probe just a little further about Cecilia's final moments, and Beck – wanting to repay the man for his kindness, his generosity, his attention – would let it all spill out. And after that, the gossip bloggers and tabloid magazines would go on high alert in Vetta Park. They would arrive *en force* and make it nearly impossible for the detectives to do their jobs.

After all, it was one thing for a major celebrity to die at a young age; it was quite another for that celebrity to be chased off of a cliff.

Just as Weaver started to talk about Dalton Beck – how his aesthetic had shifted in one day, how he was lapping up the attention, how the final, fatal moments of Cecilia's life had benefited only one person, Hobbs shared her views on the subject.

"What if he's making the whole thing up? What if Cecilia didn't say anything at all, or just said '*help*'? What if Beck wanted to inscribe himself in the story, and so he came up with a story of her being chased off the cliff?"

Martinez and Weaver stared at Hobbs with blank expressions. Weaver, frowning, fingered the whiskers on his chin, while Martinez clasped his hands together on his lap.

Hobbs continued. "We haven't found any evidence of any other car. No other tire marks. That doesn't rule out the possibility of another car, but it doesn't make it a slam dunk either. There have been no other reports of suspicious vehicles. I'm not saying he *is* lying; I'm just saying I think we should consider the possibility. I mean, maybe once we find out what Cecilia was doing in Vetta Park, we'll have a clearer picture of what was going on. In the meantime, Dalton Beck is really basking in his fifteen minutes of fame."

Martinez nodded and asked, "Can we get him in here? Question him again?"

"Sure can," Weaver said. "But if he sticks to his story---"

"Can we polygraph him?" Hobbs asked.

The Vetta Park police department, though small, did employ one polygrapher. Hired to help investigate crimes, the man mostly met with new police hires as a formality. The problem was, there wasn't enough crime in Vetta Park to warrant a full-time polygrapher, and courts didn't rely on them as evidence anyway. But employee turnover was an issue within the department, and the polygrapher found himself quite useful questioning recruits on their otherwise-secreted background particulars.

Weaver nodded. "We can question him and do the polygraph if he cooperates. But if he lawyers up, I'm going to reassess whether it's strictly necessary."

"Well, if he lawyers up, we'll know there's more to the story," Hobbs said. "He should want to clear up our suspicions about him."

"Spoken like a true detective," Weaver said with a wink, and Hobbs nodded and looked down at her notebook. The truth was, plenty of innocent people hired lawyers and plenty of guilty people waived their right to one under questioning. Hobbs had no idea which way Dalton Beck would go, had no idea whether he was telling the truth or not. But watching him glow under the patina of television lights, his eyes widening as he told and retold his story, Hobbs worried that he was enjoying his fame perhaps a bit too much. And, besides, you couldn't just trust witnesses nowadays – now that every third person seemed to be vying for some version of their own celebrity. Wasn't it better to know for sure?

Chapter Nine

Los Angeles, California
September 17, 2022

THEY FLEW into LAX the next morning – Hobbs, Martinez and Nick. During the flight, Hobbs relayed the ground rules to Nick. She spoke with authority, as if these instructions had been codified for years, as if she'd had any clue how to watch over a reticent fifteen-year-old with plugs permanently occupying his ears.

In fact, Nick was wearing his earphones during Hobbs' diatribe, but he insisted that the music was turned down and he was listening to every word.

And there were many words. Hobbs went on for at least thirty minutes. She explained that Nick was getting his own hotel room as a privilege but there had better be no drugs, vaping, alcohol or girls. Nick nodded at all of this – his vacant eyes focused on the stowed seatback table in front of him.

Hobbs further explained that there would be long periods of time when she and Martinez would be out on the job, and Nick was expected to do his homework from his hotel room during that time. He wasn't allowed to leave the room without her explicit permission. There would be no long walks with newfound friends acquired from dating apps, no jaunts with the hotel chambermaids, no joyrides with other teenage vagrants.

Nick snickered and nodded again, gave Hobbs a face that indicated she was overthinking things, perhaps basing her knowledge of youthful proclivities on delinquents who ended up in the police station or old teenage movies.

If Nick had asked, Hobbs would have gladly admitted that yes, teenage movies were her prime source of expertise on the topic. That – and her day job – had convinced her of the louche underworld of kids with underdeveloped frontal lobes and too much time on their hands. If it wasn't drugs or alcohol, they'd be rummaging through medicine cabinets for prescription meds. Or driving too quickly down narrow streets. Or scamming naïve octogenarians out of their credit card numbers.

Hobbs didn't think the worst of Nick, but she knew too much about kids his age to fully trust him by himself for hours at a time in a hotel room in a bustling city. She did have one point of leverage over him, however, and that was the alternative to this arrangement. All Hobbs had to do was say the word, and Nick would be on a one-way flight back to St. Louis – back to the reluctant arms of his dad and stepmom. So when Nick rolled his eyes, exhaled a gust of breath and impatiently said, "Aunt Berta, relax! I'll be fine!", she partially believed him.

"I'm supposed to be providing you with schooling while we're gone," Hobbs continued. "So your instruction will be online. I read that our hotel has good Wifi."

Nick nodded again, and it was clear to Hobbs that the boy's mind was elsewhere. He had probably heard the spiel from numerous adults in his life before, and one more repetitive mantra about staying away from toxic depravities was not going to make a difference.

Once the plane landed in Los Angeles, a flurry of commotion prevented Hobbs from checking in with Nick again. He trailed behind the detectives, earphones in his ears, eyes scanning his near-tropical surroundings with adolescent boredom.

They rented a car and checked into the hotel. It was actually a motel – without a central lobby or other harbingers of refinement. What it lacked in amenities, it made up for in location, however. The detectives had chosen this motel for its proximity to the Santa Monica Police Department, but it was also several fortuitous blocks from the ocean. Hobbs could practically smell the salty air when she was opening the door to her room.

Check-in didn't take very long, and thirty minutes later, Hobbs and Martinez showed up at the Santa Monica police station. Frazier and Oliver met them at the entryway, and Hobbs had to mentally note how wrong she'd been about the former's appearance. He was African American – light skinned – with a lean physique and wide brown eyes. Oliver, on the other hand, was exactly as she'd predicted. He had closely cropped blonde hair, a clean-shaven jawline and broad forehead.

Both men were tall and affable, and after the handshakes and pleasantries, they led Martinez and Hobbs to a glass-walled conference room in the back of the station.

Once they were seated across from each other at a conference table, Frazier and Hobbs produced twin accordion folders and swapped papers. They discussed police reports, interviews with neighbors and attributes of the Vetta Park Quarry. They swapped photos – the Vetta Park detectives detailing the impact damage to Cecilia Cinvenue's fancy Italian sports car, and the Santa Monica detectives revealing the inner sanctum of Cecilia's luxurious estate.

Hours passed, and the detectives ordered pizza for lunch. Hobbs thought about the lonely kid sitting by himself in his hotel room, but when she called him, he insisted he was *fine*, that the free doughnuts and coffee at the hotel's front office had more than satiated his appetite, and that he was busy doing an online assignment. She allowed herself to be mollified by this, but as soon as the detectives confirmed their next assignment and recessed for a few hours, she grabbed Martinez and raced back to the hotel.

Nick was -- as promised – lying on his bed in a fog of sedation and screen hypnosis. The television was blaring music videos, but Nick was still absorbed by his cell phone, his omnipresent earphones firmly rooted in his ears.

Hobbs wrenched open the window shades and took a few steps back from the blinding assault of naked sunlight. Staring at the hypnotized lump immobilized beneath hotel quilting, Hobbs rethought everything she had demanded of the boy earlier in the day. She had thought about the dangers lurking outside of the hotel room, but the biggest danger appeared to be the adverse effects of not leaving one's bed for hours.

"Get up," Hobbs said. "We need to get outside."

"I *did* get outside," Nick mumbled. "Remember? I left the room to get doughnuts."

"Yes, I remember, but you need to get out of this room and *do something* now that we're back. We don't need to be at Cecilia's candlelight vigil for a few more hours. Let's take a walk to the beach."

Nick offered a feeble, "Huh?" – too absorbed by his video content to properly protest.

"Maybe Ray will join us too," Hobbs suggested optimistically, but when she phoned her partner, he insisted that he was going to call his wife at home and then take an hours-long nap.

"Okay, it's just us then," Hobbs said.

A few minutes later, she and Nick left the hotel and headed west. They crossed several streets of dense traffic, cars choking up on each other while their tailpipes leaked. They passed an outdoor shopping area, a grassy patch of wooden benches, spandex-wearing joggers and moms with strollers. Finally, they reached the sandy shore of Santa Monica beach.

Hobbs didn't have a blanket with her – hadn't given their excursion much advance contemplation – so she and Nick sat near each other in the sand. The light brown silt pooled and sifted around her feet, while rays of sunshine warmed her chest and neck. The cloudless sky was absolutely perfect, a flawless backdrop to the wet suit-cladded surfers cresting and subsiding in the surf.

"It's gorgeous here. Isn't it?" Hobbs asked, but it was really a comment more than a question. She wanted to engage the boy in conversation, but he had become engrossed with the task of building a sandpile in his hands while also allowing trickles of sand to leak from his fingers.

Nick looked down and busied himself with the task, and all was silent for a few minutes until he said, "I don't think it's that gorgeous. I mean, the beach is pretty but look around at all the homeless people and trash and the parents yelling at their children not to run into traffic. I'm glad I don't live here."

He spoke conclusively but it was the kind of defeated attitude that reminded Hobbs of *sour grapes*. This land of ubiquitous sunshine and ocean spray, weather and topography offered a certain consistency that Nick had never known his whole life. It took a lucky person to live in L.A. And Hobbs knew it was home to a thousand strivers, people who laid in bed amid Midwestern thunderstorms and Dakotan snow showers and dreamed of making it big and moving west.

Hobbs wasn't surprised to hear Nick's avowal of distaste for Santa Monica. He had probably never endeavored for grandiosity – or even geographic beauty. He seemed to harbor the kind of ambitions that were dulled out by fatigue, apathy and thousands of hours of video game playing. Nick's version of ambition seemed to extend only to making it to the next level in a simulated world.

"Hey, Nick. What do you want to be when you grow up?" Hobbs asked.

Nick smirked and allowed a dribble of sand to seep through his fingers. "Why do you care?" he asked.

"Just curious."

Nick laid down in the sand and made a sloppy angel out of the loose formation that encircled him. He was fully horizontal but he still managed to noticeably shrug – enough to loosen the dappled sand around his shoulder. "I don't know," he said, as his eyes trained on the cerulean-blue sky. "I never really thought about it."

"Well, think about it now," Hobbs pressed. "If I told you that you had to choose, where do you see yourself in ten years?"

"Ha! Ten years? Out of my parents' house; that's for sure."

"Okay...what else?"

"Well, I suck at pretty much everything, so...I dunno...I guess working at the gas station up the street. You know, working the register, probably getting high all the time with my friends...umm...I mean..."

Nick sat up sharply in a fit of self-awareness. Suddenly he was cognizant – not just of what he was saying but who he was saying it *to* – an enforcer of the law, and even worse, a relative and advocate of his middling father.

"Do you get high a lot now?" Hobbs pressed in a forced-soft voice, trying to keep the conversation as casual as possible. This was not a department-underwritten interrogation, wherein she needed to break down a hesitant subject. This was a lost kid – her nephew no less, who seemed to medicate his isolation with easy distraction and artificial substances.

"Not really," Nick said. Then he corrected, "Sometimes."

"So, why do you see yourself just getting high and earning minimum wage in ten years? Why not focus on college and getting a high-paying job or on having a girlfriend or engaging in a hobby?"

"I don't have any hobbies, except video games," Nick responded quickly. "Fine! I'll do that too. I'll play video games, get high and work at the gas station."

"But why not—"

"You know, not everyone has the same wishes for themselves, Aunt Roberta. And, even if I did want to go to college, I'm not smart enough. Okay? Just let it be!"

"But who says you're not smart enough?"

"EVERYONE!" Nick yelled. His voice – so baritone and loud, was jarring enough to attract the attention of nearby beachgoers. He stood up sharply and took out his anger on the sand, uprooting mounds at a time and heaving them into the air. A soft breeze carried the sand several centimeters before the heap disintegrated into the whirlwind around him.

When the tornado settled down a few moments later, Hobbs could see that Nick's face was tear-stained. Her heart ached for him, and she tried mentally to draw a line from this angry guy to the sweet little boy she once knew. Little Nicky Hobbs had been full of pleasantness. His uncomplicated demeanor, his easy affections, his earnest communication made him so easy to love. Somehow, this mad, sand-throwing creature was the same person as they squeaky-voiced kid who'd thrown his arms around her and asked her for a train set, who'd wondered what it would be like to have a third foot, who'd played hide-and-seek until his fatigued body kept him lodged underneath the dining room table long after the game was over.

Hobbs wondered, what unruly force had turned that adorable boy into an anxious, unhappy teenage kid, convinced of his own futility and idiocy? Perhaps it was the natural course of time – a biological pit stop on the path from boy to man. Perhaps it was – as Nick claimed – the voices around him – parents, teachers or even friends – murmuring into a synchronized crescendo. Perhaps there were no external voices – just the piercing silence of would-be caretakers…allowing Nick to form his own negative opinions about himself.

Whatever the source, Hobbs could plainly see the aftereffects. Nick stormed away from the ocean in wide-stepped footfalls, not bothering to glance behind him to see if his aunt was following him. (She was.). He jaywalked indifferently across busy streets, allowing his fate to be decided by some greater, hidden force.

Luckily, kismet was in Nick's favor that afternoon, as cars slowed to a standstill when he stamped past them.

After thirty minutes, they made it back to the motel, and Nick hastened up the steps to his room and slammed the door behind him. He didn't have the wherewithal to close the curtains, however. When Hobbs looked inside, she saw the same figure that she'd seen earlier in the day – a body-shaped lump underneath a flimsy motel quilt, earphones affixed and screen aptly situated. This way, Nick and Nick alone could control who got through to him.

HOBBS, MARTINEZ AND NICK SHOWED UP AT WESTWOOD REC shortly before 7 p.m. The sun was lingering in the sky, providing scant illumination for the swarms of children chasing each other through the park. The detectives and the teenager followed a mass of candle-bearing mourners until they reached a tree clearing and an overturned milk crate.

Hardly the stuff of professional vigils, Hobbs thought to herself, as she nodded sympathetically at the few tear-stained faces whose eyes caught her own.

"This is going to be really sad," Nick announced, kicking his toe into a patch of exposed dirt.

Hobbs looked over at him but didn't say anything. It had been a battle just to get him to accompany them – a confrontation that involved candy-related incentives (disregarded), promises about Los Angeles landmarks (couldn't care less), and ultimately – the only strategy that ever worked: the threat of a one-way airline ticket.

When she was in the middle of the fracas, Hobbs questioned herself about why she was forcing this reluctant child to attend the vigil of a celebrity he'd barely heard of and knew nothing about. But – in the two days since she'd assumed the role of guardian – she'd come to see her role as a sort of motivator. Her goal was to get Nick out of the hotel room – at least long enough to allow housekeeping to spray lavender-scented mist over the nimbus of odor surrounding the teenage boy.

After their time at the beach, Hobbs made up her mind to invite Nick to anything that wouldn't interfere with the investigation – and that included a hastily arranged candlelight vigil, keynoted by a former lover / employee of the deceased.

When the sun finally sufficiently descended and the hordes of rowdy kids finally stopped their games, a cluster of thirty people or so gathered closer around the milk crate. A well-muscled, dark-haired man then ascended, lit his candle and lowered his head. The man's hair was a tousled mop of curls and his skin was patterned with black and white tattoos and baroque jewelry.

"My name is Marco Bagnetti," the man said in accented English. "And Cecilia Cinvenue was my girlfriend."

The crowd of people held up their candles and murmured approvingly, and Marco launched into a tear-soaked eulogy of a woman worthy of sainthood. According to Marco, Cecilia quietly gave out food at homeless shelters during the weekend, rescued stray dogs from euthanasia and donated her red-carpet dresses to local women's shelters. He also spoke of the playful, spontaneous aspects of Cecilia – features that only those who were in close contact with the actress had the pleasures of observing.

When Marco finished speaking, he held his eyes closed

and frowned while the other vigil-goers muttered affirming condolences in his direction. Marco opened his eyes and encouraged others to speak, then descended the milk crate and found a space in the front of the group.

Other speakers assumed the makeshift lectern and spoke about what Cecilia's television shows and movies had meant to them. Hobbs noted that the speeches – while poignant – did not convey the sort of closeness that Marco's had. The other attendees were all simply admirers of Cecilia and nothing more.

When the speakers had finally finished, when the sun had – finally – fully set and the park was so dark that the lit candles formed a visible constellation of ardent patronage, Marco Bagnetti called the vigil to a close. Martinez and Hobbs approached the man but they were whisked aside by well-wishers and mourners.

For twenty minutes, the detectives waited while a line of vigil attendees hugged and patted Marco, squeezed his shoulder, and repeated how sorry they were for his loss.

At last, the vigil emptied out. Just as Marco slung his milk crate over his shoulder and pivoted towards an open field, Hobbs and Martinez approached, badges in hand.

"Marco, I'm Detective Hobbs and this is Detective Martinez, from the Vetta Park Police Station in Missouri," Hobbs said. "Can we speak with you for a few minutes?"

Marco's chiseled face seemed to lighten and he swallowed hard before answering. "Em, okay, sure," he said.

From the corner of her eye, Hobbs could see Nick's expression and it wasn't too different from their subject's. Nick looked transfixed – his eyes rounded and his mouth slightly open as he watched his aunt do her job from a twenty-foot periphery. He looked as though he were just realizing that the whole police detective spiel – with all of its official-sounding regalia -- was genuine and not elaborate cosplay.

"Do you want us to talk right here?" Marco asked, and

Hobbs noticed that his voice was deep but shaky, his arms trembling as he gripped the milk carton close to his body.

"There are some picnic tables underneath a streetlamp over there," Hobbs said, her arm and index finger outstretched. "Let's sit down over there so we can see each other better."

Marco obliged and the three of them walked over towards a pair of tables. Marco took a seat on one of the benches and Hobbs and Martinez arranged themselves opposite him.

"I think that you are probably here because of Cecilia's accident," Marco said.

"Yes, that's right," Martinez said.

"Em...well, I wasn't there," Marco said. "I don't know anything about it. I've been in L.A. the whole time."

"No one's accusing you of anything," Martinez said. "We just want to ask you a few questions."

"What would you like to know?" Marco asked.

Hobbs pulled out her spiral-bound notebook and leafed through it. "You said that Cecilia Cinvenue was your girlfriend?"

"Oh...em...yes I did." Marco's face reddened and he ran his fingers through his hair. To Hobbs, he looked childishly shamed, wide-eyed, a cherub whose hand was caught in the candy drawer. "What I mean to say is... we did have a relationship that was more than friends. I'm not sure how you say it here in English."

"When's the last time you spoke with her?" Martinez asked.

Marco rocked back and forth in his seat. He rolled his eyes towards the top of his head as though he were counting something. Then he brought his fingers to his face and extended them slowly. "Let me see...one, two, three...I think maybe the beginning of August is the last time we spoke, so that would be...six weeks."

"And you called her your girlfriend?" Martinez asked derisively.

Marco brought his hands down and brusquely flattened them on the table. "I do not think you understand what it was with Cecilia. She wasn't my girlfriend in the typical...*em American*...sense but I was her assistant for that past three years. She would call me sometimes – especially during pandemic – and we would talk for hours. Or she'd tell me to come over, and we would be...you know, *together*..."

"Intimate?" Hobbs clarified.

"*Si*, intimate. And I think I'm the closest thing she had to a boyfriend in the past few years...since...you know...since she broke up with that *stronzo*...and she was lonely."

Hobbs frowned. "I beg your pardon..."

"*Bastardo*...Em...Billy.   Billy Sloan." Marco said. "*Bastard*."

"Why are you referring to Billy Sloan as a bastard?" Martinez asked.

Marco shrugged. "I have some reasons.   Billy and Cecilia...they were not a real...how do you say...*authentic*... couple. First, he was not good to Cecilia. He never treated her the way she deserved to be treated. He didn't pay her much attention. And he did things like...he forgets her birthday. So I took her out for her birthday. You know, I would get her coffee every morning. I drove her everywhere. I bought her gifts. Flowers."

"So, you didn't like Billy because he was a bad boyfriend?"

"That's just one of the reasons. As I said, I have more reasons."

"Did he have an angry temperament?" Hobbs probed. "Maybe prone to violence? Maybe she and Billy had a bad break-up?"

Marco brought his fingers up to his face, interlaced them, pondered this question for a few moments. Finally he said, "Em...Billy was...Em...how do you say. Look...is not mine to say…but Cecilia already said it. She…em…let me just say that she did do something to Billy…about two month ago. Something I probably shouldn't talk about…"

Hobbs knew the exact moment of this discourse, as she'd been in this position countless times before. They were at the apex of a roller coaster – the millisecond just before the train plunged to its descent and their witness / suspect expelled shadowed, long-hidden truths.

Marco's voice weakened until it was barely above a whisper. "Billy Sloan killed somebody. It was years ago. He told Cecilia. Cecilia kept his secret until two month ago. And then…Cecilia told this…this…secret about Billy…to a reporter."

Hobbs sat back on her bench for a moment, let the words sink in. Marco, with his heavy accent and tortured conjugations, had delivered that sentence flawlessly, almost as though it had been rehearsed. This was a sentence meant to stun, worthy of the silent air that followed it. It was a comment that bred heaps of follow-up thoughts, questions that darted into Hobbs' mind as quickly as she could expel them.

Billy Sloan…*a murderer?* Of course, all she knew about Billy was the pristine, carefully curated image that high-gloss Los Angeles professionals in well-appointed offices wanted her to see. He was so carefree and easygoing. He had shaggy hair and a wide smile, perfect teeth. Hobbs recalled slow-motion Billy in a decades-old ad, his bangs waving carelessly as he toppled to the California sand in an attempt to sell sugarless gum. Could this beachgoer, this California dream, this former golden boy…be a murderer?

Hobbs stared at Martinez and then repeated the first part of the allegation. "So…Billy Sloan…murdered someone—"

Marco's eyes widened and he abruptly shook his head. It was as though the allegation…delivered from Hobbs' lips…carried more weight and implication than when he had said it. And certainly – now that a law enforcement detective authoritatively restated this information – it was up to Marco to either defend it or debunk it. He chose the latter.

"Oh, no no. I'm sorry, my English isn't so good. He...em...he...em...he *hurt* somebody. I think badly. Oh, maybe...maybe he killed them. I don't know. I don't know any more. I'm so sorry."

"How did he hurt – or kill – the person?" Hobbs asked.

Marco shook his head. "I don't know."

"Who was the victim?"

"I don't know. I'm sorry. I don't know anything else about it."

They were all quiet for a beat and then Martinez sighed impatiently. "So, let me get this straight...Billy, at one time, hurt someone badly...as you say. And maybe killed them. But you don't know how. You only know that this happened because..." Martinez paused and allowed Marco to fill in the blank.

"Cecilia told me. And she told me to keep it quiet. Made me swear *on my life*. And then she goes and tells a reporter."

"Let's back up for a moment. Cecilia told you that Billy did this. But she didn't give you any other details about this?"

"No...em...yes...em...what you say is correct."

Martinez continued. "And then, Cecilia kept this secret until two months ago, at which point, she told Billy's secret to a reporter?"

"Em, yes."

"Which reporter?" Hobbs asked.

Marco stared at Hobbs. "Em...A very pretty girl. Her name was Margaret Scott. I was...what's the word...I had drink something, some wine...but I remember what she said to me. She whispered this secret to me...this secret that Cecilia told her."

"So the reporter whispered to you that *Cecilia told her* that Billy Sloan had hurt – maybe killed – someone..." Hobbs said. "She whispered this to you...when? During an interview?"

"Oh, no, no. In a dance club. And then we went to bed after."

"I see. Thanks for your candor. Can you give us this reporter's phone number?"

"I cannot do that. I erased her from my phone after she left my apartment. But you are the police...so you can find it."

"Why would Cecilia leak a secret like that to a reporter?"

"I don't know."

"Well...this is quite the allegation that you've alleged against Billy," Hobbs said. "If it were true, why hasn't this reporter published it? Why haven't we heard about it?"

It was a rhetorical question, but Marco answered anyway...predictably.

"I don't know."

Marco was proving more and more useless...and problematic. It was as though he'd lobbed a Molotov cocktail in Billy Sloan's direction and galloped away. He didn't know the *why* or the *when* or the *how*. All he knew was how to pin a motive on another former boyfriend of Cecilia's.

Hobbs decided to see how far Marco would go in his accusations against Billy Sloan. Typically, this was a tell for guilty parties; they often had another suspect lined up...another piece of sugarcoated deception to feed to hungry detectives.

"Do you think Billy Sloan killed Cecilia? For revealing his secret?" Hobbs asked.

But Marco didn't take the bait. He shook his head again and repeated, "I don't know." He moved his gaze from Martinez to Hobbs, no less intense. "I have told you everything I know about it," he said.

Hobbs decided to try a different approach. She leaned forward, closer to Marco, and spoke in a soothing voice. "Sounds like you and Cecilia were really close."

"Si, yes...I was close with her. *Yes.*"

"So, why hadn't you spoken to each other in six weeks?" Hobbs asked.

"Because…she…she…fired me," Marco said. "She said I try too many times to get auditions or work or jobs by contacting her…em…what's the word…associates. Who were very busy. Too busy to deal with me. That's the reason she gave. We stopped talking after that."

Marco leaned back and Hobbs could see – even in the dim lamplight – tears forming in the man's eyes. He brought his palms up to his face and wiped away the moisture, leaned his head back, swallowed hard and covered his face.

"I'm so sorry for your loss," Hobbs said quietly, while internally, she tried to fashion a murderer out of this heart-broken L.A. casualty. There would be time to flesh out Marco's allegation against Billy Sloan. While she had the Italian would-be actor right in front of her – pitching and keening with authentic-seeming melancholy – she had to consider whether he was the one who had chased Cecilia off the cliff.

Could Marco Bagnetti have been so betrayed by an unexpected firing that he picked up a telephone and ordered a hit on the movie star? Hobbs thought it seemed less than likely. Professional hits were brisk and clean – the proficiency of bullets and the pristineness of missing persons. Hobbs had never been aware of a hit man chasing someone off a cliff.

Could Marco have committed the crime himself? Perhaps Cecilia's decision to dismiss him had been unforgiveable. Maybe he consoled himself of her absence with shallow replacements. Perhaps a new girlfriend or confidante; someone else who would appreciate the lavishing of coffee and birthday dinners. Maybe he found a new minimum-skilled job as a delivery person or day laborer.

None of these efforts to move on could possibly have filled the vacuum caused by losing Cecilia Cinvenue – both as a revenue source and as a lover. And maybe, once Marco eventually came to this realization, he decided to follow the movie star. Following, pursuing at first…not stalking…exactly.

He would have shown up at her house and begged for the return of his job. And the more desperate he was, the more resistant Cecilia would have been. She would have rejected him…kindly at first, and then more assertively. She would have minimized him until he was just another admirer in the crowd – no more special than the attendees at her posthumous candlelight vigil, with knowledge of her no more intimate than what she flaunted on the screen.

Could Marco have withstood this type of rejection, or did he follow her…all the way to Missouri? All the way to the edge of a serrated cliff? He certainly checked a lot of boxes: infatuation, unreserved devotion…and with an anguish endemic to jilted former lovers.

So, Marco was certainly still a person of interest…even though he seemed so innocuous and unguarded. Love – or was it obsession? – made regular people do crazy things.

"Marco, how did you take the news of being fired?" Hobbs asked.

Marco straightened and wiped his face again. Splotches of ruddiness gave the appearance of guileless innocence. His face hardened and his voice seemed lower by half an octave. "Em…what – did you think I did something? Yes, I was upset but I never would have hurt Cecilia. Never! And if you want to look at my cell phone and my emails and… and…give me a test to see if I am lying…then fine! While you're here talking to me…you should really talk to is Billy Sloan. Or Terry Mahoney. Talk to those guys. And then figure out who did this…and…and push *them* over a cliff! Okay!"

"Okay," Hobbs said, but it was less a response to Marco Bagnetti and more of a soothing mechanism to stem the man's anger. If Marco actually offered up his cell phone and email – as pledged – Hobbs felt that she and Martinez could get a pretty good idea of whether this jilted ex-assistant had become a calculated killer.

Martinez leaned forward and squeezed one of Marco's shoulders. "We're sorry to make you upset like this, Marco. We just want to get to the bottom of what happened to her. I promise we're almost finished. Just a few more questions now. You mentioned Terry Mahoney. What can you tell us about Cecilia and him?"

The young man levelled his posture under the warmth of Martinez's gesture. He wiped the moisture from his face and took a few more deep breaths. "So…Terry Mahoney. I think in Hollywood, he makes all the decisions. I cannot tell you exactly – because Cecilia didn't like to talk about it – but I know they had…let me say…something more than a professional relationship. So, she was in one of his movies, years ago. *Soldier of Payback*. And after that movie, Cecilia was a bigtime star. And if you ask me, I could never tell whether maybe she hates or maybe she loves Terry. He had some kind of…something…em, how do you say…some kind of *pull* over her. So, I think you should talk to him."

"Okay, thanks Marco, we'll do that," Hobbs said. "Um… one more question. Can you think of anyone Cecilia might have been angry at? Someone she had a very antagonistic relationship with, or really despised? Besides Terry and Billy…anyone else? Maybe a few years ago they got into an argument?"

Marco frowned and crossed his arms across his chest, rocked backward and flattened his lips together. The air was silent for a minute, while he appeared to be mentally canvassing the friends, lovers and acquaintances who had crossed paths with Cecilia. Eventually he uncrossed his arms and shrugged – his face darkening as the moonlight slinked behind clouds. "There is one more person, I think. Maybe. She had a strange last name. I think it was Shear-something. Em…Shearwater."

Hobbs snapped back when Marco uttered the name, as though her spine had been jolted. She exchanged a brief glance with Martinez. The name was too familiar to be a coincidence, and this was the type of factfinding bullion that detectives sometimes waited months or years to find. A name – evoked of its own will – that was plucked from the graveyard of investigative dead ends. A name that had previously meant next to nothing.

"What can you tell us about Ms. Shearwater?" Hobbs asked. *Sparrow Shearwater.* Hobbs remembered the woman's first name, but she didn't want to say it to Marco. She didn't want to feed any piece of evidence to the young actor – even seemingly banal metrics…name, age, residence.

"I cannot say much," Marco replied. "I don't know too much about it…except that they were close friends one time and then more lately, they were not good friends. Not at all."

Hobbs thought about the words scribbled across Cecilia's secreted diary: *Oooh, I am so angry, I could scream. Let it be known, here, on this date, June 25, 2021, that we are at war!*

Was Cecilia sad about the loss of this friendship…or infuriated? Could the women have had more than a friendship? And what about the fact that Sparrow Shearwater had been the first one to the Santa Monica police station, all draping garbs and heartfelt sorrow, eager to offer up three names to the waiting detectives?

Hobbs knew she had to explore more about the connection between Sparrow and Cecilia, but Marco – after tendering the woman's name – was of absolutely no help. He didn't know the nature of Sparrow's relationship with Cecilia, or the nature of its disintegration. He didn't know much at all, in fact, except that everyone else in Cecilia's orbit was less trustworthy…less authentic…than he was.

After a few minutes of pleasantries – designed to put the actor at ease and leave the door open for future follow-ups -- Hobbs and Martinez ended the interview. Marco drifted across newly mowed grass and towards the parking lot. A low mist had settled over the recreational area, making his silhouette look vaguely ethereal. Both detectives watched Marco trot towards his car – his pace accelerating the further he got from his interrogators – until he finally reached the sedan, tossed his milk crate inside and drove away.

Once he was out of sight, Martinez turned to Hobbs and asked, "Do you believe his story about Billy Sloan killing someone? And Cecilia telling a reporter about it? Seemed like a pretty obvious way to pin a motive on someone else."

"Yeah, almost too obvious," Hobbs said.

"So, what do we think the odds are that the guy we just talked to chased Cecilia Cinvenue off of a cliff – or hired someone else to do it?"

Hobbs shook her head and sighed. "We should look at Marco's phone and email, just like he said. That'll give us a lot of information. The fact that he pointed us towards Billy, Terry and Sparrow Shearwater …it's helpful and also a little bit suspicious. And he really seems unlikely to be a killer but…you know what? Hollywood is a very strange place… especially for people trying to make it here. I just don't know."

Chapter Ten

Santa Monica, California
September 22, 2022

DETECTIVES FRAZIER, Oliver, Martinez and Hobbs gathered around a rosewood coffee table in the back of the Santa Monica Police Department. The conference room abutted the precinct's kitchen pantry, so every so often, wafts of pastry and tea drifted into the alabaster-walled room.

Hobbs yawned and yearned for a cup of coffee. She had kept herself awake for the past four evenings, watching old movies on the hotel's cable television. Every morning, she made a silent pledge to herself that she'd assist her nephew with his online homework after she got back from work…and every evening, she broke her promise.

The problem was…the days were long and exhausting, and she had no wherewithal at the end of it to sit down and teach geometry, or chemistry, or whatever fifteen-year-olds were studying these days. Plus, Nick insisted that his homework was easy and that he was sailing through without her help. He claimed the online videos were sufficient.

So…Hobbs spent her days investigating, talking, researching, driving through Los Angeles's sinewy and traffic-strained streets. At the end of it, she had only enough energy to share a take-out box of pizza or fast food with Martinez and Nick and then retreat to her room – where effortless relationships and uncomplicated families played out for her on the motel room's television.

This particular morning was the four detectives' final in-person rendezvous. At 3 o'clock, she, Nick and Martinez were scheduled to board a plane to Las Vegas, where they would interview the once-legendary teenage star Billy Sloan.

Hobbs suffered from a sheltered adolescence, but even she had known about Billy Sloan by the age of twelve or thirteen. Friends' bedrooms featured the simmering, blue-eyed actor splayed across walls with fresh masking tape. He was a brooding young man with faint stubble -- his legs suggestively spread while he relaxed on a bearskin rug.

Hobbs tried to imagine what shape this striking young man had evolved into, but the decades had clouded her ability to properly conjure the teenage Billy Sloan, let alone an age-enhanced image. Online images presented a diversity of looks for the actor – mostly still shots gleaned from his variety show. Perhaps he was a soulful musician with heavy eyeliner or a top-hatted magician with a cunning streak. She wouldn't know for sure until they were face-to-face. But before she could think about Billy Sloan, the detectives had to address the matter of Dalton Beck.

While seated around the conference table, Martinez informed the other detectives that he'd been in touch with Captain Weaver and Lt. Dean Adams at the Vetta Park Police Department. Hobbs shivered at the sound of her former boyfriend. Since their breakup – since his walkout after learning of her last-minute guardianship of Nick – Hobbs hadn't spoken, written to or texted Dean Adams. But she did think about him often.

Adams had always wanted to visit Los Angeles, and –

before the breakup – they had made empty, fruitless plans to walk along aquamarine waves of the Pacific, hike the cliffs of Malibu and take the train up to Santa Barbara. All these visions were as empty as the savings accounts Hobbs and Adams had set aside for such an extravagant trip. The detectives liked to dream but couldn't really afford to realize their imaginings – not in terms of money or days off work.

So, Hobbs walked past a palm tree and thought of how her handsome former flame would look in the tree's shadow. She smelled the ocean and wondered how far her ex-boyfriend would have tried to swim. She realized all their shared visions unilaterally – as the designee for the trip out west. In her thoughts, she and Adams had fulfilled all the California dreaming they had at one point set out to do. But reality was an incisive obstacle. In the absence of Dean's steady companionship, Hobbs didn't even want to communicate with him. It was too hard.

"What did Vetta Park PD say about Beck?" Frazier asked.

Martinez glanced over his notes. "Beck allowed himself to get polygraphed – without a lawyer, even – and he came out clean…stuck to his story. Said no more than ten seconds elapsed between Cecilia's last words – *I was being chased* – and the car fire, which he said started in the engine. He also said she looked kind of beat up – had a bruised left eye and a gashed forehead…although he didn't get too good of a look at the rest of her before the car lit up. Obviously, her body was too decomposed by the time the Medical Examiner was involved to determine whether her facial injuries occurred beforehand or were a result of the crash. But getting back to Beck's session with the polygrapher…our expert concluded there was no evidence of deception."

Oliver shook his head. "You thought he might be lying because—"

"Let's just say he's been enjoying the limelight," Martinez said. "But it looks like he checks out."

"What about Cecilia's cell phone? Were you able to get in and analyze that?"

"Her cell phone was shattered and fried to bits. Nothing recoverable."

"Any results from toxicology?"

"Yes," Martinez said. "Just came back in this morning, and Cecilia Cinvenue was completely clean. No evidence of any substances. No alcohol, drugs, prescription drugs or anything of the like. Nothing."

These words cut harshly through the room, and Hobbs had to admit that even she was surprised. Their jobs would have been made so much easier by the presence of a hallucinogenic or a blood alcohol level that far exceeded the legal limit. In fact, in the absence of any other evidence explaining this mystery, Hobbs had assumed from the start that Cecilia Cinvenue's toxicology report would answer unresolved questions.

As a convention, Hobbs believed the simplest explanation with the fewest parameters was typically the answer. It was the case in almost all the crimes she had solved, almost all the investigations she had helmed.

This was Hobbs' first suspicion: Cecilia Cinvenue had been treating herself to illicit substances…as was the pursuit of so many people in Hollywood. Cecilia had come to Vetta Park seeking…okay, Hobbs didn't know what exactly, but certainly a side effect of her visit was privacy. Vetta Park was such an uninteresting patch of Midwestern land, such a lackluster nucleus of suburbia, that no one knew Cecilia was visiting the town and no one had photographed her there. Hobbs had suspected that the movie star – owing to the relief of a life unwitnessed and the splendor of a few days off work – decided to indulge in an off-market medication or two.

After all, movie stars were not a fixture of Vetta Park, but drug fatalities certainly were. Street drugs – laced with opiates, fentanyl, heroin and who knew what else – were as easy to obtain as ever in Vetta Park, and perhaps Cinvenue had gotten her hands on a few. Then, once the hallucination was in full bloom – once the big violent monster was growing and chasing her from her earth-bound stupor, Cecilia Cinvenue had taken flight.

A drug-induced hallucination…that's what Hobbs had suspected chased the movie star off a cliff. But she had been wrong.

"Should we get Sparrow Shearwater back in here?" Hobbs asked. "Marco indicated that the end of their friend-ship was a fairly big issue in Cecilia's life."

"We can get her back in here…" Frazier said, leaning back in his chair. "But we already grilled her at length about the dissolution of their friendship, and she would only give us a bunch of spiritual mumbo jumbo."

Hobbs nodded and looked down at her notes. "Okay, so the interview that Marco alluded to…the last reporter that Cecilia spoke to when she revealed about Billy—"

"I already spoke with the reporter this morning," Frazier said, in a voice of clipped immediacy. He then looked up from his notepad and gave Hobbs a soft smile – a tacit gesture that his eagerness wasn't a reflection of any derelict duty on her part.

"Margaret Scott with the *Hollywood Ledger*," Frazier contin-ued. "Cecilia's last known interview. Margaret said that Cecilia did, in fact, leak *a big secret* about Billy Sloan to her. She wouldn't specify what. She mentioned that this revelation of Cecilia's…was even a bit off-topic, that Cecilia seemed ready with an agenda to share this bit of gossip."

"But the *Hollywood Ledger* didn't run with it?" Martinez asked.

Frazier shook his head. "Margaret said it's not the *Holly-wood Ledger's* business to print unfounded rumors about other celebrities. They're a highbrow publication and not a tabloid. And the fact that this allegation seemed agenda-driven,

Margaret said they didn't want to get involved with whatever was brewing between Billy and Cecilia. Even though it probably would have sold a lot of magazines."

Hobbs brought her fingertips up to her forehead and massaged her temples. "So Marco was right," she said. "We don't know exactly what Cecilia said, but we do know that she tipped off a reporter...with *something* on Billy Sloan. And that gives us a fairly strong motive against Billy."

The room was silent for a few moments – an unspoken acknowledgement of the significance of assigned motive. For Hobbs, it seemed all too easy. First Shearwater had appeared – disheveled and heartbroken – all too eager to name three persons that the police departments needed to look into.

And then – perhaps because their investigation needed a jump start, perhaps because these three gentlemen played such a pivotal role in the movie star's classic tragedy – the detectives had formed a ring around their people of interest. The three main men in Cecilia's life became the locus of their inquiry...a circle that eventually expanded to include Shearwater herself.

Hobbs had certainly never had a case like this before, but she had investigated cases in which all the suspects pointed fingers at each other. Such situations were messy, problematic. The detectives had to unravel stories and motivations, person by person, like the unknitting of a complex, layered knot of yarn. And typically, when she reached the end of the destitching and unraveling, there were deceptions and collusions, alliances and clandestine plots. Maybe Hobbs shouldn't have been surprised that such a high-profile victim as Cecilia Cinvenue would have an intricate, convoluted story buried in her demise. Didn't the movie star deserve such a fatality – a soap opera of colliding characters, events and motivations? Would a simple cat-and-mouse account be a letdown?

Frazier tapped on the desk with his pen. "Let's get back to it," he said. "Last item on our list is Mr. Marco Bagnetti. Our

IT team went through his emails and texts and transcribed voicemails."

"And--?" Hobbs asked.

"Well…he enjoyed the company of ladies," Frazier said. "Plenty of them. But if he had any sort of vendetta against Cecilia, or she against him, he sure didn't exhibit it electronically. Everything he told you guys matched what his phone and email records showed. Including the lack of a connection with any person or business in Vetta Park. Or east of the Rockies, really."

Hobbs nodded and said, "I see." This bit of information didn't surprise her at all. Marco Bagnetti seemed most guilty of infatuation and status climbing. How much did he love Cecilia and how much did he view her as a vessel to greater things for himself? He had fashioned himself as a *boyfriend* – the moon in Cecilia's orbit, one of few close confidantes – but Hobbs wasn't sure whether he provided an ear for Cecilia's darkest ponderings or simply fetched things for her.

Maybe Marco Bagnetti was as close to a boyfriend as Cecilia would get – someone who would venerate her, work for her, love her – blurring the lines between a commercial transaction and an emotional one.

Could Cecilia have loved Marco back? Could she have hated him enough to launch a crusade against him, worthy of impetuously printed words of aggression in her journal? Hobbs did not think that likely. If anything, Cecilia's crime against Marco was her rebuke of him, her lack of reciprocation of his affections, his eventual firing.

Such a disavowal could launch a murderous campaign, but that didn't seem to be the likely outcome here. As Frazier explained, Marco's devices had proven his whereabouts on the morning of Cecilia's accident, and there was no evidence that he'd hired someone to do the dirty work for him. There was no evidence that he considered her guilty for the crime of not revering him the way he revered her. As Frazier described it,

Marco's emails about the star were always fawning, flattering. Until the end, Marco Bagnetti was just grateful to bask in his rose-colored memories of Cecilia.

After a few more minutes of pleasantries, the four detectives wrapped up the meeting. Hobbs collected Nick from an empty cubicle near the front of the station, and they – along with Martinez – grabbed a cab to LAX.

The flight to Las Vegas was mostly pleasant – a smooth ride until the airplane caught some disrupted air sailing off the Spring Mountain Range.

While the plane bounced and jolted – cutting through the clouds with indifferent fortitude, Hobbs kept her calm and stared out the window. A white, puffy haze coincided with the sharpest jerks, and Hobbs knew that – statistically speaking – it would only be a matter of minutes before landing.

Hobbs knew something else, statistically speaking: Toxicology reports of major celebrities were rarely completely clean. Much had been discussed at that morning meeting, but Hobbs' mind kept returning to that nettlesome toxicology report.

Cecilia Cinvenue had been distant in the weeks before her death – from both her Italian assistant/lover (whom she'd fired) and her spiritual guru (also fired). These privations undoubtedly would have left a vacuum – which many people in Cecilia's position would have filled with drugs or alcohol. But in the absence of those substances, in the absence of close confidantes, Cecilia had found *something* in the dusty, half-vacant industrial buildings at the edge of Vetta Park. Roberta Hobbs didn't know exactly what. But she was a seasoned enough detective to know that a spotless toxicology report was not an investigative dead end. It was – to the contrary – a potential clue.

Chapter Eleven

Los Angeles, California
1992

CECILIA CINVENUE HIKED northward on wobbly feet. She was fifteen years old – a starlet in her own right, a fraction of her former self. Cigarettes, diet pills and no-sugar soda had diminished her frame until she was a sinewy waif. She still climbed like a champion though – her determined feet cresting over rugged rock, her obedient body carrying her further despite frequent objections from her vacant insides.

The rocks beneath Cecilia's feet gave way to a gravel, dirt-colored path and then the steps became easier. She didn't yet have a driver's license or a permit, or – come to think of it – most of the milestones of middle adolescence. So she couldn't have visited Temescal Canyon Trail by herself even if she'd wanted to. Next to her, matching stride for stride, muscles practically oozing from his tight white t-shirt, was gorgeous teen heartthrob Billy Sloan.

Yes, it was *that* Billy Sloan – the one who played the oldest son on the nation's top family sitcom, the one who had already successfully transitioned from small screen to big – with roles in three studio-backed high-budget films and one surprise Emmy nomination. (He lost – but still, it was just an honor to be nominated).

Billy Sloan's airbrushed face glossed the covers of almost every teenage rag, and the piercing shrieks of young girls accompanied his presence within a mile in either direction. That evening, however, no one but Cecilia, their immediate families and their respective teams knew about this outing. It was the brainchild of public relations reps looking to maintain their clients' relevance and generate a little buzz ahead of the November sweeps.

Billy wore a thick jacket and a baseball cap slung low across his forehead, so that only a true fan – one who had memorized the curvature of his jawline and knitting of his eyebrows – would recognize that it was him. The autumn air gusted around them, relocating snapdragon leaves and pseudorontium herbs into spiraling eddies. Cecilia shivered and clutched her sides.

"Here – take this," Billy said, offering his jacket.

Cecilia gladly accepted, although it was several sizes too large and swathed her in black leather and pine-smelling cologne. Now it was Billy's turn to shiver – with only a t-shirt protecting him from the elements. Head lowered, he stuffed his hands in his jeans pockets and huffed further along the path.

Cecilia caught up to him and brushed his elbow. "I'm warmed up now. Do you want it back?"

Billy stopped, looked at her and smiled. Cecilia could see how millions of young hearts melted at the sight of his wide lips, his chiseled cheekbones. He was only a few years older than her but the gap in their ages felt to her like a decade. Billy Sloan was seventeen years old but carried himself with the seasoned confidence of a man. He was tall and broad-shouldered, husky-voiced and vaguely paternal. She had only met him a few times before their Temescal Canyon outing and he'd always given her advice as though he were a veteran, even though the career guidance amounted to little more than fortune-cookie caliber cliches. *Don't give up on your dreams, Cecilia! The sky is the limit for you.*

Cecilia was hoping to get something more substantive out of the teen idol during their outing, but he seemed to like hiking in silence. As they climbed, Billy's head remained pointed to the ground, perhaps to evade recognition by the few other passersby or perhaps he enjoyed keeping his thoughts to himself.

After an hour or so, they reached a clearing, with a wooden bench perched several feet from the edge of a rugged precipice. The bench was facing southward, and Cecilia and Billy wordlessly agreed to take a seat and marvel at the ocean-lined view. The sun was setting over the Pacific, shading the sky into a multihued marvel of watermelon-pink and orange. Beneath the sky, Cecilia could see as far south as Marina del Rey – its white condominiums jutting up – and as near as Pacific Palisades – with all the buildings, palm trees, and little houses in between. If she were the romantic type, Cecilia would have seized on this opportunity to get her first kiss. After all, what better take than the story of two reticent TV stars, embracing under the auspices of a placid November evening, with west Los Angeles spectacularly splayed before them?

But Cecilia wasn't in a particularly romantic mood, so she shifted towards the back of the bench, her knees pointed away from Billy and facing the peaking waves. Billy didn't seem particularly interested in making out with her either. He crouched forward and rubbed his exposed arms, his head still aimed at the ground.

A cluster of teenagers materialized around them and marveled at the striking scene. They laughed and chased each other, exchanging silver flasks and cigarette stubs. Cecilia's heart panged at the sight of them – an ease of interaction that she would never know. The gaggle ignored Billy and Cecilia initially, but she knew the reckoning would happen and it certainly did.

A red-headed young woman took a big drag on her cigarette and nearly choked on her exhalation – a volcano of breath and words released at rapid speed.

"Hey! You're! You guys! You guys! They're! Ohmygod! Hi!"

Billy toed the dirt beneath his sneakers and gave the young woman a half-smile, half-squint that made his face look as striking as ever. "Hey," he said.

The young woman pointed and shrieked and when her friends flanked her, they laughed even harder and exclaimed their affinity for and devotion to Billy all at the same time. A few peeled off from the main group and mobilized in front of Cecilia, repeating the same behaviors. It was fawning and flattering, certainly, but the type of interaction that was difficult to respond to. Cecilia felt like she and Billy were part of the display. Here was Los Angeles and all its trimmings: gorgeous sunsets, foamy ocean water, marvelous hiking paths…and two young celebrities carefully curated on a park bench – all fodder for the teenagers' future storytelling.

When the group had finished with Billy and Cecilia, they moved on and headed further up the mountain. Cecilia imagined what it would be like to switch places with one of the teenagers. To be the outspoken, red-haired nymphette, dragging from cigarettes with abandon, shouting to her friends in a way that was so carefree, so *uncontrolled*.

Cecilia's entire diet consisted of cigarettes. She still remembered the first time her agent, Anita Livingston, folded one in her hands. She remembered the two-colored narrow cylinder streaking tobacco smells across her palm.

How old was she, the first time a trusted adult encouraged her to take up the habit? Thirteen or fourteen? Just on the cusp of radical hormonal change that had seen her hips widen and her breasts swell? This was anathema to the crew of handlers who knew best how to keep her in the show. Perhaps Cecilia should have been outraged at the offer of a cigarette, but instead she was delighted. She felt like she'd been brought into the clutch of adult secrecy – that this contraband was an initiation into a world she was all too eager to inhabit.

Cecilia took the cigarette and developed a habit – one that complemented the recent downsizing of her meal size. Since her weight loss pledge, Cecilia had restricted her intake to meals the size of her enclosed fist and the complete elimination of carbohydrates, sugar, dairy and fats. This left almonds in her diet – dry, sliced, flaky almonds that older actors taught her how to chew painstakingly slowly in order to prolong the taste. There was also diet soda, which did little to quell her gastrointestinal urges but produced a lot of burps and hiccups.

It was the cigarettes that really did the trick. Just a month into her new diet and Cecilia had earned the praise of her parents, her team, her costars, and enthusiasts across America. The acerbic fan mail stopped, as it was replaced by everyone telling her how great she looked. The fans didn't know about the cigarettes or the nearly complete restriction on food consumption. They only knew that they liked what they saw – a wraithlike beauty, slinking across their screens with weightless efficacy. Everyone seemed to like it.

Cecilia sat back on the park bench and again thought about the red-headed stranger. Had Cecilia behaved like that – in public, no less – she would have been breaking a thousand imperatives drilled into her since the day she landed her big role.

She couldn't stridently call out to her friends, freely puff and drag, or wear oversize jeans and a baggy sweatshirt. She couldn't leave her house without thinking about facial angles that photographers would exploit, body poses that tabloids would manipulate into pregnancy speculation.

The irony was, Cecilia had dreamed and prayed for fame

– and she sure had basked in it at the beginning. She loved the expensive perks, the high-speed life, the entry into a members-only club, which catered to a rarefied list of rich and beautiful.

But once the shininess of this new life wore off, Cecilia saw it for what it really was – a prison with no parole board hearings. Her home was filled with nice, expensive things because she couldn't easily leave it. This level of fame was an invitation to be inspected and controlled. Nothing would come freely anymore – no decisions to indulge in a late-afternoon confection, no make-up free jaunt to the local coffee shop (at least, not without consequences), and certainly no carefree hike up Temescal Canyon. She was there with Billy because two executives believed that such a storied dalliance would generate buzz and amplify visibility. That was it.

At least Billy was pleasant enough to be around. He didn't say much, and when the group of adolescents had long since ascended the hill, he turned to her and smiled. "Well, that was interesting."

Cecilia nodded at him and curved back to the blue-green waves. Despite the setting sun and colder temperatures, Cecilia could still make out a few surfers. Their full black body suits made them look like tiny, silhouetted dolls, and they ebbed and bobbed carefully as if executing a meticulous choreography.

"You looking at the surfers?" Billy asked.

Cecilia nodded again. "Yeah, they look amazing. I don't know how they do it."

"I think I'm going to play a surfer in my next movie," Billy said. "I'm supposed to start working out with trainers next week."

"Oh yeah? Another movie, huh?" Cecilia's voice was tight, and she counseled herself to rein in her jealousy. "How'd you manage that?"

"It's a Terry Mahoney movie. You know him?"

Cecilia looked at him and shook her head.

"He's the big Hollywood cheese. He makes pretty much every successful studio movie on the planet. Get on his good side and your ticket is golden."

"Do you think you could introduce me?"

"To Terry? Absolutely! I bet he'd love to meet you."

Cecilia thanked him and turned her gaze back to the surfers. They performed the same motions as always, as though they were string-puppets controlled by an invisible thread. The night darkened too, a blue-black murkiness overtaking the brilliant dyes that the sun had left in its wake.

Before long, Billy drove Cecilia back to her house, and although they didn't kiss or hug or engage in any of the routine physical affections that their teams had been hoping for, Cecilia did feel a sort of optimism about the whole experience. She didn't see Billy as a romantic interest in the slightest, but instead he was a gateway to future fulfillments. Also, Billy was sweet and easygoing – with the type of disposition who could never hurt anybody. He was safe.

It was 1992 and the world lay in high-flying producer Terry Mahoney's guarded, gated, star-laden palm. All Cecilia needed was Billy's introduction and the future she had dreamed of for so long would be hers.

Chapter Twelve

Las Vegas, Nevada
September 23, 2022

THERE WAS a buzz about the Las Vegas strip on that Friday. Or maybe it burned with energy every day. Roberta Hobbs didn't know, since she'd never been to Las Vegas – or even Nevada – before. But she let her eyes swim over the pools of people pacing along wide, smoothly paved sidewalks, their faces reflecting the opalescent glow of nearby buildings.

Everything was pulsating as if it were alive; everyone was moving, as if tourists had a show or exhibition or a casino to get to. Roberta could have stopped on a stretch of sidewalk and just observed: show ladies in six-inch heels and feathered boas, water cannons that discharged lake water with buckshot precision. There were signs and marquees as far as the eyes could see, peddling their anchor performance in bright florescent lettering.

On one such marquee, Hobbs saw the words: *Billy Sloan: Master of Trickery*, and she clasped Martinez's shoulder and pointed at the casino. "There it is," she said. Underneath the main letters, in smaller, caps-lock font: *50% net proceeds go to the Elijah Gatlin Foundation.*

"Who's Elijah Gatlin?" Nick asked, and Martinez and Hobbs both shrugged. Hobbs consulted her phone as the trio ascended a footbridge and walked over endless columns of impatient traffic. While she read – carefully avoiding the tourists taking pictures, parents pushing strollers at a leisurely pace -- she learned that Elijah Gatlin was a middle-aged man who'd died from brain cancer in 2010. Several years later, Billy Sloan set up a foundation in his honor, with proceeds going to cancer research funding.

Hobbs read out loud while the trio made their way inside the casino. She read about Billy's fundraisers and galas, described photos of his presenting an enlarged check to a group of besuited medical professionals – eager and doting while being flanked by the appreciative members of Elijah Gatlin's family. She read excerpts from interviews in which Billy described the toll that cancer had taken on his own family tree.

"I guess he's kind of a do-gooder," Martinez said, as they arrived at the crowded casino lobby. The lobby was grand and anachronistic. Ornate Corinthian columns connected a tessellated carpet with vaulted ceilings. Hobbs looked up and saw painted recreations that reminded her of ancient Roman buildings. She, Nick and Martinez got in line while they observed the commotion surrounding them.

"This is busy," Nick said, and Hobbs agreed. As the line snaked forward, she wondered how many other people in queue were there to seek their fortunes, a modern-day Westward rush for those seeking gold.

Finally, they reached the front of the line, and greeted a bird-faced man with a gold nameplate and a ready smile behind the lobby counter. "Can I help you?" the man asked.

Hobbs, Martinez and Nick smiled and gave their information. They learned they would be staying in three adjacent rooms on the nineteenth floor. The path to the correct elevator banks took them past a sensory-disorienting array of slot machines and blackjack tables, ringing notes and high-pitched clatter. Even the elevator was bedlam. They crowded together with a crush of others – gamblers, pool-goers, squealing children and moralizing parents. To Hobbs, the elevator seemed like a miniature replica of the casino itself. Stripped of game tables, restaurants, pools and other distractions, the box-shaped conveyance revealed Vegas's denizens at their most authentic moments. Everyone seemed to talk as though no one was listening, even though the clatter was impossible to avoid.

Only when she reached her room, did Hobbs discover silence, and she tried not to ruin it by shrieking at the magnificent birds-eye view of the cityscape below. It was hard not to gape, however. Beneath her, those magnificent choreographed fountains continued to cough up synchronized arcs of water, a credible replica of Paris's Eiffel Tower stretched northward, and a large phosphorescent hot air balloon seemed to glow, even in daylight.

"Wow," Hobbs breathed into the spotless glass door.

"Hey, Aunt Berta! Check out my view!" Nick called from the doorway. Hobbs accompanied him back to his room and observed the same gleaming panorama.

"I've never seen anything like this," Nick said, and Hobbs just nodded and smiled, although she also felt pangs of accomplishment that she had introduced Nick to both his first plane ride and his first trip outside of the Missouri-Illinois gateway. The trip to Los Angeles had been warm and tropical, but Los Angeles was too sprawling to afford a single ingestion of its unique splendor. Vegas – on the other hand – allowed itself to be observed in a one magnificent take.

After a few minutes of quiet beholding, Hobbs left Nick to the auspices of his technological devices and met Martinez at the elevator bank.

They rode together to the lobby, chatting about the view and the recent renovations to casinos along the Strip. Hobbs spoke with confidence – like an expert – even though her reservoir of knowledge about the topic stemmed from the few recent podcasts she'd listened to in previous weeks while working out.

Once on the main level, Hobbs and Martinez walked through another set of slot machines, clanging bells, card tables and dim lights. They ascended two escalators and pivoted back a few yards, walking on dark carpet that reminded Hobbs of bowling alleys of the 1980s in her Kansan suburb. Just when she was convinced that they had gotten turned around somewhere along the way and were unquestionably lost, a glossy-haired woman in a pantsuit met them in front of a wooden doorframe. "You must be Detectives Martinez and Hobbs," she said. "I'm Billy's manager and I'll take you back to see him."

Hobbs and Martinez obliged and followed the woman through industrial-frame doors and long hallways. They walked until they reached a wooden door with the all-caps nameplate *BILLY SLOAN*.

The woman rapped on the door. "Billy?" she said tenderly. "The detectives are here."

The door flung open and a tall, blue-eyed, coral peach-complected, stubble-jawed man appeared. Hobbs smiled at the recognizable face. Billy hadn't aged much in the decades since his gaze brooded at her from his bearskin-rug recline.

"Hi, I'm Billy," the man said tightly. "Nice to meet you. I know you're here to talk about Cecilia. Please. Come inside."

Hobbs and Martinez shook Billy's hand and introduced themselves as they made their way inside his dressing room. A quick survey of the room revealed very little about its principal inhabitant. There was a well-lit mirror and an ivory desk, two worn, black leather couches and a coffee table.

Hobbs and Martinez took seats on the couch and Billy

Sloan grabbed the desk chair and straddled it, facing them. He crossed his arms over the chair's back and frowned. "Look, we can get right into it. When I got the news, I couldn't believe it. I've been crushed ever since I heard. Cecilia was such a beautiful person. I can't imagine why she would do this."

Billy's eyes filled with tears and he brought his thumb and pointer finger to the bridge of his nose to stem the flow. He looked utterly dejected, but Hobbs had to remind herself that this was an interview with an actor. He was skilled at crying on demand, at shaping his tear-stained face into a believable sulk.

"What can you tell us about your relationship with her?" Martinez asked.

"Uh...not much, recently," Billy said. "You know, we were together... I guess it was 7 years ago that we split up and I hadn't talked to her too much since...except to...you know... wish her a happy birthday and stuff like that."

"Why'd you break up?" Hobbs asked. "Who broke up with whom?"

Billy craned his neck back and glanced around the room. He studied the pale white walls as though he were a guest, probing his surroundings for the first time. "It's a bit...complicated..." he said.

Hobbs hoped that the incipient silence would compel Billy to finish his sentiment, that she and Martinez wouldn't have to wrench the release of Billy's despondent thoughts.

Martinez couldn't resist. "Yes?" he asked.

Billy rubbed his eyes. "I can't tell you who broke up with who because it was very mutual. And when I say that, I mean that...well, back in 2009 or 2010, there were all these tabloid rumors going around about me. I'm sure you remember..."

Hobbs frowned and shook her head and Martinez did the same. In 2009 or 2010, she was fully immersed in the louche world of Vetta Park's drug trade and petty criminals. "No, I don't remember the rumors," she said.

Billy looked straight at her then and clasped his hands together tightly above his knees. Hobbs sensed that a confession was imminent, and she relaxed into a more comfortable posture on the leather couch.

"Well, all these rumors were going around about me that I was gay," Billy said. "And my team thought it would be good if I was linked with someone – a female – to, you know, dispel the rumors. Obviously, there is nothing wrong with being gay, and to be clear, I'm not gay, but you know, in Hollywood, it can affect your status as a leading man in romantic films, which was kind of my specialty at the time. So, my manager asked me if there was anyone I wanted to be paired up with... and I thought of Cecilia. I'd practically grown up with her, and I never knew her to have a boyfriend. Don't get me wrong, she definitely got with men – more than most, I'd say – but never one steady, single guy. So, we thought maybe it would help both of our careers if we were...you know... together." Billy's voice trailed off.

"So...you're not gay?" Hobbs asked cautiously.

"No, I'm not. My agent and manager just thought I should be in a romantic relationship to help my career – which was hurting from the rumors – and Cecilia happened to be the lucky lady."

"Were you and Cecilia ever really together?" Hobbs asked. "Or was it all just...to maintain the image?"

"Um...we gave it a go a few times," Billy said. "During that five-year period that we were said to be together. You know, when we were drunk and bored and lonely. But nothing ever amounted to anything. Really, she was more like a sister to me."

"Can you tell us a bit more about what Cecilia was like, during the time you two were pretending to be a couple?" Hobbs asked.

Billy lowered his head. "Well, we were both kind of in a bad place. I was trying to figure out who was spreading rumors about me, and also resurrect my movie career… which, as you can see, never got resurrected. And Cecilia was always kind of sad. Even around people, she was lonely. She seemed to me to be always searching for something…looking for love, or should I say *sex*, in the wrong places. Lots of different guys. And she dabbled in drugs too, recreationally. Nothing serious."

"What kind of drugs?" Hobbs asked.

"Sometimes coke. Sometimes Oxy. Lots of booze. But she wasn't crazy about it. She wasn't addicted or anything. I don't think."

"Okay, Billy, the next question…you know I have to ask it. I would be remiss if I left your dressing room and didn't ask it," Hobbs said.

"Okay. Go ahead."

"Did you have anything to do with Cecilia Cinvenue's accident last week?"

"No. Absolutely not." Billy's denial was quick and blunt, delivered with a hastiness of certitude and a direct stare into Hobbs' eyes.

"Where were you last week, September 14th and 15th?"

"I was here. I rehearse on Wednesdays and perform on Thursdays. There's, like, a hundred people who can vouch for me. And I'm sure someone has video of my performance. Trust me, I had no idea Cecilia was in Missouri, and I wouldn't even be able to find it on a map."

The last words were delivered with a kind of self-deprecating chuckle – the antics of a heedless Hollywood native whose geographic skills left much to be desired. But it was also the recycled trope of California natives, who claimed not to waste their time visiting flyover country.

Hobbs refrained from citing the many exploits of the Show-Me state, and instead lowered her face towards her notepad while she jotted. "Can you give us the names of one or two people who can vouch for you?"

"Sure," Billy said, and he motioned for Hobbs' pad. After furiously writing with a left-handed scrawl, Billy handed the pad back to Hobbs. She noted that he had written down the names of three people – ever the over-deliverer.

"Thanks. We'll follow up with these folks," Hobbs said.

"No problem." Billy made a relaxing motion – a back-wards lean that could have prefaced his ascent from the chair – the termination of this interview. However, Hobbs and Martinez stayed in their seats. They had more ground to cover.

"Billy...I'm sorry to keep coming back to this...but is there any reason you and Cecilia may have been angry at each other...or, more specifically, she may have been angry with you?"

Billy frowned and shook his head. "No, definitely not. We loved each other."

Hobbs cleared her throat and stared at Billy with a concentrated gaze – a look that he tellingly shrank from. "Bil-ly..." Hobbs said. "A reporter has let us know that Cecilia revealed something very *disturbing* about your past."

A myriad of different expressions surfaced on Billy's face. First surprise...then, when he caught and suppressed that emotion with flattened lips and wrinkled brows, he seemed almost comically entertained by this idea. He lifted his head, and – again, matching Hobbs' intense stare – suddenly became serious.

"Oh. Okay," Billy said.

"Well...we know that this event happened in your past, and I have to say, that it makes you look fairly suspicious."

Hobbs was knowingly coy about revealing too much, because, when it came right down to it, she had no idea what this disturbing thing was. Was it murder or an accident? A street fight or an episode of domestic violence?

Billy shrugged his shoulders and looked at her then – his

face the same innocent, carefree veneer that she remembered from tabloid magazines decades ago.

"Okay," Billy said again.

"Can you think of why Cecilia may have done this?" Hobbs asked.

"I don't know why Cecilia does what she does. You said you spoke to the reporter. Is the story about my *disturbing past* going to run?"

Hobbs leaned back and shook her head, never taking her eyes off Billy. "I don't think so," she said. "I think the outlet decided not to print it."

She thought about this little tidbit of information and hoped it would stir something inside of Billy. That she could have kept to herself and claimed ignorance about the reporter, said she didn't know. But instead, Hobbs had answered honestly and quickly, and this release of information would provoke a quid pro quo. Whatever *terrible thing* they were all indicating, all dancing around without revealing…this wouldn't be publicized, but it could be told to the detectives. They were safe, honest, trustworthy. He could speak to them.

But Billy didn't oblige. Now stiller, he exhaled softly and massaged the edges of his lips. He didn't say a thing.

"Can you think of why Cecilia would have done that?" Martinez asked. "Revealed your secret to a reporter? Was she mad at you?"

"*No*," Billy insisted. "Like I said, we were great. We had no issues with each other."

Martinez and Hobbs let Billy's improbable insistence hang in the air – the absurdity that someone would rat on someone they loved for no particular reason. The detectives didn't glance at each other for signs of which tactic to take because they didn't need to. They had choreographed this part of the dance countless times before – typically with felons and drunks and other offenders at the fringes of society.

Never could Hobbs have imagined that she would be in

this position with Billy Sloan. It was as though some natural universal arrangement had been upended. But she didn't hesitate.

"Billy, we *know* you aren't giving us the full story. Obviously, if Cecilia was going to break your trust in that very telling way, there would have to be a reason for it. You're not giving us a reason, which makes us suspect you even more."

Billy shrugged his shoulders. "I've told you everything you need to know. I've answered all your questions."

"Did you kill someone in your past?"

Billy scoffed. "No."

"Did you hurt someone?"

He shrugged. "Sure, everyone hurts people. It's a part of life."

"Did you physically hurt someone?"

He smiled. "Look, I grew up with brothers. We were always wrestling and fighting. Did I hurt them? Probably. Did they hurt me? Definitely. Have I hurt other people throughout my life? Sure…I've skied into people on the slopes at Aspen. I've put some people in a headlock who maybe didn't appreciate it. I've done a few stunts wrong that probably resulted in a few bruises. If you ask me to tally up the number of times that I've hurt someone, I'm not even sure I could. I'm only human, you know."

"Ever intentional?" Hobbs asked.

"No! of course not."

"What else can you tell us about this…this…secret that Cecilia revealed?"

"I have no idea what Cecilia said. If whatever she said isn't in print, it probably had no substance. I've told you everything I know."

Hobbs recognized this phase of the interrogation: *the impasse*. This was the moment before suspects asked if they could leave or requested their lawyer. This was the moment that all of Billy's constitutional rights would be laid bare, that the detectives showed their hand and revealed that they had absolutely nothing. Hobbs knew that Billy was hiding something, but this knowledge was as intangible as the drifting, smoke-fissured air. This knowledge would not allow her to keep Billy in the room if he chose to leave or to scare him into complying. She had to try a harder tactic.

"Let me tell you what I think. I think that you and Cecilia had a falling out. I think something happened and she decided she was at war with you. She told your biggest secret to a reporter and you got angry and followed her to Missouri, and chased her off of a cliff...or you had someone else do it. That's what I think."

Billy shrugged again. He was unruffled – almost calmed – by Hobbs' theory. "That would make a good storyline, but it's not the truth. We never had a falling out. I loved Cecilia until the very end."

Martinez pointed his index finger at Billy. "Well, out of all of our people of interest, buddy, you're the only one with a motive!"

"I think that just means you need to do some more detective work," Billy said. "If I'm your main guy, you have a lot more work to do, because I didn't have anything to do with Cecilia's death."

They were quiet again, the detectives registering Billy's haughty defiance. They had threatened him with a tactic that typically made suspects yell and deny, assert their innocence in steadfast avowals. Billy, by contrast, had shrugged his shoulders and sighed, languidly looked at them and affronted their detective work.

It was obvious to Hobbs that this approach was having the opposite effect on Billy. She decided to move on, to see how readily he would finger someone else in the circle of Cecilia's acquaintants. "Can you think of anyone she may have had an issue with? Anyone she may have hated or who hated her?"

Billy still stood up, but instead of moving towards the door, he sauntered to the far edge of the room and faced away from them. He looked almost to be praying to an unobserved deity or reenacting a memory of being sent to a time-out corner. When he pivoted and faced them again, his face was angry – flared nostrils and tight jawbone. The detectives were finally seeing the emotion – the infuriation – that their previous allegations had failed to muster. The fury materialized when he was pointing at someone else.

"Well…" Billy said. "There is one guy I can think of, who didn't treat Cecilia especially well. And she was mad about it. But if he finds out you got his name from me, I have absolutely no hope of ever returning to Hollywood."

"We hold everything you say in the strictest confidence," Hobbs repeated. But she had a sense that she already knew the identity of the person Billy was about to name.

And she was right when Billy resumed the chair-straddle and stared directly at her. "Terry. Mahoney." Billy said.

"What can you tell us about Terry?" Hobbs asked.

"He is an absolute sleazebag. He was and he still is."

Again, Hobbs waited for Billy to continue without prompting. She had suspected the name *Terry Mahoney* to be uttered from Billy's lips – either him or Marco Bagnetti. After all, their small group of suspects continued to name each other – a circular firestorm of thorny bullets.

Yet the utterance surprised her at the same time. It was 2022, after all – and all of Hollywood's corrupt and immoral players were supposed to have been swept up and exposed with the #metoo campaign. Through it all – all the op-eds and published reports, all the social media revelations and whispered, random-blog inferences – Terry Mahoney had emerged unscathed.

"What is it about Terry Mahoney that Cecilia had an issue with?" Martinez asked.

Billy shook his head. "I don't know. I asked her a bunch of times and she wouldn't tell me. Even though I'm the one who introduced the two of them years ago. All she would tell me is that she really hated him. But she never told me why."

"Do you think Terry might have had something to do with Cecilia's death?" Martinez asked.

"I don't know," Billy said. "But if I were you, I'd definitely talk to him."

"Do you know where we might find him?"

Billy shook his head. "If I knew that, I probably wouldn't be here, pulling rabbits out of hats for the matinee crowd. No idea."

Hobbs and Martinez thanked the man, stood up and headed towards the door. What Billy didn't know was that the Vetta Park detectives – as well as their Santa Monica counterparts – had already made several unsuccessful attempts to pin down Tarry Mahoney.

The elusive producer was filming *on location* – a locale that his handlers had difficulty agreeing on. Perhaps it was Dubai, Dubrovnik or Rome. After all, he was in the middle of filming a particularly intense action movie franchise, which involved crisscrossing the scenic spots of Europe and into the U.A.E.

Multiple attempts to convey the gravity of their investigation had heretofore gone unrequited with Terry's people. Terry's handlers said all the right things: they understood that this was an important investigation; they offered Terry's condolences for Cecilia Cinvenue's devastating and unfortunate tragedy. And they said that they'd get word to Terry to get in touch with the police detectives in either Missouri or California as soon as possible.

And still…the call from Terry hadn't come, and it was increasingly clear to Hobbs that he was a key person of interest in the case. Typically, she dealt with slippery suspects by appearing unannounced on their doorsteps, search warrant in hand.

But this was a different situation than one Hobbs had ever dealt with before, and the pursuit was seeming more elusive and more expensive than ever. She could hardly imagine submitting a request for a plane ticket to Dubai, or more vaguely, *somewhere in Europe*. They would need to get more aggressive with the studio, the movie financiers, the Hollywood mechanisms that greased the wheels of this particular film. They would need to issue shutdown threats and get in touch with Interpol. If Terry wasn't going to materialize on his own behest, they needed to make it happen.

Billy Sloan shook Martinez's hand at the doorway and touched Hobbs on the shoulder...as though all their previous contretemps were forgiven. "You guys can check out my show tonight if you want," he said. "We have some comp seats that are pretty good. Our box office manager can get them to you."

Hobbs thanked the performer and politely declined. "We're not allowed to accept any gifts or favors in these situations."

"Oh, right. Of course, I get it."

"But don't worry. We wouldn't miss your show. We already got the tickets on our own. You may see us in the last row of the balcony seats."

"Great!" Billy said. "Well...see you later then...I guess."

Hobbs and Martinez smiled at Billy, left the dressing room and began the long walk back to their hotel rooms.

THEY WERE LUCKY ENOUGH TO FIND A QUIET ROOM IN THE casino – one that had a formidably large conference table and telephone in the center. Martinez sat in one of the chairs and dialed the Vetta Park police department, while Hobbs paced impatiently behind him.

It wasn't that the interview with Billy had left her confounded, or that she was bothered by the holes still lurking in this case. It was the idea of speaking with a certain man who was no longer her significant other – one whose deep, confident voice would take her back to their hasty breakup in her apartment.

Dean picked up on the third ring. "Vetta Park, P.D. This is Dean."

Hobbs leaned against the neon green-painted wall while Martinez and Dean maneuvered through pleasantries. *Yes*, Vegas was just as big and shiny as Martinez had imagined. *Yes*, Vetta Park was still enduring its moments of fame as the location of Cecilia Cinvenue's untimely demise. Dean spoke of a circus that had only swelled in fanfare after Martinez and Hobbs had left. There were even more pesky journalists and more news vans crowding narrow streets, curiosity-seekers who flocked to the rock quarry and tried to mentally recreate Cecilia's final moments. The turn of events had created such a fiasco that infuriated construction workers could no longer adequately do their jobs.

Dean spoke of having to ferret out traffic cops to prevent the probing fans from finding their way down into the rock quarry – averting a cascade of tragedies that could mimic the initial one.

While Dean spoke, Hobbs tried not focus on how much she missed the sound of his voice. She was glad to be standing behind Martinez, so he couldn't see her expression. Hearing Dean passionately exclaim about personnel assignments and the eventual designation of the rock quarry as a cultural landmark were almost too much to bear. She took a few moments to get hold of herself and took a seat next to Martinez at the table.

"So now that you've interviewed him, what do you think about Billy Sloan?" Dean asked. "Think he chased Cecilia off the cliff? Or got someone else to do it?"

"It's possible," Hobbs said. "He certainly had the motive to do it. He didn't seem like a murderer, but I can't say for sure. He was really evasive about his past. No doubt, there's more to the story that he's not telling us. And there's one more person we need to speak to before we get a complete picture of what we're dealing with."

"Who would that be?" Dean asked. "Or do I already know?"

"You already know the name," Martinez said. "Terry Mahoney. He's the key to this case. We need to talk to him."

"But…Weaver said you're heading back here tomorrow?" Dean asked.

"That's right," Martinez agreed. "Terry's been a bit hard to locate."

"I see," Dean said, and Hobbs tried not to interpret these two tiny, insignificant words as anything more than conversation fodder, that there was no register of optimism or glee in Dean's response to the confirmation of their arrival.

It's over, she told herself, even though she didn't quite believe it. She and Dean had been over too many times before for her to pack this relationship in a coffin and write its eulogy. In fact, if anything, this ebb and flow of togetherness followed a pattern that was almost ritualized. It was late September, and the days were getting shorter; therefore, she and Dean were right on track for their early autumn falling out.

After Halloween, holiday preparations would commence, and the ex-couple would be reminded of ritual family gatherings and easy couch-laden comforts before a crackling fire. If not every single human in the universe reminded them of the impending holidays, the mantle was assumed by every restaurant and commercial establishment they entered in the months of November and December, every radio disc jockey and every single ad on television.

The holidays were quite simply impossible to avoid, and just as inevitable as their eventual observance, Hobbs and Dean would find their way back to each other. Hobbs believed that…even though there was nothing tangibly tying her to Dean at that moment. Even though her parental assumption of Nick was still a foremost factor in her life and had no end date. She had to believe it.

"Anything else you want to discuss?" Dean asked. It was innocently worded and open-ended, and Hobbs wished to exile Martinez from the room and discuss *a lot of things* that had been swimming around her mind for the previous week. But she was a professional and she answered professionally.

"One more thing," Hobbs said. "You've been looking into what Cecilia was doing in Vetta Park just before she died?"

"Yes, that's right."

"I have a hunch that she was at a rehab center. I know there are discreet rehabilitation centers scattered across the country. They're really expensive and designed for utmost privacy. I wonder if the Vetta Park Light Industrial District has one."

Martinez frowned, as this was the first he had learned of Hobbs' hunch. "I can't imagine a celebrity center in the Vetta Park LID."

"No one can. That's exactly why it's the best place for one. Smack dab in the middle of the country, equally distant from Los Angeles and New York, and a convenient thirty minutes from Lambert St. Louis Airport…and twenty minutes from Mid-America Airport, which I know has private jet service."

"Interesting," Dean said. "Well, that's a good place to start. I'll look into it."

"Great," Hobbs said.

"You guys doing anything interesting in Vegas tonight?"

Hobbs and Martinez looked at each other and smiled. "We're going to see Billy Sloan's show," Martinez said. "We're not charging the department for the tickets, but maybe watching his song and dance routine will give us some insight to the investigation."

Dean bid them good luck and they got off the phone. Hobbs didn't have any real hopes for the evening – none relating to Cecilia at least. She hoped that getting tickets to a big Vegas show would be a highlight for them and an evening to remember for Nick.

As it turned out, that night was, in fact, an evening to remember...but not in any of the ways that Hobbs had expected.

THE LIGHTS ON THE CASINO FLOOR SHINED AND BLINKED; THE din of chimes and clinking change was as loud as ever. Hobbs walked proudly through the corridors, flanked by Martinez to her left and Nick to her right. She felt like a benevolent aunt – mostly because Nick had shown as much interest – joy? – as she'd ever seen from the boy after she invited him to Billy Sloan's variety act.

And now, Nick looked as much like a young man as ever. That afternoon he had begged Hobbs for a certain stipend to allow him to buy clothes commensurate with the evening outing. Hobbs found it hard to say no. Typically, Nick wore the same uninspired wardrobe as though it were his uniform – dark hoodie, dark sweatpants and sneakers. His outfit choices seemed designed to allow him to camouflage with the furniture, to disappear within loose-fitting cotton fibers and a cinched hood.

So when Nick reemerged from his junket with a long-sleeve button down dress shirt (black, of course), black slacks, black belt and dress shoes, Hobbs had nodded appreciatively and prevented herself from suggesting that there were several other colors in the rainbow palette that were perfectly accept-able for menswear.

Now, as they walked through the casino en route to Billy's show, Hobbs was grateful for her earlier reticence. The black attire *worked* on Nick, insomuch as it matured him – at least to the unknowing eye. He wasn't a bored kid, lazing wearily on sofa cushions, tranquilized by cartoonish figures on a rectangular screen. He was a young man on his way to a Vegas show — a certain swagger in his step, a certain glint in his dark brown eyes. To Hobbs, it seemed that this outing portended to a future in which Nick was a responsible, capable man. She could see the pathway, at least.

When they eventually made their way to the theater, they found their seats and waited for the show to begin. Hobbs noted that it was a sellout crowd and that most of the attendees resembled her — demographically, at least. When Billy appeared on the stage — wearing silver, speckled pants and a high-gloss fuchsia shirt unbuttoned to the mid-torso — the crowd went wild with applause. Hobbs and Martinez exchanged raised eyebrows while Billy gyrated and twirled alongside a battery of sparsely-clad female dancers, to the tune of disco music.

Hobbs wasn't a huge fan of the disco number, but the rest of the crowd disagreed with her, as evidenced by their hoots and shrieks. When Billy disappeared after the first two songs — leaving the showgirls to demonstrate their pirouetting and jetes — he emerged at the end of their number in a sweatshirt and light blue denim. This was the Billy Sloan Hobbs had remembered — the one who had been tacked to her bedroom wall and stared at her with brooding intensity.

A stagehand procured a stool and guitar, and Billy sat down and demonstrated his musical chops vis a vis mawkish love ballads. He finished one song and then peered into the audience, flashed a coquettish grin and said he was going to choose a woman from the audience to bring on the stage for his next song.

Hobbs sunk into the stitched burnt-orange carpeting of her seat and prayed that Billy hadn't done any advance work to determine her seat location. But a few moments brought welcome relief. There were more than enough women clamoring to be Billy's chosen muse, and the performer chose an eager, white-haired septuagenarian to accompany him on the stage.

By intermission, Billy had sung two songs to the woman and taught her how to do a few steps of the waltz. The early energy of his show had lapsed, and Hobbs could hear position-shifting creaks from many of the seats around her.

"Can I go back to the room?" Nick asked, once the lights were turned up. "No offense or anything, but I'm kind of bored."

Hobbs nodded to him and then braced herself for sixty minutes of a second act. Once the boy departed and the lights dimmed again, Billy took the stage in a three-piece suit with black bow-tie and kitschy top hat. He wowed the crowd with a few card tricks, told several jokes and rounded out the show with a personal anecdote about growing up in Hollywood.

Hobbs and Martinez joined the rest of the attendees in raucous applause, but as she left her seat, she had to admit to a certain relief that the whole thing was over.

It was several minutes later when she and Martinez were walking back to their rooms...a moment when Hobbs – perhaps out of habit – scanned the chiming slot machines and gaming tables across the casino floor and caught sight of... Nick. Playing blackjack.

"Ray," Hobbs said weakly and took hold of her partner's elbow.

"I see him," Ray said, and then the two of them rushed across the casino floor with militaristic determination.

Nick – wide-smiled and jaunty – had somehow acquired a hat, which he was using to obscure the ripple of his shoulder-length hair and a pimple-burdened forehead. In front of Nick were stacks of casino chips.

"Nick," Hobbs said sternly from behind the boy's shoulder, and something about the surprise or austerity in her voice caused Nick to nearly topple back from his stool. He took note of the adults — *the police detectives* — on either side of him, and his face registered a slide of conflicting emotions.

At first Nick smiled even wider and said, "Hey!" but then — seeing not the slightest amount of levity in either of their faces — he acquired a hangdog expression and said, "I'm leaving."

"That's right. You are," Hobbs affirmed, and took a few steps backwards to allow Nick to leave quietly while maintaining a shred of dignity.

Nick scooped up the chips into his hands, like a castigated thief just trying to make off with whatever plunder he could bear. "Let me just cash out first—" he was starting to say.

Hobbs placed her hand on Nick's wrist and squeezed. The chips spilled out of his fingers like reactive dominos. "You will absolutely not," she said softly and firmly. "You are currently in the act of committing a crime and I will not tolerate it. The money stays here."

The table dealer — a middle-aged woman in her fifties or sixties, wearing a pecan-brown silken vest over black shirt-sleeves — kept her head down and scooped up the chips that had been emancipated from Nick's grasp. The woman didn't say anything, but Hobbs could see a pit boss and two security guards amassing at the edge of the room and pointing in their direction.

"But I won, like, hundreds of dollars!" Nick protested, in the voice of a fifteen-year-old kid. At once, the protective luster of grown-up casing had worn off, and teenage Nick emerged, huffing and whining and seeming as incongruous at a blackjack table as ever.

The pit boss and security guards approached the table, and Hobbs instantly felt guilty. Not for Nick having to sacrifice his small fortune, but for the table dealer, whose lowered head and pained expression conveyed contrition and self-scouring. Her job was now at stake.

One of the security guards — a portly man with a dark

blazer and overflowing belly, pointed at Nick with the antenna of his walkie talkie and then at the dealer. "Did this kid show you ID?" the man demanded.

Her chin still pinned to her neck, the dealer nodded and said softly, "Yes, he did."

All eyes turned to Nick. "You *what?*" Hobbs asked, still trying to keep her voice down. It was one thing for the table dealer to look the other way while a kid who was likely teetering on either side of twenty-one took a spot on the stool. It was quite another for the kid to have willfully displayed a fake I.D. that substantiated an age he was still almost a decade away from realizing. Confiscating this contraband would be another goal for the evening.

Nick – finally realizing the severity of the situation, finally accepting that he had been caught...and no smooth talk or clandestine flash of U.S. currency was going to alter his fate – dropped his chips and marched away from the table.

"That your kid?" The security guard asked curtly.

"He is in my care, yes," Hobbs said. "And my partner and I are police detectives, and we will make sure this never happens again."

The security guard looked back at the dealer. "Did he give back all his winnings or are there more?"

The dealer shook her head. "He'd only been here a few minutes. All his winnings are still on the table."

The security guard affixed his walkie talkie to his belt and smoothed a hand over his shiny forehead, revealing annoyance or perhaps relief. The winnings were all on the table, so there was no greater matter to press. He and the other security guard sauntered away, and the pit boss admonished Hobbs to prohibit her son from ever setting foot in their casino again.

Hobbs – who typically found herself on the other side of law enforcement matters – wasn't accustomed to being chastised. Yet, instead of correcting the man that Nick was actually her *nephew*, instead of saying that six-foot tall fifteen-year-old boys with a well thought out agenda could be tough to supervise at times, she nodded and said she'd keep a better eye on him.

The pit boss took down her name and phone number anyway, just in case a review of the videotapes revealed a stealthy sneak of blackjack chips. Hobbs gave this information and then she and Martinez walked away to find the teenager. When Nick hadn't materialized by the time she made it back to her room, and when her fist slams against his hotel room door met with no response, she gave him a call.

Nick picked up just before the rings were to give way to voicemail, his voice indignant. "*What?*"

"Well…Ray and I are at the rooms and you're not here…" Hobbs said.

"So?"

"*So?*" Hobbs took a deep breath and gritted her teeth. "Nick. I just told a member of the casino's security team that I'd keep a better eye on you. Luckily, they aren't going to press charges against you. But you *are only fifteen years old*, and I do need to know where you are −"

"I went for a walk outside. I'm right in front of the hotel."

Then Nick dropped the call, and Hobbs stared dubiously at her cell phone.

"He didn't say where he was?" Martinez asked.

"No, he did. He's right outside," Hobbs said.

"Oh, that's a relief."

"You can take the rest of the night off, Ray. Thanks for your help. I've got it from here."

Martinez wished her goodnight and eagerly sprang back to his hotel room with the alacrity of a child. Hobbs then took a few moments to herself inside of her hotel room. She found the minibar and topped off a plastic cup with a heavy pour of white wine. The alcohol felt refreshing as it coated her esophagus; the minutes-later buzz was a welcome solace. She eventually threw the empty cup in the trash and went downstairs.

After leaving the building's lobby and exiting the parking area, she found Nick perched by the edge of the Strip's walkway. He seemed calmer, but he was gazing at passersby with a concentrated intensity—locked jaw and fixated eyes.

Hobbs perpendicularly weaved through the crowd and then found a place to stand right next to him. She decided to approach with a disarming greeting. "Hey."

"Hey."

They stood in silence for a few minutes and watched the crowd of people. It was late – certainly much later than Hobbs typically went to sleep – but the crush of humanity was as spirited as ever. While Hobbs and Nick stood and watched, heavily costumed ladies sauntered by, as did bachelor and bachelorette parties, middle aged revelers and older couples who reminded Hobbs of her parents. She wanted to break the ice by offering a platitude about the energetic nature of Vegas tourists, but Nick seemed hostile to all forms of small talk.

Finally, he spoke. "You know, I was winning back in there. Like, hundreds of dollars. You made me give up hundreds of dollars that I really needed."

"Nick, you would have never been able to keep that money. Security was on to you. They showed up just after Martinez and I did. And trust me, you're much better off having Ray and I diffuse the situation than having it escalate, with you winding up in a Las Vegas jail cell."

Nick huffed. "They would've never thrown me in jail."

"With a fake ID? And illegally gambling while you're underage? They absolutely would, Nick."

Nick pressed his lips together and scowled but didn't say anything in response. He crossed his arms over his chest so tightly, that he seemed to Hobbs like a mummified statue – one that risked tipping over in the face of a strong wind. For a few moments, they stayed like that...until Hobbs couldn't stand the silence any longer.

"How long have you been playing blackjack?" she asked

him, and she realized that her tone was way more interroga-
tive and less inquisitive than she'd desired. Really, she just
wanted to break the stasis, but the words tumbled out of her
with the probing familiarity of the precinct interrogation
room.

Nick threw his arms up. "*Oh God*! You make it sound like I
have a gambling problem or something! I just learned how to
play *today*! *Okay*?"

Hobbs let another few moments pass to let some of the
tension dissipate into the warm early-fall air. A group of
twenty-something women passed by, and Hobbs took note of
their drunken posture and giddy pace, their dress of sequins
and high-heeled boots. She smiled at their lightheartedness,
their buoyancy. To them, the night was an open-air reverie, in
which all things passionate and intoxicating were possible. To
Hobbs, the night represented an arduous conversation with an
uncompliant teenager – one that would at some point address
the confiscation of his fake ID. Oh, to switch places with any
of these women.

"I just learned today. Okay!" Nick repeated.

"Okay," Hobbs said quietly. And then, if there was a way
to soften the tone of this dialogue, to wave the white flag of
accord, she offered, "I'm impressed that you did so well after
just learning how to play today. That's pretty amazing."

"Whatever," Nick said and knocked the toe of his shoe
against the concrete wall. Hobbs wasn't certain, but she
thought she could detect a fleeting smile of self-satisfaction on
Nick's face. Perhaps her compliment had somehow sliced
through the shell of hostility.

Nick then busied himself with the task of kicking the
concrete wall. It was a ritual mission with no apparent end
point and no side effects. When he finally grew tired of that,
he pivoted, crossed his arms again and picked up the conversation. "I watched a few videos on counting cards while you
and Ray were at your meeting. It isn't too hard. You just have

to memorize which cards have already come out of the decks and whether there are more likely face cards at the end, when the deck is low. You need to have a really good memory. Which I do."

"Mmmm. I see," Hobbs responded, and she refrained from offering more. As the spigot of Nick's ruminations was finally opened, and his thoughts were at last being let out, she hesitated to do anything that might close him off again.

"You don't know what it's like to finally be good at something after sucking at everything," Nick continued.

Hobbs desperately wanted to counter this narrative. *Nick, you don't suck at everything*! But she maintained her commitment to silence, to letting him just talk.

"I have failed at pretty much every high school class that I have ever taken," Nick said…and then, he pivoted again and took out his frustration on the cement wall.

"Everything! I suck at reading. I suck at writing. I suck at math. I suck at Spanish. I hate PE because it's filled with know-it-all jocks who think they're the best at everything and that they rule the school. I hate! It! All!"

Nick accentuated every fragment with a glancing kick to the wall. Tears had formed at the corners of his eyes and they spilled down his face. He then placed his arm across his eyes and faced the wall, as if beseeching its absolution, entreating it to cover and forgive his shame.

People continued to stream by, unnoticing. Hobbs couldn't decide whether their unconcern was hospitable or cruel. She wanted to reach out to her nephew, to lay a gentle hand on his shoulder, to counter his self-effacement, to draw him into a hug…but she had no idea how her actions would be received. She was way out of her depth – a parental imposter with no previous experience to draw upon. But it wasn't easy to watch his suffering from the standpoint of a few feet of distance and several decades of age.

Nick turned to face her again, squeezed his eyes and

pinched the bridge of his nose. It was as though he were wringing out every last bit of moisture. "I'm sorry," he said softly. "I'm just not used to being good at anything. And that time in the casino...I know you hated it...but, to me, it was... it was good."

Hobbs nodded. "You don't need to apologize," she said, "I get it."

Nick looked down and kicked the air in front of his shoe at an invisible soccer ball. "How's your case going?" he asked, seeming eager to change the conversation.

"Oh, well, you know..." Hobbs responded. She felt that they were still early in the investigation, although they had uncovered a few valuable leads. But the spoils of celebrity sleuthing meant absolute silence when it came to discussing the case with outsiders...and this designation, unfortunately, applied to her nephew.

"Have you learned a lot about Cecilia Cinvenue?" Nick asked.

"Yeah...sure."

"Like where she grew up, what high school she went to?"

"Yep. But I guess I knew that about her even before working on the case, since I remember her being a child star."

"What kinds of things do you know about her?"

Hobbs smiled. "I know what everyone else knows. I know, for example, that she hates broccoli." She knew this bit of Cecilia Cinvenue trivia...as the starlet made her aversion to the vegetable a staple of the interview circuit. When Cecilia famously went on a late-night talk show in her mid-20s, the host goaded her into a broccoli-eating competition, with the promise of thousands in donations to the charity of the winner's choosing.

Cecilia had scrunched her nose and stuck out her tongue in such an adorably reluctant way, her facial gestures launched photographs and viral memes well after the contest had finished. That she won the contest and bequeathed a Los

Angeles children's hospital thousands of dollars for her efforts only added to the halo of brilliance encircling the star.

"What's Cecilia's favorite movie?" Nick asked.

This was another easy one. Cecilia was a known *Harry Potter* fan – unabashed in her zealotry. The movie star had trumpeted the release of each book with her own fawning review, famously dressed up as wizarding characters for Halloween and name-dropped Hogwarts students and administrators during press junkets as though these characters were friends of hers.

Hobbs answered Nick's question quickly…since the question was a layup, the topic as trite as asking her to spell *dog* or *cat*. It was only after Hobbs responded and Nick lowered his head to stare at the streaming cavalcade of shoes, boots and sneakers, that Hobbs questioned why Nick would ask such things.

"You want to know why I'm asking?" he repeated. "Because everyone on this planet knows everything about Cecilia Cinvenue. We all know where she's from, what she likes to eat, what she reads. You know, we even know what she *doesn't* like to eat. When Cecilia spoke, people *cared about what she said*. They took notes. And this rich-beyond-words, beautiful movie star wasted all of that caring. She took all of that caring and…probably drunk and high…drove her car off a cliff. What an absolute waste."

Hobbs took a deep breath and stayed quiet. She willed herself to speak nothing of the star's immaculate toxicology report. If this were an attempt to siphon non-public information about the case, Nick was very good. It took all of Hobbs' energy not to contradict his perception.

But Nick soon made clear that his conjectures were not the result of a self-appointed enquiry into Cecilia's motives. He was thinking about himself.

"What are *my* favorite foods, Aunt Berta?" Nick asked. "What movies do I like? What foods do I hate?"

"Um…well…" Hobbs felt put on the spot, and slightly unnerved by his questions. It wasn't just that she didn't know these basic things about her nephew, but that she felt unfairly indicted by her lack of information. In the years since he'd become a teenager, Nick had made himself unknowable. He hid behind a hoodie and a screen and grunted answers to even the most basic questions. If Hobbs couldn't answer basic biographical questions, it was as much his fault as her own.

"You don't give up a lot of information about yourself," Hobbs said. "I would like to know these things about you, Nick. Maybe, going forward, I can try to be more inquisitive and you can try to be less annoyed by my inquisitions."

At least this brought about a chuckle from the teenager. A rare break from the evening's sullenness. But Hobbs soon realized that Nick's chuckle was joyless – a reflexive response to her naivete.

"I'm not talking about *you*, Aunt Berta," he said. "You had no choice but to take me in after my dad basically dumped me on your doorstep. I'm talking about my parents. My mom who ran off with some guy to Canada and never calls. My dad who remarried and spends his time keeping his new woman happy and maybe a little bit with his new kids and not at all with me. Do you think he would care what vegetables I liked or didn't like? What movies I want to see? He wants me to shut the hell up and leave him alone without bothering his new life. There is no one in the world who cares about me, Aunt Berta. No one who knows anything about me. Anything real. And I'm not saying that so you'll feel sorry for me; it is a fact."

Hobbs wanted to refute Nick's comments, but the boy was too many layers deep in his pool of self-loathing to even want a verbal flotation device. He turned to look back – not at her, but at the wall – whose smooth surface bore no scars from the violence he'd inflicted earlier. "I'm going back to the room," Nick said. "Sorry to bug you with all this. Weird night."

He then pulled a card out of his pocket and thrust it into her hand. Hobbs looked down and saw that it was a fake Missouri driver's license. The photo was authentically Nick — with a reasonably believable 2001 birthdate — but the laminate was curling at the edges and the font styles were just a bit off. If the table dealer had just scrutinized this piece of forgery more closely, perhaps the whole night's events may have been different.

Hobbs placed the fake ID in her pocket as Nick turned towards the hotel and began walking back. She watched her nephew traverse the parade of revelers until he was on the other side…and eventually, swallowed by the magnificent doors of their hotel.

Hobbs knew she needed to get back to her hotel room. A good night's sleep was an essential prerequisite for what would be a day of travel and analysis…even on Saturday. But she took a few minutes to watch the crowd before following her nephew inside. She leaned against the concrete wall and thought about its resemblance to all of the adult figures in Nick's life. It had withstood his lashing with callous indifference. And when he'd turned around to embrace it, to cry against it with desolate, long-hidden emotion…the ash-gray slab responded as it always had…stoic, uncaring, and just waiting for him to hurry up and be pushed back out into the world.

Chapter Thirteen

Los Angeles, California
1996

CECILIA WAS NINETEEN YEARS OLD – a thin waif of a beauty. She was a gazelle on limber, sun-toned legs, with long blonde hair pouring down her back and wide blue eyes. She had fully inhabited the role that many observers had questioned the inevitability of. When she was a cherub-faced ten-year-old, when her two front teeth grew in a bit chunkier than the teeth surrounding them, when she turned thirteen and every ounce of flesh and body fat seemed poised to grow in an inauspicious direction – doubters assumed that this child star would realize her unsightliness and fade into oblivion.

But Cecilia proved them wrong – not just by becoming beautiful but by consummating an exquisite splendor that had been hidden for many years by oversize sweaters and high-swept ponytails. When she emerged at an awards ceremony – a sleeveless red gown accentuating her narrow waist and flawless skin – the interviewers who were lined up across the red carpet seemed incapable of reining in their flattery. They asked her about her style, her favorite designers, her beauty regimen. Cecilia answered every question faultlessly…as her carefully curated instructors had trained her to do. She told them her style was relaxed and comfortable, that she liked big box retailers instead of high-price designers, and that her beauty regimen was to sleep as late as possible and drink lots of water.

Cecilia's down-to-earth nature made the interviewers love her even more, and they boasted about her accessibility – even as P.R. managers whisked her to the next stop. Perhaps lost amidst all the sycophantic praise was the realization that Cecilia Cinvenue could not possibly be as average as an everyday American nineteen-year-old, no matter now pedestrian she claimed her life to be.

When the awards ceremony was over and all the photos and articles were splattered across glossy magazine covers, Cecilia's mother called her into the home office the following week and declared the awards show a success. It didn't matter that Cecilia had left the ceremony empty-handed. "They love you!" Betty exclaimed.

Cecilia thumbed through the magazines and tried to quiet the inner detective that spotted a bulge of skin creeping out from red embroidery, the rounding of a face that was only supposed to display a sloped, lustrous cheekbone. These thoughts made her crave a cigarette and she took a deep, lusty inhale of a Marlboro before replying with a casual: "I know."

"You are an absolute star!" Betty marveled, and Cecilia responded by quickly finishing her cigarette – stubbing the tobacco fibers against a red porcelain ashtray – and picking up more celebrity-centric magazines.

It didn't do much to see her gleaming face, high-fashioned clothes, well-styled hair staring back at her. Not anymore. The first time she'd caught sight of her photo in a celebrity lineup of Avant-garde trends – perhaps two years earlier – she had jumped up and down, squealed with glee and summoned her mother. It wasn't just the photo but the meaning of her inclusion. It said something about the company she kept and the weight of her styling decisions.

But – as with most things it appeared – that which she'd initially loved, she had grown to hate. Being a style icon meant taking risks and those risks just as often resulted in *worst dressed* spreads as in flattering ones. Even leaving the house in sportswear presented an opportunity for the photographers to pounce. The problem was, all of her years in Hollywood hadn't habituated her to the custom of being picked apart. If anything, she was more sensitive about her appearance than ever, and loathed the idea of disappointing people.

If there was a bright side to Cecilia's fashion sensibilities, it was that all of the attention had garnered more opportunities. Already, she had two independent movies under her belt, both of which had been filmed during her television show's hiatus. Both films' reviews had been mostly favorable, even though box office returns were abysmal.

Cecilia's hit television show, *The Family Next Door*, was finally coming to an end and it was time to focus on what came next. That was the impetus for the afternoon meeting with Betty, the meat of the matter, whereas Betty's cache of supermarket magazines was simply the appetizer.

When all the magazines had been rummaged through and Anita Livingston came on the speakerphone, Cecilia listened carefully as her agent listed opportunities. These were just preliminary ideas, Anita was careful to say, and she could supply scripts and names if any of the suggestions whetted Cecilia's appetite.

Cecilia listened, but all these variegated prospects had the same basic problem. She was either an accessory to the story or the writhing, simmering half-nude sexpot of the story. She wanted a script that would demonstrate her acting chops, one in which she could deliver poignant monologues that would tear at the hearts of tear-stained moviegoers and members of the Motion Picture Academy alike.

And what had Anita found for her? Roles in which she could taunt and tease – and ultimately seduce – rich school-boys, married dads, hard-working cops, corrupt politicians. Cecilia wanted empowerment and female-driven narratives. Her agent tried to argue that being a seductress *was* empower-ing. After all, what was more galvanizing than luring a princi-pled Senator away from his wife?

Cecilia wasn't interested. "What about Terry Mahoney?" she asked. "The producer? I met him once and he told me he was interested in casting me in an upcoming movie. Remember?"

There would have been no way for Anita to forget that meeting because the young star reminded her of it regularly. Cecilia had met Terry at a house party two years earlier at the invitation of Billy Sloan. She remembered the colossal brick-structured nestled within the Hollywood Hills, high-vaulted ceilings, lacquered furniture and stainless-steel sculptures that seemed more at place in a museum.

She had followed Billy through the estate and out the back doors, where tables and couches flanked an infinity pool that seemed to stretch towards the San Gabriel Mountains.

At the center of all things, a tall white-haired man sat on a couch, while tray-carrying caterers and partially garbed young women orbited around him. There was an aura surrounding Terry Mahoney, but Cecilia wasn't sure whether this was a halo of good fortune or a nimbus of immorality. Perhaps it was both.

She fought to get Terry's attention that night – competing against the white-powdered substance that disappeared into his nasal cavities, and the gorgeous Hollywood girls-in-waiting who basked in his interest.

When it was finally her turn, Cecilia approached carefully and took a seat next to the man. She tried to introduce herself, but Terry Mahoney already knew who she was. With a quick inhalation, he pitched his head back and lost himself to the vortex of swimming pool shenanigans that were occurring just behind him.

Cecilia tried to regain his focus. "Can we talk about the movies that you have coming out?" she asked. "As you know, I'm an actress and I think I would be good—"

Terry rocked forward and aligned his head with the rest of his body. Then he turned to look at her as though for the first time…perhaps surveying her, assessing her, writing her in to one of his scripts. He smiled amiably and said, "You are quite a vision, Cecilia Cinvenue. I would be lucky to have you in one of my movies."

Cecilia was shocked and buoyed by this response – this entire interaction. She didn't have to sell herself to the producer, didn't even have to *introduce* herself. He already knew who she was, and perhaps was even familiar with her body of work. She started to dig into the logistics – *what movies he was planning to work on? Which of her people should contact which of his people?* – but the night was young and electric, and Terry was having none of this.

He stood up and shed his gold silk shirt, carefully removed his gold necklace depicting a diamond-crusted cross and took off his jeans. When he was wearing only boxer-briefs, he plunged headlong into the pool and splashed the young party-goers who had been carousing with champagne flutes in their hands.

That was the endpoint of her interaction with Terry Mahoney. The night ended with Cecilia alone on the couch, calculating and strategizing – while the object of her observation took off into the pool shack with one of his party guests.

She refused to see the night as a loss, however. After all, she *had* met Terry Mahoney, he knew who he was, and he'd expressed an interest in having her in his movies. Luck! He had said he would be *lucky*! Cecilia repeated this to herself as she endlessly rewound their communication in her mind.

Over the ensuing months and years, Cecilia repeatedly

reminded Anita about this brief but consequential meeting at the party. And Cecilia's agent reminded her that access to Terry Mahoney was hard to get, and that she was doing everything in her power to place Cecilia's headshot in front of the powerful man.

Now they were in Cecilia's home office, reviewing opportunities that held no promise or excitement for the young woman, and her thoughts alighted on a topic that had been flitting around her mind for the past year.

"What if I went to college?" Cecilia asked. "I'm nineteen. I could go and get a four-year degree and then get back to acting once I graduate."

Cecilia didn't know the first thing about college – not in any tangible way. She knew from movies and television shows that it consisted of grassy campuses and ivy tendrils that snaked across elaborate brick buildings, eager students with thick backpacks half-slung over their shoulders. She knew that it was an expansion of educational attainment, a commitment to a field of study, or perhaps a broad field of many studies.

What she didn't know – what nagged and wrenched at her – was the goings-on of social activities behind dormitory walls. So many movies presented these affairs as cautionary tales – the tainted drink, the lusty resident advisor, the thieving roommate. But Cecilia knew there were social aspects – normal, regular, non-movie fodder interactions – that she hadn't navigated since she was in elementary school.

There were times when she wanted to take a break from all the acting and immerse herself into an entirely different life – one that involved sitting in a classroom, eating dining hall food and joining friends for Saturday night keg parties. She wanted to be one of the girls in the college tapestry – striding across an open field on her way to an event...smiling at the guy or girl next to her, her sweatshirt proudly displaying the name of the university. That was Cecilia Cinvenue – always the loyalist, even to a phantom university. But she was also a

Renaissance woman, able to employ a number of skills. She could place acting on a shelf – as though it were a beloved book that she'd one day rediscover…and live like a scholar for four years.

Maybe Cecilia didn't know much about college, but she knew it was a departing ship – a milk bottle with an expiry date. Sure, she could take up classes at any point, but this was the only time she would be *college-aged*, the time she could blend in on a dorm floor or house party.

Cecilia's mother and Anita then assured her that she had it backwards: actually, it was *college* that would always be there and *acting* that required her to strike while the iron was hot… while *she* was hot.

"You make it sound as though I'm going to lose my looks and be unemployable in, like, ten years," Cecilia said with a chuckle. She had always perceived her acting career as a carefully constructed brick building that was capable of extending towards the sky. She had built the foundation and established her name and a notable body of work. So if the bricklayers took a break for a short while, the bones of the building would always remain. Unless television-watchers were collectively assailed with some form of acute amnesia, they would remember her.

Cecilia could see the anxious look on Betty's face and could hear the consternation in Anita's strained voice. The woman at the other end of the speakerphone stammered and cleared her throat a few times, and Cecilia then realized that there were unspoken truths in her profession – that those who spoke with authority preferred to keep quiet about.

But Anita told her anyway, in the frankest voice possible:

Cecilia was fighting against the tide; she was a salmon swimming upstream, the agent explained. From the moment she became a fully, legally realized adult, physics, biology and economics were working against her. Disciplines that Cecilia knew very little about and would have no ability to study – at least not for the next several years.

Physics – in which a gravitational pull was bound to deform and disfigure her body into middle age and senior citizenry – and biology, in which every interaction she'd had with the sun would press moles, freckles and wrinkles into once-impeccable skin. And then there was economics: the law of supply. Basic human reproduction ensured an assembly line of beautiful and eager young women who only wanted to take Cecilia's place in the most expedient way possible. The way Anita described it, these young beauties were being dropped off on Hollywood doorsteps as though they'd been farmed and ordered from a catalog. The assembly line would continue uninterrupted into eternity, while Cecilia had started depreciating as soon as she was of legal age. She was bound to spend her adult life chasing a superficial, unattainable goal that sun exposure and genetics had predetermined for her. *This* was why she couldn't go to college.

To an outsider's ear, this all sounded perfectly ridiculous. Age and experience were supposed to make a person better at their job, not the other way around. And yet, Cecilia understood her agent's words – had probably understood them in some fundamental way, even before the woman had said anything – and she didn't bother to bring up postsecondary education again. She saw that she needed to continue to pursue acting while she was still only nineteen – that each revolution around the sun would limit her choices and abilities in ways that she wasn't yet able to imagine.

"I'll keep at it," Cecilia said. "But none of those roles sound interesting to me. Can you please do one thing for me and I'll never bring up going to college again?"

"Sure," Anita said. "What's that?"

Cecilia paused for a moment and then made her request. She hoped that the fuss about college had attached a sort of gravity to her demand. If nothing else, she was demonstrating her doggedness about her future. Perhaps her agent would no longer see this as a sweetly-laced appeal and instead as a huge, steel-erected roadblock – one which would have to be cleared to make way for future acting roles.

She spoke with insistence. "Can you get me a meeting with Terry Mahoney?"

Chapter Fourteen

Los Angeles, California
1999

TERRY MAHONEY'S movie set was conveniently located on a stretch of beach twenty miles south of LAX. They filmed under the severe beams of merciless sun – sweat pouring off of sculpted, tanned bodies. The film had endured several name changes in its year of development, but the latest one seemed to stick: *Soldier of Payback*.

Cecilia was one of the soldiers – a mercenary leading a team of lithe stone-faced enforcers. They were plotting to enact revenge against a villain who had persevered in one of the earlier film franchise installments.

When she'd first read the script, Cecilia had come up with plenty of questions and plot holes. How could the villain possibly still be alive after sustaining ten bullet holes and a dynamite explosion? How had this team of limber-legged gymnasts become her militia when she barely spoke with them? In fact, almost all of the words in the script were shouts and sound bites – good for the film's trailer, bad for any semblance of plot continuity and character development.

Cecilia was to be given top billing and prominent movie poster placement in a studio-backed franchise film, so she kept her mouth shut about her character's irrational dialogue – which probably amounted to less than a hundred words in the whole script. She voiced her lines with sexy intensity and declared her hackneyed instructions to the army with feigned intensity.

During filming breaks, Cecilia retreated to her trailer and ran lines while she cooled off, away from the harsh trenches of sand and sweaty extras and crew milling about. At one point – towards the end of filming – Terry Mahoney rapped on the metal-frame, aluminum door.

Cecilia swung the door open and was surprised to see the man. Although he had cast her in this movie, Terry's big-brother influence over the film occurred in high-level office rooms and meetings where Cecilia wasn't allowed to enter. All she saw was his downstream influence – his name invoked like a commandment from the Heavens. When Terry wanted things a certain way, *they happened*, even though the man himself seemed no more than a lurking shadow to the principal operation.

Now Terry Mahoney was standing on the steps to her transitory mobile home, fanning himself with a few pages from the script. He looked authoritative – white hair cropped neatly into place, t-shirt tucked neatly into slacks. "Cecilia," he said, when he saw her, by way of a stony-faced greeting.

Cecilia invited him inside and tried to calm her heartbeat, which now seemed poised to gallop out of its chest cavity. Terry Mahoney made all things happen, and she wanted desperately for him to like her, to see her worth, her talent.

"Terry! So great to see you!" Cecilia said. "What can I do for you?"

Terry sighed, pulled up his slacks and took a seat on the plush red couch. "I want you to accompany me. This evening.

I have a dinner with some investors. My assistant will give you the details."

Cecilia felt a wave of anxiety rush out of her, felt the blood flow return to her organs. "Oh, yes, I would love to attend. Thanks so much for thinking of me...."

But Terry was already halfway out the door of her trailer. He had come to extend the invitation and apparently had no mind for the response.

Later in the day, after filming had wrapped, Terry's assistant laid out all the pertinent details for the evening's dinner: Cecilia was to look *hot* – a nice formfitting dress – the shorter the better – with high heels and plenty of makeup. The assistant displayed no shame or sheepishness in listing these requirements of the outing. These film investors were very important to Terry, she explained, and they wanted his girls to look a certain way.

His girls. Cecilia was caught between feminine outrage and grateful inclusivity. She didn't know exactly what it meant to be one of Terry's girls, but when the stretch limo appeared at her apartment complex later that evening, she felt like she'd been promoted to a higher echelon of celebrity.

The limo whisked Cecilia to a non-descript four-story building next to a strip mall off Sepulveda Boulevard. From the outside, the establishment looked as ordinary as its adjoining retail shops: a dry cleaner, a sushi place and a bagel shop. But once inside, Cecilia could see that the building was a private restaurant and club. Its darkened windows offered total secrecy, and cordoned-off back rooms led to other cordoned-off backrooms.

Cecilia followed the restaurant's host through the labyrinth of rooms until she reached the last one. It had couches and banquettes, coffee tables overflowing with expensive spirits and half-empty bottles, dollops of powder scattered across surfaces, sparsely clad servers tending to expensively dressed men. When Terry caught sight of Cecilia, he waved her over with muted enthusiasm.

"Gentlemen, this is Cecilia Cinvenue. I think you remember her from *The Family Next Door*. She's starring in my next movie. Going to be a big-name actress, this one."

The men smiled at Cecilia, stood up and gave her kisses on the cheek. She felt the hand of one of men cupping her backside while they embraced – and had to resist the urge to deliver a swift elbow to the man's ribs. The man pulled away and sat back down, and Cecilia chose to say nothing. Her thoughts were churning with inconsistencies: Terry Mahoney's uncharacteristically complimentary introduction, which filled her mind with grandiosity and optimism. And then there were the groping, well-dressed businessmen, eyeing her like she was a piece of fruit that they wanted to sample.

The entire club was a rejection of her hopes for the evening. She had imagined a wide, circular dinner table, across which ideas and visions would be exchanged. But the amatory music – breathed over the speaker system – was too loud to allow for any real conversation.

What was worse, Cecilia had hoped she would be a central member of the evening's conversation. But the discussions were to take place in whispered fragments among the men, directly exhaled into each other's ears. Cecilia was simply window dressing, like all the other women there. She was no different from the ladies leaning over to transform U.S. currency into rolling papers, the ones strutting in six-inch stilettos while acrobatically balancing heavy bottles on oval trays. She was no different from the dancers, scattered across the flat surfaces of banquette backs.

And her suspicions were confirmed when one of the investors beckoned her with a wave of his fingers and suggested that she join the other ladies on the banquette. Cecilia obliged, carefully climbing up and finding her footing.

She proceeded to dance in the least awkward way she knew how, mimicking the gestures of the young woman beside her.

The music in the club had a beat that Cecilia tried to attach to her motions. She had never felt less sexy before in her life. Why had she jumped up on the banquette so willingly? Because she was an actress – accustomed to being directed by formidable men, to having her actions molded by others. Also, her life's goal seemed to be to accommodate, to please, to entertain.

What would have happened if she'd just said *no*? Was that even an option? If she'd threaded a path through the club until she found the front door and never looked back? The dark streets of West Los Angeles would engulf this solitary girl – clad in a sequin-sewn mini-dress, with high heels that could not accommodate a footpath of more than a city block, and a face that was too recognizable.

And so she stayed and she complied – bending and twisting, dropping down when the beats seemed to call for it, mirroring the practiced veteran just inches away from her.

If Cecilia was trying her best, the men weren't buying it. She saw their chuckles, their furtive whispers, the way that Terry Mahoney – face flushed – whispered into the ear of his co-conspirator, eyes never leaving Cecilia's body.

When the first song ended, Terry approached and pressed a small round pill into her hand. "Take this," he ordered, and motioned for one of the men to pass over one of the bottles. "You can wash it down with this."

Cecilia did as she was told, swallowed the pill neatly and smoothed it down her esophagus with a chug of vodka from the bottle.

Twenty minutes later, she was inside the music. She felt the beats in her bones, felt the vocals as warm tingles throughout her arms. Her body waved and crashed as though it were liquid – magma that melted and poured in tune with the music. There was no one else on the banquette, in the club, in the universe except for her – Cecilia and the music – and she felt it as deeply as she'd ever felt anything.

The music was a parole board hearing, a liberation officer. It allowed her to move and sway without judgment; it freed her from the limits of the physical universe. Suddenly she was unencumbered…and when the man on the couch approached her, the one who had groped her, the one whose eyes now seemed to burn right through her…she readily accepted his embrace and rocked to the beat against his rigid embrace.

It was such a cathartic feeling for one who was so controlled to be uncontrolled…to let the events happen as though they were ordained. That pill had allowed her brain – her always racing thoughts – to take the night off and give in to predestiny. For the first time in her life, Cecilia Cinvenue didn't need to think. She could just *be*. She was free.

"Your pupils are really dilated," the man said, and handed her a cup with a liquid inside. The liquid was swarming, moving to the beat, beckoning to her, tantalizing her.

"It's just water, I promise," the man said. "You should drink it."

Cecilia looked up and stared at the man. He was blurred by the dark walls behind him, a chalk drawing so smudged, it was hard to see where the lines formed. The cup sat languidly in Cecilia's hand, until the man took her wrist and brought the clear plastic rim to her face.

"Drink it," he said again, and Cecilia did. She couldn't have verified the contents of the beverage except to say that the liquid was smooth was clear – not that that mattered. In fact, nothing really mattered in the dusty air of this vibrating club, except that she could move freely. Her thoughts were no longer attached to the brain's frontal lobe. They were engines of their own rapaciousness, unable to be restrained or condemned.

The man pressed his body against Cecilia and moved to the beat of the song. Cecilia wasn't sure whether this was a new song or the same one as before – just that the music's beats occurred both inside and outside of her – like air, like the liquid she had just consumed, like her churning, twisting thoughts.

She matched the man's rhythm, if for no other reason than that he was physically constricting her and to push him away would require more planning than she was able to muster.

Her mind wasn't there anyway; she was spinning in a tempest of her own invention. The creatures on the couch morphed into oblong objects, as did the swiveling woman who may or may not still be next to her. Everything was sped up too, as though a fast-forward button had been pushed. The song was faster; the moves were faster; her heart beat faster; even the objects on the couch moved faster. The only thing that was really alive was Cecilia; everything else was Kafka's Metamorphosis, capable of transforming into an insect…or a rodent… or an inanimate fixture of the room.

Cecilia could comprehend then that she was truly *alive*… fully, acutely, preternaturally alive. She finally *felt something* – something other than the dull condemnation of her own self-reproach, other than the tedious repetition of her usual work-day, other than her unspoken qualms about not measuring up. She was finally, at nineteen years old, *alive and feeling*.

This realization carried her into the next few hours – when she danced to the next few songs, and when she went home with the groping man – for no other reason than the solicitation had been offered. It was the next step in a night of *obliging* – was it obliging or obligation? She did what was asked of her because that's who she was. Because Terry Mahoney had invited her out. Because he'd stuck a pill in her hand. Because all her decisions occurred in the cyclone of fate, and thoughts and judgments relating to consequence she couldn't have lassoed back into her mind even if she'd wanted to.

The following morning, Cecilia Cinvenue woke up alone

in a king-size bed in a dark hotel room. A note on the pillow pronounced that the man had already caught a flight back to New York City, but he'd reserved the room for an extra day, and she could stay as late as she liked. She didn't even know the man's name.

Cecilia crumpled the note against her chest as her previous actions came rushing back to her, a levee that had been lifted.

What pill had she taken the night before and why did she suddenly feel so depressed? What had she done with the man, and more importantly, what did Terry know? What did Terry think of her now? Should she have declined his initial invitation to dinner with investors? How could she have known? Only an imbecile would refuse a fabled rendez-vous where ideas would be shared and careers would be advanced.

Cecilia knew that saying *no* at any stage of the evening would certainly have come back to hurt her, professionally at least. The question wrenching at her mind was this: What would doing everything that they'd asked of her – everything this industry expected of her – end up costing her?

THE PARTYING CONTINUED. WHILE FILMING TOOK PLACE across the Southern California sand – and eventually into boxy, warehouse-like buildings that were designed to mimic the interior of American life – Terry Mahoney took Cecilia under his wing.

She felt protected and cosseted by his attention, which he dished out in an unrestrained, unembarrassed manner. Initially Cecilia was *one* of Terry's girls, but after the party with the investors, Cecilia had become *the* girl. Not the girl he slept with. Not the girl he flirted with. In fact, he barely even spoke to Cecilia, and she carried with her the constant fear that if he ever tried to engage her in conversation, he'd be disappointed by the result.

Cecilia was Terry's girl by nature of her comportment by his side. When Terry had investor dinners and yacht parties, he invited Cecilia along, and extolled her acting talent and her rising star power before plying her with the dust, drink and pharmaceuticals that would keep her galvanized for the night.

For Cecilia, everything that was happening was a fast-moving train. Had it only been six months since she'd begged Anita to place her head shot in front of Terry? Six months since the available script options had been so disappointing, since she'd considered a complete career overhaul and focus on her education?

In six short months, she had become the reigning Holly-wood starlet of the moment, the vision of fame and excess that she'd prayed for – even after her initial forays into Holly-wood royalty.

This was another measure of royalty altogether. She quickly became accustomed to the click of camera shutters, the high-pitched shriek of her name, the insatiable request for autographs, the ubiquitous vision of her face splattered across tabloids – endlessly conjecturing about her state of pregnancy, depression, family dysfunction, money woes or boyfriend status.

Two or three times a week, Cecilia Cinvenue accompanied Terry Mahoney to his lofty galas and afterparties. Their asso-ciation wasn't sexual, but vaguely avuncular and surprisingly procedural. If his job was to lift the gates into this cherished world, her role was to beautify it, to appease his friends, to smile for the cameras, to swallow whatever he put into her hands.

From what Cecilia could tell, this relationship was recipro-cal. She liked the feeling of appreciation and acceleration – this piquancy for life that heightened her senses and dulled her appetite. She liked dancing under the multihued orbs of the disco ball, and allowing a faceless man to carry her off into the bedroom.

Only in the morning did she feel the customary shame and regret, the *comedown*, which assistants promptly placated with coffee and Zoloft.

On the off-nights, when there was no party and no dinner, Cecilia felt even worse. Her life was so full, so fast, and also so empty. Earth's entire population wanted her in its clutches and yet she was incredibly alone. On these nights, she satisfied her self-loathing with a few bottles of Pinot and poorly written poetry.

How many drugs had she taken, and of what variety? She had no idea. How many men had she slept with? It was impossible – *inadvisable* – to do the math. Interviewers constantly asked her if she was seeing someone and she gave them the stock answer that years of preparation and instruction had perfected.

There's no special someone in my life. I'm just focusing on my career right now.

Both were true statements, adages that single actors and actresses had been imparting for years. Yet, to Cecilia, it almost seemed *too* revelatory. This focus on her career didn't just mean late nights and long hours. It meant yacht parties and fast sex, casual drug use and sycophancy to the richest people, who made all the decisions. How could there ever be a boyfriend in this equation? He would either be too admiring of her or too disgusted by her, too wary of this lifestyle or too immersed in it.

Cecilia wanted nothing to do with the men inside this existence – not once the transactional nature of their liaison was over with – and yet, she couldn't relate to anyone outside of it.

What was worse, while Cecilia frequently despised the world she was part of – a world which had knighted her with excess and prestige – she also coveted it. Was it her competitive nature that compelled her to want to be the best at everything? She wanted to be in the rarified upper echelon of Hollywood actresses, and such status didn't just come from effective script reading and good vocal composition. At least, it hadn't for her.

Consistent with the consumerist nucleus of all professions, succeeding in Hollywood required branding, marketing, selling oneself. It wasn't enough for Cecilia to trod across a sun-soaked beach and deliver a poignant six-paragraph speech while toting a forty-pound weapons cache on her back. Once the filming had wrapped for the night, she had to shed the rebel's combat uniform like a snake's skin and put on thigh-length dresses with fishnet nylon stockings and two layers of mascara.

This twofold existence required a surplus of energy and modicum of sleep, and Cecilia considered herself lucky that circadian cycle suppressants came in medicinal form. She could swallow a pill and dance and fuck and listen to the hottest producer in the hottest industry tell everyone what a star she was.

She didn't even have to think. Her racing, craving, tortuous mind could adjourn.

Cecilia could swallow a pill and close her eyes and feel the thrum of time heave forward, like an airplane during turbulence. She could feel something – so much of something – after years spent feeling nothing.

She told herself she was living, finally living! But sometimes, when the high wasn't enough, when the dance music stopped, when the hotel room in the morning was colder and emptier than expected, she wondered whether she was actually dying.

Chapter Fifteen

Vetta Park, Missouri
September 24, 2022

MARTINEZ, Hobbs and Nick landed at Lambert Airport shortly after noon on Saturday morning. The flight had been bumpy, but it had also made good time; they were caught in the throes of a wrathful but efficient tailwind that delivered them to the gate ten minutes early.

When Nick and Hobbs arrived back at her apartment, Hobbs booted up her laptop to check emails from the previous few days. Most of the messages were spam or charity requests, but she did catch sight of a note sent from Nick's school, flagged with high importance.

Nick had already made himself comfortable in his bedroom when Hobbs arrived, laptop in hand, as though it were a ventriloquist dummy that was going to speak on her behalf.

Hobbs wasted no time. "Nick!" she exclaimed. "Your school just emailed me that you haven't submitted any of the work they assigned while we were in LA!"

While such a dereliction of duty would have sent Hobbs

into a seizure when she was Nick's age, the boy *harumphed* and rolled over on the bed, his sweep of hair flopping over his ears.

"Nick, did you hear me?" Hobbs insisted. "You have work that you need to turn in before Monday."

"Bro. *Yes*, I hear you," Nick mumbled into the headboard, and then brought his arms up to cover his head. Apparently, his hair alone wasn't doing the trick of confounding Hobbs with his indifference. Only a complete facial covering would convince his aunt that he was finished with the conversation.

"Don't call me *Bro*," Hobbs said. "I am your Aunt Roberta and you will address me as such." Her voice was deep and authoritative – the type of intonation she used on young offenders in the system.

"Okay, fine, whatever," Nick said from underneath his manmade facial sheath.

Hobbs was aware that he so plainly wanted her to leave, and it was in this moment that she was so certain she shouldn't. She sat down on the bed and put a hand on his ankle. He quickly jerked his full body away so that he was facing the wall – a bowed, faceless parabola that simply wanted one or the other of them to disappear.

Hobbs opened up the laptop and read from the sternly-worded email. She emphasized the words that emblazoned the top of the message with pointed severity.

"Notice of missing assignments!" Hobbs read. "Teachers have flagged the following assignments as missing: Algebra 1 Activity 6 Packet. History: Industrial Revolution and Political Change. Write a draft essay looking at Capitalism, Socialism and Communism and address the similarities and differences within these economic and political systems. Remember to include annotations in your body paragraphs…Nick…Nick, are you even listening to me?"

He wasn't listening. Or if he was, he was making a great show of ignoring her. With each of Hobbs' words, Nick seemed to slink fuller into the bed, more deeply secreted beneath the quilt and bedsheets. It was only when she stopped reading and looked at the rumpled mass beneath the covers that he poked his head out and said, "I heard everything you said...*Aunt Roberta.*"

"So...you'll complete your assignments now?"

"I have until Monday. I'll do them over the weekend. First, I need to do this game. Logan's waiting for me to get on."

He then brought his phone out from under the blankets, turned it sideways and started assailing the screen with his thumbs. Hobbs had no idea who Logan was — a friend from home? A friend from his new school? — and she also wondered about the utility and consequences of snatching his phone. Maybe it was better to take Nick at his word — that he would in fact complete the assignment — instead of provoke a battle she wasn't sure she would win.

Hobbs sat and watched her nephew for a few more moments. The tranquilizing effect of whatever game he was playing enabled him to ignore her completely. She pledged to don the function of parental authority — to check in with him after an hour or two and kick him off his gaming device. She decided she would set up the dining room table as an office of sorts. She would reboot an old laptop with word processing and spreadsheet software, and place pens and pencils on either side.

All these silent assurances were made with the purest aims of follow-through. Perhaps Hobbs really would have set this plan in motion if her phone hadn't rung moments later, a breathless Dean Adams on the other end.

"Dean?" Hobbs asked. "What's wrong?"

"It's Terry Mahoney," Dean said. "We tracked him down in Dubai and he's giving us five minutes of his time for a phone interview later today. How quickly can you get to the office?"

HOBBS MADE IT TO THE PRECINCT THIRTY MINUTES LATER. THE rain was cascading down in sheets, and although she darted quickly from the parking lot to the front door, she still arrived soaked and dribbling, silently cursing the futility of her umbrella.

Dean Adams was the first person she saw. He looked as gorgeous as ever, as though their distance had deleted the commonplace, the conventional from his appearance. His hair was a curled mop – a once-pompadour now curled from precipitation. But instead of looking shaggy – as she was certain she did -- he wore it with confidence and it added vivacity to his aesthetic.

Dripping from the rain, hair matted to her head, this was not how Hobbs wanted to see her ex-boyfriend after their week's hiatus. But Dean greeted her professionally – as though he were platonically grateful for her safe return from travels – and gently guided her towards the conference room.

Martinez and Weaver appeared minutes later, and soon it was just the four of them seated around a circular table that held a conference phone in the center. The foursome sat silently and stared at the phone as though it were a jack-in-the-box that might startle them at any moment.

Typically, they would have engaged in idle chatter, but that afternoon, there was none. They had chased Terry Mahoney for too long to be distracted by small talk, and so all their energies poured into the device at the center of the table, which finally rang after ten agonizing minutes.

Dean leaned forward and pressed the speakerphone button. "Vetta Park P.D.," he said.

If they had any hopes that a comprehensive interview would ensue, these aspirations were dropped when it was clear that the voice on the other end of the phone was one of Terry Mahoney's assistants. She assured the authorities that Terry was due to get on the line at any moment...but the minutes of reticence soon multiplied, until Hobbs was sure they had sat and stared pointlessly at this inanimate object for thirty minutes.

Dean cleared his throat and leaned forward, and Hobbs thought he was about to register his own protest, when a distant voice finally communicated from the speaker.

"Hello. This is Terry," the voice said. He sounded gravelly and distant – like a lifelong smoker at the end of a long tunnel. Behind this voice, Hobbs could hear shouts and clang – properties of a high-traffic movie set.

Dean took charge. "Terry, hi. Thanks for giving us a call. I'm Lt. Dean Adams and with me are two of our detectives, Roberta Hobbs and Ray Martinez, and the captain of our precinct, Joseph Weaver..."

Whispered rumblings made clear that Terry Mahoney had no mind or patience for this sort of cordiality. Hobbs could still tell that Terry was making demands of those around him, even though his voice was low and mottled with static. There was no contrition about his decision to speak over Dean's introduction. When he returned to the line to address the Vetta Park P.D., his voice was insistent, impatient.

"Uh guys, I'm in Dubai working on set and I've got, like, two minutes here. Is there something you wanted to ask me?"

"Yes, we wanted to talk to you about Cecilia Cinvenue," Dean said.

"Yeah? What about her?"

Dean looked around the table, and Hobbs could see the consternation set across his face, the glare of uncertainty in his eyes. She knew the foursome was prepared for a typical police interview, which at times could stretch well into the hours. There needed to be an arc of progress – an initial softening that molded into firmness when the subject stalled the investigation with reluctance.

Two minutes would not allow for initial pleasantries, nor a

build-up of trust that could be shaped into firmness. They would have to cut right to the core of the interview, start in the middle, their questions lobbed like pointed ammunition.

Weaver took the helm, perhaps thinking that his gentleness would smooth over the interrogation.

"Well, two minutes isn't really enough time," he said. "But in the interest of getting the hard stuff out of the way, we'll have to ask…where were you last Thursday, September 15?"

Terry didn't hesitate. "I was here. Dubai."

"I see," Weaver said. Then he asked, "How would you define your relationship with Ms. Cinvenue?"

"My *relationship*? We didn't have a relationship."

Dean, Martinez and Hobbs exchanged irritated glances. Terry Mahoney was going to make this as difficult as possible. Hobbs realized that their two minutes of allotted dialogue would entail pinched responses and off-topic distractions. Already, Terry was yelling at someone who was in his physical vicinity, declaring to them that the duration of his phone call wouldn't exceed another minute.

"Your *association* with Ms. Cinvenue," Dean clarified. "Tell us what that was like."

"Look, guys, we didn't have an association or a relationship or however you want to call it. I cast Cecilia in a few of my movies…I guess it was back in the 2000s. And I guided her career and helped her out during that time. But that's it. I never dated her. To be honest, I have no interest in a washed up forty-something who probably snorted too much blow and lost control of her car. Sorry I can't be more helpful."

The line went dead and the occupants of the room looked at each other. Terry Mahoney's interview hadn't given them anything apart from insight into what a callous bastard he was. His rising impatience, his air of authority – even over police detectives investigating a potential homicide – and his casual use of the term *washed up forty-something* – as though women over a certain age were afflicted with a sort of disease that men like Terry were wise to keep their distance from.

"We need more than two minutes with that guy," Weaver said, and all heads in the room nodded. Hobbs figured that Weaver's use of *that guy* was meant to strip the producer of some of his self-assurance, a reminder that Terry was just another person who would be forced to heed to their authority…if it came to it.

"Do we have the budget to fly to Dubai?" Dean asked, and Weaver responded by interlacing his fingers and looking down.

This non-answer was indeed an answer to the question. Their tiny municipality whose meager tax dollars had recently funded a junket to Los Angeles and Las Vegas could in no way afford to dispatch these detectives to the Middle East. Not even for a high publicity case involving the death of a celebrity.

"I think I read somewhere that Terry was expected to attend the New York Film Festival at Lincoln Center," Martinez said optimistically. "It starts next week."

Captain Weaver looked up sharply and smiled. "Great! We'll do that then. New York's a lot closer than Dubai. I'll have Rochelle look into which dates he'll be there and she can arrange the travel for you and Hobbs."

They all nodded in agreement and stood up from their chairs, setting about their day. The small talk surfaced when Martinez and Dean began a lighthearted debate about the health of the St. Louis Cardinals pitching rotation, and Weaver chimed in with sporadic exhalations of support or disagreement.

Hobbs made her way to her cubicle. It wasn't just that she had no strong opinions on the Cardinals that were worth lending her voice to the discussion. She was also bothered enough by the subtext of their interview with Terry Mahoney to not want to alight on superficial topics.

Her consternation was twofold: First that their primary

person of interest was elusive and ornery. They were relying quite heavily on several words in an online newspaper attesting to Terry's appearance at an upcoming film festival. Perhaps he would honor this obligation – or he might choose to stay in Dubai. Hobbs hated that the Department's lack of funds prevented any assurance of taking him in for questioning — and she knew that Terry would exploit this pecuniary disadvantage.

But secondly – and perhaps more importantly – Terry's demeanor had revealed specks of truth about what it was like to work in Hollywood. In only a two-minute call, he had demonstrated his brusqueness, his intolerance for disappointment, his demanding nature. If this man had taken Cecilia Cinvenue under his wing and guided her career for ten years…what had that period of time done to her? And – when it was over – what had it left her with?

———

The night was bathed in a neon glow. Hobbs lay awake under the duvet and stared at the ceiling. She thought about getting up to adjust the curtains from the blaring street lamps, but the effort of drifting away from her warm bed seemed too much. In the next room, she could hear Nick's patter of breath. He wasn't a snorer, but Hobbs' job had inured her ears to miniscule detection. In a quiet room, she could hear the minutest whisper, the clap of the air condition clicking on or off. In some cases, she heard these distant sounds as though they were right next to her. And her undistracted mind – the whirring, spinning neurons and synapses that always came to life right when she was trying to go to sleep – did a handsome job of connecting the dots.

Which dots were being connected in that humming, droning apartment that night in late September? No matter what had happened that day, no matter which part of the investigation into Cecilia Cinvenue's thorny life vexed or confused Hobbs, her thoughts always came back to Dean.

Dean Adams. Her thoughts of him ricocheted around her mind. She projected his muscular likeness onto the pale, pearl-colored ceiling. Memories of his voice tingled her ears. She wondered whether he was sharing his bed with anyone, whether he thought about her, whether he missed her.

When the phone rang and it was Dean on the other end, Hobbs at first wondered if she had somehow inexplicably summoned him, if her single-minded thoughts had evoked some invisible stirrings within the universe. When he said her name, his voice sounded more baritone than she remembered, more yearning. At that moment, if he'd asked to come over, she would have opened the door unhesitatingly, told him all was forgiven.

But, as he soon made clear, his phone call had nothing to do with pining or lust. He wanted to talk about work, and his breathlessness was due to an important breakthrough in the case.

"I looked through every single business license application in the Vetta Park Light Industrial District going back decades," Dean said. "It took me forever. But you'll never guess what name I came across, for a business less than two miles from the rock quarry."

"Which business?" Hobbs asked.

"Shearwater Enterprises," Dean said. "It's an LLC Partnership, owned by none other than *Sparrow Shearwater*. Her name is all over the signing documents."

"So, she lied," Hobbs said.

"Yes, she lied. Or, at a minimum, she *omitted*. She knew exactly why Cecilia Cinvenue was in Vetta Park. But she proactively visited the Santa Monica detectives as soon as Cecilia died to point the finger at three other guys. She's the one we should've been looking into all along."

"Can we have Frazier and Oliver pick her up?"

"It's two hours earlier in LA, so I already gave a call in to those guys and they sent a team out to her place to bring her in."

"Oh good."

"Actually, no. The uniforms said that her car was parked in the driveway. They rang the bell and no one answered, but the front door was slightly open, which they thought was strange. They said they went inside due to concern about Sparrow's well-being, but the place was empty. In fact, it looked pristine. No sign of Sparrow, or her keys or her purse. The fridge was empty, no sign of any trash. And she's turned off her cell phone."

Hobbs rested her cell phone on the pillow next to hers. She tried to decide whether the detectives had been outsmarted or outmaneuvered. Maybe the answer was both. From what little she knew about the spiritual guru, Sparrow could have taken off to lead an ayahuasca retreat in the hidden hills of northern Mexico. Or maybe she had killed Cecilia and was now going to live a life of surreptitious evasion.

But what motive would Sparrow have had for killing Cecilia? And why was her front door left open?

Hobbs picked up the phone again and discussed the next-steps logistics with Dean. They would investigate the physical dwelling of Shearwater Enterprises. They would speak with their LA counterparts about getting a warrant for a search of Sparrow's domicile and electronics. They would issue an all-points bulletin to alert other law enforcement agencies to be on the lookout for Sparrow Shearwater.

Hobbs hung up the phone with Dean and collapsed on her mattress, which made a springing sound from the impact of her movement. She was no longer thinking about Dean at all in a sexual context, and instead, her mind was swirling with thoughts about the case.

The one person of interest who was most available to

them – Billy Sloan – was also the only one with a clear motive for killing Cecilia. What was his secret and why would Cecilia try to publicly reveal it?

Then there were two shadowy figures – Sparrow and Terry Mahoney – who factored into this case in ways Hobbs didn't fully understand. Their motives and their actions were concealed by the inability to get them into a room. Sparrow had proven herself unreliable and Terry made it his business to be unavailable.

And lastly there was Marco Bagnetti. Hobbs kept vacillating on the Italian actor – whether he loved Cecilia Cinvenue or just loved the access she bestowed on him. What was this young, ambitious man capable of?

Sparrow, Billy, Terry, Marco – all of whom certainly must have known about each other. Had they ever worked together? Would they ever conspire with each other, and why?

In the adjacent room, Nick's respirations rose and fell to the beat of a peaceful metronome. The streetlights outside finally cut off at some point in the early morning, and the halogen-washed room became dark. The bed was warm and the duvet felt like a padded embrace, its beading adhered to the curves of Hobbs' body. All these factors should have entranced Hobbs into a peaceful sleep. But it was hours before sleep finally came.

Chapter Sixteen

Los Angeles, California
2009

CECILIA CINVENUE – once America's ingenue, a universally beloved star who could melt the world with a flash of her dazzling smile – was now an expired, damaged good. By December 2009, she felt the lapse of her useful shelf life. She sat in Anita Livingston's office and stared out the window at the nomadic foot traffic traversing Century City Mall, a nubbed cigarette dangling from her lips.

So much had happened since *Solder of Payback* – so much fortune and misfortune. The success of her Terry Mahoney opus had thrust her into the stratosphere – made her a name that every single American knew how to pronounce, made her a face that people hid in bushes and long tree limbs to capture.

Cecilia had always dreamt of the euphoria that accompanied this type of success, but in actuality, work begat more work. There was no rapture, only diligence. She was too enclosed inside the cresting whirlwind of fame to see her way out of it – too managed by pedagogues, professionals and trainers to see beyond them.

The scripts and offers poured forth, and Cecilia and her mother spent hours together, discussing her options, deciding on projects. Cecilia's bloated paychecks had enabled a change in scenery. She sold the family house and purchased a brick and Spanish tile behemoth nestled into the hills of Pacific Palisades. The backyard pool was a marvel. Vast and enthralling, dotted with waterfalls and statues, its sky-blue waters poured out of the swimmer's line of sight – almost as if feeding the Pacific Ocean.

Cecilia absolutely adored the pool, but just as much, she enjoyed sitting poolside. Smoking and reading scripts, she would lounge under the protective shade of a vinyl umbrella and wait for her mother to appear.

The older woman always made her entrance through the sliding glass doors with a cappuccino in one hand and sheafs of clipped papers in the other. Then the two would discuss projects under the searing California sky as though nothing were off limits. Cecilia's options were as considerable as her imagination would allow. Every day that she vacillated over scripts, reading and debating with careful consideration, it seemed that more showed up at her house, on her agent's desk, passed clandestinely to her mother during a restaurant meal.

Cecilia recalled those early days of struggle as though they were a faded memory belonging to someone else. She was too elevated, too entangled in this world of infinite opportunity to recall the years of auditions, of rejections. These days, it seemed that anyone would give her anything she wanted.

Was she happy? During interviews, and at the behest of P.R. mavens, she was "overjoyed", "thrilled" and "grateful". Privately, she still struggled to adjust to this odd and extraordinary life. If she were to select an adjective, it would be "busy", and – ironically – this state of being often prevented her from carefully considering her mental health anyway.

In the decade that followed *Soldier of Payback*, Cecilia starred in three more Terry Mahoney vehicles (she was his "muse", he often averred), two romantic comedies, a comic book adaptation, and a character-focused indie film that she only took at the behest of her beseeching mother.

It was at the end of 2008 when disaster struck. Not a global destabilizing economic or political tragedy but a mini-earthquake, confined to Cecilia's world. She had starred in Terry Mahoney's *Terminal Revenge*...and it had flopped... earning a small fraction of its anticipated worldwide box office. Up to that point, the studio heads had been so certain of Cecilia's bankability that they'd greenlit this project with her as the only marquee lead. The film's failure was more than just an economic loss. Coming on the back of her lackluster indie flick, it sent invisible signals in shock waves across the industry that Cecilia Cinvenue's star had burned out.

Cecilia was as surprised as anyone about her sudden drop in cachet. She had done all the things they had told her to... the radio and television interviews, the constant promotion, the social media postings. She'd worn clothes that gaped a bit too loosely in the chest for her liking, laughed at the radio DJ jokes and inappropriate interviewer questions. She had smiled and chuckled when she really wanted to roll her eyes and arrange an escape route. All these things that had once reaped reliable results no longer did. She was suddenly a baseball pitcher with the yips...unable to wield a fastball after decades of consistency.

It was an actor's missive to keep working, and Cecilia certainly had no shortage of scripts sent her way. But after *Terminal Revenge*, there was a difference in the types of roles and the types of scripts. She was no longer going to command the lead; her best options were to support the younger, more prominent actresses or to be one name in a grand ensemble cast of actors.

To Cecilia, her currency deflation felt like a catastrophe,

but she was surprised by the casualness with which Anita handled it. It was as though Cecilia's devaluation were part of a natural course for Hollywood females – an innate sequence in her evolutionary timeline. It was the big earthquake that was bound to hit California's shoreline sooner or later. It was exactly the course that Anita had prescribed when Cecilia suggested college at the age of nineteen.

Because misery loved company – or maybe because the world had a way of taking that which Cecilia thought was a gross misfortune and heaping an *actual* disaster on top of that – in the beginning of 2009, Cecilia's parents died in a car accident.

It was the type of news that she struggled to digest at first...convinced that she was the target of a cruel prank or elaborate hoax. She learned about it when two uniformed officers showed up at her door in the middle of the night.

The officers – their dejected faces angled downwards as if they couldn't bear to witness her reaction – told her in furtive voices that her parents had misjudged a metal barrier on Mulholland Drive and had careened over the edge.

Cecilia accepted this news but didn't believe it. She allowed it to wash over her, hasten her blood flow, redden her face, but she still expected her parents to arrive home like they always did. It didn't seem to sink in until the morning, when Betty and Richard's cherry red Ferrari never made it into the driveway.

By then, friends and distant relatives were showing up. News had a way of spreading quickly when the paparazzi were involved. Cecilia could hear the chop of helicopters suspended over the house while she welcomed well-wishers armed with casseroles she would never eat.

It was amazing what could happen in twelve hours. At ten p.m., Cecilia had gone to bed after reading through scripts, tucked into the coziness of her brocade duvet cover and the belief that life would continue apace as it always had. By ten a.m., the cosmic shift in her existence was marked by hosting an impromptu gathering of devastated individuals – none more devastated than her.

Two weeks later, Cecilia buried her parents and retreated to the emptiness of a manse once teeming with life. The world seemed to move on as well. Her parents' passing warranted a quick news article and sympathetically worded eulogy, but within weeks, it was already old news.

Cecilia was alone in her house and alone with her grief. She spent the spring and summer drifting in and out of consciousness, aided by top-shelf liquor and copious quantities of marijuana. There were men too – mostly tall, handsome types who evaded her celebrity firewalls by connecting on social media sites and dating apps. They were invariably awed by her substantial house and her team of personnel. Most couldn't shield their amazement while their eyes scanned the high-beam ceilings and elegantly appointed furniture beyond the front foyer. They fawned over her while she offered them a drink, winked flirtatiously, gave them a tour that ended in the same room of the house every time.

These men drifted in and out of her life. They were outfits that required continual replacement. Some were more than happy to accept this arrangement and others lobbied to stay on and try out for the role of boyfriend...but Cecilia was too emotionally unglued to get attached to any of them. She needed them to fill the physical cavity left by her parents' absence. The house was too big for Cecilia to exist simply by herself, and every morning that she awoke to silence was a reminder of what she had lost. It was better to bask in the noise of no-strings-attached lovemaking, better to drown in the excess of Bloody Marys and Long Island ice teas with a companion who readily poured the drinks.

Scripts still came to Cecilia during the summer of 2009, but she had no mind to read them. They were emblematic of all that she'd lost and all she would never be able to achieve.

When Anita suggested that Cecilia hire a replacement manager, Cecilia scoffed and drank all day. Who could replace her own mother? Betty may not have been the most perfect manager – may have been a pushy, zealous *stage mom* – but she was Cecilia's own. She loved and protected Cecilia with a ferocity that could not be matched by a friend of a friend.

By early fall, though Cecilia was caving. She sensed the movement of the earth by the slow drop in temperatures, the fog that occasionally rolled in from the ocean. Time was moving ahead – everyone tangled in their own personal matters – and the young starlet who had once commanded the screen was now being forgotten. The world didn't care that Cecilia was orphaned, unmoored and depressed. By then, she hadn't worked on a project in almost a year, and even her alcohol-flooded mind understood that her absence from the world's visual cortex could cost her dearly.

She would have to make a move to stem the freefall…and so she finally hired a replacement manager at the behest of her henpecking agent. This new manager, Daria Sloan, was a wiry middle-aged woman, with tight red curls and gauzy skin. She took Cecilia to lunch near her Century City office and told richly-woven fables about their future synergetic dealings.

Cecilia listened and poked at her salad, trying not to contemplate how her working life going forward was going to be vastly different from the past. She agreed to review ten scripts that had been collecting dust on her dining room table over the ensuing two weeks. But when the lunch ended, and Cecilia arrived back at her house, reading scripts was the absolute last thing she wanted to do.

She heard the echo of her shoes on the marble floor, felt the vast emptiness of the unused kitchen. With tears streaking down her cheeks, Cecilia poured herself a heavy Screwdriver – four shots of vodka and one teaspoon of orange juice. Once the spirits sunk in, she felt her mood lighten. A text on her phone buzzed with the flirty axioms of a gentleman caller. This man was a newcomer to Los Angeles – Marco Bagnetti.

Marco Bagnetti: a beautiful man with high cheekbones, olive-toned, glowing skin and hazel eyes. He was a young actor who'd enjoyed moderate success in his native Italy and decided to pin his fortunes on a relocation to the City of Angels. A westward expansion that would summit in gold country…like so many other strivers before him.

But, in many ways, Marco was different from the others. He was vulnerable and artistic – alternatively penning poems about their relationship and singing songs about Cecilia while strumming his sitar. Occasionally, he brought literary classics to Cecilia's house and together they pored through Shake-spearean sonnets and Dickensian tragedies.

In America, and certainly in Los Angeles, Marco Bagnetti was a nobody – as faceless as any of the city's residents. And even though his face was absolutely stunning, beautiful people seemed to be a commodity in this town. No one shrieked or tremored when Marco Bagnetti walked down the street in this neighborhood. Not like they did in Milan or Venice.

When Cecilia was with Marco, she marveled at his candor, his openness. Marco spoke quite freely about his desire for physical connection, and his reluctance for any emotional entanglements. At times, he seemed entirely freed from the grounded world, running his tongue across Cecilia's body with wanton abandon, shaking her from her conventional routines with exotic madness.

His body was covered in tattoos, and to Cecilia, this seemed to be the ultimate release from their contractual professions. To Cecilia, her body was an unmarked sanctuary that belonged to the masses. She had no rights to color over it, to puncture it, to alter it. To Marco, his body was his own business, and it would be up to the film producers to decide whether to airbrush over his decorations or cover them up with CGI or costuming.

Marco also auditioned with attitude. He had conditions, even before he landed contracts. When Marco discussed these clauses with Cecilia, he spoke of artistic integrity and not sacrificing one's principles. But Cecilia had worked long enough in this business to know better. Most actors – herself included – would have sacrificed a non-vital organ to get work. They exaggerated their abilities and stalked decision-makers. She would never have laid down such rules as not playing the role of a loser in battle, not dying on-screen and not having her voice dubbed over until she'd had three attempts to perfect her dialogue.

And this was the reason Marco couldn't get much work. The rumor mill churned reports of his difficulties before he even reached audition rooms. He claimed the higher road – idealistic platforms that weren't going to be sacrificed – and wore these dogmas like the badge of a fearless soldier just before being killed in battle.

By 2009, Marco Bagnetti's prospects were even worse than Cecilia's. Objectively, Cecilia was still commanding a high salary, was still a face everyone wanted to see. That she wasn't the top-billing lead in a high-budget studio film anymore was a hindrance that seemed to bother only her. By contrast, Marco wasn't offered anything that he didn't have to audition for, and ninety-nine percent of those endeavors led to rejections.

It became so bad that he resorted to leaving scripts on sheets after their passionate encounters were over; he brought up movie opportunities and people he wanted to meet on their romantic dates. Cecilia knew that she didn't have a future with Marco, and she felt almost embarrassed by the fact that her industry connections would carry no weight when it came to casting him. If he was using her to catapult his own pros-perous career, he would eventually realize the futility of the endeavor. In the meantime, she could enjoy his company and try not to think too hard about who was using whom.

That late-autumn afternoon in 2009 – after her awkward lunch with her new manager -- Cecilia invited Marco over to her Palisades mansion and arranged a buffet of libations on her kitchen counter. There was sweet and dry vermouth, tequila, vodka, bitters and bourbon, and three rolled joints of weed, just to round it all out.

While anticipating Marco's arrival, she carefully avoided looking at the unattended piles of paper on her dining room table. Better to focus on the here and now and not try to think too hard about the future. The scripts could wait.

Chapter Seventeen

Century City, California
2010

THE CLOUDS DRIFTED low over the west L.A. sky, and darkened Anita Livingston's grand office. Her desk sat against a long rectangular window, facing outward, framing Century City Mall as though it were a landscape to behold.

As a lifelong L.A. inhabitant, Anita was used to the sun. The sun provided a vivid accompaniment to whatever news she was delivering. If it was good news, the glowing star was a useful backdrop, enhancing the future, brightening the atmosphere. If it was bad news, the sun was a sharp instrument, unrelenting – the harsh light shined on the buckled body of an actor who needed to improve his or her game.

On that morning in January, however, the news was bad and the sun was subdued. There was a dimness to Anita's face as she sucked in a cigarette and breathed the smoke evenly out of both nostrils. She passed an ashtray full of stubs across her desk to Cecilia and offered the actress a cigarette.

Cecilia obliged and stared out the window. She knew what was coming.

"The news isn't good," Anita said. "And I hate to be the one to tell you this but I'm the only one. Daria's going to be a great manager but she's only been with you for a few months and she doesn't know you well enough. I've worked with you for years, haven't I?"

The question was rhetorical but Cecilia nodded anyway. She knew the news would be bad because of the way Anita was prefacing it – avowals of love, reminders of the timetable of their working relationship. The absence of Cecilia's parents had left a hole so gaping that no earthly remnant could fill it. Anita had been doing her best to balance tough love with maternal affection. She frequently sent texts for no other reason than to check in, sent flowers to remind Cecilia that she was loved.

But Cecilia wasn't loved – not in the way she needed to be. Not the way a parent loves a child. She accepted these gestures from Anita with gratitude, but they didn't amount to anything. And when Anita took a giant drag from her cigarette, and gave Cecilia a look of sympathetic devotion, the actress sank from her agent's gaze and continued staring out the window. She didn't need the older woman's admiration, her superficial plugging of a wound that should never have been there in the first place. She just wanted to get whatever news was forthcoming and leave the office.

"People are talking," Anita finally said. "Industry people. They're saying that you're sleeping around, you're with a different guy every night."

Cecilia shrugged her shoulders and took particular interest in a family of five about to enter a department store across the street. It was a rather fitting juxtaposition, their breezy, uncontrolled togetherness, and her stifled stillness. "So," she said.

"So!" Anita said, and then stubbed out her cigarette. "So!" she repeated, and then stood up and walked over to a leather sofa – three dark-mahogany cushions bookended by square armrests. She motioned for Cecilia to join her, but the young woman was now fixated on the goings-on of regular life outside the office building. Anita's vacancy from her chair had provided an unmitigated vista of the bustling high-end commerce of Century City Mall. And Cecilia much preferred to focus on the comings and goings of complete strangers instead of the disillusioned face of a woman who knew her too well.

Anita stayed on the sofa and lectured to Cecilia's back. "I think you know how important reputation is, Cecilia. You're at a real crossroads in your career and I don't want to see you mess it all up with this nonsense. A celebrity's popularity and appeal...these are critical to not just casting but brand endorsements, speaking engagements and book deals. If you sleep around, Cecilia, it's going to affect your ability to land any of those deals and contracts going forward. It's so different from the way that America...and the global market...thinks of you. And I'm sorry to be so frank about it, but that's the truth."

Anita hadn't said it – specifically – hadn't defined *celebrities* with precision or granularity, but Cecilia knew she was saying *female*: female celebrities. It was women who couldn't afford this type of reputation. And instead of acknowledging her agent's words or accepting these facts which Cecilia already knew...the actress's mind whirred with images of all the male celebrities who reveled and caroused consequence-free, frozen images of their lip-locked faces adorning countless celebrity tabloids. And Cecilia, who had been careful to conduct her trysts at home – at least after Terry Mahoney had stopped inviting her out – was now forced to reckon with the taut friction between her chosen profession and her preferred defense mechanism.

"I'm not taking a different guy to bed every night," Cecilia said defiantly.

"Sweetheart, this is a small city. Everyone talks. You know Terry Mahoney has a big mouth. If you're banging his friends and acquaintances, you can bet that everyone's going to know about it. And if you're meeting guys and inviting them to your house, thinking you're keeping it discreet, you're not. Men have big mouths too and they like to talk. Women have the reputation for spreading gossip, but men do it just as much. Especially if they've just had a night with America's Sweetheart. America's *former* sweetheart."

The last sentence burned, a red-flame wave that started in Cecilia's neck and trickled northward to her face. She felt the sting of what she'd lost – what she was in the process of losing. The thorny remark that Anita had just thrown across the room – the aching designation of *former*... maybe it was better to be nothing at all than *former*.

Cecilia stood up and marched over to the couch. She inhaled her cigarette and exhaled sharply in the direction of the room's door. Anita's office looked as claustrophobic, as hostile to her as ever – walls covered with framed movie posters and signed head shots that mocked Cecilia with wide smiles, stress-free self-importance.

"I have been seeing someone," Cecilia said, taking a seat across from her agent. "He's an actor from Italy. Marco Bagnetti. He's trying to make it over here."

"Ah, Marco Bagnetti. Name rings a bell. Do you love him?"

Cecilia smiled slyly. "I don't *love* him...but I..."

"Then dump him. Immediately. I already know about Marco. He's using you to open doors, but those doors will never open. He's beautiful all right, but he's way too demanding and high-maintenance and his English isn't good enough. He'll be back in Italy by the end of the year. Cut him loose and settle down with someone. Lay all of these rumors to rest."

Cecilia smirked and shook her head. "Fine. I'll just throw a quarter in a fountain and make a wish for a stable, highly-functional, good-looking man who isn't put off by my success to show up at my front door. I didn't realize it was that easy."

Anita moved closer to Cecilia and clasped her fingers together. Cecilia could tell by the woman's excitement that something was brewing – something strange and foreboding, something she probably wasn't going to like.

"Well…" Anita said. "There is a certain actor who you used to be quite close with. Someone tall and handsome, and brilliant and successful, who just got out of a relationship. And his manager contacted Daria and me and asked to set up a meeting with you."

Cecilia scoffed. "What? Who?"

Anita beamed. "Billy Sloan!" She said the name as though she were announcing lottery winnings, her face bright with excitement.

Cecilia sat back on the couch and thought about Billy Sloan. She and Billy had shared a childhood of audition rooms and callback hopes, of yearning to be part of this greater life and then vacillating once they realized what they'd gotten themselves into.

She and Billy had been closest in the early nineties when they were in their mid-teens. They talked on the phone, went on hikes, shared their desires to be the most famous, the most celebrated, the top of the Hollywood echelon.

Nothing in particular drove them apart but they started spending less time together after Cecilia was cast in *Soldier of Payback*. At first, Cecilia thought he was retreating due to jealousy over her successful film, and she found that wholly unreasonable, since he had been the one who introduced her to Terry Mahoney in the first place.

But then she realized it was her lifestyle that made Billy recoil. It was her new habits, pals and pursuits. His path had been easy: an uphill, linear climb. Television stints begat movie roles, which begat movie leads. Everything Billy did stretched forward, built upon his previous work. And his personal life was easy too – a series of monogamous three-year relationships with beautiful unknowns. These young women slung against his shoulder during expensive dinners and awards ceremonies, grateful for their moments of fame. They showed off shiny pearl-white teeth and skinny legs, long, smooth hair and unspoiled skin. They wanted nothing more than to bask in the shadows cast by their leading man, and when their three-year tenure was up and it was time for a new young dish to inhabit the role, they crept away as pristinely as they'd arrived.

Maybe it was Cecilia who had drifted away from Billy. Cecilia – with her clandestine drug-fissured junkets and audacious wardrobe. Cecilia, who always feared she was one tabloid story away from Hollywood revocation. Her body of work resembled a roller coaster more than a ladder – one with a steep initial uphill and plenty of tips and turns thereafter.

Yes, it was Cecilia who resented Billy's simplicity – how the sun always shined on him, how easy it all was. How he had held up his end of the bargain to command the higher ranks of Hollywood royalty and how he watched as she partied her way away from her end of the bargain. She hated how he watched – and most certainly judged – all the terrible mistakes she made in real-time. He was part of the rarefied crew of insiders who knew the truth about her. Of course she had stayed away.

Cecilia finally responded. "Are you sure Billy is okay with this meeting?" She asked. "Because I don't think I'm his type and he seems a bit too—"

She hesitated to fill in the blank. What was the right word? Uppity? Uncomplicated?

Anita sighed and placed her hands over Cecilia's hands. "Yes. *He's* the one who suggested meeting up with *you*. It's win-win for both of you. Don't worry so much, my dear. I'll set it all up."

Cecilia nodded and agreed to the meeting with Billy. She

could certainly understand what she would gain from a meeting with Billy Sloan. If guilt by association was a thing, there was also *innocence* by association. Just by standing next to Hollywood's cherished everyman, Cecilia could redeem herself. Billy's dazzling, beguiling clout would lift her out of the drug-and-booze doldrums she faced in Terry Mahoney's wake. What Cecilia didn't understand was…what was in it for Billy?

MARCO BAGNETTI DID NOT GO QUIETLY. HE RAGED AT CECILIA in thunderous Italian while hurling his possessions into a drawstring knapsack. There wasn't much of his at her Palisades mansion anyway – some Dickens, some Shake-speare, a book of sonnets by William Wordsworth and a small, painted ukulele. While Marco threw these items into his bag, he roared at her – a cascade of words she couldn't translate but didn't need to.

Cecilia tried to appeal to Marco's rational side. They were never really a couple, never agreed to anything beyond a phys-ical relationship, and this connection that they shared had run its course.

But Marco couldn't be pacified and continued to fulminate – a volcano of piercing phrases and what Cecilia could only assume were Italian profanities. She didn't know if he was angry at the loss of her or the loss of what he perceived she could do for him. It was as though Marco had wrapped up his potential future successes in this affiliation with Cecilia, and now that she was cutting him loose, he would be adrift…a stranger in the mean streets of Hollywood.

Marco finished packing up his items and continued to storm all the way down the grand spiral staircase and towards the front door. He was all arms and fingers – pointing, gestur-ing, vaguely hostile. To Cecilia, the only words she understood

– the only words he spoke in English – were the ones he said just before he slammed the front door behind him. Words that could have been a promise of his future Hollywood triumph or a thinly veiled threat to Cecilia.

"You haven't seen the last of me!"

CECILIA DIDN'T REALIZE HOW MUCH SHE HAD MISSED BILLY Sloan until he showed up at her door. He was still as gorgeous as that nineteen-year-old California boy -- shaggy blonde hair now cropped into a slicked back hairdo, gawky stance now molded into a manly, sculpted posture.

Cecilia shrieked at the sight of her old friend, and he scooped her into a bear hug and twirled her around. For a few seconds, she was weightless, aloft, delirious with elation.

"Cecilia, how I've missed you!" Billy said, and once he put her down, she took a few steps to the side and welcomed him into her home.

"It's beautiful, just beautiful," Billy marveled, as his eyes swept over the vast foyer, the twin sloping staircases, the expensive fixtures, the priceless artwork hanging from the walls.

Cecilia made her way to the bar area and offered Billy a cocktail, but he held up his hand and sweetly requested water, no ice.

She obliged and watched him drink. He looked so youthful and childlike – anachronistic in his innocence. Billy Sloan was the last uncorrupted remnant of teenage Hollywood…her teenage Hollywood.

"So…why did our managers and agents suggest this get-together?" Cecilia asked.

Billy finished his drink and properly found a coaster for the glass. He laced together his fingers and stared directly into Cecilia's eyes. "They didn't suggest it. I suggested it. You're gonna think I'm crazy, but…I think we should get together… you know, be a couple. Just for a little while. It'll create a public relations frenzy and help both of our careers."

"Oh…You think we should be a couple for real or be a couple for pretend?"

"For pretend."

"Oh…okay." Cecilia wasn't sure what else to say.

Billy broke his gaze and stood up. He locked his interlaced fingers behind his head and stared through double glass doors at the mansion's library. It was a vast room, rarely inhabited, with rows of unread books and rolling ladders. "I have a secret," Billy said to the inert fixtures.

It was at that exact moment that Cecilia knew what Billy's secret was. She understood why he festooned his elbow with an army of eager almost-famous young women. She knew why he carefully guarded his private life, why his acting path had been so carefully curated. She knew why he was requesting this fictitious pairing. It all made sense.

"I know your secret," Cecilia said…not to truncate his confession but to ease the words from his mouth. If he could count on her understanding, perhaps he could work up the courage to tell her directly, instead of speaking confidences into the cold air, which would then carry the sound waves to Cecilia's ears.

Billy didn't say anything so Cecilia continued. "Billy…I know you're gay and that this relationship you've set up for us is to shield your image. When I first thought about it, I was kind of opposed to the idea. But I've thought about it ever since and I think I want to go ahead. I think it would be good for the two of us. This house gets lonely and supposedly I have some image repair to get to as well. At least that's what Anita says. So, I say we go for it."

Billy turned around and stared at Cecilia. She could see the newly formed emotion at the edges of his eyes, the blotchiness of his normally smooth skin. He walked over to Cecilia and took her hands in his, never averting his gaze. Then he sat down next to her and cradled her shoulders, as though protecting her from incoming fire.

"You think I'm gay?" he asked. "I guess that wouldn't differentiate you from anyone else in America right now. But…no…no. That's not it."

"Wasn't that your secret?" Cecilia whispered, and she looked up and stared at him. Their faces had never been so close before…so close that there was barely an inch or two of distance between them. There was no need for whispering – after all, they were the only occupants of an expansive room – but somehow, the situation called for it. It was as though deeply dormant truths deserved the pageantry of continued secrecy in their revelations – as though saying it out loud too quickly would violate the secret's ethos.

"No, that's not it," Billy repeated. "I don't think you're going to be able to guess this one. It's a big one. It keeps me up at night and I think about it all day every day. It could ruin my career, and I can never have anyone know."

"Oh, wow. What is it?"

Billy stood up and paced a lap around Cecilia's bar area. He looked up at the ceiling while he patrolled – as if looking heavenward for answers or perhaps to stem the tide of tears. "I think I killed someone," he finally said, and then stopped in his tracks to see her expression. Then he said, "Indirectly. It's the worst thing I've ever done. I wish I could go back in time. I wish I could change it."

Cecilia tried to disguise the look of shock that she knew she was revealing. She wanted Billy to feel unguarded, free of judgment. But the news was so far from what she'd expected him to say, it was all she could do to sit frozen in place and wait for him to continue.

"About a year ago, there was a big mass shooting in LA. Do you remember it?"

Cecilia frowned. "Kind of. I mean, there are so many

these days, I tend to lose track. Are you saying you had something to do with a shooting?"

Billy shook his head. "No, of course not. But the shooting happened right by where we were filming and my manager told me to go to the hospital and visit the victims. You know, visit the beds, take pictures, give autographs, all that P.R. shit."

"Okay."

"So I go, and I'm meeting all these victims who are lying in their beds, and one of the guys I meet is this Elijah Gatlin guy. He seemed like a nice, normal guy. Pretty young wife, two young kids. He nearly jumped out of bed when he saw me… told me he was my biggest fan and he used to watch me on TV all the time and that – even though he'd been shot – this was the greatest day of his life."

Cecilia smiled. "Okay. So…"

"The photographers and journalists are all there with their cameras, clicking away and taking notes, and I guess I got carried away making promises. I told him we were friends for life, and I gave him my manager's number and told him to call me anytime. Oh man, Cecilia, I even wrote down my home address for the man. I don't know what I was thinking. There was all the news hype and the journalists and photographers and this gunshot victim confined to his hospital bed who knew every one of my shows. I got so carried away; I told him I would always be there for him, and I said a whole bunch of other shit. I wasn't thinking straight at the time."

"Oh no," Cecilia said. "I think I can see where this is going."

"I know, I'm such an idiot. I don't know what I was doing. And, as you can probably guess, this guy starts calling me. *A lot*. Fans like that can be scary and you know it. People don't realize but we know. So he starts calling me…and…and I just avoid him. I tell my manager, don't take his calls, dude. Then, Elijah shows up at my house. Climbs my gate. I didn't have a security system, Cecilia. I had a gate and *he climbed it*. That's how determined he was. He caught me totally by surprise. He starts asking me all kinds of questions about where I've been, why I've been avoiding him, can we hang out, can I make good on these things I said, blah blah blah. He tells me he has brain cancer and his dying wish is to go to some movie with me or something like that.

"That just set me off. I felt very uncomfortable, very vulnerable. In my defense, people do kidnap and kill celebrities. I can't have mega-fans just climbing my gates and showing up at my doorstep, right? You know how it is. I told him to get the hell off my property or I was going to call the police and get a restraining order. I called him a bunch of names. I told him he was worthless, that I'd never be friends with him. Ugh, I told him I was glad he had brain cancer. I said a bunch of horrible things that I didn't even mean. I just wanted him to go away and never contact me again. Then he went home and hung himself. He left a note saying that it was because of everything I'd said. He left behind a widow and two young kids."

"Oh…no…" Cecilia said.

"And I found out because his widow called and told my manager, who put me on the phone. His widow said Elijah was already dying of brain cancer, that it'd be easiest to tell everyone he took his own life because of that. She told me that he loved my shows so much, could I please show up to the funeral. It would've meant the world to him. So I went – because I felt so bad, so responsible – and all of his childhood friends kept coming up to me and telling me what a great guy I was for showing up, about how much I meant to Elijah, that he used to always emulate me when he was younger. I saw his two little kids crying. His widow, his parents were crying. Cecilia, it was all so terrible." Billy returned to the couch, placed his head on Cecilia's lap and wept quietly.

Cecilia brushed his hair back with her fingers, wiped away his tears with her thumb. "It's okay," she whispered. But she wasn't sure whether it was okay, or what it all meant. She had expected a confession of sexual preference – a confession she could address and placate, one of the oldest stories in Hollywood.

But Billy's confession was another creature altogether – one that seemed too large, too hairy, too beastly to exist in her ivory-colored bar area, well-appointed and clean, innocent.

Billy continued to sob, his head shifting back and forth while he heaved. "I'm such a terrible person. I can't be in a real relationship anymore," he said. "I can't be with anyone because I can't tell anyone. And my agent –and everyone else – thinks I'm isolated because I'm sexually confused right now and I'm just fine to let them keep thinking that, because I can't tell them the truth. I can't tell them what I've done. Cecilia, journalists still ask me about my friendship with Elijah Gatlin based on that hospital visit. They treat me like a saint. If word ever got out about what really happened, it could mean the end of me. The end of my career. You have to try to understand how much this means to me. Cecilia, you have the power to destroy me. You can never say a word to anyone. If you did…I don't even know what I would do. Let's just be a couple together and then I'll figure this all out, okay? I trust you. I've known you for so long. You're one of the only people I can trust. Let's just put a public image out there and at least that part of our lives will be uncomplicated. Can we do that?"

"Yes, yes, we can do that," Cecilia said, still stroking his hairline. "Let's show the world what great actors we are. We can be a very convincing couple and no one will think other-wise. And then you can sort out everything else." She leaned forward and kissed the top of Billy's head. "You have nothing to worry about, I promise you. Okay? I would never betray you. Never. Your secret's safe with me."

Chapter Eighteen

Vetta Park, Missouri
September 26, 2022

THE LATE-AUTUMN SUN beamed into Weaver's large office, lighting triangular-shaped patches of carpet beneath the laminated wood table. Around the table, Weaver, Hobbs, Martinez and Adams reclined in creaky chairs while they thumbed through copies of organizational documents.

The documents were so uninformative that Hobbs considered it almost comical that someone had taken the trouble to copy and collate three versions of them. The papers consisted of Tax ID numbers and labels, grossly generic descriptions, barely legible signatures.

What they could glean from the information was that Sparrow Shearwater had set up a wellness center. She was the founder and owner of the enterprise, and her subordinate, Paula Fekete, managed the day-to-day operations.

If Sparrow Shearwater was a social media enthusiast – a woman who frequently uploaded videos and messages of herself imparting spiritual sermons – Paula Fekete was quite the opposite. Very little about her was known or revealed online, and the detectives had to resort to law enforcement databases to learn that Paula was a native of Mezőladány, Hungary, and that she'd come to the United States as a teenager. Paula's license photo revealed a narrow, beaky face framed by straight, dark hair. She had wide-set blue eyes and a haunting gaze. She didn't smile.

Assembled around the table that morning, the foursome discussed what they didn't know, which seemed to be just as telling as what they did. Attempts to speak with both Paula and Sparrow proved fruitless. Paula had a listed phone number that dispatched phone calls directly to a mechanized voicemail box. As for Sparrow, the detectives were able to narrow her whereabouts to a rainforest deep within a Brazilian jungle – and this was only because they happened upon an itinerary that the guru had shared publicly.

If the schedule was to be believed, Sparrow would be unlocatable and unavailable for the remainder of the week. Of course, the detectives realized, the itinerary could have been an electronic decoy – a brilliant mechanism to buy time while the woman planned her escape. They kept the APB in place and continued to connect with Sparrow's voicemail. And their Santa Monica counterparts maintained a dispatch to Sparrow's apartment twice a day – just in case.

"So, we don't know much about Shearwater Enterprises," Dean said rhetorically, and the others around the table nodded. Earlier that morning, Dean, Martinez and Hobbs had visited the building listed as the center's domicile. It was brick-layered and industrial, and appeared mostly vacant from the outside. There were no cars parked in a nearby lot, no signs of life except for windswept, dried out leaves that had descended from nearby trees.

Hobbs had buzzed an oval-shaped button near the front door, but there was no response. While they waited, she looked around at the surrounding area. There was a nearby trainyard and tall electrical tower. Across the street, another nineteenth-century, rectangular brick building seemed to be in the latter stages of deterioration. Several windows had been ruptured, several bricks were missing and a minor trash heap had amassed at the building's foundation. It was a wonder – and probably a hazard – that the structure was still standing.

Hobbs found the neighborhood not only remote but entirely depressing. Even though the sun was out, the area still seemed gray and dusty, seeping of Midwestern decay. She wedged a business card into the front door of the building and they left.

Now, at the meeting in Weaver's office, they rattled off suspects and theories. The strongest motive was the idea that Cecilia had been killed because she was in the process of revealing secrets.

"Think about it," Dean said. "What do people do at rehabs, at wellness centers? They sit in a big group circle and they reveal secrets. We already know that Cecilia revealed a big secret of Billy's before she went into rehab, so we know she wasn't the best at keeping things to herself. Do you know what I mean?"

Hobbs knew exactly what he meant. As they discussed Cecilia, Hobbs envisioned the scenario in her own mind. Cecilia, seated in a rusty folding chair inside of a warehouse-like room. Far from the cushy rehab centers of Malibu and Santa Barbara, this placed would have reeked of disinfectant and collected dust and cobwebs in the corners. It was the price of privacy.

Hobbs imagined Cecilia taking a deep breath and beginning to share. There was Billy's secret, of course, but there were also others. This was 2022 – the extension of Hollywood's reckoning, and who knew more about Tinsel Town's inner workings than its own long, adored sweetheart?

Perhaps Terry Mahoney was communicating with someone inside the rehab center – a starstruck patient, a rebellious orderly. Perhaps there was a reason that Terry's name kept surfacing in interrogations about Cecilia's antagonists...and yet the man's reputation was spotless. Maybe he needed to keep it that way.

Perhaps Paula Fekete was sending information about Cecilia's disclosures up the line – first to Sparrow Shearwater and then to Terry Mahoney. When it got to be too much – when the information got to be too damaging – Terry gave word to put an end to the leaks. To put an end to Cecilia Cinvenue.

Of course, all of this was pure speculation, and Hobbs was careful never to embark too swiftly down a path without the evidence to back it up. She was aware that she had little, but trusted that more would be forthcoming. This was how these cases almost always went.

The detectives were just finishing their summation of the Shearwater Enterprises legal documents when the phone in Weaver's office rang. Rochelle – the red-headed, chain-smoking, gravel-voiced newbie, called out, "Hobbs! Call for you! I patched it through to Weaver since you're in there!"

They all exchanged glances with each other. It had been two hours since Hobbs had left her card in the industrial building's front door. Hobbs could see hope and expectation mirrored in the others' eyes. She pressed a button on the table's center receiver and said in a practiced voice, "Roberta Hobbs, Vetta Park P.D."

"Is this Roberta Hobbs, the guardian of Nick Hobbs?" the voice on the other end asked.

A gust of disillusioned exhalation circulated from the table. Hobbs looked down at the documents in front of her and said flatly, "Yes, this is she. Is there something I can help you with?"

The voice was nasally, older-sounding and annoyed. "I'm calling from the main office of Vetta Park Central High School. You need to come and pick up your son...er...your child that you're the guardian of. He's been suspended and he needs to be picked up by a parent or guardian."

"I'm a detective and I'm in the middle of a serious case here," Hobbs said. "Can it please wait until the end of the day?"

The woman was unpersuaded, impatient. "Ma'am...*as I just said*...a parent or guardian of Nick Hobbs needs to come to the high school and pick him up *right now*. He's been suspended."

"Fine. I'll leave work and I'll be right there."

Hobbs switched off the phone and gathered her jacket. As she was getting up, she realized she hadn't even asked about the reason for the suspension. She supposed it didn't matter; she would get all the sordid details when she reached the high school.

While Hobbs was getting ready to go, she felt all the eyes in the room on her. It made her feel weak, amateurish, a kid at the grownups table. She was careful not to look in Dean's direction, lest she grasp the relief he likely felt that this wasn't his problem...the unspoken confirmation that he had made the right decision not to get involved.

While Hobbs was dashing out of Weaver's office, she overheard Martinez yell after her, "Welcome to parenthood!"

NICK WAS WAITING FOR HER IN THE FRONT OFFICE OF THE HIGH school. He had cinched his black hoodie so tightly around his head that it almost seemed like a helmet – a dark fabric helmet that concealed his forehead and eyes. At Hobbs's approach, Nick shifted positions – from a front slouch to a back lean. He seemed to always be slouching and leaning – any posture except for upright, at attention. He flicked a pencil up and down on the table and frowned, waiting for her to speak first.

She didn't hesitate. "Well. I'm here." The words came out bitterly, barbed. She sounded harsher than she'd intended, but Nick didn't react. He continued leaning and flicking, scowling, yawning.

"Ms. Hobbs? You're Nick's guardian?" the woman behind the counter asked, and Hobbs saw that it was the same woman as the registrar who had given Nick his schedule.

Hobbs nodded and walked over to the counter. "Yes, I'm here. I got a call that said I need to bring Nick home due to a suspension. Can you tell me what he did?"

The registrar frowned at Hobbs and then produced a slip of paper. It was the paperwork for Nick's suspension – the codifying document for his transgression. Hobbs skimmed it over and saw that there were a multitude of infractions. *Truancy, smoking in the bathroom, cursing at his teachers.*

"Nick!" Hobbs said, reflexively, as if this were her own child who had disappointed her with out-of-character behavior. Did she know Nick well enough to proclaim this as a departure from his usual conduct?

"The ninth-grade principal is in a meeting right now," the registrar said. "You can sign this and take him, or you can wait and get more details from Dr. Holland."

"Oh, I'll wait," Hobbs said – almost zealously – and then took a seat at the small round table next to her nephew. She turned to look at Nick but he wouldn't match her gaze, focusing instead on the small, wooden flakes of the pencil.

After five minutes, Dr. Holland emerged and invited them inside his office. It was a windowless room, painted walls decorated with diplomas and certificates, redolent of an inspiring scholar. Holland was middle-aged, bespectacled, Black man. He had angled cheeks and wide-set eyes. His voice was deep while he recited the litany of charges against Nick.

It seemed that Nick had decided to skip all his morning classes, and use his free time to smoke cigarettes and vape in the men's room. When a teacher discovered him and delivered him to the office with the penalty of an afternoon detention, Nick did not return to his classroom, humbled and rehabilitated. Instead, he left his second period class to return to the scene of the crime and resume his activities.

A different teacher discovered the young man, lips wrapped around the paper cylinder, flicking ash into the sink without a care as to the fumes emitted. The teacher would later say that Nick was acting as though he was trying to be caught, and such was the teacher's surprise when Nick refused to leave the premises. As Dr. Holland described, Nick refused even to stub out the cigarette, and responded to the teacher by hurling a string of expletives and invectives at the educator.

Perhaps sensing his physical disadvantage, the teacher phoned the front office for assistance. Subsequently, a fleet of well-trained officers and counselors bolted to the men's room, and it was only upon realizing the inevitability and degree of his punishment that Nick decided to comply.

Dr. Holland leaned against the edge of his desk and looked harshly at Nick. Nick was seated on a peach-colored sofa at the edge of the room, and he'd arranged himself to avoid eye contact with his principal.

"Nick, do you have anything to say for yourself?" Dr. Holland asked.

Nick vaguely shook his head and stared blankly at the walls. He continued his reticence while Hobbs signed the suspension paperwork and apologized to the principal on his behalf. While she walked briskly through the school and into the parking lot, Nick moseyed carefully behind her – as if taking note of the building and its features for the last time.

It was only once they were seated next to each other in the car, on their way to the police precinct, that Nick said something.

"Those assholes," he said, into the folds of his hands. He spoke so quietly that Hobbs wasn't sure he'd spoken at all.

"I'm taking you to the precinct because – as you know –

I'm in the middle of an important case," Hobbs said harshly. "Dr. Holland gave me classwork that you can do in one of the cubicles."

Nick sighed and brushed his chin with his hand. "Whatever."

Hobbs continued: "And, you're going to finish that classwork and bring it back tomorrow."

Nick finally gave a reaction – a real reaction. He was a firecracker fuse that had just been lit, a grenade that had just been launched. He shot forward in his seat and tore his hoodie off his face. Peripherally, Hobbs could see tear-stained cheeks, cowlicked hair. "I'm NOT going back there!" Nick yelled. "School doesn't do anything for me!"

"Well, Nick, that's just the thing!" Hobbs yelled back. "School isn't supposed to *do something* for you! It's not a trick pony! It's not there to entertain you! The onus is on YOU to apply YOURSELF to school! School isn't going to DO ANYTHING without you deciding to make it work! It's an object, an application, a noun. YOU are the sentient PERSON who must FIGURE OUT how to make it work! No one is going to chase you down to make school work for you! That's YOUR job! And by the way, our society is just fine with its citizens failing…and dropping out of school is DEFINITELY the first step!"

They were quiet in the car for a few moments – no sounds except for the whirring of the car engine. Nick shifted positions so he was leaning against the passenger car door, almost hugging it to the extent his seat belt would allow. Hobbs saw him put his right thumb and forefinger over the corners of his eyes and she felt a pang of sympathy. Perhaps she had been harsh to suggest a future of societal withdrawal and decay for Nick, but she had seen too much in her work to suggest otherwise.

When they arrived at the police station, Hobbs parked her car and sat with her hands on the dashboard. "You need to go back to school tomorrow, Nick. I can't have you stay with me if you're not going to go. If you cut any more classes, I'm going to have to send you back to your parents. And I'm not saying that to threaten you. I'm saying it because if you're making bad decisions, I can't be any part of it. I care about you too much to allow you to skip classes under my watch. I hope you understand."

Nick unclicked his seat belt and leaned forward, resting his forearms on his thighs and his forehead on the dashboard. He looked hunched, fetal, with knotty hair that waved in different directions and a curved spine. Ten seconds went by, and then he sat up straight, sighed, and tilted his head so he was finally looking at her.

"I'll go back," he said. "But I hate it there. I'm not learning anything."

"I think that's the right decision," Hobbs said. "And I appreciate it. And I'm sure you *are* learning, even though you don't think you are. I mean...Vetta Park Central High may not be the best public high school in Missouri, but it is accredited and you do spend seven hours a day there...when you go to class. So, I can't understand how you wouldn't be learning anything."

"Well...then..." Nick said. And then he huffed and mumbled something under his breath before opening the passenger door and walking inside the police precinct. Hobbs stayed inside the car for a minute, trying to interpret what he had said. Eventually she settled on: *Why can't I leave?* But there was a small part of her that thought he might have asked: *Why can't I read?*

Chapter Nineteen

Los Angeles, California
2015

IN CECILIA'S OPINION, the Five Years of Billy were good ones. That's what she called the span of time when she and Billy were cohabitating, smiling for cameras, arriving together for red carpet events – mussed and primped, garbed in designer clothing, grinning at each other over cameras and microphones.

At home, they were boring, uninspired. Cecilia watched reality television and smoked outside – alone on the master bedroom balcony – while Billy filmed on location or worked out at the gleaming, newly-constructed Pacific Palisades gym.

Like so many real girlfriends and boyfriends throughout the country, Cecilia sat quietly and waited for her fixation to come home. She lingered on the downy chaise longue and scrolled through her phone while she waited. Other nights, she sat on the king bed's fluffy bedspread and waited, all the while entertaining fanciful dreams.

Cecilia imagined an eager and vigorous Billy Sloan

lumbering through the house, looking for her. She envisioned fervent eyes and rapacious lips – his passionate, hungry body on top of hers. For perhaps a handful of times during their half-decade together, these imaginings came to fruition. Although only when Billy was inebriated and lonely, nursing a chipped heart and shattered ego. In the morning, he was always apologetic and regretful, filled with reasons why what happened shouldn't have happened…and why it never would again.

Cecilia only nodded and half-smiled while Billy post-coitally ruminated about the complications, the potential disaster of their love affair. She saw everything differently than he did. She dreamed about their time together and held on to the memories like a prized keepsake – a film reel of moments that needed to be relived until Billy got drunk and despondent again…and revitalized the highlights loop with fresh moments.

Most days…after filming was finished, after meetings had been adjourned, Cecilia sat by herself and watched the sun sink behind her backyard's luscious tree-lined landscape. Her time with Billy had improved her career, just as her manager and agent had predicted. It had moored her, fastened her to the earth and the living, gave her a reason to come home at night.

That Billy and Cecilia were only play-acting was a mere preface to the true story. As Cecilia imagined it, Billy would wake up one morning and realize that his soul mate had been sleeping upstairs from him this whole time. She had been bringing him coffee in the morning, smiling as they practiced lines, laying her body next to his while they watched movies. His true soul mate was Cecilia Cinvenue. It had to be.

This was why that rainy April morning in 2015 was all the more devastating. Billy visited Cecilia in her bedroom and called off the whole thing. They were breaking up because he had found true love in the arms of a twenty-year-old aspiring dancer. She was raven-haired and lithe, unburdened by the emotional residue of deceased parents, childhood employment or vice addictions. Her name was Lana Ainsley— a florid sounding designation – according to Billy – whose initials he had tattooed onto his forearm. He rolled up his shirtsleeve to show the markings to Cecilia: a cursive, swirling L A, inside of a giant red, cross-hatched heart.

Cecilia listened to her fake boyfriend carry on about his genuine girlfriend and felt herself sink into the carpeting. She felt heavier than ever, as though this news had weighed her down with its sizeable gravitational force. She felt uglier than ever, stupider than ever. How could she have thought that Billy would consider her a real romantic partner? He had already brandished himself with Lana Ainsley's initials – already permanently adhered her to himself. This girl who was born almost two decades after Cecilia. This girl who couldn't possibly opine about major late-twentieth century issues with Billy or laugh with him about childhood sitcoms from the 1980s. How had Billy fallen for her so completely...so quickly?

As for Cecilia, what was she except for a landlord? A sometimes-lover when the blood-alcohol level was right? She had provided him with a cover story when he needed one... for years...and all the emotions and affections from their time together belonged to her alone.

Billy continued to carry on about Lana, oblivious to the effect his words were having on Cecilia. Did her face not betray her devastation? Was she that good of an actress?

"I also want to thank you..." Billy was saying. "For helping me through that rough spot. It was a really tough time for me and being able to be here with you helped me out a ton. You know, after Elijah's death and everything. I'm in a completely different place now...ready to move on with my life."

"I'm glad I could help." Cecilia said. And then, she couldn't help herself but to ask: "Does this mean you're moving out?" She hated asking the question…hated thinking about the day Billy would pack his items and leave her alone in this colossal house, having to hear her mutterings echo off of empty walls once again. But just as fully, she hated the idea of Lana Ainsley stepping foot inside of the residence – defiling its architecture, its history with her puerile meanderings.

"Yeah…I think I should," Billy said. "I'm in a much better place, and I feel like I'm ready to move ahead with my life. Lana talked to me about ways that I could honor Elijah Gatlin's memory. Like I could set up a foundation in his honor and the proceeds could go to cancer research. This way I can do something for him – for his family – without having to reveal…you know…what happened."

"Does Lana know what actually happened?"

"Oh yeah. She knows everything. She said she wouldn't tell a soul and I trust her."

Cecilia nodded and looked down at the floor. She knew then that it was over – the bond that connected Billy to her. Someone else knew of Billy's dreadful secret. It was no longer a foreign language that only the two of them shared…no longer an invisible line that no one else could cross. Someone else had been brought into the fold – someone far too young to under-stand the ramifications of a ruined career, the smarting of a tarnished reputation. That Billy had shared his biggest secret with his new lover told Cecilia everything she needed to know.

"Are you guys moving in together?"

"Yeah, we're planning on it. We were looking casually and then we found this cute two-bedroom condo in Westwood. I think you'd like it."

Cecilia recoiled at the thought of having anything to do with Billy and Lana's romance – even something as benign as liking their place of residence. She could feel herself spiraling – her thoughts birthing worse thoughts. She was unloved and unlovable. She was both impossibly fat – as her earlier years had predicated – and gangly-skinny, as the number on the scale indicated...somehow simultaneously. She didn't know exactly what it was about her that made her so unworthy...but there was certainly something about her that kept the laudable suitors away. Something that kept Billy chattering and gabbing about his new girlfriend – lost in a haze of love and lust – oblivious to Cecilia's heartache.

There was something wrong with Cecilia...unnamed, unknown, but certainly *there*. Her fallacy was on display but unfixable – a lifelong deficiency that had no cure. She lay in bed the night that Billy devastated her with his newfound exhilaration and silently chastised herself for ever loving the man. Another shortcoming.

In the morning, Cecilia fixed herself a cocktail of gin, vodka, rum and triple sec, mixed with a teaspoon of soda. When she was numb enough that everything around her blurred into a haze of imprecise colors and textures, she picked up her phone and dialed Marco Bagnetti.

AFTER BILLY MOVED OUT, THE VOID IN CECILIA CINVENUE'S mansion was larger than man-size. It was an enormous gaping chasm, an abyss in the earth that illicit substances and frequent hook-ups could only cursorily mend. They didn't plug the hole at all; all they did was distract.

If distraction was the best that Cecilia could do, she went at it full-throttle. Whenever she felt the needle-sharp flares of craving, there was Marco and then Marco's bodyguard and then Terry Mahoney's old friend and also men she had met online. There was cocaine and Oxy and gin and vodka. There was powder and dried leaves, capsules and tinctures. All kinds of distractions to keep Cecilia sedated...to keep her thoughts occupied...as though the unaltered, unobscured mind of

Cecilia could do some real damage. Best to prevent it from itself.

During this time, Cecilia didn't work. She had always considered herself a pillar of good on-set behavior. Even during her earlier episodes, she had always found a way to get herself to work on time...to endure her lines and directions with reasonable proficiency.

But this time it was worse than it had ever been. She couldn't get out of bed on time in the morning or muster the mental strength to memorize lines. Her head constantly throbbed; her throat was dry; her muscles were sore. Only returning to the well of iniquity provided temporary relief from her symptoms, and this illogicality sustained her cycle of bad judgment and regret.

Terry Mahoney made an unannounced visit to her home one day. An associate had told him about Cecilia's decline and he afforded three minutes from his hectic schedule to drop by and give Cecilia a name.

Sparrow Shearwater... This woman was the spiritual guru who counseled the stars. She was practically a sorceress. She had healed many of Hollywood's exclusive A-listers, all discreetly. She would heal Cecilia under the cloak of a new friendship, and no one would know.

Terry pressed a business card into Cecilia's palm and hovered near the doorway – his time almost up.

"Why are you doing this for me?" Cecilia asked – surprised at the towering icon's interest in her convalescence.

Terry looked down at his watch while he responded. "*Hollywood Ledger's* doing a feature on you. My sources told me the writer's going to come down hard on me for introducing you to drugs, booze and bad boys. Now, we all know that's bullshit, but my team wants me to talk to the guy and give him a different narrative. So fine. I'll give him ten minutes. And... you know...I'm not going to give specifics...but I do plan to say that I tried to steer you on the right path…gave you the best name in the business."

"Oh…I see. Thanks."

"Cecilia, I'm not messing around, okay? Give Sparrow Shearwater a call. She'll save your life."

SPARROW SHEARWATER WAS NOT EXACTLY WHAT CECILIA expected. Cecilia had thought she'd be meeting someone tangentially medical – a middle-aged woman in ironed scrubs, her hair knotted behind her back in a tight bun.

Instead, Sparrow emerged through the front doors of the coffee house like a specter that a Ouija board had summoned. She wore a large printed tunic that gaped over her narrow frame. Her black hair was held back with knots and beads, but still flowed down in a wispy cascade, covering her shoulders and back. Sparrow's skin was a flawless alabaster, age-obscuring. She could have been twenty or forty years old. Her face was oval, cheekbones hollowed, eyes large and hazel. Cecilia figured that Sparrow could have found work in the entertainment industry…if she weren't a healer.

"You must be Cecilia," Sparrow said warmly, in a voice that reminded Cecilia of a soothing balm.

"Yes, that's right."

Sparrow smiled and revealed two rows of gleaming white teeth. "It is so nice to meet you."

She took Cecilia's hand in hers and sat down opposite the actress. Cecilia noticed that they weren't engaged in a handshake, but rather a hand grip. The healer held on to Cecilia's hand and pressed her manicured fingertips onto Cecilia's palm. It felt oddly intimate. When the waiter came by to take their order, Cecilia seized the opportunity to rescue her hand and place it in her lap. She wasn't ready to be gripped, to be held.

"I'll just have hot green tea, please," Sparrow said softly.

Cecilia ordered coffee and waited for the waiter to leave before saying, "Terry has said many wonderful things about you." This was kind of a lie, as the producer had only afforded Cecilia a few minutes of his time in the previous eight years...but it was the common language of her profession to talk up relationships, to amplify connections so they could serve an individual purpose. But if Sparrow was charmed by this adulation, she didn't show it.

"I'm very pleased to meet you, Cecilia. And you should know that one of the hallmarks of my business is a commitment to absolute secrecy. No one will know anything about your time with me, just as I will never speak of my time with any of my other clients."

For the next thirty minutes, Sparrow spoke of her ideology, her methodology, her personal history and her unusual beliefs and alternative remedies. She spoke so quickly – and darted from topic to topic – that Cecilia found it hard at times to take it all in. It was a whirring, well-researched, well-rehearsed diatribe that bounced from topic to topic and contained the buzzwords that Cecilia would expect from a spiritual guru. Sparrow spoke of archetypes and dreams, of shadow personalities, of personas and personality types, of the full human experience, of the importance of considering one's own death, of the value of alternative medicine.

For Cecilia, this lecture was a welcome relief. Without exception, when she met new people, all they wanted was to know more about Cecilia – not in a caring way but in a way that made her feel they wanted a piece of her. They wanted photos, signatures, stories. They wanted to take home a specimen and show it off to their friends. Cecilia typically felt exhausted from new encounters, but with Sparrow, it was different. Sparrow didn't want anything from Cecilia. She just wanted to talk.

Also, most of the people that Cecilia met fit into a few

common categories. There were fanatical fans, industrious Hollywood types, entrepreneurs who wanted her to showcase their wares, photographers, writers who wanted a good story. Sparrow wasn't like anyone Cecilia had met before. She was soft and languid. When she spoke, her voice was calm and pensive. She made Cecilia want to listen.

"It's very fortuitous that I have an opening in my schedule right now," Sparrow said. "Typically, I'm booked for months, if not longer. But I don't believe in coincidences. Do you? I think I'm meant to be at this place exactly at this time. I think I'm meant to be your healer, your redeemer. I'm meant to help you out of whatever physical, mental, emotional constraints you find yourself in. The bondages that are keeping you from self-actualization. Of course, it's entirely up to you if you want to think about whether to embark on this journey with me. We would start with a two-day retreat at Joshua Tree. We could even do it this weekend if your schedule would allow. Get out of L.A. and into the fresh desert air, which is very therapeutic and very restorative. You can let me know in the next day or so whether this is some-thing you'd like to do. Don't let me know right now. Give yourself time to reflect on whether this is a path you truly feel ready for."

Before they parted, Sparrow again gripped Cecilia's hand and stared deeply into her eyes for a few moments. Then she turned around, mounted her motorcycle, adjusted her helmet and drove away.

After Sparrow's departure, Cecilia felt deflated. It wasn't the usual feeling that she had after meeting new people for the first time. She didn't feel as though she'd been prodded and provoked, nipped at with casual indifference by someone who was *wanting* something from her.

Rather, it was Sparrow's lack of wanting that had caught Cecilia's interest so keenly. The healer didn't ask Cecilia about herself or even request a decision right away – so certain was she that this was the type of relationship which deserved a proper mulling over.

Sparrow's departure had underscored the certain emptiness of Cecilia's life. During their coffee meeting, Sparrow's energy had been buoyant, contagious even, but now Cecilia had nothing. She felt the vacuum when she started her car and wheeled out onto the Pacific Coast Highway. She felt it when she entered her mansion and heard the noise of shoes on marble echo throughout the high ceilings and wide corridors. Sparrow had asked her to wait for an answer but Cecilia knew she was ready. As soon as she went upstairs, she grabbed her suitcase and started packing for Joshua Tree.

CECILIA AND SPARROW STAYED IN TENTS IN THE DESERT — TWO octagonal, nylon and polyester constructions, with zip-lined doors that faced each other. The National Park itself was otherworldly, a moonscape of dust and painted rocks. Cecilia was certain she had never been anywhere more beautiful. Sure, her job had taken her to many remote locations on various continents. But those places were inundated with trailers and fake backdrops, illuminated with white halogen bulbs and teeming with on-set crew.

Joshua Tree, by contrast, was an absolute marvel in its emptiness, its vastness. Cholla cacti jutted out of sand-colored ground. Panoramically, everything Cecilia could see belonged to nature: mountains, vegetation and cumulous clouds. It was as though her entire life had taken place in a fabricated locale, and only now was she *finally* unchained from that fiction. Only now, thanks to Sparrow, could she finally experience the reality that everyone else so easily possessed.

The first day that they arrived, Sparrow and Cecilia said very little to each other. This was by design; Sparrow wanted Cecilia fully immersed in the natural world. As Sparrow explained, for Cecilia to fully discard her demons, she needed to complete the first step of the Purity Program. This meant shedding the trappings and remnants of the commercial world. It meant immersing oneself in nature – *forest bathing* – and listening to the calls of wildlife and trilling birds.

While Cecilia sat in front of her tent and listened to the warble of a canyon wren, she thought she had never felt so satiated in her entire life. Everything up to that moment had been clutter, consumerism, noise. Now she was utterly silent and utterly pacified. She reclined on her camping chair and let the sun wash over her face and bare-limbed body. She tried to divert her thoughts from the harmful, age-accelerating effects of unalloyed sunlight on pale skin. As Sparrow explained, the sun was a venerated energy source, vital for replenishing the body's crucial nutrients and minerals. Beneath a giant floppy hat, Sparrow explained that the sun was to be celebrated – not feared.

The day progressed into evening and the two women smoked cigarettes as they watched the sun set behind distant jagged mountains. Dinner was cold cuts and meat sticks, but Cecilia didn't mind. She nibbled on a crescent of chilled ham while she thought about the important words and phrases that Sparrow had sporadically mentioned during the day: self-actu-alization, spiritual fulfillment, purity, enlightenment.

Sparrow brushed a fold of hair behind her ears and stripped the edging from her slice of ham. "I want you to think about a question," the guru instructed. "Think about the most important question for you right now. The one thing that you most want to comprehend and yet you're most in the dark about." She folded the slice in half and looked up at Cecilia. "Look, we're in the dark right now, aren't we? There's no light around us except for the stars. So, think about a question for which the answer will help guide you from darkness to light."

Cecilia rubbed her hands together and thought about a question. The sun's passing had dropped the temperature at least twenty degrees. She wanted to go inside the tent and seek warmth, but she feared that doing so would negate the effects of the cold, natural atmosphere on this experience. So she reminded herself to remove the physical from the mental…to focus only on her thoughts and not on her discomfort.

Cecilia first thought about her mother. Betty Cinvenue, a svelte, doting figure, who had always rushed into Cecilia's room when the small child wailed from nightmares. Who comforted the young girl, and raked her lean, freshly polished fingernails through Cecilia's dampened hair. Betty Cinvenue, who refused her daughter a single slice of cake at the child's own birthday party, who ran through pages of audition lines with her daughter and wouldn't allow the child to quit, even when she was curled over with exhaustion.

Cecilia knew that Betty loved her intensely. She remembered her mother's worried face – rummaging through her purse at the local store's cash register – looking for phantom cash that didn't exist to pay for makeup and pageant dresses. Cecilia remembered thinking that no one would ever love her like her mother did.

But – at the same time that she felt Betty's fierce love, she felt the woman's fiercest cruelty. Betty was judgmental and critical – a venomous tongue that insisted on diligence, a mother who encouraged cigarettes and anorexia, a natural beauty who spoke about her daughter's plastic surgery as though Cecilia's face were a renovation project.

Betty was also as loving as anyone had ever been to Cecilia. She was permanently in her daughter's corner – a tireless advocate, a devoted ear, a manager, an advisor. Betty was Cecilia's angel and also her devil. The benign ghost who told her she could do anything and the angry phantom who told her she wasn't enough.

Cecilia missed her mom terribly and she also hated her. Could these conflicting emotions exist within the same person? Usually, Cecilia was able to bury her anger beneath obliging inner monologues. But this night, as the darkness covered all the scant possessions in their orbit – all the camping materials, the octagonal tents, even the lightly swaying vegetation – Cecilia only saw black. She felt the true grief of being orphaned by someone by someone who had given her so much, and also taken so much. Her chest swelled at the idea – this unwelcome thought – that she would never see her mother again. It was almost too much to bear.

In the darkness, Cecilia felt the sharpness of emotions she had spent her life burying. In the darkness, no one could see her face. It was a trick of Tinseltown for Cecilia to hide her face in the daytime. Scores of fans, photographers, movie buffs, autograph seekers...everyone on this earth, it seemed, wanted nothing more than to look at Cecilia's face. Her face was always illuminated anyway, eyes blinking under abnormally bright lights, her every muscle twitch absorbed by the fervent public.

But in the darkness, there was no one and nothing. She could be her ugliest self, the most awful creature, and no one could see or judge. It was a sacred blessing – this hiding of the sun – that allowed her to shine the brightest. She could finally think about who she was and what she wanted.

What did Cecilia Cinvenue want at that very moment? To stop torturing herself with diverging memories and eulogies – to let her mother rest peacefully and focus on the living.

The *living*. Aside from Sparrow (who didn't really count since Cecilia had hired her), only three living people existed in Cecilia's constricted world. Three men – all tall, deep-voiced, well-postured, but so different from each other. There was Marco, with his mop of black hair and rakish wardrobe – perhaps the most gorgeous to look at, but the least concerned with her. He would pick up the phone on a moment's notice to have a tryst at Cecilia's mansion, but he couldn't be counted on for anything else. If Cecilia needed something – even so benign as an attentive ear – he was already lost. When she started talking, she could see the glaze in his eyes, the subtle head bob that indicated he had tuned out, already absorbed in the manifestations of his own thoughts.

Then there was Billy Sloan, with whom she had shared five of the best years of her life. Perhaps Billy was the one who had hurt her most – the actor who had so competently played the part of her lover that she believed him. The one who had fake-adored Cecilia for years, only to discard her when a twenty-year old, libidinous nymph sidled up to him.

And lastly Terry Mahoney. Was Terry Mahoney the best or the worst of the bad actors? He had simultaneously launched her career and ruined her. He had introduced her to the powerful life – given her the means to afford a shiny Palisades mansion and the pills to descend into a well of self-loathing. Even when he went through the motions of caring, it was only due to public relations. His intentions were clear from the beginning.

After ten minutes of ruminating about the three living figures in her life who were closest to her, she realized her question.

"Should I ask it out loud?" Cecilia asked.

Sparrow closed her eyes and gently moved her head from side to side. "No, Cecilia," she said. "This question, which you've carefully formulated, is for you and you alone. It is for you to ask and you to answer."

Cecilia nodded and asked the question silently.

Who cares about me?

It was the most important question she could think about, the nagging thought that shadowed her throughout her life. Even when her parents were alive, this question ate at her because she thought she knew its inauspicious answer. *Was she ever cared about?* It was a sentiment that brought tears to her eyes, restored a state of self-victimization that she tried her entire life to evade. She was so rich and so famous, so beautiful, so beloved and so lucky. She lived in a gorgeous multimillion-dollar mansion in a sought-after neighborhood with views that overlooked an endless, exquisite ocean. She had what so few others in the world had. Was that enough? That needed to be enough. It was all she had – all she would ever have -- and it needed to be enough.

Sparrow sat up and suddenly asked, in a soft voice, "If you died tomorrow, Cecilia, what would you leave this world with?"

Cecilia paused for a beat and then started listing her film credentials but the spiritual guru abruptly cut off the actress's catalog of accomplishments. "No, no, no… this is a different type of exercise. I want you to reach into your very eros, Cecilia, *your life energy*, and think about your definition in just a few sentences. You need to ask yourself what you've given to this world and what you've taken from it. What has your existence meant in a very fundamental way? If your tombstone could say just a few lines that defines the nature of you, what would it say?"

"That's a very…thought-provoking question," Cecilia said.

"It was meant to be."

"I don't think I can answer that right now."

"You weren't meant to. You'll need to think about it. But here, now, unfiltered, uninterrupted…is the perfect time and space to be asking yourself this question. I'm heading into my tent now. Goodnight Cecilia Cinvenue."

Sparrow left and Cecilia was alone, staring up at the pure night sky. She had never seen stars flicker so brilliantly or heard the wind howl so raucously. It was only hours after she'd been left alone that she came up with the answer to Sparrow's question.

Cecilia was so tired – eyelids drooping, legs that felt like weighted shackles – that she wasn't sure her incoherence would allow her to repeat the words to Sparrow in the morning. But she was so certain of the refrain's contents that she saw them as though they were etched into marble already – scratched in Gothic Script font with blistering clarity.

HERE LIES CECILIA MARIE CINVENUE.
   Always adored, never valued
   Always followed, never heard
   Always loved, never accepted

Chapter Twenty

Vetta Park, Missouri
September 27, 2022

TUESDAY MORNING STARTED out cloud-covered and dreary. It was the first notification that autumn would be forthcoming, the first chill in the air that foretold of colder weather and darker mornings.

Hobbs arrived early to the precinct – eager to demonstrate her commitment to the job after having to leave the previous day's meeting in such a hurry. She had left Nick at home, still asleep, his rangy arms and scuzzy hair seeping out of twisted covers and blankets.

She had left a list of chores she wanted him to complete on a note taped to the refrigerator. The first three items pertained to school. He was to catch up on all his classes, study for upcoming exams, write down due dates for upcoming deliverables.

Even as she wrote out the tasks, Hobbs knew they would never be completed. Still, she felt vaguely parental just codifying them – providing a list that she could later point to and say that she tried. She knew that Nick would spend his entire day on a screen playing video games...and when she mentioned the list, he would say that – despite repeated trips to the refrigerator – he hadn't seen it.

At the office, the florescent lights flickered brightly over masses of paper and empty cubicles. Within half an hour, everyone trickled in. First came Weaver, who nodded sharply at Hobbs as he treaded past her, into the kitchenette for his morning coffee. Then Ray Martinez, followed shortly by Rochelle. Her halo of red hair drifting away from her autumn jacket was not to be missed, nor was the loping way she darted through the central corridor to smoke cigarettes near the dumpsters behind the building.

Lastly there was Dean Adams, who took his time removing his jacket and carefully hanging it on the upright, metal coat rack. Hobbs studied him as he fastidiously shed his outdoor layer. Something about his precision with this mundane task fascinated her. He was gorgeous in his complete obliviousness of being watched and in his utter devotion to finishing the task at hand. Hobbs felt a deep pang of melancholy as she looked at him.

Luckily, Captain Weaver distracted her before she could descend too deeply into this mineshaft of regretful decisions. He appeared beside her desk, full coffee mug in hand, and caught her up on the previous day's developments.

The big news was the discovery of Sparrow Shearwater. She had returned from her Brazilian expedition the previous afternoon and appeared surprised to discover several messages, emails and texts from the Santa Monica and Vetta Park police departments...not to mention accounts from irritated neighbors about uniformed police officers who blocked their driveways in marked patrol cars.

Sparrow called the Santa Monica station but was unable to reach either Det. Oliver or Det. Frazier. When she then contacted Captain Weaver, they arranged for a Tuesday late-morning conference call, with all the interested parties roped in.

That call happened just after 1 p.m. Central time. The Santa Monica detectives exchanged pleasantries and greetings with their Missouri counterparts while they waited for Sparrow to join the call. Hobbs, Weaver, Adams and Martinez sat around the circular conference table in Weaver's office, just as they had done the previous day. They even sat in the same chairs as before – as though assigned seating was an unspoken criterion.

After ten minutes, Sparrow got on the call. Her voice was breathy, mottled, and she spent two minutes detailing an anecdote to explain her atypical lateness.

"It's all good," Frazier reassured the woman. "But why don't we cut to the chase, since we've all got limited time here. Why didn't you tell us about your wellness center in Vetta Park? When you came in to talk to us, you didn't say a word about it."

"What?" Sparrow asked. Her voice was still raspy, but her tone of voice had changed. She seemed defensive.

Hobbs wondered to herself whether Frazier had jumped the gun by going in for the kill too quickly. When she and Martinez ran interviews, there were typically small-talk introductions, offers of snacks and soda, or little pieces of useless information that they shared about themselves. Rapport building often disarmed persons of interest, led them to drop their defensiveness and open up. Then again, these self-aggrandizing Hollywood types always had a time crunch. Perhaps this was why Frazier had jumped in.

"I don't know what you mean," Sparrow said. "Yes, there's a wellness center in Vetta Park, but I came to you to let you know who I thought was responsible for my good friend – my *former* good friend's – death. The center has nothing to do with it."

"We asked you if you had any idea why Cecilia Cinvenue

would have been in Vetta Park and you said no," Frazier said pointedly.

Sparrow answered quickly. "Well, I have no idea why she would have been in Vetta Park. Could she have been at the wellness center? Sure. Could there have been another reason? Sure. Maybe she has family there, or one of her many boyfriends. I didn't tell you because I didn't know."

"You don't know who's at your own wellness centers?" Hobbs asked.

"No, of course not. I have a general manager, who...her name is Paula Fekete...and *she* runs the center in Vetta Park. If I kept track of the participants there, I wouldn't be able to run my company. You know, I have a much higher-level role. I run the Brazilian retreats. I hold seminars. I meet with high-level clients one on one. I don't have time to put my hands into every little aspect of my enterprise. That's what Paula's for."

"So you had no idea whether Cecilia was at your wellness center?" Hobbs pressed.

"At the time, no."

"And now?"

There was a silence on the other end of the line, the moment when Sparrow's reluctance clashed with the reality of being questioned by the police. Hobbs couldn't see the woman, but she imagined the internal machinations of figuring out how to answer their questions in the most ambiguous way possible.

Sparrow finally spoke in a small voice. "Well...sure...I've spoken to Paula since then. And, yes, Cecilia was at our wellness center before she died."

"Who else was at the wellness center?" Frazier asked.

Sparrow scoffed. "I beg your pardon?"

"We have reason to believe that someone else at the wellness center was involved in Cecilia's death," Frazier explained. "We're going to need to know who else was there."

"Well, I'm sorry but I can't share our wellness center's list of patients with you," Sparrow said. "Discretion is at the heart of our very existence. If I shared that with you, I would be out of business."

Hobbs leaned forward and bent her head while she spoke. "We'll have to get a search warrant for your wellness center documents and get the client list. Our judge will give it to us by the end of the day."

"Fine. Get a warrant. Until then, I can't tell you anything about anyone who was there. It's my job to protect the privacy of my clientele. It's what I'm known for."

Hobbs glanced across the table and exchanged a look with Weaver. They had a judge in Eastern Missouri — or rather, *he* had a judge. An older gentleman, with graying scraps of hair around the ears and years of adjudication under his belt. When Weaver requested a search warrant, he always got it. Sometimes in minutes, sometimes in hours, but the judge always came through. With Hobbs' stare, Weaver firmly nodded in response. He would take care of it.

Frazier took the helm of the questioning. "When you came to see us, you gave us three names of people we should investigate in connection with Cecilia's death. Do you remember that?"

"Yes, of course."

"Do you still feel that those three are people we should investigate?"

"Yes, of course. I haven't changed my views on them."

Hobbs leaned forward again. "Can you tell us why you named those three individuals? Sorry, I wasn't present when you first spoke with my counterparts and I want to make sure I have everything right."

Sparrow sighed heavily — a noticeable lament of this inane police drudgery. She spoke in a condescending voice — in a slower manner — as if Hobbs' question revealed the detective's hearing deficiency. "Well, there were only three people in

Cecilia's life who were close to her…aside from me. And she and I had a falling out, so I wasn't so close to her recently. I named Terry Mahoney, Margo Bagnetti and Billy Sloan. I don't think any of them were particularly good to her…but I can't tell you anything more about them."

"Do you think any of them might have tried to kill her?" Hobbs asked.

"I have absolutely no idea. I don't know any of them that well. I don't know what their relationship was like with Cecilia at the end. I can't say."

"Do you know who Cecilia was really angry at? Perhaps a little over a year ago…she may have vowed revenge or war on someone? Do you know more about that? That would have been before you two fell out."

"I can't say."

"You don't know or you can't say?"

"I can't say."

"I see," Hobbs said. "Well, I'm sure we'll get everything we need to know when the warrant allows us to look at all the files." She noted to herself that the spiritual leader's equivocation had at least revealed a certain knowledge. That Sparrow knew more than she was saying, under the shield of privacy. She knew who Cecilia had been deeply angry at, and probably much more than that.

Also, Hobbs had tried to sound vaguely menacing in her phrasing, with emphases on *everything* and *all*. She hoped to convey that Sparrow's reticence was working against the spiritual leader…that their search warrant would enable a sweeping investigation in which the police would learn more than was strictly necessary for this case.

But Sparrow was unmoved. "Are we done?" she asked.

"No, we're not done," Frazier said. "If you and Cecilia had a falling out, why was she staying at one of your wellness centers?"

"I'm as surprised as you are, detective. Like I said, I only learned that she was at the wellness center afterwards. I had thought she had no interest in what I had to offer...no interest in warding off the material, transcendental dysfunctions that were imprisoning her inner spirit. She never listened to my advice when she was a client of mine."

Hobbs was wary of descending into spiritual speak. She thought she detected a change in manner and tone from the spiritual leader as well. Sparrow's voice deepened and her cadence slowed. Now, she was no longer the surprised, defensive woman fielding queries from a battery of law enforcement. She was once again the leader, the head of an enterprise, with mystical preaching to instruct the foolhardy detectives.

Hobbs wanted to put an end to it. "We're going to get that search warrant from a judge," she said. "In the meantime, you'll need to get on the phone with Paula Fekete and have her let us into the facility and sit down with us for an interview."

"Okay, fine," Sparrow said. "I'm not trying to be difficult. I'm just trying to protect my clients' privacy."

"I understand," Hobbs said. "But if you truly want to get to the bottom of Cecilia's death, you'll make the meeting with Paula happen today. Not tomorrow, not the day after, but today. Got it, Sparrow? *Today*."

PAULA FEKETE MET HOBBS AND MARTINEZ AT THE FRONT door of Shearwater Enterprises. As they ascended a narrow staircase with maroon carpeting, she explained – somewhat apologetically – that she had received their business card but was waiting for the go-ahead from Sparrow before talking with police.

Paula was a lean, lithe woman, with short blonde hair and a short dress to match. Her voice was high-pitched, slightly accented, unhesitant. She hopped up the stairs with alacrity.

When they reached the top of the staircase, Paula opened a wide door and revealed a large, mostly vacant room with high walls that reached ten or twelve feet before hitting the ceiling. The walls were painted snow white – a shade so pale and pristine, it reminded Hobbs of a sanitarium. On the ceiling, exposed wooden beams intersected with silver pipes, and halogen bulbs dangled down. In the corner, near a giant window, the radiator whistled. There was a kitchenette with a humming refrigerator, a slab of white marble demarcating the center island.

Hobbs instantly thought of temperature controls in a room like this. Was it impossibly drafty in winter? Insufferably hot in summer, with all the humidity washing off the Mississippi River? She thought about Cecilia Cinvenue's final few days in this industrial, impassive clinic.

"So, Cecilia Cinvenue was here, huh?" Hobbs asked. Something about the pristine state of the room had caused her to shed the desire for small talk. She wanted to inhabit Cecilia's life in this place, understand how the actress felt, what she saw.

"Yes, yes, Cecilia was here," Paula responded. Something about the eagerness in her response – that she hadn't cited potential HIPAA violations or patient confidentiality rules – made Hobbs suspect that Paula didn't have the same privacy concerns as did her mentor. She decided to press as far as the woman would allow.

"Was Cecilia here the day she died?" Hobbs asked.

"Yes…yes she was. So unfortunate. I cried for days when I heard the news."

"Can you think of any reason why Cecilia would have driven off of the cliff into the rock quarry that day?"

"None at all. I thought she was making great progress here."

"Can you tell us a little bit more about what goes on here? I know it's a wellness center. Can you please elaborate for us on how you treat your...patients?" Hobbs stumbled on the last word, not sure whether she should refer to them as patients or customers. Adherents? Subjects?

Paula nodded and led the detectives to a pile of yoga mats. She selected one from the top – a dark blue, rectangular piece of rubber – and placed it in the center of the room. Then she sat down, lotus-style, and waited for the detectives to follow suit.

Hobbs and Martinez both selected yoga mats and arranged themselves on the floor facing Paula. Hobbs glanced at Martinez and sensed her partner's discomfort, the tiny paunch of his belly dripping over his belt buckle. Throughout their career, they had assumed many positions and situations in the course of interviewing people, but Hobbs was sure they'd never before been arrayed on the floor like this. She and Martinez were leaning forward, stretching their limbs, staring at a perfectly-postured subject whose straight spine afforded a certain authority. After a few seconds of watching them shift and shuffle, Paula started talking.

"Well, Sparrow has devised rather unconventional methods for our clientele and that's why we're successful," she said. "Our clients don't sit around and talk about their griev-ances in a big circle. We marry the physical to the emotional. If someone has a tough childhood, they are 'reborn' in this facility. If they're addicted to drugs, we give them a regi-mented allocation in this controlled facility and slowly taper down the potency. Not cold turkey, like other facilities. If our clients are addicted to sex, we follow the ageless practice of girding the loins with a leather belt until they're able to mentally move beyond their impure impulses. If they're addicted to alcohol, we allow them to drink, but put horse-radish root powder or some other bitter spices in the concoc-tion to affect the connection within the mind. As you can probably tell, our aim to modify – to *revolutionize* – our clients' association and conditioning. As Sparrow teaches, our addictions are unnatural mechanisms that hold us back from connecting with the divine. And we can alter our addictions by changing our conditioning."

Hobbs and Martinez exchanged a look to see who would ask the next question, but Paula continued.

"And how do we connect with the divine? It's not just a physical craving we seek but mental and emotional as well. This is where Sparrow's sweat lodges and retreats are very helpful. Once our clients have curtailed their physical, their *outward*, addictions, we teach them about healing from within: how to face their shadow selves, how to confront and heal from their previous traumas, how to become connected with their spiritual egos. Oftentimes, this means self-renewing in nature, existing without distraction. You see, detectives, Sparrow's teachings deliver our clients to the most essential states of their natural being. We teach restraint, self-control, self-reliance, temperance, chastity, kindness, humility, freedom from all vices. We have tremendous success with our clients – many of whom are A-list celebrities – and we are very highly regarded."

"I'm sure you are very highly regarded," Martinez affirmed, while Hobbs looked down at her notes and allowed for a few moments of quiet before asking the next question.

"Can you tell us *exactly* what Cecilia was doing the morning she died?" she asked.

Paula smiled. "It was the same as every day before. She woke up around seven o'clock and had a wheat germ smoothie for breakfast. We meditated together and had a short detoxifying session, where Cecilia spoke about her chakras."

"Her...chakras?"

"Her energy centers. We spoke about unblocking her sacral chakra. It's located just below the belly button."

"Was she in any kind of emotional or physical distress?" Martinez asked.

"Detective, no…not at all. It was a very good session. Once we completed it, I left to take a shower in my bathroom. When I came out afterwards, Cecilia was gone. I found out the news a few hours later. It was devastating." Tears welled in the corners of Paula's eyes.

"Did you try to follow her, once you discovered she was gone?" Hobbs asked. She carefully avoided using the word *chase*, with its prejudicial implications.

"Detective, no! I wouldn't chase anyone. Our clients can come and go from this facility as they please."

"So you were the last known person to see Cecilia Cinvenue alive?"

"Well…last or second to last. My husband, Nathan, was here too that morning. He was working from home in our bedroom. He told me he made himself a cup of coffee in this pantry area…" Paula raised her left arm and made a motion towards the kitchenette. "He told me they just exchanged greetings and then he went back into the bedroom. He never saw her after that."

"We'll need to speak with Nathan as soon as possible."

"Certainly, Detective. He's working from home again today. I'll call for him."

Ten minutes later, the front door squeaked and a dark-haired, broad-shouldered man walked into the room. He approached carefully, as though weighing each step, and made pointed eye contact with each detective while shaking their hands.

"I'm Nathan Fekete," he said, and Hobbs noticed that his voice was deep, his grip was strong, and his English – similar to Paula's – was slightly accented.

"Nice to meet you, Nathan," Martinez said. "What can you tell us about Cecilia Cinvenue's last morning here? The day she died?"

Nathan crossed his arms over his chest and Hobbs noticed the bulge of biceps pressing against his tight gray t-shirt. He seemed so bulky and muscled, capable of anything, a giant when compared to the diminutive movie star.

"I can't tell you much," Nathan said. "It was the first time I'd met Cecilia. I came upstairs to fix a cup of coffee and she was here. We said a few words and then I left."

"What were those words exactly? Can you remember?"

"Umm, let's see. I think I said, 'Good morning. I'm Nathan Fekete, Paula's husband.' And then I think she said something like, 'Hi. Nice to meet you. I'm Cecilia.' Then I went over and started making my coffee and while it was heating up, I think I said something like, 'It's a beautiful day outside.' And then she said something along the lines of, 'Yes, it's very sunny.' Or: 'Yes, it is a beautiful day.' And then I got my coffee mug and I went back downstairs."

Nathan spoke in such a deliberate and studied way that Hobbs was somewhat certain they were being mocked. She figured that Nathan had prematurely decided that there was no substance in his morning conversation with Cecilia, and so was delivering the recap of their dialogue with a drawn-out lilt. Hobbs didn't care so much about his attitude, however, as about the meaning of his words. Nothing about the conversation with Nathan – as he detailed it -- would have implored Cecilia to get in her car, would have caused someone to give chase. There had to be more that he wasn't telling.

"Can we have access to your cell phone?" Hobbs asked. "Take it for a few days and then give it back to you?"

She thought that Nathan might recoil, demand to know if he was a suspect in Cecilia's murder, object to the idea of turning over a beloved device to law enforcement and demand a warrant. But instead of protesting, he simply nodded and turned it over – a sleek rectangular device with a black cover.

"Thank you," Hobbs said, and she turned it around in her hands a few times before placing it in her back pocket. The

Vetta Park's technology team would be able to determine Nathan's whereabouts on the morning of Cecilia's murder. If he had, in fact, chased her down the rock quarry, then they could reverse engineer all of it – the chase, the specious kitchenette conversation and the morning meditation with Paula. All of it was suspect.

"Am I done here?" Nathan asked. "I honestly don't have anything else to say about Cecilia. I've told you everything."

"It's very important that we figure out exactly what was going on the morning Cecilia died," Martinez said. "Can you tell us about her demeanor? How did she seem?"

Nathan shrugged. "She seemed...relaxed..."

"So, you come into the room...this famous movie star who you've never met before is in here, while your wife is taking a shower. You say 'hi' to the famous movie star, pour yourself a cup of coffee, talk about the weather and then leave the room. After you leave, this movie star decides to get in her car and drive off the cliff at high speed into a rock quarry, killing herself. Does this make sense to you?"

Hobbs left out the part about someone chasing Cecilia since – somehow – that hadn't yet been divulged. Nuggets of knowledge not yet in the public domain were of the utmost value...and had to be shielded from casual mention to potentially suggestible witnesses and suspects. The current of information needed to flow the other way.

Nathan shrugged again. "No, it doesn't make sense to me. But I've told you the truth about exactly what happened from my perspective. I can't tell you anything else. Please have my phone back to me as soon as possible." He didn't pause to ask again whether he was done, to seek their permission. With a decisive nod in both of their directions, he left the room, allowing the big entrance door to swing wildly behind him.

Paula – who had been quiet during the questioning of her husband – now stood up and wandered over to the kitchenette. She poured three glasses of ice water and guzzled down the first with only a few swallows.

"Nathan is a wonderful man," Paula said decisively. "He would never hurt anybody."

"You can understand why we're interested in the two of you," Hobbs said. "As the last two people to see Cecilia before she drove off a cliff."

Hobbs paused after that statement for dramatic effect. She wanted to emphasize that the movie star had not just killed herself but had done it in this elaborate fashion, and that being the last two people to see someone alive carried a certain weight. It automatically made them people of interest, people who knew the most, people who could point to the causalities of the morning, perhaps also people with the most to lose.

Paula stood, unmoved, her lithe body balanced against the kitchenette counter, her glass of water sweating droplets onto her fingers. She shrugged – just as her husband had done under questioning. "It's all very mysterious," she said. "And I don't understand why she would do it."

"Were there any other patients at this wellness center?" Martinez asked. "Maybe someone else who would have interacted with Cecilia during her time here?"

Paula shook her head. "No other clients were here. Under Sparrow's teachings, we only see clients on a one-to-one basis. That also differentiates us from other centers. Our clients get the maximum individualized attention, and a program that caters solely to their needs. This is why we're so successful and we have such a long waiting list..."

Martinez lifted his hand as if to truncate Paula's sales pitch. Paula's response had become mechanized, as if well-rehearsed, and it was the last thing the two detectives wanted to hear.

Hobbs took a deep breath. "We understand that before

she came out here, Cecilia had leaked a big secret of Billy Sloan's to a reporter—"

"Ah yes. Yes, Cecilia told us all about that."

"She did? Can you tell us what she said?"

The question was a longshot, an inquiry that Hobbs felt she had to ask, but was unlikely to get a response to. Most therapists and confidantes she knew would never reveal the details of their client discussions without being pushed to do so – certainly not those professionals who prided themselves on confidentiality.

But Paula wasn't like the others. She leaned upwards and stretched her torso and arms, like a ballerina adjusting her posture until it was perfect. Her face brightened while she answered.

"Yes. It's one of the first exercises of self-realization that we practice at this clinic. Discuss your constrictions regarding the act of pursuing help. You see, help for the physical body is accepted in Western culture, but mental and emotional counseling is – sadly – quite stigmatized. Cecilia was very nervous about coming here, for fear that the news would damage her reputation. She was very guarded about her public persona, even though it was simply a mask."

"So...Billy..."

"So, Cecilia told me that on a phone conversation before she left, she expressed her fears to Billy with regard to a feature piece in the *Hollywood Ledger*. She was afraid that reporter's investigations would reveal her stay with us, and as we know, she very much wanted to keep her time here a secret. She was ashamed of it, even though we told her there's no shame – only redemption – in seeking healing. Billy told Cecilia that he had made peace with a tragic incident regarding a fan from years ago, and that if Cecilia wished to talk about that with the reporter – to throw off the scent from herself – she had his blessing. Cecilia discussed this in our session on selflessness.

That when Billy released his own burdens in the mission of aiding Cecilia, he was fulfilling ascetism...that is, self-denial... and it brought him even closer to a higher spiritual plane."

"Umm." Hobbs took a moment to page through her notes, and when she glanced over at Martinez, she saw that he was doing the same. They needed to adjust to this news... delivered with deadpan monotony, but worth the weight of a gold piece. That Cecilia's admission to the reporter had been an act of altruism on Billy's part was a scenario Hobbs hadn't remotely envisioned.

It was certainly plausible...believable. Paula had no reason to lie about Cecilia's fears of being outed, her conversation with Billy. This admission placed a terminus on one of their theories – Billy as a suspect – but it also raised other questions.

"What can you tell us about this incident?" Hobbs asked.

"I only know that the gentleman involved was named Elijah Gatlin. Cecilia mentioned that Billy had set up a foundation in his name."

"Elijah Gatlin...the cancer victim?"

Paula shrugged in response and continued to stare wide-eyed at the detectives. It made sense to Hobbs that Paula wouldn't have delved further into the minutiae of Billy's troubles. Her subject was Cecilia – the striking, vice-addled, worry-stricken movie star.

This latest deliberation led Hobbs to her next question. "Is there anyone Cecilia might have been really mad at? Maybe someone she felt like she was at war with?"

Paula nodded. "Oh yes, Cecilia was extremely angry at one of the producers of a movie. I think his name was... Terry...Maloney or Mahoney? I learned this from Sparrow, quite recently, and not from Cecilia herself. Perhaps this anger would have been a grievance for us to work through with Cecilia during her time here. Unfortunately, we simply didn't get the chance to work through Cecilia's inner healing as I would have liked. We didn't have enough time."

"Do you know anything about her anger with Terry Mahoney?" Hobbs pressed.

Paula sighed. "Only that, according to Sparrow, it was a vast and immense anger, a cumbersome weight that burdened our young Cecilia. It was a boulder that she continually had to push up a mountain, only to be confronted with, time and again. You see, only when we work through our emotional states, only then can we see how we're being hindered, how we're failing to reach transcendence of the egoic mind..."

Martinez lifted his hand again and Paula paused. "It sounds like you don't know anything specific about Cecilia's beef with Terry Mahoney," he said.

Paula nodded. "Sparrow would be the source for that information."

Sparrow was a dead end – at least for the meantime. Her knowledge of privacy laws and warrants, the limitations of police interrogations, meant that Hobbs and Martinez weren't going to get to the heart of Cecilia's wrath anytime soon.

But they weren't at a total loss. There was Terry Mahoney himself – the imposing, condescending, bigwig Hollywood producer. Perhaps he thought so highly of himself that he was above condemnation, that all his decisions were appropriate and acceptable simply because they came from him. Perhaps he believed himself so above reproach that he wouldn't see the need for a lawyer. The man who seemed permanently pressed for time...perhaps Terry would answer Hobbs' queries if only to swat her away – this pestering gadfly who insisted on questioning him about Cecilia.

After they left Paula's loft, Hobbs and Martinez agreed with each other that Terry Mahoney was their next big step. "This time..." Hobbs said. "We'll need to get a lot more than four minutes of his time."

Chapter Twenty-One

Burbank, California
2021

CECILIA SAT at a patio table and waited for Terry Mahoney to finish his lunch. He was at his usual spot at his usual restaurant – a place Cecilia knew from when she'd been one of his chosen girls. The memory now seemed like it had occurred centuries ago.

Of course, Cecilia had become a different person during the intervening years. When she was one of Terry's girls, she was a drug-addicted mess – a whirling dervish of late parties and early mornings, exhaustion placated by blue, bullet-shaped pills and white powder. She had spun into the arms of Terry's companions and drank alcohol as though it was her only source of nourishment. She consumed and dabbled until she woke up the following morning, disoriented and dehydrated, clutching the covers close to her tiny body until it was time to get dressed and go home.

Now, at the age of forty-four, things were different... mostly. Six years of Sparrow's tutelage had taught Cecilia about the importance of immersing herself in nature and abandoning material possessions and superficial influences. She knew the meanings of Sparrow's teachings, even if she didn't always utilize them in practice.

But it was hard to abandon her vices altogether. For starters, Marco was always, unfailingly, an option. He would show up at her doorstep ten minutes after a phone call. He'd be breathless and tanned, muscled and eager, with a bottle of wine in one hand and a script in the other. Sparrow insisted that Marco was an emotional blockade, that he was too self-absorbed and ambitious to provide Cecilia with emotional fulfillment. But the times that Cecilia summoned Marco, she hurled herself against his body with the eagerness of a wild, famished carnivore – ignoring the warning signs that Sparrow so adamantly imparted.

Cecilia also tinkered with drugs and booze...not religiously, not like she'd done before. It wasn't an addiction anymore, she was certain. It was a choice. The time between movie roles seemed to grow longer as Cecilia got older, and she needed to coat the endless hours with a placating varnish. It wasn't an addiction but a diversion, something to complement the lonely hours of television-watching from her big, empty bed.

Sparrow was aware of these tumbles into superficiality, and she was angry about it. She threatened to fire Cecilia as a client, quoted mantras about backsliding and mind-body disassociations. Every time Cecilia ingested, snorted or quaffed, she knew what was coming. There would be a period of euphoria, followed by an insufferable vacuum. She would call Sparrow – aching and disoriented – her voice dripping with apologetic pathos. Sparrow would come over and nurse Cecilia back to health, all the while lecturing the movie star on her choices.

During these moments, Cecilia always delivered apologies

and promises – not just to her spiritual guru but to herself. Awash in her own bodily misery, barely able to endure the physical withdrawal symptoms and the guilt and shame that accompanied her decisions, Cecilia would resolve never to make the mistake again. At the time, she even believed her shaky assurances. Sometimes her periods of sobriety lasted months or years. From 2018 until 2020, Cecilia did not have a single drink; she didn't snort or inhale a single drug; she was entirely celibate. Then the global Covid pandemic materialized, the entertainment industry fell briefly into a dormant stasis, and Cecilia assumed all her previous bad habits. Staying clean was much harder than she could have ever thought.

But 2021 brought with it a sliver of fresh hope. It wasn't just that vaccines were available, but that everything that had been immobilized during the pandemic appeared to be coming alive once again. It was a renaissance of sorts.

This was true for the film industry as well. Once again, Terry Mahoney would be helming a big-budget, action-adventure movie. The working title was *Thieves of Stone and Ashes*, with principal filming to take place in Croatia, Italy and Dubai.

Cecilia's agent, Anita, had vaguely mentioned the film, and that the studio was looking for an established actresses to play the lead female protagonist. Cecilia thought herself perfect for the role. She was as *established* as any other actress, a quick-limbed runner, a solid marksman, an athlete. Like many other actresses, Cecilia was a shapeshifter; she could be a lithe, beaky bird of a woman or a toned, barefaced ass-kicker. She could be both at once. And she had worked well with Terry Mahoney before. After all, *Soldier of Payback* had garnered hundreds of millions of dollars at the worldwide box office, and that was back in 2000. Without question, Cecilia Cinvenue was the right person for this role.

The problem was, Terry Mahoney didn't see it that way.

He didn't even afford Anita the time it would take to explain his difference of opinion. Someone in his office handed down the judgment to Anita's secretary: *not interested.*

This seemed to rest perfectly fine with Anita. She delivered the rejection to Cecilia as preface to a litany of roles the woman *could* audition for. These were minor characters and backup players...women whose one-liners roasted the comedic central figure, women whose twenty-five-year-old daughters commanded the scripts.

Cecilia was not ready to accept subjugation, so convinced was she that *this particular* role was made for her. But Terry Mahoney had long since stopped returning her calls. In fact, she hadn't seen the man since his arrival at her front doorstep that day back in 2015 – impatient, insistent, with Sparrow's business card in hand.

What Cecilia did have was a certain knowledge of Terry's consistency...that when he was in LA and otherwise unoccupied, he ate lunch at a large Italian-American restaurant in Burbank...one whose outdoor seating spilled onto patios and terraces, and whose wrought-iron railings were festooned with Christmas lights regardless of time of year.

When Cecilia thought she saw Terry's hefty frame move through the curtained interior, she pounced. Inside the restaurant, she caught him on his way out of the restroom. He took one look at her and threw his head back, eyes synchronously rolled to the top of his lids. He huffed out, "Oh Lord," and threw his hands up.

"Terry...I'm sorry..." Cecilia said.

"You're here to talk to me about *Thieves*, and baby girl, as I told your agent, it ain't you, honey. The studio doesn't want you and I don't want you." When Terry talked, his blonde hair seemed to shift in a subtle choreograph, the wisps tapping at the bottom of his neck.

Cecilia shook her head. "But it *could* be me. If you gave me the chance. Just let me read for you, for the casting agent, for the studio…"

"Why do you think you can do this? Because of *Soldier of Payback*?"

"Yes! That was a huge hit! And we could do it again!"

"Cecilia…" Terry was staring at her intently now, more sharply than he'd ever done before. Even when he was a mentor and she was his muse, his gaze always seemed to lope sideward, assessing the others in the room. But now he was looking at her so directly, she could see the dark pupils of his eyes, encircled by cornflower blue. If she focused on the color, she could train her thoughts to see innocence, humanity, instead of vitriol…instead of the meaning and manner of his words.

"Cecilia, that was *twenty years ago*."

"I know, and I've only improved, during those years. I'm fitter than I was then, more athletic. I'm more in control, as you know. I have so many more movies under my belt…so much more experience. Anita told me that you wanted someone who's a known entity with the public, and Terry, *I am a known entity*."

Terry sighed. "Cecilia, we're looking for an actress in her late twenties or early thirties. What are you…forty…."

"I'm forty-four. But I know I look and feel a lot younger. Terry, give me a chance to prove myself."

"Cecilia, I don't know how to tell you any other way. The answer is *no*. And since no one else is going to tell you, I'm going to be the one. You're expired, okay? I need to get horny sixteen-year-old boys into movie seats. You only mattered when people wanted to fuck you. You're not that hot anymore. No one is asking Anita to make a twelve-month calendar with your pictures so they can pass it around the locker room, okay? That should be your first clue. And if you think that more *experience* is what we're after, baby girl, then this world isn't made for you."

Cecilia remained frozen in her stance while Terry whirled past her, presumably back to his seat. He had said everything he needed to say, and there was no longer a need for convincing. Cecilia understood as though Terry had entered her very soul, as though he'd evaluated and assessed her, and delivered his honest verdict with heartbreaking clarity.

She felt sweaty and shivery, and when she looked down, she could see that her legs were shaking – narrow, willowy stalks that struggled to sustain an emaciated frame. Once Cecilia was able to move again, she raced home in her car and poured her thoughts into her diary. She wrote tough-sounding epithets like: *This is war! Some people are the absolute worst people and deserve to be obliterated from this planet. It is ON!*

But the truth…the underlying, unwritten certainty…was too upsetting to even be put into words. The truth made her sob into her hands once the journal had proven a futile source of consolation. She poured herself straight vodka, served with a painkiller on a gold-rimmed platter. It felt indulgent, gratuitous. Any ingestion felt like undeserved gluttony.

Cecilia finally saw things for what they were. That years of experience, self-analysis and sound judgment meant absolutely nothing. The industry wanted a fresh, smooth face, a young starlet whose gravity-defying, unaged aesthetics sold magazines and calendars. All the exertion in the world couldn't erase Cecilia's birthdate. She had spent so long working on herself, thinking it meant something.

And could she even blame Terry Mahoney? He was just parroting a basic axiom of nature. Was it nature or culture? Could she blame Terry Mahoney for wanting to sell movie tickets? Profit-seeking investors were surely pressing him for a payoff. Could she blame Terry for the gender and age disparities in the industry, in the modern workforce at large? Could she blame him for relegating older women to supporting roles? Or was he just a cogwheel in this ruthless industry? In her journal, she had lashed out against Terry because the man was realizable, knowable, and frank. It was too awesome for Cecilia – in her alcoholic and drug-fired stupor – to truly consider the power imbalances that plagued her world. A world that, as Terry claimed, wasn't made for her. Not anymore.

Chapter Twenty-Two

St. Louis Lambert International Airport
September 28, 2022

ANNOUNCEMENTS BLARED over the loudspeakers at Lambert International Airport, while Martinez, Hobbs and Nick sat at their gate and watched the hustle of proximate and distant travelers. In Hobbs' view, they were lucky that a prominent film festival was to take place in New York City at the end of the month. It drew Terry Mahoney back stateside, made him accessible to them. Hobbs felt relief that she didn't have to beg Weaver for permissions and budget extensions to visit far-flung places she'd only ever seen on a map. She didn't have to fret over leaving Nick to his own devices for an extended period of time or deciding whether to pull him from school.

New York City was a three-hour plane ride. It was the city of dreams, a dense archipelago comprised of islands and boroughs. On one such borough – Manhattan – a stately, imperial building on the city's Upper West Side housed the annual New York Film Festival. Hobbs knew that Terry Mahoney would be there presenting a new release. She imagined his relaxed smile, radiating towards a rapt audience. She imagined his face, bathed in halogen-washed light, soaking up all the adulation that moviegoers, fans and industry insiders had to offer.

Their plan was to encounter Terry at the end of the evening. Once he'd presented and spoken, posed for pictures and given sound bites, they would confront him near the exit. They would do so quietly, with quick flaunts of their badges and hushed voices – so as not to arouse the suspicions of nearby reporters.

But first, they had to get there. At the terminal, Hobbs and Martinez looked out of a fingerprint-smeared window while mechanized voices droned into the din. Outside, parallel jetways stretched towards rain-soaked pathways, like legs of a spider. Somewhat disturbingly, there were no planes attached to any of the jetways. Perhaps the arrival of a massive gray storm cloud had something to do with the lack of airplanes.

"I don't think we're taking off any time soon," Martinez said, and he nodded vaguely towards the foreboding weather on the other side of the window. "I think they're saying to check the app for updates."

Hobbs looked at Nick, who was focused on a game on his phone. The boy's head was propped in its usual position: neck craned downward, ears wrapped in noise-canceling headphones.

"Hey," Hobbs nudged her nephew. "Can you look up this flight on the app and tell us what's going on?"

She closed her eyes and lolled her head back, relaxed her body as if preparing for the long haul. Diverging flight announcements fused into one garbled missive, as if spoken in a foreign language. Still if she could close her eyes for long enough, breathe deeply enough, the announcements shifted into a kind of white noise…background hums and chants that hastened her descent into sleep.

"Hey," Nick said and nudged her back. "I think there's an announcement about the flight. Here's the phone."

"I'm drifting out," Hobbs said, her eyes still closed. "Read it to me."

"No, no. You should read it for yourself."

"Nick. Is the plane we're supposed to board on fire? Have the pilots announced a strike? Are we expecting a monsoon?"

"Uh, no. Nothing like that. I don't think"

"Then read it to me. I'm too tired to open my eyes."

"Um. Okay. Um...Fl...Fla...Fly...Flight 2035...has been delu...dela...de-something...due to bad wet...bad wetty... bad...wait a second...bad weeth...wait...ok...bad wet...bad something...con...continent...confirm...conduct? Whatever. I don't know. *I don't care! Whatever!*"

Nick hurled his phone onto the floor and jetted out of his seat. He took several large paces towards the commercial corridor and then Hobbs lost sight of him. She figured that he was blowing off steam and would return sooner or later. Not just because there were limited places a fifteen-year-old could decamp to in an airport, but because he had left his cell phone behind. This most vital of organs, this treasured device...Nick would come back for it within the half hour.

In the meantime, Hobbs raised the phone from the floor and read the display. *Flight 5082 has been delayed due to bad weather conditions in the St. Louis area.*

"Looks like we'll be delayed for a while," she said to Martinez.

"Um. Yeah," Martinez responded, and when Hobbs looked at him, she could see that his face looked grayish in the airport light, his eyes were lowered.

Hobbs ran her thumb over Nick's phone and said nothing. She and Martinez sat there for a while, as though they'd just seen a ghost, some type of sinister apparition. This phantom loomed over them while they separately pondered what they both knew. When a woman appeared before them – mussed gray hair, St. Louis Cardinals shirt in vivid red, they almost didn't notice.

"You two look like the bearers of bad news!" the woman remarked. "Is it the flight? Has it been canceled?"

Martinez took a few moments before answering. "Uh, no ma'am. It's just delayed due to weather. I'm sure the flight will take off soon."

The older woman nodded at Martinez and walked away...past open backpacks, cell phone cords and fast-food wrappers on her way to the gate agent.

"It's not the flight," Hobbs repeated to herself. And then she saw her nephew out of the corner of her eye. Nick was seated alone at an adjacent gate, his bangs drooped over narrow eyes, face red-swollen and tear-stained. The sight of him made Hobbs' heart clench, her eyes well. He was the picture of a boy navigating a complex world, the closed, padlocked doors in his future as yet unseen.

What had been canceled as they sat at the airport gate on that blustery morning? Not a flight that was simply delayed, still sending hordes of people into frenzied phone calls to colleagues and family members.

For Hobbs, it was the cessation of a long-held dream – that anything was possible with hard work and a positive attitude. It was a belief – which now seemed so sanguine, so naive, that her nephew could turn his life around.

Perhaps Nick didn't know it yet but Hobbs knew. Literacy was the conduit for American consumerism, the gateway for upward mobility. It was an assumed acquisition, a commonality that everyone – even those at the very basement of the economic strata – seemed to possess.

Without literacy, Nick was a child without a future. The more Hobbs watched her nephew rub his fingers across his puffy, reddened eyes in his airport chair, the more her heart sunk. As she observed him, she realized that he had known all along. This knowledge of his deficiency fueled his rage against authority figures, a child fighting alone against the scaffolding of a fissured education system, a school *that did nothing for him.*

He had tried to tell her but she hadn't understood. Just one of many unwitting adults in his life, she now realized. At the time, she'd been too trusting of conventional structures, too confident about the way things worked. A child as boisterous and creative as Nicholas Hobbs – the kid with the loud voice and full-framed stature – how could he fall through the cracks? When did he start to fall behind and did anyone see it or try to remediate it?

A crackling announcement sounded over the loudspeaker and the gate agent updated their departure time to within ten minutes.

Hobbs could sense the collective exhalation around her, could hear the high-pitched timbre of the voice next to her relaying the good news to the person on the other end of the phone call. "Thank goodness!" the woman said. "Oh, I'm so glad!"

There was relief all around her – blanketing her – and all Hobbs could feel was numb. She weakly smiled at Martinez and gave Nick a head motion that indicated she wanted him back at her area to begin boarding the flight. In the absence of guidance and insight, she was still able to provide the kid with direction. It was the least – and the most – she could do.

WHEN THE PLANE FINALLY DEPARTED ST. LOUIS, THEY WERE two hours behind schedule, and taxiway traffic added another thirty minutes to the tardiness. When they finally reached New York, Hobbs, Martinez and Nick scurried through LaGuardia airport, their backpacks swinging from their shoulders like off-tempo metronomes.

Hobbs almost appreciated the lateness – and subsequent need to rush – as it allowed them to focus on the most immediate logistics. There were traffic patterns and taxi queues to consider, optimal routes to take into Manhattan, the stirrings of big city life outside their snow-stained windows.

At the hotel, as soon as they had their three separate room keys, Martinez touched the back of Hobbs' elbow and asked for a few minutes of her time. She sent Nick up to his room and sat across from Martinez at a window-adjacent booth at the edge of the lobby. He looked forlorn, his moustache downier than usual, the wrinkles more pronounced.

"I want to talk to you about Nick," Martinez said.

"Oh…yeah, sure. What about him?" Hobbs knew exactly why Martinez wanted to talk about Nick and yet she didn't want to speak about it at all. Her fear wasn't that speaking would give life to the issue; she was a realist and she knew there was no rationalizing or diminishing what they both had witnessed. It was that Nick's illiteracy felt like a shock to her, a slap that she had yet to digest. It was too young and raw, a red-speckled tumor in her heart, and she didn't yet have the right words for it.

Martinez took a deep breath. "I think he might have dyslexia, or a similar reading disorder."

"Well, I mean…sure." Hobbs tried to laugh but it sounded like a chirp; she tried to seem unconcerned but it came out sounding forced. Glancing outside, she sought endorsement from the crowds of pedestrians – some of whom were merely feet from the window. She thought at least one of the New Yorkers might look over at them – these two figures in a fluo-rescent-lit hotel chamber – but none of the passersby paid them any notice. They were too absorbed in their own matters.

"You say *sure*, but do you really know what I'm saying?"

Hobbs looked away from the window and back at Martinez. She stared at him with piercing annoyance. "Yes, Ray, I get what you're saying. The boy has a reading issue. Yes, I saw that at the airport. I'm not an idiot. I just don't know what to do about it. I've never before encountered a fifteen-year-old who hadn't learned to read. I mean, maybe he has to go back and repeat some grades. I guess I'll hire a tutor for him to get him up to grade level. That's all I can think of."

She could hear it in her voice – the annoyance layered over anxiety. Everything about Nick's earlier attempt to read violated her basic understanding of milestones, schools, grades and parenting. She felt like she suddenly didn't know or understand the younger generation, couldn't rely on the basic tenets of ninth grade adolescence that she'd believed were a given.

His palms flattened on the table, Martinez stayed quiet. When a minute had passed, he pressed his hands together as though he were conducting a physics experiment, as though he were praying.

"Roberta…" Martinez said softly, and Hobbs noticed that he used her first name, that his normally chaotic cadence was slow and measured.

"Yes. What?"

"This is more than just not having learned how to read. What I'm telling you is that I think Nick may have a reading *disability*."

Hobbs was quiet for a moment and thought about Martinez's words. Which was worse: having never learned to read or having a reading disability? It didn't take long for Hobbs to render her verdict: the latter was worse. If Nick had simply never learned to read, that could be an indictment against an incompetent school system, but it said nothing of the individual. It meant that Nick was malleable, fixable. That she could make a few calls, hire a tutor, and voila…like a baking recipe that had finally contained the correct ingredients, there was a path from effort to solution.

But a reading disability was an individual – as well as a collective – denunciation. Hobbs didn't know much about reading disabilities, but what she did know made her anxious.

This word…dyslexia…this diagnosis…it suggested constant remediation and lifelong struggles. It meant this basic human achievement…reading…might be forever elusive for her nephew. She couldn't think about that, couldn't consider Ray's casual suggestion…so uncomplicated when the person in question wasn't a loved one. She pushed back.

"Ray, you're not a doctor or a reading specialist. You're a detective. What makes you feel qualified to diagnose Nick with dyslexia?"

"I'm not diagnosing him; I'm suggesting it, and the reason I feel qualified is that I have dyslexia, myself."

"Wait. What?" Hobbs said softly. She sat back and studied her partner. She canvassed their years together and tried to recall instances of Martinez reading. Her mind produced grainy images of her partner slumped over a sheaf of paperwork, eyes darting and spine stooped. She saw him punching buttons into a keyboard, eyes flitting across a monitor. Paperwork was a necessary accessory to police work, and Martinez had always accepted the drudgery without pause or complaint. "I didn't know you had dyslexia," she finally said. "I think I would have known."

"Oh, well, we blend in quite well with the population," Martinez said with a smile.

"Ray…seriously…"

"I am being serious. Yes, I have dyslexia, and I still have trouble reading, but as you can see, I do okay. I've had a lot of interventions throughout my life. I've been lucky. I wouldn't be the guy you see before you today if not for that. And I'm telling you, just hiring a tutor isn't going to cut it for Nick. You need to get him tested."

"Where? At the high school?"

Martinez shook his head. "I don't think so. There's a school in St. Louis called The Patton School. It's for smart kids with learning disabilities. I went there on scholarship many years ago. You should give them a call when you get back to Vetta Park."

Hobbs nodded and said that she would, then curved her head until she was looking around the hotel lobby again. She saw guests milling around as usual, perching towards or away from the check-in area and the concierge. No one noticed the twosome sitting by the window, partners but not a couple, one of whom looked like she'd just been given a terminal diagnosis.

"Roberta..." Martinez said softly again, and Hobbs brought her gaze back to look at him. She wondered if he could see the physical indications of her broken heart... perhaps a pallid face, or mottled collar line.

"Roberta, it isn't so bad," Martinez said.

Hobbs shook her head. "It's just...every time I think the kid's going to be ok...I get fresh new evidence that he's *not* going to be ok. That his whole life is going to be a struggle for him."

"Roberta, yes, he might struggle, but Nick is going to be just fine...Listen to me...Nick is a good kid at heart. He just probably doesn't learn the way classes are taught in a traditional classroom setting...just like I didn't. It's not so bad, Roberta; it's just *different*. There are so many successful people in the world with dyslexia. It can be a huge burden but it can also be his biggest gift. Trust me, Nick is going to be alright. He's a tough kid...especially if he gets the help he needs now."

"Well, sure, now I'll do everything I can. I'll call that school...The Patton School...and get him tested, and I guess we can go from there. But why has it taken this long, Ray? This kid is in *ninth* grade...in high school! How could he get to this point without anyone speaking up about him? Without anyone realizing? Ninth grade and he can't even read?"

"I have a feeling it's more common than we think, unfortunately." Martinez said. And Hobbs nodded and thought to herself, while the cadence of arrivers and departers created a din of rushed voices around them. She thought about Nick's absent mother, his distracted father. She thought about an overworked school system in rural Missouri, a punitive-oriented system in Vetta Park.

Martinez's next words floated through her like an incisive salve – words that married what she felt with what she knew but hadn't yet admitted to herself.

"His whole life, Nick never had anyone looking out for him," Martinez said, his lips crooked into a vague smile. "But now he does."

Chapter Twenty-Three

Pacific Palisades, California
2022

DESPAIR EVENTUALLY CAME FOR CECILIA. It wasn't a morose, bottomless pit – not as she'd felt in the unsufferable weeks after her parents' death. Rather, it was a slow roll – the type of emptiness that inhabited her stomach and then moved northward – to the heart, the ears, the eye, the brain. It was a methodical virus that planted taunts in her mind. She wasn't worthy. She wasn't valuable. She wasn't enough.

Cecilia knew that her long periods of inertia were the catalyst for her sadness. Big, gaping holes had to be filled with something. There was no human connection in her sweat-bathed bed linens. Not even the California sun could leach through blinds that were closed and covered with darkening shades.

She sat alone in her bed and smoked cigarettes, watched daytime television and thumbed through magazines without pausing to read any of the text. When lonely times became insufferable, she called Marco.

Marco Bagnetti – the one constant in her life. He wasn't a

confidante or source of inspiration. Despite his affinity for poetry and classic literature, he wasn't interested in growing with Cecilia. He didn't want to teach her or learn from her, didn't want to create a bubble where the two of them could fuse into a couple.

In contrast, after all these years, he still seemed to value Cecilia to the extent that she could open doors for him, career-wise. And he was more than willing to maintain a physical relationship, despite the fact that their lovemaking had transformed into routine machinations of two people who actually cared very little for each other.

Cecilia hated her dependence on Marco, hated that she always rang him when the loneliness of her bedroom got to be too stifling. She hated that he always, invariably appeared, as if he were a mechanized automaton rather than a sentient being. His dependability caused her to hire him as her personal assistant. She thought she would appreciate his accessibility – the readiness with which he tended to her errands. But after a few months, she realized the pointlessness of all of it.

What was Marco supposed to do, except respond to her texts in his stilted English, read her (dwindling) fan mail and stand by on reserve in case she invited him into the bedroom? The gaping holes of her lack of work – lack of purpose – were only intensified by this eager monitor of her life.

"Dump him," Sparrow told Cecilia one morning. Cecilia was sitting poolside, her hands occupied with a cigarette and a ceramic ashtray, while Sparrow paced in the freshly mowed grass at the edge of the mansion's back lawn.

"You have to dump him," Sparrow repeated, after Cecilia said nothing. "He's keeping you from your sacred nature. He's disrupting your vibrant energy field, Cecilia. It's because of Marco that you haven't worked…that you're not working right now. He's a crutch – a parasite. He's feeding off you. Don't you see that?"

Cecilia breathed a cloud of smoke into the air and didn't respond.

"He's slept with two of your friends – that we know of, Cecilia. And he's using you to try to advance his Hollywood career. How do you not see that?"

Cecilia narrowed her now-watery eyes. She saw only the drifting billow of smoke right in front of her. It formed a cloud – obscuring the pristine Los Angeles panorama, sullying the pure California air. When the wind wafted her smoke cloud away, Cecilia puffed again. She felt like she was making an art of the practice.

"You can keep ignoring me, Cecilia, but I'm telling the truth and you know it. You need to fire Marco as your assistant. And you need to dump him too."

Cecilia looked over at Sparrow and studied the woman. She inhaled and puffed, drawing out the cycle, blowing her air towards Sparrow even though the wind invariably carried it in another direction.

Sparrow looked intense and over-clothed. It was a seventy-five-degree day and she was wearing a tunic and long robe, pearly beads that stretched below her belly button, rings on each finger, rings in her nose and lips, patterned tights and threadbare sandals.

"Why are you ignoring me, Cecilia?" Sparrow asked. "What obstacle before you is preventing you from listening?"

Cecilia finally spoke. She quashed her cigarette and stood up, with a promptness so swift, it caused a few moments of lightheadedness. Then she said, "Come on," and led Sparrow into the house and towards the front door.

While she was escorting her spiritual guru out, she knew that everything the woman had said was completely true. Still, she couldn't bear to hear it, to face it, and when she was finally in the circle driveway at the front of her house, she delivered the verdict that stunned both of them. Not only wouldn't she part with Marco, but it was really Sparrow who was the source of Cecilia's problems.

"I don't think we can continue this," Cecilia said. "I need to fire you as my spiritual advisor. It's been great and all, but all good things come to an end, I guess." Cecilia then turned around and closed the door on a stunned Sparrow Shearwater.

Back inside the house, she didn't even shed a tear. She knew that Sparrow would clamor to get back into her good graces, that she would allege dissociated fugue or sophisticated brainwashing or leave voicemails claiming some other spiritual mumbo jumbo to recoup her most famous – most lucrative – client. But Cecilia knew what Sparrow didn't; their relationship was officially over.

Perhaps this move seemed sudden or cruel, but Cecilia needed to break the association – like severing an artery. For some reason, she needed to go deeper into the well – to taste the very flavor of desolation – and that meant dissolving her lifelines, her dependencies.

In her kitchen, white powders that resembled sugar taunted her from their plastic baggies. Tawny-brown tinctures summoned her to distill them into plastic cups. And on her cell phone, a certain ambitious Italian actor was calling her repeatedly and beckoning her to pick up.

It had to end. Cecilia had gone too far this time – taken on too much. Marco was not one to pull back, to try to save Cecilia from her depravities, and for this reason, she kept him around. But he wasn't good for her, and she knew that too.

The days blended into nights without the advent of clocks, of sunshine, of normal circadian rhythms. There was no structure to any of Cecilia's indulgences. *Breakfast*, *lunch* and *dinner* meant nothing to the evaporating actress.

Marco was there beside her, rolling herbs and papers into joints, pouring drinks and giving her lascivious, sideways smiles as they lounged in her jacuzzi. And sometimes he wasn't. Sometimes she awoke from a stupor to find him gone. She would stumble around the nest of tossed clothes and expended papers until she got too tired, collapsed into her bed and waited for him to return.

The timeframes of Marco's departures – was it minutes? Hours? Days? – Cecilia spent self-medicating and filling her mind with reality television. Anything to take her awareness off her throbbing head, her stinging, smarting body. She was engaging in the exact *opposite* of Sparrow's careful teachings, indulging in everything the spiritual leader had advised to avoid.

But it had to end, and Cecilia knew it too, even without Sparrow's homilies ringing in her ear. During one of Marco's disappearances, Cecilia couldn't dodge the string of annoying texts and unanswered calls from acquaintances. Marco had copied Cecilia's contacts list and was foisting himself on her connections – using his lover as a means to a profitable end.

She had discarded him before and she could do it again – this despite her weakened physical state, her garbled words and gauzy thoughts.

When Marco returned, Cecilia shouted at him that they were *over*! Unlike Sparrow, Marco didn't protest, didn't argue, didn't even appear surprised. He gathered his belongings while whispering Italian epithets, gestured vaguely at Cecilia and then left. A gust of wind – or perhaps Marco's passive-aggressive pretense – slammed the front door hard behind him. Unlike the first time, this time, he set off without yelling about his inevitable return.

Then it was just Cecilia and her drug-induced paralysis. Cecilia's diet of drugs and alcohol could only go on for so long. Her senses couldn't take the sledgehammer to the brain, the constant swirl of motion even when she was lying in bed, the sweat flashes, the dry mouth. It was as if she'd become a shell of a person; her habits had stripped her of her humanness and her body was protesting.

But who could help Cecilia now? She had no one. In previous years, she'd have called Sparrow Shearwater, but now that was a sailed ship – as final a verdict as the door she'd closed on her former advisor.

Still, Sparrow had said something about a rehab center. Cecilia remembered it in sentence fragments, pieces of lucidity that floated into her mind when she thought about an escape hatch from her debauched life. Yes, there was a discreet wellness center in the middle of the country, Cecilia was certain about it.

Only when her unalloyed thoughts returned to her, when the shock of her latest bender had burned through her body, did Cecilia remember where in the notes app of her phone she'd stored the information.

Shearwater Enterprises, LLC

Vetta Park, Missouri

There was a phone number too, and when Cecilia dialed it, a soft-spoken voice picked up after two rings.

"Wellness center," the voice said, and Cecilia felt those two words flood her body as though they were magical elixirs, already repairing the ailing woman.

"Are you associated with Sparrow Shearwater?" Cecilia asked, and then she listened as the accented healer described the nuances of practicing under Shearwater's tutelage and their commonplace ownership agreement.

"But, if I came to your center for treatment, would you have to tell Sparrow Shearwater that I did?"

"Not if you didn't want me to," the woman said, and to Cecilia, this was another current of relief, words of pure magic delivered by a sorceress. The woman introduced herself as Paula, and she assured Cecilia of her commitment to secrecy, of her adherence to the principles governed by Sparrow's teachings, of her ability to enlist Cecilia as a client the following week.

Cecilia didn't need to hear anything else. When she ended the phone call with Paula, she sobbed with relief, hugging her starved body while she quavered. Despite all her poor decisions, all her hastily amputated relationships, all her noxious bludgeons to the body, relief was coming. She just had to get to Vetta Park, Missouri – wherever that was – and make it happen.

TWO DAYS BEFORE CECILIA'S DEPARTURE, ANITA LIVINGSTON called.

"Cecilia! They want to do an article about you!" Anita said. Her voice was feathery, eager, and it reminded Cecilia of attachment to the living. For days, the actress had been holed up in her house as if waiting out a storm, trudging through her ornately furnished rooms as if wading in a soup of pathos. And here was Anita, brimming with life, announcing an upcoming interview as though it were a roadmap to success… to a rightful reinstatement.

"I don't know if I'm in the right headspace to speak with a reporter," Cecilia said, and then she mentioned – with nebulous equivocality – that she was taking a trip and would be unavailable for a while. She said that she was in a period of uncertainty and unaware of her future. It reminded Cecilia of the time she had floated the notion of going to college – back when her career was red-hot. She felt then as she felt now – a rickety mass of inexact constitution, a wavering, ignorant mind. She had been nineteen years old then, and now she was forty-four – a stunning arc of a lifetime in between, and yet, she still had no idea what she was destined for. All she knew was the immediate future – she had to get to rehab and get her head straight. She had to stop indulging and self-sabotaging. She knew that at least.

"Cecilia, if you want a career to come back to, you need to do this interview. Don't tell the journalist that you're in a bad place emotionally. They don't need to know about any of it. Look, if you plan to go off the grid for a while, just say you're taking a big trip with some friends...somewhere exotic, somewhere remote. And make sure to emphasize that you're *open to new opportunities* when you get back. You'd love to try comedy. Highlight your skills. What am I saying? I don't need to tell you any of this. You're a veteran. You've got this."

Cecilia agreed to the interview and ended the call. She took a shower and let the water's warm beads drift off of her while revisiting the conversation. What was more laughable, that Anita had suggested friends? None existed anymore – certainly not the gaggles of midlife women that Anita had envisioned...their hairlines held back with bandanas, backpacking packs adhered to their bodies, eyes floodlit with the promise of adventure.

Was it preposterous that Anita had suggested a foray into comedy? Anita was forever seeking new paths for the stalwart actress, while Cecilia clung to what she knew. She could cry and lament, deliver provoking soliloquies and perform low-impact acrobatics only with the help of a stunt double. Comedy was the furthest thing from Cecilia's skillset.

And how about that skillset? What could Cecilia actually do...except for act? She couldn't speak any other languages. She couldn't dance, couldn't hold a beat, carry a tune or play an instrument. Her entire professional life was funneled into one single vocation that was simultaneously trying to push her out.

And yet, as Cecilia toweled off and slunk into her nightgown – an ivory rag of cotton that silhouetted her frame – she knew she would have to act her heart out during this interview. She couldn't bear to disclose her upcoming stay at a wellness center, to risk the scorn of a devoted fan base who somehow loved her without delving too deeply into the details. They loved a lighthearted, flush-faced Cecilia...one who laughed easily and lived happily in a lovely world.

Cecilia looked around her colossal master bathroom and could see that the world she inhabited was, indeed, lovely. It consisted of the brown, rugged-sloped Santa Monica mountains, visible from her porcelain tub. It consisted of walk-in closets filled to the brim with designer wear, sink basins crowded with expensive makeup and jewelry. It consisted of a woman at the center of the room, blonde-haired and wide-eyed, with perfect skin and body to die for. It consisted of a woman who was completely lost.

BILLY SLOAN WAS THE NEXT PERSON TO CALL. "I'M GETTING married!" he told Cecilia joyfully. His voice was so loud and exultant, Cecilia could practically feel it gust through the house...a house it was hard to believe he had once occupied.

"I'm really happy for you. Congratulations!" Cecilia said. But she could tell that her salutations sounded flat – a terrible actor reading a stale script. "So, Lana's the one, huh?"

"Yes, she's it. She's everything," Billy said, and then proceeded to list Lana's set of traits and unique charms – the qualities that made him certain about what he'd suspected from the moment he saw Lana Ainsley across the fitness room floor.

If Billy was trying to convince Cecilia, she needed no further explanation. The man was clearly in love – from the seraphic anecdotes to the rising lilt in his voice. It was an exhilaration she had never witnessed in the five years he'd lived with her.

When the conversation got quiet, Cecilia tried to think of something to say but came up empty. She didn't want to press for any details about the nuptials: time, date, place, dress designer. She didn't want to think about the proposal: Billy on one knee, of sober expression and vulnerable heart, his fingers wrapped around a velvet box, from which a giant diamond surely shimmered. She didn't want to think about Lana Ainsley's gleeful response, the way the young woman must have jumped and shrieked, the plans she was surely making for a euphoric future.

Billy cleared his throat and said, "Hey, Cecilia, I've been meaning to call you for a little while. It's not just to tell you about the engagement. I also wanted to tell you that I'm really sorry."

"Sorry? For what?"

"I'm sorry, all those years ago...I know..." His voice trailed off and he sighed. "I didn't...love you the way you wanted me to. I didn't feel the way you felt about me."

They were both silent again and Cecilia didn't care to fill it the way she typically would. She didn't want to scrape at topics and rejoinders that would put Billy at ease over his confession. Was it worse that her secret of loving him was entirely obvious to him at the time? Or that her love for Billy Sloan went entirely unrequited? Or was it worse that he was now apologizing for it – in the most awkward, demeaning way? He had just uttered an apology for his lack of feelings for Cecilia, enveloped in his engagement announcement with another woman. Billy deserved the silence.

But he broke it after a tediously long minute. "Well, I just want you to know that I enjoyed living with you, and I appreciate how you helped me out. I hope you're doing okay."

And then the well broke, and Cecilia poured forth with everything that *wasn't* okay with her. Her voice was visceral, strained, as she catalogued all of the ills in her life. It was only because Billy had evoked *appreciation*, had suggested *wellness*, that she felt compelled to set the record straight. She mentioned her addictions, her loneliness, and her plans to imminently depart for a rehab facility in nowhere, Missouri. And – lest he laud her recuperative efforts with characteristic optimism – Cecilia mentioned that *The Hollywood Ledger* would soon be doing a story on her.

"My agent insists that I cooperate and have the interview before I go," Cecilia wailed. "And they're going to interview people I know, and before long, someone will mention drugs and sex and rehab. Or maybe I'll mess up and mention rehab, instead of lying and saying I'm going *away with friends*, like my agent wants me to. And then word will get out and I'll be so ashamed, Billy. Even more over than I already am. If that's possible."

"Cecilia…" Billy said, and Cecilia squeezed her eyes closed and rested her forehead on the palm of her hand. In that position, immobile and unseeing, she imagined her name the way Billy had uttered it. It sounded soft and smooth, the downy blanket she used to snuggle under when she was younger. She wanted him to say her name again – not from wanton lust but from affection. She could imagine that it meant more even though it was only an utterance – spoken in lieu of a caring response.

But Billy surprised Cecilia with what he eventually said. "You helped me with my secret so many years ago, and now I'm going to help you with yours. Tell the reporter about me. About Elijah," he said.

"Billy…you know I would never…"

"No, I want you to. I'm ready to face the music about it. I'm not hiding from my past anymore. I've even spoken with Elijah's widow about it and gotten her blessing. Tell *The Hollywood Ledger* that Elijah hung himself after climbing my gate and confronting me on my doorstep. That'll open up a dialogue about superfans and celebrities. It'll be like catnip. It'll run for days. No one will care that you're in rehab, trust me."

Her eyes still closed, Cecilia shook her head. "That's really kind of you."

"Well…it's been taking up space in my brain for so long now, I've got to let it out. I need to live authentically. And I've been thinking about how to come clean about it, and I think this is the perfect way. So, don't look at it as a favor I'm doing for you. See it as a favor you can do for me."

"Thanks Billy," Cecilia whispered, and they ended the call shortly after.

Cecilia threw herself onto her four-poster bed mattress and rested her eyes on the frame's mahogany pattern, recalling the phone conversation. She knew that she would divulge Billy's secret when the reporter called – but couldn't figure out whether this would benefit her or him, both or neither. She knew she was supposed to feel gratitude for Billy's request, but all she felt was grief. His was a gesture of kindness – despite what he said – but it was also born from a lack of love, of lust, of mutual adoration. It was the gesture one made when bidding farewell…when moving on to bigger and better, and leaving one's previous world behind.

MARGARET SCOTT FROM *THE HOLLYWOOD LEDGER* PHONED Cecilia the day before the actress left for rehab. Cecilia had been busying herself with at-home projects – cleaning the kitchen, tidying the bathrooms, ensuring closed window shutters and locked doors. When Margaret called, Cecilia looked down at her phone, took a deep breath and answered.

"Hello. This is Cecilia," she said, sweetly. She remembered the character she was meant to play…the smiling, awestruck sweetheart, the lovely innocent.

Margaret Scott introduced herself, and Cecilia imagined a picture based on the reporter's voice. She envisioned a tall, dark-haired woman…long like a fireman's pole. She envisioned a woman who carried a spiral notepad under her arm and dug deeply into people's lives. She envisioned a woman who insisted on getting to the bottom of things, and she shuddered as she answered Margaret's first few questions.

Of course, the first few questions were the softballs…no different than the hundreds of other interviews Cecilia had done over the previous thirty years. She explained her child-star upbringing as a romanticized idyll…the quality time she had spent with her beloved mother, reading scripts in their backyard. Cecilia spoke fondly of *The Family Next Door*…how it had been a launching pad for her future successes, how tightknit the cast was.

Cecilia realized that Margaret Scott was not the feared hard-charging journalist when the woman missed several opportunities to probe Cecilia's sentimentalities. When was the last time Cecilia had spoken to anyone from *The Family Next Door*? If pressed, Cecilia would have to admit that it had been decades…that she, herself was considered the most successful product from that family sitcom, and her costars seemed to have faded into Hollywood dust as soon as the cameras stopped rolling.

But Margaret went soft on Cecilia, at least at the beginning. It was only when the woman started questioning Cecilia's singledom that she started to grow uncomfortable. She hadn't prepared herself properly for this part of the interview, or perhaps she was just tired of delivering the same answers: *She was single and happy. She was waiting for the right person to come along.* And then, perhaps out of desperation to cast aside the reporter's inevitable vision of her as a decaying celibate, she provided Marco Bagnetti's name and contact information.

The move was impulsive…an attempt to provide corroboration for her claims that she was a blithesome, passionate woman. But the more she thought about it, the more she realized her mistake. Marco would undoubtedly seduce the reporter. He would charm her at dinner with his luscious, flattering assertions. Then, he would take her to a dance club and press his body against hers, before they hastily departed and fell into a tangle against his cardinal-red, satin bed sheets.

And what would the ultimate end-product story about Cecilia look like? Cecilia panicked as she envisioned an article detailing the lascivious romance between America's sweetheart and this drug-fancying, chain-smoking, serial skirt chaser.

Her thoughts caroming in varying directions, Cecilia aimed to stem the damage, and that's when she let out Billy's secret. There was no transition to ease into the news, no contextual motive. Margaret Scott had asked Cecilia about upcoming projects and Cecilia responded by leaking the tragic story of Billy Sloan and Elijah Gatlin. It was easier than admitting that she had no upcoming projects. It was better than lying about a phantom backpacking trip with invisible friends through inaccessible back country. It was preferable to admitting the truth.

Margaret Scott was quiet after Cecilia made her divulgence. Despite a few *umms* and *hmms*, Margaret basically said nothing. She took her time coming up with a follow-up question – no doubt weighing whether to pivot into an entirely different article than the one she'd been assigned to write.

And when she finally did think of a question, Margaret asked about preferred fashion labels and red-carpet hairstyles. They were back to superficialities – Cecilia's likes and dislikes, daytime routines and favorite television shows.

When the interview ended, Cecilia thought about what she'd disclosed and what remained hidden. She thought about the easy questions in the wake of her stunning disclosure and wondered what would eventually be printed.

Such frivolous questions could be an indicator of good or bad. It could mean an article of fluff and deference…a public relations manager's dream. Or it could mean a few paragraphs of monotony buried in the last pages of a publication.

Cecilia had no way to know until the final product came out, and she wasn't even sure she wanted to read it.

As she was finishing up her chores, getting the mansion ready to be uninhabited for several weeks, Cecilia reassessed the contents of her interview and revised her answers. There were no second chances, she knew. What she had said and done were as good as printed in stone.

Still, she held out faint hope that the bombshell she'd unleashed would be of such great shock value that the story on her own life wouldn't run at all. *Maybe they'll forget about me,* Cecilia thought. *And I'll sit for another interview after I come back from the wellness center. I'll be clean and sober and happy by then. That one definitely will be better. I'll be better. I'll be unstoppable.*

Chapter Twenty-Four

Lincoln Center, New York City
September 28, 2022

THE NEW YORK film festival contained a life that was entirely foreign to Detective Hobbs. Perhaps she was too sheltered, too myopic, too tethered to her Midwestern life. She could only gaze as busy people brushed past her. So many of them were sprucely, expensively fashioned, as if wearing clothes specifically tailored for their lean frames, candle-thin legs and torsos. They were tall and rangy and trotted by like long-limbed giraffes in the Sahara. They waved and smiled into cameras, beckoned the intimates in their entourage and paraded past.

Terry Mahoney was one of the people hurrying and waving, surrounded by associates on all sides. He walked so quickly, Hobbs could only see a flash of blonde atop a bulky body. She knew it was him because of the whispers and murmurs of cinephiles on either side of her. Once he charged into a theater, Hobbs and Martinez followed. After a few minutes of asking around, the detectives were buoyed to speak to someone in the know – a bespectacled, owl-faced young man who labeled himself as one of Terry's assistants. The assistant discouragingly ran through the schedule of Terry's next few hours – a film screening and a panel discussion – neither of which lent themselves to a police interview.

However, the assistant assured them that Terry would make himself available once the festivities and trivialities for the night were finished. Their best bet was to bide their time in the lobby bar of the Mandarin Oriental Hotel and wait for the famed producer to show up.

Hobbs and Martinez followed the young man's suggestion and left the film festival. Once inside the hotel's lobby lounge, they sat patiently on lemon-yellow chairs with upright backs, and stared outside at the magnificent New York cityscape.

Terry Mahoney showed up four hours later. He brushed into the lounge area and headed straight for the bar. Drink in hand, he made a beeline for Hobbs and Martinez, even though he'd never seen them before.

"Detectives," Terry said by way of a greeting, then took a giant swig of his beverage and placed the empty glass on the rectangular table in front of them.

"How did you know it was us?" Martinez asked.

Terry scoffed and held his arm out, as if revealing the other patrons in the lounge. "It's pretty obvious. And you aren't drinking. What can I do for you?" His diction was quick and stilted, like a metronome on a speed setting. Hobbs waited a moment to decelerate the pace of the conversation before responding.

"We're here to talk about Cecilia Cinvenue," Hobbs said. "We weren't quite finished with our questions during our last conversation when you hung up the phone."

Terry toyed with the glass on the table, rotating it in a clockwise orbit between his two hands. "Alright then," he said. "You have me at your disposal now. What's up?"

Hobbs sat back and responded with a slow, even cadence. "Well, we checked out your alibi and confirmed that you were in Dubai at her time of death, as you told us. So, we know you weren't directly involved in it...but that doesn't completely absolve you either. We have reason to believe Cecilia's death involved foul play, and that you had a role in it."

"I had a role in it?" Terry's voice swelled. "Can I ask what that role was?"

"Why don't *you* tell *us*?" Martinez said.

Terry laughed and ordered another drink from the bar. When he came back, he seemed amused, his movements jaunty. He downed the second drink and smacked the glass against the table. It struck Hobbs as revelry instead of anger, the comic end of a long day.

"I got nothing for you," Terry said. "I had nothing to do with her death, and I can't think of why you would suspect me."

"Well, Terry, it has to do with motive," Hobbs said. "Cecilia wrote in her diary about hating you, about going to war with you, about taking you down. You're the only one Cecilia seemed to feel this...anger...about. And we all know that you're a powerful guy with a lot to lose. Maybe she came at you and you decided to take her down. To shut her up. To save yourself."

Terry looked carefully at the detectives – first at Hobbs and then Martinez. Hobbs deigned to think that this was the moment Terry decided whether to cooperate or request a lawyer. She had been interviewing persons of interest for so long, she knew how to identify this moment. It was the point at the apex of the wishbone, the moment subjects fully realized who had outsmarted whom. But, whereas most people in Terry's condition grew anxious and red-eyed in the face of policy scrutiny, the movie producer was as relaxed as ever. He laughed emphatically, the crow's feet around his eyes compressed, his upper body trembling with amusement.

"You should be in the screenwriting business," he told Hobbs. "Seriously. You've got a great imagination for fiction."

"You still haven't answered the question," Hobbs said. "Why was she so angry at you?"

"Uh, because I wouldn't cast her in *Thieves of Stone and Ashes.* She wanted to read for the lead and I told her that was absolutely preposterous and that she had lost her mind."

"Why wouldn't you let her read...does that mean audition?"

"Yeah, it means audition. And no, I'm not going to cast a forty-five-year-old woman for an action-adventure lead. At the end of the day, I need to *sell tickets* to the movie. But Cecilia... she got her panties in a bunch about it. And I guess she decided that we were *at war* and she was going to *take me down,* as you say, which is really funny when you think about it."

"Why is that funny?"

"Detectives, come on!" Terry stood up and brought his glass back to the bar, grabbed a cocktail napkin and ran it against his upper lip. When he returned, he pushed his chair in and kept his palms against the edges, as if wrapping the seat backing into his fold. When he spoke, his voice sounded lubricated but still urgent – the dialect of a powerful man, always being lobbied, always besought. He spoke with the confidence of a commanding boss – whose age only deepened his voice, enhanced his standing.

"Detectives... I've got a million things going on right now. I've got to finish this movie that's already over-budget and prepare for an upcoming release and wrap up what we've been filming in Dubai. Like I said, I haven't seen Cecilia in years. I don't really care about her either. Look, the truth is, she'd open her legs for anybody. She slept with half the cast and crew of her last film, developed quite a reputation for herself. Maybe you should look into *that* instead of me. And besides, I don't know what you mean by *foul play.* She said she was going to take me down? *How?* How was she going to take me down? You think she was gonna #metoo me? Everything I do is consensual, I promise. Ladies are begging for it, and I never hit on her once. You think I killed her because she was going to take me down? She had *no power*! And no value in this town. Not anymore. Nothing she said or did meant anything. Hate to be so frank when speaking of the dead, but it's true. Truth is, I wouldn't be bothered by her when she was alive, and I'm not going to be bothered by her now. So…unless I'm under arrest, we're done here."

Terry gave the chair a final squeeze and took a step back, nodded at both detectives and sauntered, unaffected, down the hall towards the elevators.

———

THEY WERE BACK IN VETTA PARK THE FOLLOWING DAY – seated around Captain Weaver's office table in usual formation. Hobbs sat across from Dean, flanked by Weaver and Martinez on either side. In front of them were sheafs of paper detailing their most important interviews: Marco Bagnetti, Billy Sloan, Sparrow Shearwater, Paula Fekete and Terry Mahoney. Outside, tree branches swayed against Weaver's window, bared from winter's tentative approach, stooped under a cloudy sky.

Captain Weaver shuffled through the papers' edges, as though they were a deck of cards. He massaged the tips of his moustache, which seemed to Hobbs to be whiter and longer than usual – a nod to the avuncular demi-god of ancient fables, or perhaps simply a lack of desire for facial grooming.

When Martinez began to detail the merits of the interview with Terry Mahoney, Weaver cut him off by shaking his head and gesturing with both palms extended. "I don't need every detail," he said sharply. "I just need to know what our biggest lead is."

Martinez and Hobbs exchanged glances and Hobbs looked down as she prepared her answer. She studied the top page on her stack as though it could provide any guidance – a mysterious clue hidden on the top page. Finally, she said in a blunt voice: "We have no leads," and she allowed that admission to sink into the musty air before explaining.

All their persons of interest had verified alibis, which placed them hundreds of miles away from Vetta Park on the morning of Cecilia's death. No forensics placed anyone else at the scene. No computer or cell phone inspection revealed foul play. And, perhaps, most telling, no one had a motive to kill Cecilia Cinvenue.

"What about her will?" Weaver asked. "Even if she squandered every penny, her mansion alone is worth several millions."

Martinez responded. "Her will named her parents and hadn't been updated since their deaths. So, her estate is going into probate, and most likely, it'll go to her closest living relative or relatives. But so far, no one's come forward to make a claim on it."

"Okay, so no obvious financial motive. What about her boyfriends? She had plenty, if I recall."

Hobbs responded. "She had many men in her life...but I wouldn't use the term *boyfriends*. Billy Sloan had long since moved on with someone else. Marco Bagnetti just used her as a stepping stone, as far as we can tell. And Terry Mahoney hasn't wanted anything to do with her since...gosh, probably since she turned thirty."

"What about a photographer or a deranged fan? Maybe someone wanted to take her picture or get close to her and she sped away?"

Dean cleared his throat. "Captain, I've looked through every surveillance video of every establishment in the Light Industrial District that I could find. There was only one speeding car and that was Cecilia's. And the tire forensics support that conclusion as well. One car."

"So, we don't have anything suggesting she was *actually*

chased off of that cliff?" Weaver demanded. "Am I right about that? Absolutely nothing."

"We'll look through the whole case file again and see if we missed anything," Hobbs offered. "But, Captain...I wouldn't say we've got *nothing*. I think we have a pretty good picture of Cecilia Cinvenue's last moments and her life as a whole, for what that's worth. We'll also look into the suicide angle, which now seems like the likeliest reason for her going off that cliff. You know...maybe Cecilia was surprised and embarrassed to see Dalton Beck at the bottom of the cliff and just came up with a story."

Weaver nodded, pressed his lips into a frown and then dismissed the meeting. Back at her desk, Hobbs placed her head in her hands, closed her eyes and thought about what she knew. In her thoughts, a magnificent water nymph materialized – golden hair drifting over bony shoulders, wide eyes with a nucleus of blue that captured the light, that flirted with ever-present eyes, ever-flashing cameras.

Hobbs envisioned this portrait of a beautiful, famous woman, who was simultaneously revered and trapped in a lonely life. When Hobbs thought about Cecilia's addictions, they plagued the detective as if she, herself, were the sufferer. Hobbs saw remnants of her own life in Cecilia's stories of unrequited longing...the unhealthy cravings, the uncertainties of purpose. Before Cecilia's death, it would have been unfathomable to Hobbs that she could have anything in common with the famed movie star, but now she saw Cecilia as she really was. When Cecilia's car went off the cliff, it was as if her humanity poured forth. She was a tragic figure, but a relatable one...a human one.

And the sad conclusion of all of Hobbs' detective work was that no one in Cecilia's life cared to pick up the pieces of a dying star. Everybody in Cecilia's circle went about their business while she decayed in front of them. Perhaps it wasn't their fault; perhaps Cecilia chased them away. Maybe the star erected crenelated walls in the face of their suggestions, ignored their advice and set about her personal, self-administered remedies. Maybe loving Cecilia Cinvenue was too much of a task for the people in her life, and they couldn't be blamed.

If Hobbs' job was to point the finger at a person or persons, it brought her no vexation that she wouldn't be able to do that in this case. It seemed that the dehumanizing traits of an entire industry were to blame ...and Hobbs couldn't very well throw long-accepted norms into the slammer. Nor could she prosecute Cecilia's confidantes for their self-absorbed ways of life.

Hobbs would give the case a once-over before closing the book on it, but perhaps all this indefatigable investigation was due to her reluctance to accept an easy truth: that Cecilia Cinvenue had driven herself off of a cliff. The more she thought about it, the more Hobbs realized the hardness that lived inside of that conclusion. No one cared enough about Cecilia Cinvenue – not to listen to her as a child, not to love her as an adult, not to accept her aging body, not to ensure her spiritual well-being. And, perhaps most importantly, no one cared enough about Cecilia to chase her off of a cliff.

Chapter Twenty-Five

The Patton School, St. Louis, MO
October 3, 2022

HOBBS SHOWED up to The Patton School at the appointed hour on Monday morning, with Nick trailing her footfalls by several feet. The boy looked downtrodden that morning, a gray face to match the gray skies, a frown that he buried as he pointed his face towards the ground.

In contrast, The Patton School was magnificent, all shimmery glass and opalescent decorations. The school itself was a rectangle with a rotunda peeking out from the back, a moat of lush vegetation with hemlocks and pine trees, a red-bricked front entrance where the Admissions Director came to meet them.

"Hello, hello!" she said eagerly. "I'm Joanne Flaherty."

While Joanne shook their hands, Hobbs noticed that the woman was petite and delicate, with tiny fingers that threatened to crack beneath their grip. She had alabaster, sun-deprived skin. She smiled warmly.

"You must be Nick Hobbs," Joanne continued, leading the

duo inside. "We're excited to meet you this morning. I just wish the weather were more cooperative."

Hobbs nodded in agreement, and then was immediately distracted by the slatted, ornamented interior. The lobby was gorgeous, unlike any school Hobbs had been inside before. Children's artwork had been carefully curated to create a visual topiary. On every surface, verdant green and emerald paintings depicted forests and woodlands. Paper and cardboard stars hung from wooden ceiling beams. Hobbs expressed an adulatory, "Wow," as she surveyed the synthetic indoor landscape.

"Oh, I know," Joanne said. "We have a lot of talented artists in our student body." Then she pointed down one of the corridors and smiled at Nick. "Why don't you come with me and we'll do a quick assessment. Your aunt can wait in the library."

Nick obliged and Hobbs found the school library through a narrow doorway adjacent to the front office. Once inside, she marveled at the creamy, well-scrubbed surfaces, the towers of books arranged in towers of stacks. The library itself was a dome, canopied with skylights that let in the gray cloud-concealed light. Hobbs found a book to occupy her time and was surprised to find that three hours had passed before Joanne Flaherty met her inside and escorted her to a meeting room inside the Admissions Office.

They found seats – Joanne behind a long, cinnamon colored desk, and Hobbs in a wooden, broad-beamed chair. Before revealing the results of the assessment, Joanne mentioned Nick's various strengths: he was polite and well-mannered, hard-working, tenacious. She also said she had dropped him off at the school gymnasium, where he could join a pickup game of ninth grade basketball while the adults discussed the results.

"I feel like you're about to tell me bad news," Hobbs said cautiously.

"It's certainly not *bad*," Joanne said, with a rising intonation that typically – in Hobbs' practiced opinion – accompanied the delivery of bad news. "But, based on this morning's assessment, I believe that Nick would greatly benefit from enrollment here at The Patton School. He clearly struggles with phonemic word recognition – that is, matching letters to the sounds they make. He has difficulty spelling and writing, and a very, very hard time reading words he's unfamiliar with. In many cases, he wildly guessed at the word based on the first letter or two. And his self-esteem…" Joanne dropped off, and Hobbs wasn't sure whether that was to preface this bit of the assessment with gravity, or to give Hobbs the opportunity to jump in and halt whatever the Admissions Director was about to say.

But Hobbs maintained her expression and composure, a cross-legged stance and stoic face, and allowed Joanne to continue.

"His self-esteem is quite depleted," Joanne said, as though self-esteem were a jar of water that could be consumed throughout the day, a once-teeming goblet that they'd caught at its low point. "I think it's because this has never been properly assessed before, and I'm guessing he's really struggled academically. I hate to be so blunt, Ms. Hobbs, but Nick described himself as 'dumb' and 'an idiot'. Our assessment shows that not to be true, of course. Nick is, in fact, very smart and very creative. He just learns differently, and it's a way that conventional schools, unfortunately, don't teach."

Hobbs thought about her nephew. She imagined the soul-searing life of a child who showed up to class that was effectively taught in a different language – a boy who stayed lost while everyone around him easily absorbed the information. No wonder he felt dumb.

"Are you saying that you think Nick could go here?" Hobbs asked.

Joanne nodded. "Yes, and in fact, we reviewed the rough

estimates of his father's financials that you provided, and if that information is close to accurate, Nick would even qualify for full financial aid. We have many alumni with deep pockets and a generous endowment, and so we're pleased to be able to offer scholarships to students just like him."

"Oh...okay." Hobbs said.

"Why don't you have Nick come for the full school day tomorrow," Joanne suggested. "See how he likes it?"

Hobbs nodded, said of course she would, but she felt a bit flabbergasted by the pace of everything, this news that seemed like a steamroller plowing over everything in its path.

It wasn't just Nick's life that would drastically change if he enrolled at The Patton School; it was Hobbs' as well. Her brother Harlan lived hours away, on a piece of land shadowed by the Ozark Mountains and bounded by the Meramec River. If Nick were to enroll at the school, it meant that his residence underneath her roof was more than temporary. She wouldn't be able to tear him away on a moment's notice and send him back to rural Missouri. Such a first-rate school as Patton was a product of its suburban existence, abutting the industrious streets of St. Louis. Hobbs was certain that no replica of The Patton School existed around Harlan's straw-grass stretched plot of land.

When the meeting ended, Hobbs collected Nick from the gym and drove back to work. She didn't even bother with salvaging the remainder of the day for him at the local high school – not now that she fully comprehended the futility that Nick had so stridently tried to talk to her about.

During the drive, Nick chatted about what he'd learned about himself that morning. Joanne had told him he was a good problem solver, a discerning listener and a champion of big-picture thinking. In Nick's summary of the morning, Hobbs detected glints of an optimistic future– something she had never before observed in the teenager.

But while Nick spoke, Hobbs' mind was otherwise occupied…spiraling with thoughts and doubts about the future. She wanted, almost more than anything, for Nick to thrive. But what would she have to give up to make that happen?

———

Nick attended The Patton School on Tuesday. When the day was over, he trotted into Hobbs' waiting car, his backpack swinging jauntily behind him.

"How was it?" Hobbs asked, and then veered out of the parking lot, while Nick recounted a play-by-play of the entire day, with an academic level of detail. Hobbs looked at the road while her nephew spoke, but she could see from cursory sidelong glances that he was excited. He cast his arms around while he described the classes, counted on his fingers the names of classmates he could recall. He gestured and snickered, and spoke with such a quickness that Hobbs had to urge him to *slow down so she could understand* more than once.

By the time they reached the police station, Nick was tossing his backpack around in his lap, commenting on the contrast between The Patton School and the local high school. Hobbs saw several things she'd never before witnessed in the boy: interest, focus, eagerness.

"Am I not going back to the local high school?" Nick asked.

Hobbs put her car in park and placed her hands on the steering wheel. She felt like she was bracing herself for a larger discussion, an inevitability, and it was easier to look straight ahead – at the sun-spotted waxy surfaces of other cars – than look her nephew in the eyes.

"I figured, since it's the end of the day and all, just to bring you here while I wrapped up my most recent case," Hobbs said.

"No, I mean forever. Am I not going back to the public high? Am I going to Patton tomorrow? The woman said I could come back if I wanted to. She said if you wanted me to. Then I could go back."

The question of *want*. *Not so simple*, thought to herself. "Nick, I need to figure some things out. I need to check in with your dad. I need to think about my schedule. Please be patient."

"Okay. But just so you know…I really, really, really want to go back to The Patton School. Like really."

"Duly noted."

And then Nick finished with his backpack, laid it on the floorboard next to his feet and pivoted to the next topic. "So…what are you working on? Are you still trying to solve what happened to Cecilia Cinvenue?" he asked.

"I'm not really in the *solving* phase, more in the *wrapping up and doing an ungodly amount of paperwork* phase," Hobbs explained. "All because Cecilia told a random bystander that she was being chased, two police departments in separate parts of the country launched investigations. One little comment from her and our lives have changed."

"But did your life really *change* from working on this case?"

"It's hard to explain exactly why, but yes, I'd say it has." Hobbs fingered the stitching on her jacket and thought about what she'd learned from working on the case. She'd seen the intersection of a ruthless industry and a soft, searching actress. And through it all, Hobbs had felt a sort of softening of her own…soothing thoughts taking the edge off of hardened confidence, a heart that bent towards tenderness.

Nick frowned. "You know, I told one of my friends that you were working on Cecilia Cinvenue's death and he said that he had never even heard of her before she died and doesn't understand why everyone's all bent out of shape about it."

Hobbs laughed softly and didn't match Nick's gaze when he shot an absurd look at her. She knew he wouldn't understand why she was chuckling – the bizarre near-impossibility of his friend not recognizing the name of a famous movie star who'd spent three decades on a screen. He didn't understand the generational divide that turned her revered icons into old-timey footnotes, the inevitable forgetting that afflicts everyone, whether meager or famous. Cecilia Cinvenue would always exist in one form or another, even though the visceral delight that accompanied her name and likeness would fade with time.

But there was another reason Hobbs was laughing, and that was Nick's sudden interest in her case. He had never asked questions before, never made plans for *tomorrow*, never shown an interest in anything outside of his phone, and even that typically entailed a hard-faced expression, dawdling gait and lethargic mood. Now he was taking an interest – an eagerness – in the life that had been thrumming and breathing at the edges of his existence the whole time.

Hobbs exited the car and Nick walked next to her inside the building. He never asked her why she found him so amusing, and Hobbs was glad, because she knew no matter how much she tried to explain, he wouldn't understand anyway.

———————

At the police station, Nick sat politely in a chair next to Hobbs' cubicle. When she took phone calls or entertained the myriad of officers who stopped by her desk for a chat, Nick remained buried in his phone. Although his head was bent, his fingertips constantly scrolling, Hobbs thought he may have been listening to her at the same time. There was something about the way his lips discreetly curled at the edges anytime someone told a joke, something about how his eyes alighted across her desk when her focus was aimed elsewhere.

When Nick asked for a piece of paper so he could help solve the Cecilia Cinvenue case, Hobbs thought nothing of it. She absentmindedly heeded his request and left the boy to his own devices. A minute or two later, her eyes flitted across her unfinished paperwork to his scrawling and she felt her breath catch in her chest.

Leaning forward on shaky legs, Hobbs re-read what he had written, then stared at him with wide, wild-raging eyes. "Oh my gosh," Hobbs said. "Nick, let me see what you wrote."

"Oh, I'm just wasting time, Aunt Berta," Nick said. "I wasn't really serious about solving it. I mean…"

He seemed suddenly embarrassed by the attention – not just from Hobbs, but from Martinez, who had wandered over from his desk -- no doubt after hearing the low-voiced din in Hobbs' cubicle.

"Is the kid going to solve the case?" Martinez said grandly and flashed a wide smile that both Nick and Hobbs recognized as patronizing, exaggerated. He seemed eager to play a role in this ruse – the boy as obliging detective – adults practically keening in their forged flattery.

"Martinez, he did," Hobbs said incredulously. "He solved it!" Then Hobbs put her hands on Nick's shoulders and squeezed – as close to a physical embrace as she could muster, what with trembling arms and rapid-fire breaths. "Nick, you're amazing!"

Nick looked from his scribbling to Hobbs' face and back down again. He looked stunned – not sure if this was all a stunt meant to humiliate him, with a sweeping and sentimental lesson at the end. Still, he didn't seem ready to decry her adulation either. He simply stayed silent and waited for an explanation.

Martinez leaned forward and frowned. Hobbs could see the edges of his lips stir while he attempted to decipher the boy's scrawling. After a few seconds, Martinez corrected himself into an upright posture and said, "He misspelled a few words there."

"Yes!" Hobbs said. "Exactly! He showed us the pieces we were missing!"

"Umm…okay…so…if he solved it, then who chased Cecilia Cinvenue off the cliff?"

Hobbs smiled. "No one. There was only one car, remember?"

"Okay…so…" Martinez stopped and waited for Hobbs to finish the sentence. She knew that he was completely lost, as well as Nick…that no matter how many times they re-read what Nick had written and tried to tie it to the case – to anything *sensical* – it lost even more meaning.

Hobbs didn't intend to prolong the silence, but she wanted to back up her theory with evidence. While Nick and Martinez waited and lingered, stared into the distance and rolled their eyes around the room in thought, Hobbs rummaged through her paperwork until she found the page she was after. "Aha! Here it is! Ah…okay…do you remember our interview with Paula Fekete? At the wellness center?"

Martinez frowned again. "Yeah, sure."

"Well, what did Paula say were the values of the center? The principles they were always trying to teach?" Hobbs pointed at the paper. "I wrote it down: restraint, self-control, self-reliance, temperance, *chastity*. Do you remember that?"

"Yeah sure. So then, how does that mean the case is solved?"

"It's solved because it's clear now that it wasn't a suicide. Cecilia Cinvenue wanted to live. She spent her whole life trying to be what people wanted, trying to be better, trying to improve herself. No one accepted and loved her for who she was. And, in a terrible, tragic way, in the end, that's what killed her."

Martinez and Nick still looked confused, but they accepted Hobbs' version of events. It seemed that there was no correlation between their understanding and the rivulets of cryptic explanation pouring forth from Hobbs' mouth. For her part, Hobbs wasn't trying to be mysterious, but this new fragment of knowledge had appeared so suddenly – a lightning bolt of information that shocked her view of the Cecilia Cinvenue story. She wasn't talented enough to simultaneously revisit a week's worth of investigation and explain it to the bewildered men still frowning at her and remaining silent. Soon enough she would explain everything.

For the time being, she complimented Nick – his outside-the-norm writing, invaluable even when accidental – and reexamined the penciled etchings on his curled-edged piece of paper.

This what Nick had written:

I ws beeying shase.

I was beeing chase.

I was being chste.

I was being chaste.

Chapter Twenty-Six

Shearwater Wellness Center,
Vetta Park Light Industrial District
September 15, 2022

THE MEDITATION SESSION WAS COMPLETE. The chakras discussion had been enlightening – in such a way as Cecilia found intellectually stimulating, but not necessarily relating to her. The wheat germ smoothie was taking its time to digest – roiling a typically empty stomach at a snail's pace.

Cecilia sat at the edge of a cushioned sofa and examined her newly painted toenails. There was nothing to do while Paula took her shower – nothing worth reading, no property of *self* she felt like examining any further that morning. That horse had been proverbially beaten to death during her long-winded sessions with Paula.

And then – as though her thoughts had the supernatural abilities to summon apparitions from the great beyond – a beefy, dark-haired man appeared in the doorway and walked into the kitchen.

"I hope I'm not disturbing you," the man said, his voice deep like a radio DJ. His tight-fitting t-shirt, his wavy crop of jet-black hair, even the scent of coffee and aftershave -- secreting a masculine timbre that she could sense from the couch across the room. It was a quality she hadn't observed since traveling East of the Rocky Mountains.

"You're not disturbing me at all," Cecilia said. "Nice to meet you. I'm Cecilia."

The man smiled but didn't cross the high-ceiling room to seal their introduction with a handshake. Instead, he delved through various cabinets and started making a pot of coffee.

"I'm Nathan Fekete," the man said. And then he added, "Paula's husband."

Cecilia felt the final words of his sentence like a stab to the chest. It wasn't a dagger but more like a scalpel – exposing a disappointed heart, but not a betrayed one.

"Paula hates when I come up here and interrupt," Nathan continued. "But I ran out of coffee downstairs. Where is she? Is she in…?"

"She's in the shower," Cecilia said.

"Well…" Nathan stood against the counter and crossed his legs at the ankles. He said, in a slightly accented voice: "Beautiful day outside."

Cecilia stood up from the couch and wandered into the kitchen. She kept a ten-foot distance from the man so as not to seem too eager. She stood against one of the painted wooden beams and stretched her back, her chest aimed forward, her blonde locks dangling obediently past her shoulders. She knew how she looked – the effect of a curved back, wanton smile, extended chest.

Nathan Fekete seemed to disabuse all of Cecilia's preconceived ideas about beautiful people – that all chiseled, striking creatures flocked to the coasts, that they were absent in dusty, Midwestern towns. But here was Nathan Fekete, married but undoubtedly interested. After all, he had come upstairs and interrupted Cecilia's time with Paula. Was it a coincidence that Nathan had timed his "coffee" visit so perfectly with his wife's exodus to the bathroom? Cecilia didn't think so.

And yet, something prevented her from making the move – from sauntering fully into the kitchen on slender legs and sultry demeanor. It was his wedding ring – a thick gold band that flared at her every time he flicked his wrist. It was the karmic consequences of depraved behavior...the unscrupulous vice she had traveled over eighteen hundred miles to get away from.

Could Cecilia have had Nathan if she wanted? It was tough to say. He was pouring his coffee with the readiness of a man who craved something. Were his fingers shaking due to caffeine deprivation or illicit desire? In the bathroom, the cascade of water hitting the shower doors ensured their secrecy. It was fitting background music to the tryst that was possible.

Possible but not inevitable. What had Cecilia learned about herself? She turned to sex as validation. Sex was a device...a way of wresting power in a world that deprived her of it. Her sacral chakra represented withheld intimacy and sexual matters. This was the topic she had Paula had been working through just that morning. Perhaps Nathan was sent up to the room on purpose at Paula's behest...to test Cecilia's commitment to convalescence, her ability to commit to restraint.

Nathan filled his coffee mug and smiled at her as he skirted past. All things masculine trailed his stride...the slightly suggestive turn of his lips, the flex of his bicep while he held the coffee mug, the smell of him.

Cecilia felt the urge to follow Nathan out the door and to wherever he was staying. But she knew better. Instead, she recalled the tools of chastity and restraint. *Gird the loins with a belt. Remove oneself from the situation.*

Their girding hadn't even been cleaned up from the living

room from the morning's lesson about sacral chakras. The belt's loosely coiled leather lay haphazardly on one of the couch's cushions.

Cecilia grabbed the belt and impetuously weaved it around her mid-section and upper thighs. She then grabbed the keys to her Ferrari and rushed out of the apartment.

Once on the road, Cecilia drove with furious concentration. She checked the rear-view mirror as though all her addictions and insecurities were going to hurtle after her. Meticulously engineered tires squealed against the potholed streets of the Light Industrial District.

And still, Cecilia drove in a frenzy. The approaching quarry hit its danger with bent warning signs and shabby, misplaced orange cones. Cecilia drove as though she were on fire…as though her old thoughts could be outraced. She felt invigorated with the windows lowered, the gusts tearing through her now-unkempt hair. Everything in her wake was a discarded memory…alcohol, drugs, starvation, and useless sex. Everything was gone.

When Cecilia's girding came loose…the damn belt was sneaking down her thighs, tying her knees, binding her legs together – she squirmed to try to fix it but only made the situation worse. Cecilia saw the quarry with only moments to react and missed the brake pedal by inches. Or was it centimeters? The slithering chastity belt had made her lose her footing, and instead of braking, she floored the gas and went headfirst into the quarry. A moment of flight, in which the car was airborne…this marvel of machinery soaring over rocks and dust. And Cecilia – who braced her head with bony arms against the steering wheel, her eyes shielded from the cloudless sky and mossy, swaying trees in the distance – prepared for the drop.

WHAT DID ANYONE REALLY KNOW ABOUT CECILIA CINVENUE? She was forever lost – a tiny creature whose future was dictated before she was old enough to speak. She was obedient and kind, and these features served and starved her. She was always longing, always searching. She wanted a life that was no less lovely but more connected; she wanted regular people and easy acceptance, conversations with no hidden motives, quick, hearty laughter, well-curated meals. What everyone else seemed to have.

What did anyone really know about Cecilia? She was a shiny, shimmering creature, with goldenrod hair and gossamer bones. In her final moments, she flew over limestone crags and coralline rock, and when she landed abruptly on sediment and dirt, her head impacted the steering wheel with a force that made her gasp. She knew, then, that the future was prophesied, that the yearning still inside of her would never actualize. So much beauty in this world, so much to see that would never be seen.

Out of the corner of her eyes, a helpful bystander. He was thick and helmeted – his figure circling the car, fluttering across her peripheral vision. Cecilia's head throbbed and her throat felt bloody – the coppery taste pooling behind her tongue. From her nostrils, the benzene scent of motor oil, foretelling a dangerous story.

Cecilia did not want to end her beautiful life so brusquely, she wanted to live to see more blue-green mountains with snow-white lids, the Hollywood sign shimmering outside her patio doors, the flaps and folds of ocean waves in salt-bathed air. She wanted to mature and learn and grow and to live in a world that loved her back. When at last the hazy creature came around the driver's side, Cecilia whispered the only thing she knew to say – the encapsulation of all her work, her reasons, her intentions. *"I was being chaste,"* she said. And then, it was over.

WHEN A MOVIE STAR FALLS by MARGARET SCOTT
The Hollywood Ledger
September 17, 2022

CECILIA CINVENUE'S MOOD WAS LIGHTHEARTED AND optimistic during her final telephone interview. She sounded relaxed and refreshed as she spoke of her previous body of work and future deals. "I'm the happiest I've ever been," the star said.

Perhaps we'll never know what compelled Cecilia Cinvenue to take a fatal plunge off the side of a cliff in Vetta Park, Missouri – a tragic event that is still being investigated by the Santa Monica and Vetta Park police departments for evidence of foul play. But what we do know is that the light that shined so brightly in the actress appeared to be beaming through the telephone in the week before her untimely death.

"I was born into such love from my parents, and I had so much inspiration," Cecilia told us. "My mom was my biggest cheerleader, and she's the one who encouraged me to get into show business. She told me that by playing characters, I could make audiences laugh and I could make them cry. I could make silent voices talk. I could fill people's hearts. Of course, that's a lot to put on the shoulders of a little girl. But, when I was young and going on so many auditions and trying to make it in Hollywood, those words from my mom were always in the back of my mind."

What the actress and her mother couldn't have anticipated was the extraordinary level of success Cecilia would enjoy at such a young age. Cecilia's first breakout role was as a principal actress on *The Family Next Door* – a prime-time television comedy. "I had such a wonderful time filming with the cast and crew," Cecilia said. "They were like my second family and we've always kept in touch."

After *The Family Next Door* ended its eight-year run, Cecilia successfully made the leap onto the big screen. For almost a decade in the mid-2000s, she was famed film producer Terry Mahoney's muse, appearing in several of his movies. Their collaboration resulted in Cecilia's most successful film: 2000's *Soldier of Payback*, an action feature that grossed over $250 million worldwide, and cemented Cecilia's status as a top-notch movie star.

"I'm so proud to have been a part of everything I've done," Cecilia said. "All the cast and crew I worked with, all of the amazing scripts brought to life, all the characters I inhabited, these experiences have been truly magical."

As her final interview came to a close, Cecilia remained wistful. She spoke about her life with the characteristic cheerfulness that will certainly be missed. "When I think back about all that I've done, I'm proud of myself," the actress said. "I know my parents would be proud of me too. When fans get in touch with me and they thank me, it is the greatest feeling ever. It feeds my soul to know that I've made a difference. And even if I never make another movie or TV show again, it's enough for me to have accomplished everything I've done to date. It's been such a wild, crazy, fun, difficult, emotional adventure. And I'm grateful for all of it."

Chapter Twenty-Seven

Vetta Park Police Department
October 4, 2022

DEAN ADAMS MET Hobbs in the interrogation room of the Vetta Park PD at the end of the day. It was a closed-off chamber – no windows or mirrors, a heavy door the only channel to the outside world.

When Dean walked in the room, Hobbs could tell that he had prepared for the importance of the discussion. There was something about his somber face, the way he hesitantly shut the door behind him, as if preparing for an indictment.

"Everything ok?" Dean asked, with characteristic kindness. His eyebrows formed angles above his hazel irises. His stubble cast a darkened shade across an already-shadowed face.

Hobbs tried to ignore his beauty, the pull of his charm. "Yes, everything's fine," she said. "I wanted to let you know that I spoke with my brother this morning. Nick is going to live with me full-time until he graduates high school. He's going to attend The Patton School on a full scholarship. So, it's good news."

"It's good news," Dean repeated flatly, and the two of them just looked at each other across a cold, white-laminate table.

After a few moments of silence, Dean finally asked, "What does this mean for us?"

"I don't know," Hobbs answered quickly. "I guess…you can make a choice to be a part of our lives or not a part of our lives. But this is something that I have to do."

"Don't make it sound like it's not a choice you made, Roberta. You could've sent the boy home on the next bus to rural Missouri. You didn't have to basically adopt him—"

"Yes, I did!" Roberta interrupted.

"*Why?*" Dean demanded.

The bright white lights of the interrogation room, the wafting scent of bleached cleanser, the cold metallic folding chair – all these factors seemed to intensify under Dean's irascibility. Hobbs wanted to hold his stare – a duel of the nonviolent, conversational sort – but she more imminently needed to collect her thoughts.

Breaking her gaze, Hobbs stood up and paced across the room. Words amassed in her mind, but she didn't speak them. Dean eventually interrupted the silence – his voice a warm, soupy brogue, in contrast to his earlier crossness.

"Just tell me this," Dean said. "Is it because of me?"

Hobbs walked back to the table and folded Dean's hands into her own. They were cold, clammy, and she brought them up to her lips and kissed them. It was a scarce moment of intimacy for the estranged couple – a display of tenderness Hobbs rarely displayed, let alone in the workplace.

"Then why?" Dean practically whispered.

"Because…because of so much," Hobbs said. She let go of Dean's hands and folded her own in her lap. She tried again to explain. "Because of Cecilia," Hobbs said, and she wasn't surprised when Dean shook his head and tossed up his hands at the incomprehensible line connecting two seemingly disparate situations.

"I know it doesn't make any sense," Hobbs explained. "But this particular investigation got to me. I mean, when we think about Cecilia…think about everything she had and everything she lacked. She had so much of what everyone strives for – beauty, fame, wealth – and so little of what we all take for granted. The closest thing Cecilia ever had to a close relationship was a mother who turned her into a workhorse. Despite what Cecilia said in every interview, she never had someone in her corner who loved her unconditionally. And look what it did to her."

Dean shook his head. "Yeah, but c'mon Berta. We all know Cecilia's death was just an accident. She wasn't trying to commit suicide. So, trying to pin her story on Nick like it's some cautionary tale—"

"No, but she was at that wellness center for a reason. She turned to sex and drugs and alcohol for a reason. She was always searching for a way to fill that void. And Dean, believe me when I tell you, *Nick has the same void*. He never had anyone who really cared about him, anyone taking an interest in his life, anyone rooting for him. He had that void and I stepped in and filled it. And if I didn't, no one would. That's meaningful. Not just for him, but for me too."

Dean nodded and didn't say anything. After a minute had passed, he stood up and scraped his metal chair against the floor. "I guess that's it then," he said.

"Yeah. I guess so."

They hugged good-bye. It felt almost silly to Hobbs to be embracing a co-worker she would see not twelve hours later… but Hobbs also knew that when she saw him the following morning, things would be different. Dean's silky coif of hair, his disarrayed polo collar, his unfurled cuffs…these would no longer be hers to adjust. Dean's salmon-shaded lips wouldn't be for her to look forward to kissing sometime in the future.

Their hug good-bye was a farewell, a punctuation mark at the end of an amorous, doting, long-held love affair.

So, this was an ending…but it was also a beginning. When Hobbs drove into her apartment complex later that evening, the first thing she saw was a tangle of adolescent boys and young men running across the basketball court. Her eyes caught on one person in particular…his black hair fastened with a cotton headband, skinny arms lobbing a ball against the net's backdrop, sweat sheening off his body in the early evening's humidity. Nick cheered and high-fived the other guys every time he made a basket. He smiled even when he missed.

Hobbs felt she could sit in her car and watch him for hours – his easy vigor, his determination, his delight. Before long, the night would grow dark and the game would break up – all the players retiring to their respective homes for the night. But in the meantime, she was content to watch them play – to witness the fading sunlight shine on her nephew.

This is for you, Cecilia, Hobbs thought to herself. *You saved this boy and you don't even know it. Thanks for shining so brightly in the dark. Thank you for everything.*

Dear Reader,
Word of mouth is crucial for any author to succeed. If you enjoyed Movie Stars Shine Brightest in the Dark, please consider leaving an Amazon review. It would be greatly appreciated!!

It would be impos[sible] ...
supported me throu[gh] ...

Cara Goldberg ... were the first person to read the book and gave me very honest advice about what you liked and what needed to be improved. Your words – as always – improved the novel tremendously. I can't thank you enough.

Nicole Oppenheimer – my invaluable writing companion, who always gives me candid feedback and pushes me to up my game. Thank you so much for your input on everything!

Thanks to my Mom for reading and writing a review for All the Hidden Pieces, and for always being my biggest cheerleader in my writing journey (and in life!)

Thanks to my editor and stepmom, Judy Sachwald. In addition to all of the typos that you diligently spotted, you provided developmental editing that went above and beyond the task at hand. The emotional aspects of the book would not have been the same without your input. Thank you.

To my friends and family who used social media to help spread the word about All The Hidden Pieces, I can't thank you enough: Jen Jim, Marissa Rosen, Becky Marbarger,

Louise Goldstein, Lauren Abraham, Liessa Alperin, Kevin Litt and Brandon Berman. AND to all of my friends and readers who read the book and took the time to write a review, I read each one and I am forever grateful!

To my tribe of close friends, who have supported me every step of the way. Showing up, championing me, it means the world: Jayme Fingerman, Carla Nieman, Robyn LeBoeuf, Melissa Abrams, Amy Wagner, Amanda Luft, Mandi White-Ajmani, Debbie Levy, Rekha Ramanuja, Kate Hellmann and Melissa Abrams. Thank you ladies so much! Your friendship is everything.

To Dan Boccabella, my "accidental" editor. Thank you for your diligent reading!

To Kelly Becker, Jessica Brooks Garnreiter, Joann DeLurgio and Jessie Nelke: I absolutely loved discussing All The Hidden Pieces with your book clubs and sincerely thank your members for their thoughtful discussions!

To Lois Martin and all my other readers who either reached out to me with feedback or invited me to speak to your book clubs, each request and email meant the world to me!

Thanks to Sophisticated Living St. Louis – and specifically Carrie Edelstein – for giving me my first print publishing gig and Town&Style St. Louis for featuring All the Hidden Pieces.

Thanks to the readers, curators and librarians of the Indie Author Project for matching self-published books with public libraries. I am honored to be part of your tremendous community.

And of course, my family – my amazing husband, Raphael, who read the book and provided instrumental feedback, and thanks to the rest of my family for your guidance, love and support for so many years: Dad, Laura, Chris and Chris, Nancy, all my in-laws, and those handsome young men who have put up with me every day for the past decade and a half: Andrew, Ryan, and Josh. You three are my loves and my inspiration and my reason for years of non-productivity!

About the Author

Jillian Thomadsen grew up in Baltimore, and has lived in Virginia, New York City and Los Angeles before finally settling in St. Louis, MO. A former finance professional, Jillian now spends her time volunteering, teaching her teenagers how to drive, and learning middle school math (and writing!)

Jillian first got the writing bug at age seven, and has been honing her craft ever since. She has written for *TheHill*, *Sophisticated Living*, *ADDitude*, *ScaryMommy*, *Today Parenting* and *BusinessWeek*. Her first novel, *All the Hidden Pieces*, won the 2020 Missouri Author Project. *Movie Stars Shine Brightest in the Dark* is her second novel.

Get on the mailing list! Please contact Jillian at jillianthomadsen@gmail.com or go to www.authorjillianthomadsen.com.

Made in the USA
Monee, IL
11 December 2023

48825769R00198